THE GODLESS REALM

THE GODLESS REALM

Book One in "The Heirson Chronicles"

Christopher Goldthorn

Cover art designed by Christopher Goldthorn using Vondy AI (www.vondy.com)

Published 2025 by Christopher Goldthorn

Paperback ISBN: 978-1-0684484-0-9
Hardcover ISBN: 978-1-0684484-2-3
eBook ISBN: 978-1-0684484-1-6

First Edition March 2025
10 9 8 7 6 5 4 3 2 1

To my parents for all the reading, listening, and for introducing me to fantasy.

To any and all who have endured me talking about Cam and Sonia for the last nineteen years.

And, most of all, to my beautiful wife. My rose, my rock, my life. Without you I would never have visited Rhydariel again.

“Where will all the martyrs go when the virus cures itself?”

'Letterbomb', Green Day

Contents

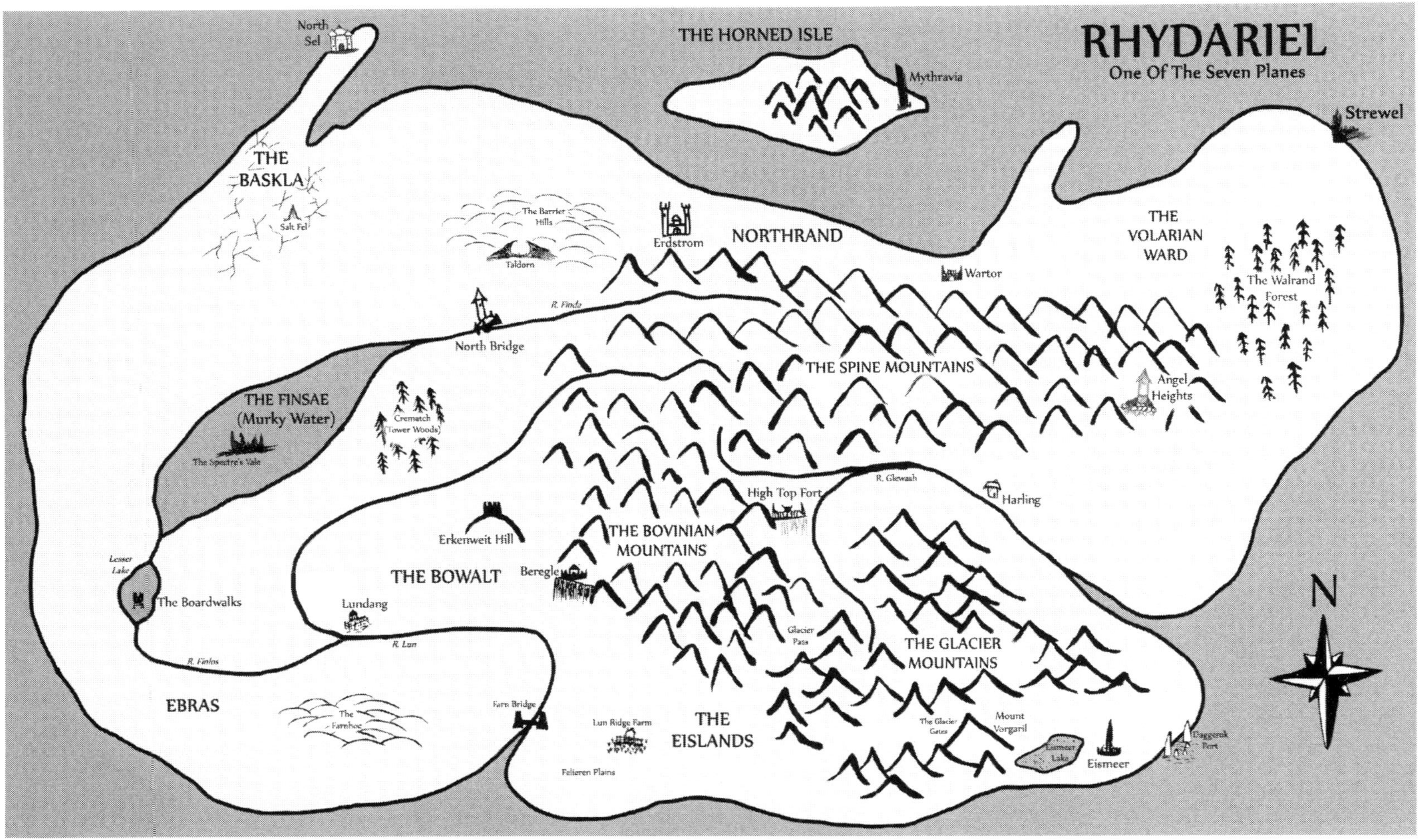
RHYDARIEL
One Of The Seven Planes
THE HORNED ISLE
Mythravia
Strewel
North Sel
THE BASKLA
Salt Fel
The Barrier Hills
Taldorn
Erdstrom
NORTHRAND
Wartor
THE VOLARIAN WARD
The Walrand Forest
R. Finda
North Bridge
THE SPINE MOUNTAINS
Angel Heights
THE FINSAE (Murky Water)
The Spectre's Vale
Crematch (Tower Woods)
R. Glewash
High Top Fort
Harling
Erkenweit Hill
THE BOVINIAN MOUNTAINS
Lesser Lake
The Boardwalks
THE BOWALT
Beregle
Lundang
R. Lun
Glacier Pass
THE GLACIER MOUNTAINS
R. Finlos
EBRAS
The Farnhoe
Farn Bridge
Lun Ridge Farm
THE EISLANDS
Felieren Plains
The Glacier Gates
Mount Vorgaril
Eismeer Lake
Eismeer
Daggerok Port
N

The Peoples Of Rhydariel

Cam McAllister – A teenager from Welverleigh in Worcestershire, England.
Sonia Coles – His best friend.

Felgaron – A swordsman.
Gismay – A farmer.

<u>The Kingdom Of Ebras</u>
Elderking Ebrahir
King Hedradour
Marshall Larin – Hedradour's Second in Command.
Araht – A warrior.
Captain Maloran – Captain of Farn Bridge.

<u>The Kingdom Of Eismeer</u>
Lord Fohenk
Captain Dunwald – Fohenk's Second in Command.
Captain Bryndain – Fohenk's best archer.
Lieutenant Aglorar – Dunwald's Second.
Lekkon – A Soldier.

<u>The County Of Beregland</u>
Lord Marn
Lady Ianor – Marn's daughter. Commander of his armies.
Lady Carial – Marn's daughter. His House Maiden.
Agazi - A merchant

Chapter One

Of Dreams And Castles

The white walls of the castle loomed up out of the fog as they had done for over a thousand years. Smooth and sheer they climbed above the muddy marshland beneath, their milky gaze casting a thoughtful watch across the mire that spewed outward in all directions; a stain that ran brown and reeking through the grasslands which used to be home to thousands.

Archers stood atop the lofty heights, keen eyes staring down at the battlefield, waiting for the order to let loose their arrows. Infantry stood behind, shaking with anticipation. Their silver-grey armour was bejewelled by gems of moisture as the fog clung to them, creating a legion of crystalline statues that stood, proud and defiant, against the thickening gloom.

Their Commander paced slowly between them, placing his hand upon each shoulder as he passed. Despite his rank, the armour he wore was plain and unadorned. He had led his tired, battle-hardened men through many perils, always against superior foes, and always they had prevailed despite the odds. This, though, would surely be their most desperate battle.

Turning his face toward the advancing hordes, the Commander took one long, final breath, and drew his blade. The sound of the metal scraping against the sheath rang out across the silent courtyard, sending a shiver through the spines of all who heard it. Though it was notched and stained beyond all recognition, he would not sheath the blade again until the battle was won.

The Commander's eyes strained to finally glimpse his foe. Their first rank was in range. His heart longed to strike out at them, soul-less abominations that they were. The second and third ranks came closer, and still he gave no order. He must wait until the perfect moment.

Soon the tenth rank was in his sights, their ungodly forms black against the silver-grey of the fog.

"Archers! Loose!"

The first wave of arrows whistled through the air, finding their marks on the battlefield below. Still they came marching out of the fog, so single-minded were their foes; for every line they felled, two more took its place, trampling over the bodies of those who fell before.

Ladders were being brought forward.

"Swords!" he cried.

The deafening shriek of metal being unleashed from nine-hundred sheaths rang through the courtyard.

A ladder clattered up against the wall right in front of the Commander. The sound of the enemy's growls rose to meet them from below. Two hands appeared on either side of the ladder, and the first form leapt like a lion over the parapet and charged him.

Both let out their war-cries and the Commander raised his sword.

Suddenly, the walls beneath their feet crumbled. He felt himself falling backwards into an abyss. His men fell with him, still grappling with their enemies. The white walls evaporated as if they themselves had become dust before his very eyes.

He looked about frantically, and saw his men fruitlessly defending themselves from the foul things. All around he heard the sounds of death.

Looking up at where he had fallen from, the Commander saw his own assailant swiftly diving toward him.

Not like this, he seethed.

He lifted his sword across his chest, the keen edge facing the terrible creature. Mere feet now separated them from each other and the foul thing bared its fangs at him.

The air around him began to fill with a red light.

The creature was upon him, screaming.

The Commander swung his sword hard towards the thing's midriff.

Red light engulfed them as the scream reached a piercing note and Cameron McAllister felt his back hit the mattress hard as he awoke. His breath was strained, and his sheets were soaked with sweat. Sitting up, still frantic, he looked around for the source of the noise. He quickly found it upon his right, and raised his hand to kill it with his sword.

The reality of his surroundings came to him.

He recognised his room and his mobile phone, flashing and vibrating with his six o'clock alarm. Sighing, Cam leant over and lightly pressed the screen. Looking to his left he saw the early summer sun filtering in through his red curtains.

He hated dreams like that.

He shook himself, running his long fingers through his mid-length, brown hair. It, too, was soaked with the fever of his dream. He was quivering. He closed his eyes and rubbed his face with his palms.

It had been a recurring dream for nearly six months now. One night it had come upon him unannounced and since then it had taken over his slumbers, becoming more in depth and unnerving each time.

He knew why: it was because of his new job.

Cam was an actor. Fresh of out university, he had begun his assault on the profession with a two-year stint touring the country with an educational show for schools but he had quickly grown tired of living out of his suitcase, taken the plunge, and left. Then had followed the horrible period of his life where he had spent nearly a year out of work, waiting for the next contract to come. Fortunately he had been able to live at home with his mother, or he was not sure he would have kept his head above water.

Then his mother had seen an advert that changed everything. It was for a character acting position at Edgeborough

Castle, a tourist attraction barely an hour from his home town of Welverleigh, and it was an eight month contract. After twelve months of exile it was as if a bright, verdant oasis had formed in the barren desert of his life.

But first he had to get the job.

The day of the audition had been positively alive with tension; it radiated from him as if he were on fire. His mother, being as supportive of him as she had been all his life, did everything she could to make things easier for him; conversation, distraction, advice. Cam had wanted none of it. He wanted simply to get it all over and done with.

The train journey had only taken an hour and a quarter, but it had felt to Cam as if he was reliving all of those twelve previous months. What if he didn't get the job? What if he forgot his lines? What if he choked under pressure?

When the train had pulled into the unassuming station that served Edgeborough, Cam stepped off as optimistically as he could and began the twenty minute walk to the Castle.

As he made his way through the small, historic town, Cam saw that the place was veined by tiny alleyways and winding single-tracked roads that ducked between and across one another as if trying to escape unseen. The Castle itself seemed to be the vessel into which all these roads, alleys, and pavements poured themselves, allowing the great medieval structure to rise up out of the rocky hill that supported its ancient stone walls.

Cam crossed the busy main road that stood before the Castle, then walked through a rocky cleft that had long ago been dug into the centre of the hill. It did not seem to truly belong there, set against the twenty-first century roads and houses that encroached upon Edgeborough's Tudor and Victorian denizens. The sun did not penetrate here, for the cleft was covered on both sides by thick deciduous trees that stood as age-old sentries held by an unspoken oath. Cam felt the gentle, cool air brush against the small beads of sweat that had begun to dot his forehead.

At the end of the cleft there stood a pair of old iron gates that were of typically ornate Victorian design. Their bars seemed to be wrapped amongst themselves as if they were vines or creepers, and their black iron stems were punctuated by gilded blooms. But between these bars was what truly held Cam's attention.

Beyond the gates lay a gentle grass verge that turned upwards towards the sky in a graceful curve, broken only by the meeting between the verdant bank and the stark white stone of the castle walls. The view astounded Cam. He had remembered coming here on school trips when he was younger, but it had been so long that he had forgotten just how impressive a structure it was. It had stood, he knew, for around eight-hundred years on that spot, and it had seen many great people and events.

The walls looked as though they could beat back any advancement; sheer and sure they loomed, defying any who dared to try and breech them. Two towers rose out of the walls, pinnacles of strength and stubborn resilience that protruded like fangs out of stone gums. Their tops stood two hundred feet above the green, weed-filled dyke that surrounded the base of the structure, lying in wait for those foolhardy enough to try and storm the keep.

The dyke itself could be crossed by means of one of two bridges; the first, nearest to Cam, was wide and led through the gatehouse, while the other was a small-walled, narrow sliver of stone that ducked behind the furthest tower and crept through the wall away to Cam's right, out of vision. Both were guarded by thick, heavy, oaken gates.

Cam had drunk deeply of this sight before he moved up the rather disappointing concrete steps towards the Castle's main entrance. Here he was greeted by the realities of a tourist attraction; turnstiles, car parks, ticket offices. The place was also covered with posters advertising the various attractions and features of the castle that would entice those who were as yet undecided to stride forward and demand entry. Cam glanced at these quickly, then walked purposefully into the restaurant that stood at one side of the small courtyard. This was, he had been told, where the audition would be held.

The next few hours of Cam's life were a blur, though he vaguely remembered that he felt the audition had gone well.

He recalled the sensation of holding the script in his hands, crisp and freshly printed. This was followed by the crippling anxiety of the next two hours he had spent wandering the castle grounds before the workshop session began, and the mix of paranoia and concentration that engulfed him it when it did.

By the time he was back on the train and returning to Welverleigh, Cam was physically tired, emotionally drained, and quietly confident that he had done all he could possibly have done.

That evening he had just sat and watched TV with his mother, trying to avoid the subject of the audition and take his mind off the fact he would probably have to wait at least five days before he got an answer.

Three days later he had been offered the job.

That had been six months ago, and the only troubling thing that had happened to him since had been the recurrence of the dream. He understood it for the first few weeks - working at a castle and acting like a medieval character all day would evoke a vivid imagination like his - but he could not understand why his mind persisted in replaying the vision over and over again.

Bringing himself back to the present morning, he threw his legs over the side of his bed and let his toes touch the rough carpet beneath. He took a swig from the glass of water which rested upon his bedside table, and shot a quick glance around his room. His collection of movies and computer games could explain his dreams, though he had owned the majority of them long before taking the job at Edgeborough Castle.

Cam let the thought slip from his head as he stood himself up and grabbed some clothes from his wardrobe. Then he went out onto the landing and trotted down the stairs.

"Cam, breakfast!" his mother's voice rang through the house to meet him.

"Give me five minutes," he replied, almost automatically,

lifting a towel from the radiator.

"You're welcome."

After washing, Cam sat in the front room of the house watching the sports channels, greedily eating the bowl of cereal that had been prepared for him. His mother sat in an armchair across from him, reading something on her laptop. She chuckled as Cam cursed the news that the first morning of the Test Match had been delayed by rain.

"I don't know why you're so concerned," she said, dryly, "you're not going to be in to watch it."

"That's not the point," Cam said, deciding to turn his attention to his phone.

"You are working today, aren't you?" his mother asked, looking at the clock.

"Yeah," came another automatic response, "but my train isn't for another forty-five minutes."

His mother closed her laptop and stood, collecting his now empty bowl from him.

"Well, it looks like you've got a nice morning for the walk."

Cam looked out of the window and saw the clear blue sky. A couple of small birds danced in the early morning sun, flitting between the branches of the trees in the gardens opposite. He smiled.

"You know me, always game for a wander."

This was certainly true.

Welverleigh was a small village on the outskirts of the larger town of King's Marton in the heart of England. It sat nestled within the rolling hills and fields surrounding the River Welve, and Cam's house was tucked away in a small corner that bordered both the town and the countryside beyond.

If he turned left out of his front door he was surrounded by farms and pastures, but turning right – as he would do so this morning – took him almost immediately into the suburbs of King's Marton. Cam enjoyed this arrangement immensely as it enabled him to stride into town and buy any and all things he required, and then simply fade away on long walks into the countryside whenever he wished.

These latter sojourns would often last hours, for Cam loved nothing more than getting lost in the fields and woods that surrounded his home. They stretched for miles away from the suburbs, with many hidden trails and paths seldom trod except for the most intrepid dog walker. It was in such places that Cam could let go of all the other, real-world thoughts he had, and just simply enjoy the gentle murmur of nature.

Not that his home life was particularly ungentle – he and his mother lived very happily and relatively comfortably together – but there was always something, either work or personal, that he just needed to escape from. Nature offered him the perfect outlet.

"Yes, well," his mother was saying as she came back into the room carrying her work shoes, "don't forget to pop to the shops and get something for your tea tonight. I've got a meeting so I may well be back later than usual."

Cam nodded, bringing his mind back from the woodland.

"Did you want me to get you anything?"

"I don't think so," she mused quietly, putting her shoes on, "but I'll message you if I change my mind."

"OK."

His mother stood and looked at him, semi-seriously.

"You have got her a card, haven't you?"

"It's not 'til next week, you know."

Cam looked up and saw his mother's expression had not changed.

"Yes," he continued testily, "one of the funny ones."

"I doubt she would expect anything less," his mother replied, a knowing grin on her face.

"If it was soppy and heartfelt, she'd wonder what I was dying of," Cam sighed, standing and picking up his bag, "so best not to worry her."

"Fair enough."

His mother embraced him warmly as they both prepared to

leave.

"Have a good day," she said.

"I will," Cam sighed, only slightly fighting the hug, "I'm all grown up now, remember?"

Her smile did not move.

"I know. I just like saying it."

Cam laughed quietly.

"I'll be here when you get home. I promise. See you later, Mum."

With one last, smiling look at him, his mother stepped aside and allowed him to reach the front door.

"Shall I lock it?" he asked as he went out into the fresh morning air.

"No, I'll be right behind you. Now, go on. You'll miss your train."

Cam smiled at her, and pulled the door closed behind him.

Very quickly he became aware that the heat of the day was already growing, despite the early hour. He unconsciously rolled his long-sleeves up beyond his elbows and stepped through the weed-ridden front lawn and into the road.

Turning right towards the town, Cam reached the end of his road and began his walk. Within ten minutes the atmosphere about him had changed; he had left Welverleigh and begun to descend into the heart of King's Marton itself. The town centre reared up in front of him, with its small shopping centre and circular flowerbeds.

Ducking through an underpass, Cam was once more bathed in lucid sunlight as he began to ascend the hill on the other side of King's Marton towards the station. Though it stood on the main line between Worcester and London, King's Marton itself was not graced by any except the slowest of trains. Fortunately for Cam there was a daily service to Edgeborough that managed to get him there long before his call-time of nine-fifteen.

As he took his seat in the air-conditioned carriage, Cam settled himself with his headphones and music, and set about watching the world go by until they reached Jason's stop.

This took about twenty minutes and, as they slowed into the platform, Cam saw his friend waiting with his bag slung across his shoulders. He spotted Cam through the window and gave him an exaggerated smile, to which Cam responded with a more subdued salute.

Cam liked Jason; he had been one of the first members of the tight-knit cast at the Castle to open the group to him, and they had been firm friends ever since. They were similar in many ways: sharing many of the same interests outside of work, and enjoying many of the same elements of their profession. If someone had pronounced them brothers Cam would not have been surprised, though they truly looked nothing alike. Cam's clean shaven, thin face looked young compared to the rugged, strong, stubbly jaw and deep-set eyes of Jason. He looked as though he had seen a good deal more of life than Cam, despite being two years his junior.

Cam watched as his friend side-stepped into the seat opposite him, hoisting his bag from his shoulder and letting it thump down onto what passed for upholstery.

"Morning," Cam said quietly.

"You alight mate?" Jason replied in his northern accent. "Missed you last night."

"Good evening was it?"

Jason, now fully settled, took out his phone, tapped at it a few times, and turned the screen to face Cam. He saw a photograph of Jason and a few others gathered around a cheap, clearly plastic trophy of some kind. Cam smiled.

"How many deep were you all there?" he asked, morbidly laughing.

"No more than three," Jason replied, feigning hurt, "what do you expect? It's not every season you win the King's Marton District Cricket League Seventh Division Third Eleven Cup, you know. Show some respect."

Cam laughed again, louder this time.

"That is certainly true. Who scored the runs?"

Jason shrugged.

“Not me, that's for sure.”

Cam's smile turned into a grin.

“There's a shock.”

Jason raised an eyebrow.

“Says the man who averages seven on a good day?”

“With bat and ball, I'll have you know,” Cam retorted indignantly.

“You wish, mate!”

Jason took his phone back and the two of them settled in for the remainder of their journey.

“How come you weren't there, anyway?”

“I hadn't seen Mum in a while,” Cam said softly, “what with summer season at the Castle and Cup games and all. She likes me doing extra stuff and keeping busy, but it's the wrong time of year really.”

Jason nodded.

“Yeah. It's next week, isn't it?”

“Right around Sonia's birthday, yeah,” Cam replied.

His friend looked into his eyes.

“Are you OK, mate?”

Cam shrugged.

“Yeah. It's never really meant much to me. I was about three when he went so I barely knew the man. It's Mum that's cut up about it, understandably. I just like to be around more when it's happening.”

“I get you. And good on you, too.”

Cam smiled.

“I don't really do anything. I mean, what can I do? It's been nineteen years. I can't change what happened, or bring him back. I just try and be there, you know?”

Jason sighed and took a swig from a water bottle he pulled from his bag.

“Still though, mate, I know plenty who wouldn't.”

Cam nodded silently.

“Yeah, I suppose.”

Jason sensed the mood and decided to change tack.

"What are you on today?" he asked, airily.

"Keeper," Cam responded, equally upbeat.

"I still don't get why you like doing that so much," Jason replied, a note of distaste in his voice.

"It's a good script," Cam replied honestly, "and I get to be outside in the sun all day. What about you?"

Jason adjusted himself in his seat and sat deliberately upright.

"I am Fingall," he pronounced in a rich and deep voice.

"That'll be a nice change for you," Cam said.

"Yeah, I was getting bored of being in the Gaol," Jason sighed, "but it also means I'm stuck with you all day, so swings and roundabouts."

"Yeah, fair comment," Cam agreed, smiling, "who else have we got with us?"

"From what I remember, we've got Nikki, Richard, and Will."

Cam shook his head.

"Nah, Will's off mate. Swapped his shift with Darren I think."

"Then we've got Nikki, Richard, and Darren," Jason corrected himself.

It was going to be a good day, Cam thought. A team of people he liked to work with, all in Fingall's Tower – one of the Castle's prize attractions – and he was performing his favourite role.

The Keeper.

The Keeper was the character the public first met on their way into Fingall's Tower and their primary job was to tell them the Legend of Fingall; an historic tale that had been told in the area for nearly a thousand years.

It spoke of the warrior Fingall, who had hailed from Morton's Edge – this being the medieval name for Edgeborough – and his quest to defeat the evil giant Galforth who had plagued the lands about for many years.

One day, after the village had been tormented one too many times by the Giant, Fingall decided that he would do away with Galforth once and for all by challenging him to single combat. Galforth, believing that his size and strength would be too much for the man to bear, accepted without hesitation. Fingall declared they would meet in a cutting in the hills barely a mile from the old village centre. Galforth agreed, and laughed as he watched the haughty Warrior stride out of the village towards the valley.

The Giant followed, deliberately taking the longest route through the village so that all would see him and be reminded ever more that any who challenged him would be destroyed. He strode so purposefully, and to so many corners of the village, that it took him four hours to reach the spot that Fingall had deigned for them to do battle.

It was this decision that proved to be his undoing.

While Galforth had danced his victory prematurely through the streets, Fingall had set about taking away the Giant's advantage.

Upon reaching the spot where they would battle, he dug a hole barely two feet wide but over four feet deep. The earth had been heavy and hard for him to move, and the labour had spent all but his last reserves. If it had not been for the help of some of the villagers who dared to rise up against the Giant, he doubtless would have flogged away any strength he had in the endeavour. They then covered the hole with a lattice of tree branches and scatterings of grass, loam, and leaves.

When Galforth's tall, muscular form had rumbled into the valley, Fingall stood himself barely six feet beyond the trap, level with the centre of the hole so as to be certain that his plan worked. The villagers who had helped him had now been joined by those who had followed in terrified awe in the Giant's wake, and a great crowd surrounded the two of them.

From his back, the Giant unslung his huge War-hammer; its haft was the trunk of a small tree which still bore the roots at the bottom, and its iron head was the length of Fingall's arms and the size the man's chest. He wielded it in both hands, and stepped forward.

Galforth's foot planted straight into the centre of Fingall's trap, and he fell.

In that moment, Fingall charged and swung his fine blade straight through the thick haft of the War-hammer. The Giant now found himself trapped and weapon-less, his arms having been caught against the walls of the hole, and his heart knew fear for the first time.

Without a moment's hesitation, Fingall sent his sword crashing down into Galforth's skull and the battle was done. He then took up the severed haft of the Giant's axe, and thrust the rooted end into the soil. From this had grown a tree so large that many said that the blood of the Giant ran within its branches. The Giant Oak, as it came to be known, was a great symbol to all the people of Morton's Edge; so much so that they adopted it as their symbol – an oak tree with a hammer's head at the base of it's trunk and a vein of red flowing through the centre.

Cam shook his head. In truth, he knew that it was probably just a tale, inspired by the size of the trees that grew around the town, written to entice tourists to visit. But a part of him always believed that Fingall and Galforth had existed.

No wonder he dreamt the things he did.

By the time he had brought himself back out of his thoughts, he and Jason had arrived at Edgeborough station. Stepping onto the platform, Cam was stunned by the level of heat that brushed against his skin. It was barely quarter-to-nine in the morning and he could already feel beads of sweat rolling down his cheeks and forehead as the sun began to climb towards its potency.

The air in the town centre was thick with the dull, damp smell of pollen. It came upon them in gusts and clumps, and they began to feel stifled and constricted by it. Eventually they came to the cleft he had first walked through six months ago. Under the pleasing touch of the cool air, Cam and Jason slowed their walk a little to allow themselves a brief respite. By the time they reached the Victorian gates that allowed the first glimpse of the Castle, they were far more comfortable.

Cam paused for a moment, reflecting.

“It's pretty cool, isn't it?”

Jason, who had already begun to meander towards the entrance, stopped and took in the sight from where he stood.

“It's not bad,” he grinned.

Cam stepped closer to the gates and pressed his face through them.

“Imagine what it would have been like back in the day. Imagine if we could see it how the people that built it did.”

Jason stepped next to him.

“It would stink, for a start,” he said, a flat humour in his voice.

“Such a poet,” Cam scoffed.

Jason laughed.

“Shall I leave you to it, or are you coming into work today?”

Cam allowed himself one last moment to enjoy the surroundings, then turned and followed Jason up to the main entrance and into the Castle itself.

When they entered the large, circular courtyard within the walls, Cam looked around and once more took in the place he was fortunate enough to call his 'office'. To his right was Fingall's Tower, where he and Jason would be spending their day. It was not originally called that, of course; it had been named after some Lord who once owned the place but Cam could not recall his name. To his left was the entrance to the Gaol, a gruesome but comedic look at some of the Castle's darker history. Cam had yet to be trained in there, and he was not necessarily that desperate to start.

In front of he and Jason now rose the Great Hall, its large double doors standing open and ready for them at the top of a short flight of steps. They strode across the marble-tiled floor within, up a spiral staircase, and came to the dressing rooms. Here, Cam unceremoniously flung his bag down in front of his locker, while Jason took a moment at the noticeboard to see if there were any changes to the rota. There were not.

Smiling happily to himself with the knowledge of a fun if busy day ahead, Cam strode to the costume store and collected his clothes for the day, then set about getting changed.

Throughout the morning, the cast of the Castle came in in dribs and drabs and did as he had done, all the while exchanging small talk and news. Cam spoke mostly to Jason, though he was now starting to get to know the other members of the team as well. Half an hour later, they all began making their way back down the spiral staircase and once more into the cool air of the Great Hall. With the assembly gathered, nearly twenty strong, the Hall rang with the echo of voices, laughter and camaraderie.

He took a moment to consider the day ahead. The first show would begin at ten-thirty, and would be repeated every quarter of an hour to thirty people until the last show at five-forty-five. He would get an hour for lunch at one, and after that he would bounce around the attraction, playing Galforth, Fingall and the Villager at various points in the afternoon.

He suddenly became aware that Laura, his manager, was speaking.

"Right, morning everyone," Laura began in her clear voice, "just to say a quick thank you to all of you who were in yesterday. It was a really good day with lots of great guest feedback, so please give yourselves a round of applause!"

The ripple of appreciation clattered around the circle.

"And just a reminder that after close today the Maintenance Team will be doing a full shut down of Fingall's Tower so that they and the Tech Team can come in overnight to fix the issues we've been having with the Galforth animatronic. So, if you guys can just make sure its a speedy close down that would be really helpful."

Cam and the other actors nodded their understanding, and Laura continued with the briefing. When she had given out all the information that they needed, he made his way out of the Great Hall and over to the western wall of the Castle where

Fingall's Tower was housed. It was not the tallest tower in the grounds, nor was it the grandest, but it was the oldest and that gave Cam a sense of pride for working in there.

"What's been the problem with Galforth?" Cam asked as they reached the Tower.

"Ah, nothing much," Jason said off-handedly, "just a bit clunky is all. And the voice modulator was doing some odd things yesterday I think."

"Easy fix, you reckon?"

"Not my circus, not my monkeys," Jason shrugged.

"Why didn't they fix him last night?"

"They had a corporate thing on. Whole courtyard was taken over. All hands on deck, from what I've heard. You got enough water? It's gonna be warm out here!"

Cam nodded, indicating his bag.

"Yeah, plenty. I'll be fine."

"Alright mate. See you later."

Jason turned and strode off into the tower. Cam watched him for a second, and then span himself round to face the day ahead. He smiled once more as he saw something that would make it even more enjoyable.

There, walking towards him, was Sonia Coles.

Chapter Two

Fingall's Tower

Sonia Coles was not an actor. Her role at the Castle was as part of the Retail and Photography team, which saw her checking tickets for the attractions, taking photographs at the various photo-ops throughout the Castle, and selling them to the public as they emerged from the attractions. It was not the most exciting job in the world, but it was a damn-sight better than where she could have been stuck to while away the slow hours of her days.

She had never really had a plan except to be successful. Quite how she was going to achieve this had never really occurred to her; she had simply wanted to find a job she liked and to be good at it. And she was very good at her job at the Castle.

She and Cam had met two weeks into his employment, and they had been friends ever since. There was a wonderfully organic feel to their friendship as a whole; nothing ever felt forced, no conversation was ever a struggle. They just knew what to say, and what not to say, to each other and when to say it.

Some, such as Jason, teased him that there was more to their relationship than they let on, but Cam felt for Sonia as a sister. He cared deeply for her, and did not deny it; perhaps she even cared deeply for him in a similar fashion, he had not asked. But there was nothing more than pure, simple kinship between them, and it warmed his heart whenever he got to share in it.

All these thoughts passed over his mind in but a split-second as he saw her walking across the courtyard towards him. She looked up and saw him, resplendent in his costume, and smiled.

"Morning miss," he called to her, bowing in mock reverence, "to what do I owe this pleasure?"

Sonia laughed quietly.

"You've started early," she chided, her smile still mastering her features, "you don't normally come out with the actor-y crap until twelve at the earliest!"

Cam stared at her, feigning hurt.

"Actor-y crap?"

They shared a short embrace, then set about getting the queue line ready for the day ahead.

"Did you hear the pre-books?" Cam asked

Sonia looked at him, a playful and inquisitive glance.

"Were you late for morning meeting again?"

Cam laughed.

"No, I just missed Laura saying them."

"You mean you weren't listening."

"That too."

Sonia rolled her eyes.

"You're hopeless. About two thousand for the day."

Cam smiled.

"Oh, not too bad then. How are you anyway? It feels like ages since we've seen each other."

This was, in part, true; Cam had just had two days off and Sonia had been away for a week before that on holiday. They had spoken in the meantime but they had not laid eyes on each other for near ten days. Cam had truly missed her while she had been away.

"I know," Sonia mused, "Tell you what though, I really needed that holiday! I feel fresh and ready to go!".

"What about Mark and Ellen? Did they enjoy themselves?"

Sonia nodded.

"Yeah, I think so. I don't think Malaga's their kind of place, to be honest, but they seemed OK."

"If they don't like it then why did they go?" Cam asked.

"Because it was my birthday present, wasn't it?" Sonia looked back at him now, a mischievous look upon her face. "They couldn't afford California, so Malaga it was!"

Cam smiled and nodded, then motioned to the far side of the courtyard where the first guests for the day were entering through the large gatehouse.

"Right, I'll go and get show numbers from the ticket tent," Sonia continued, "be back in a sec."

"Have fun," Cam called after her.

"Hey?" came a call from behind him.

Cam turned to see Jason's face waiting at the door.

"What do you want?" he replied with mocked harshness.

"Times, mate."

"Sonia's just gone to get them," Cam called back, "but I reckon we'll be steady. How's Galforth?"

Jason's smile stayed exactly where it was.

"Broken, but in kind of a fun way. The voice modulator is all over the place. I sound like I'm going through puberty again."

He waved and ducked inside, just as Cam became aware that a group was beginning to form at the start of the queue line.

"Good day, my friends," he called out to them, slipping easily into the lofty tones the character demanded, "tickets for Fingall's Tower?"

In total, the group was just over half-full; perhaps twelve people. He counted the tickets – officially Sonia's job, but she was still not back yet – and signalled them down to the rope that cordoned off the entrance to the Tower. Looking up at the clock across the courtyard from him, he saw that he had a full five minutes before the group was scheduled to start their show.

He glanced to his right and saw Sonia striding through the steadily growing crowds.

"Every half hour, or so," she said, taking up her position next to him.

"Yeah, sounds about right. What time are you on lunch today?"

"One," she replied, "you?"

"One as well," Cam said, "Duchess Room?"

Sonia nodded.

"See you there."

She smiled again, then walked quickly down to her position just inside the Tower door to take the group's photos. Cam followed her at a slower pace; he preferred to build up as much tension as his environs allowed. He pulled the hood of his cloak up around his face to add to the mysterious air, and strode purposefully down the grass alongside the queue to his starting position.

"You find yourselves at the base of Fingall's Tower," he started, deliberately startling a few of the guests, "this is a place of great reverence and legend. Be welcomed here, my friends, and know that no harm will come to you.

"I am the Keeper of the Tower. I ward the legend and the memory of Fingall, and of his great battle against the terrible giant, Galforth. The tale, however, is not mine for the telling. There are those inside who are far more gifted in the art of story-weaving, and I would not dare to encroach upon their talents. My purpose is simply to ensure that the tale they tell is not corrupted or altered by anything that may pervert its course.

"To that end, I must warn you that you are responsible to see that nothing you carry with you can cause the story to be altered. Things such as those little boxes which vibrate, make strange noises, allow you to communicate across great distances, and promote the use of words such as 'lol'!"

A gentle laugh from the group.

"They must not be used," Cam continued, "also, anything that allows the capture of imagery, moving or otherwise, with or without the flash, must not be used! The consequences for any person breaking these rules shall be severe. The consequences for the equipment shall be worse. You will, of course, have it returned to you, but I cannot guarantee it will be the same shape or number of pieces as it was when it went in."

Another, louder laugh greeted that line.

"With that knowledge, my friends, my companion here," Cam motioned to Sonia, "will capture your images with Fingall's coat of arms. You may reclaim this at the end of your tale. Go now and hear the legend of the Great Fingall!"

He ended his short performance with a flourish, then turned away and strode back towards the head of the queue.

"This way, travellers," he heard Sonia say in her saleswoman voice. He chuckled to himself - she hated having to act the part of a villager while she took their photographs.

As Cam strode back to the top of the queue line, Sonia would be efficiently photographing and filtering people into the tower. He took this moment to take his medieval-style bag from around his neck and check the contents he had brought with him; water bottle, mobile phone, walkie-talkie (in case of emergencies), all present and correct. He put the bag down amongst some barrels that stood near the head of the queue, but as he did so he heard the clatter of his phone dropping onto the path. Picking it up, he saw that his bag had developed a hole just large enough for his phone to slip through.

Making a mental note to get it sewn up at the end of the day, he replaced his phone safely on the other side of the bag from the hole, and stood to face Sonia as she walked back up the path towards him.

"Not a bad group to start," he said.

"Yeah, they'll do," she replied, then handed him a bottle of sun cream. "Here, you'll probably need this today. I found it sat by the camera in there. Must have been left here last night."

Cam took it, thanking her as he did so, and quickly applied it to all the exposed areas of his body.

"Next one's in half an hour you reckon?"

Sonia took the piece of paper containing the times out her pocket and looked them over.

"Yeah," she said carefully, reading as she went, "then a couple of back-to-backs at eleven, then single groups until twelve. Then a couple more back-to-backs and then lunch."

"Joyful," Cam said, "so that gives us time to talk about your birthday."

Sonia sat herself on the barrels and looked at him.

"What about it?"

"Well," he started, "any big plans? I know there's the party next week, which I will be there for, but anything else on the horizon?"

Sonia shook her head.

"Not really. After having a holiday paid for me, I can't really ask for much else."

"Not even a pony?" Cam joked.

"Piss off!" Sonia scoffed.

Cam laughed.

"Seriously, though, any talk of driving lessons or anything?"

She shook her head again.

"Nah, I don't really need them. I only live fifteen minute's walk away, and the trains'll do for everything else."

"Yeah, I suppose," Cam sighed in agreement, "I did miss you last week, you know."

"Of course you did," she said loftily, "I'm awesome."

"And modest."

"So modest."

They smiled, and Cam looked back at her expectantly.

"Alright, I missed you too," she said, standing.

"I know," said Cam, "you said so on your postcard."

"That cost two euros, you know."

Cam lifted his eye brows, impressed.

"I'm honoured."

"Yeah, well, it was on sale."

The morning continued on in much the same way for the next two hours, with their conversations interrupted regularly by the gathering public. Soon it became too hot for the cloak, but Cam did not allow himself the luxury of fully removing it; he simply dropped the hood from his face and shrugged it from his shoulders so that it now hung down the centre of his back.

Still, by twelve o'clock the the temperature was becoming restrictive. Even Sonia, able as she was to alter her outfit and allow herself to cool, had begun to show signs that she was uncomfortable.

"How did you cope in Malaga," Cam had asked after a particularly excitable group.

"Sun bathing is one thing," Sonia panted, "but this is very different."

They let another full group assemble and be directed down to the rope then, seeing that they still had two minutes before Cam was required to begin his speech, they took a moment and treated themselves to some water. Until now, Cam had not really noticed how parched he had actually become and the water, though warmed by the sun, was a very welcome relief. Sonia, her face ruddy with heat, sat on the barrels once again.

"Warm isn't it?"

Sonia nodded, puffing her cheeks out against the heat.

"I might see if I can swap and do sales this afternoon. At least I'll be indoors out of this heat."

"Yeah," Cam sighed, "might be a good idea. I'm actually quite glad I'm inside after lunch. I can have the fan on."

They saw to the next group, speech and photos going smoothly, then Cam drained the last of his water bottle. Since there was a short gap before the next group would begin to assemble, they took the chance to stand in the photo room, out of the sun, for a moment.

Ducking inside the entrance, Cam was greeted by the sickly mixture of the cold air of the Tower's interior, and the sun against his back. He refilled his bottle using the dispenser hidden behind a canvas curtain, away from public view so as not to spoil the magic, then Sonia passed him her bottle to do the same. Once this had been done, they turned and faced the Castle.

Seeing it framed through a genuine medieval door once again set off that part of Cam's mind that loved not only history, but stories like that of Fingall. His imagination raced with tales of glory, of heroic deeds, of battles great and terrible. Even now as he looked at the walls, with blue sky above and visitors walking along the battlements, he felt as if he could see into the very past; a glimpse of what the Castle might have looked like in its heyday.

“Ready for the next show?” he heard Sonia ask him, her voice drifting across his consciousness.

“Last one before lunch, isn't it?” he asked, absently.

“Absolutely,” she responded, “then an hour in the cool.”

Cam took another sip of his water, then put it into his bag. As he did so, his phone dropped out of the hole again and bounced on the flagstones.

“You dropped that,” Sonia said, smiling.

“Thanks. What would I do without you?”

He knelt down and once more retuned the thing to his bag, making certain this time it was as far away from the hole as possible.

“I'll see if Tammy can fix it at the end of the day.”

“Probably a good idea. Not very magical if the Keeper drops his 'little box that promotes the word lol'.”

She grinned at him.

“Angling for my job are you?” he asked.

“Good lord, no,” she laughed, “I just hear you say it all day and it kind of gets stuck in there.”

Cam slung his bag over his shoulder and strode, deliberately dramatically, out of the door and up the path to meet the group. Sonia shook her head as she watched him go, then readied herself to take more photos.

The group were much like the rest they had done that morning, and when Sonia had finished the last photo they walked across the courtyard, past the entrance to the Great Hall, and through a small, unassuming wooden door. Behind this was a short spiral staircase that led to the Duchess Room, one of the staffrooms. It was currently quiet, as the Gaol had their break an hour earlier and the other staffrooms were more conveniently placed outside the walls, so he and Sonia had their pick of chairs.

As they ate and rested, they talked little. The heat had gotten to both of them, so they were mostly just enjoying being in the shade. Cam had removed as much of his costume as was decent, and sat back in his seat while Sonia sat next to an open window taking in what little breeze there was.

The hour's rest came and went far too quickly for either of their liking, and soon they were making their way back across the courtyard towards the Tower.

Since Jason was scheduled to take over the Keeper, Cam went inside the Tower proper, up the stairs, and into the Villager Room. This was, as might be expected, themed into looking like the interior of a simple, medieval cottage, and much cooler than it had been outside. The walls were faux wattle-and-daub, and a very convincing fibreglass fire pit stood in the centre; it was around this that the group would be gathered, by Cam, as he delivered his script. This spoke of the evils and harm that had befallen the villagers at Galforth's hand, and how the hero Fingall was to save them all. Then, he would declare that one of them, usually a child, had been selected to be Fingall's Standard Bearer, and they would be handed a banner with the Giant Oak sigil upon it, and told that they must give this to Fingall when the time came.

The group would then go through a corridor that had been made to look like a dark, spooky forest, through which the slow, pounding footsteps of Galforth could be heard, and finally to 'The Clearing'. This was a large, circular room that had, once upon a time, been a Guard Room, now repurposed as the valley in which Galforth met his doom. Not only was there an animatronic Galforth awaiting their guests, but an heroic meeting with Fingall himself as he vanquished the Giant.

Cam had thought from the moment he started his job that it was a good attraction, and audiences enjoyed it, especially the families of the children chosen to be the Standard Bearer.

After a few moments, the first group arrived and he gathered them around the fire pit. They enjoyed the story, the child was nervously thrilled about being given such a responsibility, and they left chattering excitedly about the mild peril they were about to encounter on their way through the forest.

So it continued for the next hour, before Jason appeared though the door to signal Cam's move to be Galforth.

“How's it going in here?” he had asked, putting his bag against the fire pit.

“Not too bad,” Cam sighed, “nice and cool at least. How was it out there?”

Jason puffed his cheeks out.

“Warm. Glad I'm not you or Nikki. More than an hour out there would've done me in. This is much better.”

Cam grinned and raised an eyebrow.

“Imagine if you hadn't been drunk last night,” he said.

“Don't,” Jason said seriously, “I'm regretting it enough as it is.”

Cam laughed and clapped his friend on the shoulder.

“The fan's been on full, enjoy it. You're safe for the rest of the day.”

Jason nodded.

“Thanks bud. I think there's a group behind me so best get into the forest.”

Cam grabbed his bag, making certain that his phone stayed within it, and let himself out of the door into the Woodland Corridor.

This was a more claustrophobic space than the Village, with the narrow corridor bedecked in tree branches that arched over the passageway, above them a black cloth dotted with white fairy lights to add to the ambience. The sounds, and physical vibrations, of the Giant's footsteps were there at intervals, shaking the floor and reverberating in the air about him. Despite having been working there for six months, Cam had never really got used to this place; it made him uneasy, and he did not like to linger there.

Reaching the end of the corridor, he saw the oak door which led into the Clearing, but he took the very well disguised door to his left and entered the Control Room. Nikki was finishing her performance as Galforth.

To the group in the room it was a magical moment as the Giant was finally defeated by Fingall and his heroic Standard Bearer. If only they could have seen how it all worked.

Nikki was stood in the centre of the tightly packed space, in front of a monitor through which she could see the group as the animatronic Galforth would see them. The animatronic itself was controlled via a computer program and a motion suit – a set of gloves and a headpiece – that the actors wore, allowing it to mimic their movements. For the voice, there was a headset microphone attached to a voice modulator, allowing them all to have the deep, booming tones expected of a giant.

Cam smiled as he watched Nikki flailing her arms, taking a moment to appreciate just how ludicrous his job was sometimes.

"...you have bested me!" she cried in a truly dramatic tone. "I surrender to thee, Fingall!"

"Surrender?" came Richard's voice through the tinny speakers – he himself was in the Clearing Room with the audience. "I fear that it is too late for surrender. For the people of Edge Morton, I strike!"

Cam watched on the monitor as he raised his sword. Before it fell Nikki, using a button on the suit, sent the room into a momentary darkness. When the lights came back up, a scaled-down Giant Oak had appeared in the centre of the room.

Richard finished the show as Nikki began to extricate herself from the suit and microphone.

"Is it that time already?"

Cam nodded.

"Yup. You're going outside now, aren't you?"

"Yeah, time for a bit of Keeper."

"Has Richard said anything about wanting to swap?"

Nikki shook her head.

"No, I think he's happy on Fingall for now. Maybe see how he feels later?"

The door to the room opened, revealing Richard in full Fingall regalia.

"Hey Cam," he breathed, "is it you now?"

"For the next hour, yeah. Unless you wanted to swap or anything?"

"I should be fine, if you don't mind being a Giant for two hours?"

Cam smiled.

"I'm game if you are."

"Top stuff, see you in a bit."

Nikki looked at Cam.

"That's that one sorted then. See you upstairs."

Cam waved her a goodbye as he got himself into the suit. Before the group came in, he tested it to see what he could do. Jason was right, it was very clunky and sluggish, but he could make it work. After the show about to come in, there were only two or three more spread across the two hours before the close anyway, from what he remembered of the times.

These shows, and the remainder of his working day, passed without anything of note, and soon he was back upstairs in the dressing room getting ready for the journey home. It had been a good day, but he was tired now and looking forward to spending a relaxing evening at home.

Jason, already changed and hoisting his bag on to his shoulders, came and stood in front of him.

"You coming to the pub for one?"

Cam shook his head.

"I would love to, mate, but I promised Mum I'd be home when she got back. I think I'm probably out for most of this week."

Jason nodded.

"I thought as much, but it would've been rude not to ask."

Cam smiled.

"I appreciate it bud. As soon as Mum's settled again, I will definitely take you up on it. I could do with letting off a bit of steam."

A gentle hand upon his shoulder.

"You know where I am, mate."

"Yeah. Thanks. You in tomorrow?"

Jason stepped back and threw his arms out wide, a beaming smile upon his face.

"As always," he said.

"See you, then."

Cam watched as his friend turned and strolled out of the dressing room, whistling some tune to himself. For a moment, Cam could not help the feeling of sadness that rose within him. He enjoyed spending time with his friends, and he had not done it in what felt like an age. In truth it had probably only been about two weeks and he knew it, but he stilled missed it.

He puffed out his cheeks and changed back into his own clothes, then went to empty his bag. He dropped his head and cursed himself silently.

His phone was not there.

Dragging himself to his feet, he gathered up his belongings and went into the corridor. He saw Laura, his manager, chatting to one of the Gaol actors.

"Sorry Laura," he said, "but do you happen to know when the Tech lot are going to be in Fingall's Tower?"

"I think they said they wouldn't be starting until five," Laura answered, "why?"

"I, uh, left my phone in the control room. Would I be OK to go and grab it?"

She shrugged and checked her watch.

"I don't see why not. They won't have started yet."

"Brill. Thanks."

Cam turned and made his way quickly down the stairs, almost two at a time. He was already going to struggle to catch his train and be in time to beat his mother home, having to go back into the Tower was an unnecessary inconvenience he could very much have done without.

Out of the Great Hall and into the Courtyard he went, barely taking any notice of anyone else around him. By the time he had reached the door to the Tower he was sweating and out of breath.

"Hey?!"

Cam looked up, preparing to answer to one of the Tech or Maintenance personnel for being in their way, but was surprised by the sight of Sonia walking towards him.

"Oh, hey. You still here?"

Sonia laughed.

"I was about to ask you something similar."

"I left my phone in the Tower."

Sonia rolled her eyes.

"Do you know where it is?"

"Yeah," he sighed, "it'll be in the control room. That's where I had it last."

Sonia stepped past him and opened the door of the Tower, then turned back to face him.

"Well, come on then."

Cam looked at her quizzically.

"Are you coming with me?" he asked.

Sonia nodded.

"Why?" Cam pressed.

"Because," she answered loftily, "you clearly need supervision. Besides, two of us will find it quicker."

She grinned, and now it was Cam's turn to roll his eyes.

"Well, thank you for stepping in to make sure I don't do anything stupid," he said, a voice thick with irony.

"You're welcome," Sonia chimed, bobbing a curtsey.

"Get a move on," Cam said, fussing his way past her, "I've got a train to catch."

Inside the Tower was dark and quiet, and both of them were acutely aware of every single sound they made as they walked up the stairs to the Villager's Room. Sonia stopped momentarily to confirm that Cam had definitely not lost his phone here, and then they moved through the door into the Woodland Corridor.

As soon as he had stepped through the door, Cam felt

strange. He could not put his finger on what or why, but something here was different. He looked at Sonia, as she entered behind him.

“You OK?” he asked.

She looked back at him blankly.

“Yeah. Why wouldn't I be?”

He shook himself.

“No-- no reason. Just checking. They've not put the workers on, I see,” he added, referring to the dim light that now encompassed them.

Sonia raised an eyebrow at him.

“Not scared of the dark, are we?”

“A bit,” Cam admitted, “but that's not what I meant. Forget it, come on.”

He turned and continued to make his way down the passage. The pounding footsteps of the Giant had gone, and the eerie silence only added to his unease. He mentally caught himself – he knew this corridor inside and back to front, there was quite literally no reason for him to be uneasy.

Putting it down to tiredness, he strode carefully through the darkness and came to the control room door. He pushed it open and immediately felt for the light switch. The neon glow that thrummed into life around him did a lot to settle his nerves.

“There it is,” he said, spotting his phone on the floor in the opposite corner, “right where I left it.”

“Good,” Sonia sighed distractedly.

Smiling wryly to himself, Cam stepped through the space and picked up his phone.

The light snapped out.

Initially startled, Cam took a moment to adjust to the new darkness and rolled his eyes.

“Very funny,” he said over his shoulder, “but I told you I'm not scared of the dark.”

“I didn't do anything,” Sonia replied earnestly.

Cam turned around and looked at her.

“Are you sure? You didn't lean on the switch by mistake? I

do that all the time."

Sonia shook her head, and Cam could see that she was standing well away from the switch.

"Oh," he said, trying to hide his now growing disturbance, "well then."

Sonia saw right through him.

"It's probably the Tech team," she said reassuringly, "they'll need to switch the power off to do whatever it is they're doing in here, won't they?"

Cam gathered himself once more, and nodded.

"Yeah, 'course."

"You really are scared of the dark, aren't you?" Her question was sympathetic, and genuinely surprised.

"Normally?" Cam breathed. "No, not especially. But we're surrounded by fake magical stuff, in the pitch black, and I have an overactive imagination."

Sonia nodded slowly.

"Then let's go back out into the real world, shall we?"

"Yeah, that's probably a good call."

Sonia quickly put an arm around him in a show of solidarity, then they shuffled back out into the now pitch black corridor.

The feeling that something was not right hit Cam again, harder and more pronounced this time. He felt himself involuntarily shiver, but did all he could to quash the feeling and focus on Sonia in front of him. She had turned immediately right to back down towards the Villager Room, but after only a couple of steps she stopped and took a sharp breath.

"Jesus," she sighed, laughing and holding her hand to her chest, "you scared the crap out of me!"

Cam looked past her and saw a Figure at the end of the corridor. The outline was difficult to make out, but it looked like a man. He joined Sonia in her nervous laughter.

"Bloody hell, mate," he said, "you nearly gave us a heart attack."

The Figure did not move or make a sound.

“Sorry,” Cam continued, as he and Sonia slowly continued their steps down the corridor, “I'm one of the actors. I left my phone in the control room.”

Still the Figure stood still and silent. They had nearly reached whoever it was, but the outline remained unfamiliar; Cam could not make out a face or any identifying features.

“Is that you, Tim?” Sonia said. “If it is, good joke but Halloween isn't 'til October.”

Nothing.

“Tim?” Sonia pressed again, uncertainly.

Now Cam saw a little more detail. Whoever it was was wearing a hooded jacket, or maybe it was a cloak? Why would it be a cloak? Whatever it was, it was black and looked thick. Maybe a hoodie? It covered the Figure's face very well in the gloom; each and every detail was hidden.

“*Iarwë...*”

Sonia stepped back as the Figure finally vocalised something.

“Sorry, what?”

“*Iarwë...*”

Whatever it was saying was in a low hiss, barely audible even above the silence.

Cam watched as Sonia made a big point of rolling her eyes. She strode forward and lifted the hood from the Figure's head.

“Look, we get it, you're being scary, but...”

She stopped, and staggered backwards into Cam. He caught her instinctively, but could not take his eyes off the sight now before them.

Where a head and face should have been was a black, empty nothingness; an impossible void. No other features could be seen, and even the edges of the face was obscured.

“What the hell?!” Sonia breathed.

“Jesus!” Cam gasped.

The Figure took a step forward.

“Come on!” Sonia said, dragging him back towards the

control room. They burst through the door but, when Cam looked up, he realised they had instead entered the 'Clearing', where Fingall would be seen to make his final stand against the animatronic Giant, rather than the control room. Sonia ran across the space and hurled herself at the door in the far wall.

It did not move.

"Locked!" she spat, panting.

"Who the hell was that?" Cam asked between gasps.

"The hell should I know!?" Sonia retorted. "But when I find out they are gonna get a talking to!"

Looking about them they allowed their eyes to readjust to the new darkness they found themselves in. This room had a higher ceiling than the others, and was all in all larger, so there was at least some air. To Cam's right was the hidden alcove with the animatronic waiting to burst into the room and fight whoever was portraying Fingall, to his left was the plastic tree stump where Fingall would sit and await the audience and his opponent. Meanwhile, in the centre was the covered 'pit' where the Giant would fall – in reality, a circular recess two feet deep out of which would appear the miniature Giant Oak at the end of the show.

Cam held on to the ideas of 'illusions', 'plastic tree stumps', and 'shows' to comfort him; everything in this tower, however well presented, was a theatrical set. A set that he knew well and trusted. And whoever was playing tricks on them, however elaborate, was doing just that – playing tricks.

Sonia walked back over to the door through which they had entered.

"What are you doing?" he asked her, just about keeping his voice level.

"I'm not just going to sit in here and give whoever that idiot is out there the satisfaction of being scared," she said purposefully, "I've got stuff to do this evening!"

She yanked on the handle.

The door did not open.

"Oh for crying out loud!" she cried, exasperated. "You got

us! Well done! Have a medal! Now let us out!"

Cam looked around to see if there was any sign of who might be responsible for this ridiculousness. He saw nothing.

A blinding flash of light, accompanied by the fierce crackle of lightning, filled the room for a split second, and then was gone.

Sonia threw her arms up in frustration.

"Very nice," she seethed through gritted teeth, "the new effects work well. You should be very proud. Now let us out!"

Still searching for some explanation, Cam's eyes now fell upon the alcove where the animatronic lay hidden. He found himself staring into it, unable to look away.

A rumble of thunder rolled through the room, vibrating the very air about them.

"Yep, that one worked too," Sonia called out, "are we done with this now?"

In the darkness, Cam now started to see a shape appear. It seemed far off, but was creeping ever closer.

"Sonia..?" he whispered.

"Are you being serious right now?!" his friend was shouting at the top of her voice. "We're still doing this? What next, someone going to jump out in zombie make up?"

The shape advanced, slow but persistent, and grew with each passing moment.

It was the Figure.

"Sonia?" Cam breathed, louder this time.

"What?!" she demanded, wheeling round on him.

Cam motioned slowly with his head, his throat now too dry to make a sound. Sighing loudly, Sonia stomped over to him and, without following his gaze, pressed her face close to his.

"Are you going to help or am I dealing with these morons myself?"

He could feel the heat of her words against his cheek, but still he could not look away.

"There," he croaked.

Sonia turned her face and at last saw what he was staring

at.

"*Iarwë, Kynsa...*" said a voice, deep and far off.

They shared a glance and instinctively took half a step back.

"Good," Sonia said, trying not to let her nerves into her voice, "you've got the voice modulator fixed."

"That didn't come through the speakers," Cam breathed without thinking.

Sonia hit him on the arm.

"Whose side are you on?"

"*It has been a long time since I saw such as you*," the voice continued, "*though I did not expect to find you together.*"

As he listened, there was something about the words that unsettled Cam, but he could not make out what it was.

"Just drop it!" Sonia cried.

"*Kynsa I have not sought, but for Iarwë I have searched for long count of years.*"

What was it about the words? Cam's mind raced, listening intently to Figure out what it was that troubled him.

"I swear to god I am going to report the lot of you to HR!"

"*So this is where they hid you from me. No matter, I have found you now.*"

He had it!

"They're not English!" Cam hissed.

"What the hell are you on about?"

"The words. Listen. They aren't English."

"What kind of... Of course they're English! I can understand them!"

Cam shook his head.

"No! Listen!"

"*You can no longer escape me.*"

Sonia was about to unleash her anger at Cam for whatever nonsense he was drivelling, but then she stopped herself.

He was right.

Though she understood them, the words she was actually hearing were not English.

What the hell?

Cam steeled himself, focussing on his mind to ignore what the words were saying and instead hear how they sounded.

"Ovtûl ni'kahla."

"Did you hear it?" he hissed back to Sonia.

"Yeah. 'You are mine'?"

Cam nodded slowly.

"What language is that?" Sonia asked.

Before Cam could respond, lightning exploded into the room and they felt themselves pushed down onto the floor. The air became alive with bright bolts crackling loudly through the gloom. They felt wind against their skin; the fake trees and branches about them shuddering and creaking. The atmosphere became heavy and they found it difficult to breathe. Their bodies were being held down by some invisible force they they could not break.

"Cam?!" Sonia screamed.

"I don't know!" he called back.

Fighting against whatever it was that held them, Cam reached his hand out to touch hers. They grasped together tightly.

The Figure now filled the room, looming over them.

"*You. Are. MINE!*" the Voice roared.

Another, massive fork of lightning erupted and leapt about the room. Cam did all he could to follow it with his eyes, but it was too fast and flitted in and out of his vision. Finally it crashed down just behind their heads, into the recess in the centre of the room. They both cried out in fear.

Before they knew what was happening, the floor beneath them gave way and they felt themselves falling.

They Figure did not fall with them, but receded from their sight quickly. All the while Cam and Sonia knew that they were watching. They couldn't be certain, but there might have been laughter on the edge of their hearing as they fell. If there was, it was soon drowned out by what sounded like running water. It was loud and insistent, filling the void about them.

Around them the darkness began to change. Faint

pinpricks of light began to appear, as stars in the early night. At first only a few, but soon dozens then hundreds filled their sight. Where once was the black of the void was now the orange of evening, tinged at its edges by the last blue of the day.

From this newly lit and cloudless sky came another bolt of lightning, this time surrounding them as if the heavens were creating a cage of electricity about them. It ripped across their vision and the crack echoed into infinity.

Cam's hand gripped around Sonia's, and she responded in kind. He suddenly felt tired, more than he had ever felt before. His eyes were heavy and his body was a burden to his mind.

Their fall was slowing, and the rushing water had babbled itself away and been replaced by a gentle breeze that tugged at their clothes. The pleasant smell of heather began to surround them.

The view above had settled itself into a clear sky at sunset.

Without warning, something brushed against their backs, and the snapping of what sounded like twigs filled their ears. The smell of heather exploded about them as they lay, panting but unhurt, on whatever surface was beneath them.

Their bodies coming back to them, Cam now felt a chill against his skin. The breeze, though gentle, was icy and biting. He saw a slight mist as he breathed, and his lungs burned with sensation of the colder air.

"Sonia?" he coughed.

"I'm alright," she panted.

Suddenly the sound of frantic footsteps approached them. Someone was running.

Cam's head swam and he felt exhausted.

A face suddenly appeared above him. His eyes could not focus on it, but it spoke with a foul smelling breath.

"You! You're alive! Thank the Seven! Did you see it?"

"See what?" he asked automatically as he felt himself starting to lose consciousness.

"The lightning! By the Seven, the lightning! Did you see it?"

Cam felt his eyes closing. His mind and body were shutting down. He did not try to stop them.

Hands on either side of his face, shaking him.

“The lightning! Did you see it?”

Blackness engulfed his vision, and Cam felt himself speak but paid no heed to the words.

“Yeah, we saw it.”

Then there was silence.

Then there was nothing.

Chapter Three

Gismay

As his eyes blinked open, the first thing that Cam noticed was the heat and smell of a log fire. It mixed with the smells of heather, stale sweat, and cooking meat, attacking his nostrils as he lay there, sweating and desperate for a breath of clean air.

Above him was a roof of interlocking, smoke-stained logs, and even from his current position he could see the wooden walls that surrounded him. He turned his head to the side to see what other details he could make out, but an immediate feeling of nausea made him think better of it. He swiftly returned to looking up at the ceiling and decided to focus on his breathing.

After a moment, he heard the sound of feet shuffling across a wooden floor.

A wisp of breath, unclean and thick, cascaded into his nostrils, followed by the vision of a face he did not recognise. Three weeks growth of beard framed an unremarkable visage with a masculine jaw, topped by a mane of dusty brown hair.

Instinctively, Cam tried to jerk back and away from the stranger, but as soon as he began to move the nausea surged once more through his body. He felt his eyes roll back into his head as his body threatened to shutdown once more, but he managed to keep himself conscious.

If there was someone here he did not know, he wanted to be awake.

A firm but friendly hand pressed itself against his chest, urging him gently to lie still once more, and the eyes of the face scanned his body almost unconsciously. An expression that might have been approval passed across the man's eyes, then he withdrew out of Cam's sight. The sound of feet making their way across the floor once more filled the room, then came the sound of a door being opened and closed.

The footsteps receded out of Cam's hearing.

Realising he was alone, Cam slowly raised himself onto his elbows. The nausea came again, but it was lessened this time and passed in only a few seconds. Once it had cleared, he dared a glance around him.

The room was square, dark and warmed by the fire that burned in the centre, contained within a two-foot-high, rough stone column. This was about twice as wide again and formed of rocks coloured the grey-blue of a moonlit night, with tiny gems like stars punctuating their surface.

Outside of the fire was what looked like a farmer's cottage; open-topped barrels filled with various tools and implements stood in one corner, whilst sacks of grain and other produce lined the far wall. A table stood against the wall beyond Cam's feet, upon which was a simple candelabra standing vigil over a set of wooden tableware that was clearly handmade. He could feel that he was lying on a bench, covered by what looked and felt like an animal skin, and directly behind his head he was aware that a window – seemingly the only one in the room – allowed a small amount of natural light to intrude upon the otherwise fire-lit scene.

His attention was caught by a movement away over his right shoulder. Turning as quickly as he dared, Cam looked back and saw Sonia lying upon another bench. She was wrapped in thick, warm blankets and furs, though she appeared to be shivering. One limp hand hung outside the confines of the furs, the fingers twitching occasionally as if grasping for something that was no longer there.

A door opened, and the man with the dusty brown hair strode back into the room. Cam saw now that he was wearing a thick, woollen jerkin over a linen shift. His trousers were of an earthy-brown and these were covered from the knee down by a pair of mud-caked leather boots. Behind him was the silver-grey light of a dawn hidden by clouds, and the chill of winter snapped at his heels through the open door. This the man closed, then he stopped and looked Cam over cautiously. In his right hand was a leather flask. He strode over and offered the thing to Cam.

"Drink," he said in a thick voice.

Cam stared at him, then at the flask.

"Drink," the man repeated, giving the flask a gentle shake to emphasise his point.

Cam took it from him, raised it to his nose, and sniffed the contents. An unusual aroma; heather and alcohol.

"It is fresh, so you will need only one sip." The voice was cautioning, but kindly.

Cam suddenly felt the dryness of his mouth; he needed a drink. He lifted the tip of the flask to his lips and let a tiny sliver of liquid pass between them.

The effect was immediate.

Flavour burst into Cam's mouth ferociously, but its strength did not make it any less pleasant. He swilled it for a moment, then swallowed gladly. Nausea rose up in him once more, but then died away completely

"What is that stuff?" he puffed.

"Hocliquor," the man answered, "I have very little in the way of healing herbs, but Hocwede is plentiful here. However, my work will be undone if you don't rest."

"Who are you?" Cam heard himself ask.

"Gismay, friend. This is my home." He waved his hand around at his dwelling, but Cam paid little heed.

Gismay? What kind of name was that?

"Now, you must rest," the man continued, "you have been through such an ordeal that only the Seven know how you survived. But if it is their will that you do, I will see that it is done."

Cam's eyes shot a glance over to Sonia's body.

"She is much the same as you," Gismay answered before

Cam asked, “but she at least has the sense to sleep. Don't fear, I won't let harm come to either of you. Rest.”

Seeing that there was little else to be done, Cam's body decided to heed the man's words and slid itself back down amongst the furs. For a moment or two he lay there, feeling the sensation from the drink he had been given thrum through him. It was pleasant, like the waves of a warm ocean.

He hauled himself back up, a thought striking him.

“How did we get here?” he asked.

Gismay, with his back to him by the sacks of grain, spoke over his shoulder.

“I found you both just lying out there in the weeds. Not wanting to see you freeze, I put you in my cart and rode back here as swiftly as I could. Then I set about helping you as I was able.”

Cam's mouth was dry once more.

“That's... that's not really what I meant.”

Gismay turned and approached with a clay bowl in his hands. It contained a small measure of grains, seeds, and pulses, along with a slab of cheese and some bread. He offered it to Cam.

“If you will not rest, then at least eat.”

Cam's stomach cried out for the food, and he accepted it gladly. As he took his first bites of the cheese, Gismay went away again for a moment behind the fire. He returned with a clay cup filled with water, which Cam also accepted.

Gismay leaned himself against the stones of the fire pit and bowed his head, as if in contemplation.

“What's your names?” he asked softly.

“Cam. And she's Sonia. We work together.”

Gismay smiled.

“Ah, well, I am very pleased to meet you, friend Cam. And I will no doubt enjoy meeting friend Sonia as much when she wakes.”

Cam nodded, idly chewing on some seeds.

“Where are we?” His voice was pressing, but he tried not

to sound harsh.

A strange expression crossed Gismay's face; Cam could not tell if he was smiling, grimacing, or frowning. Perhaps it was a mixture of all three?

"Ah. I did wonder when that would come up."

"What do you mean?" Cam pressed, trying to keep the concern from his voice.

"You must understand," Gismay began, "that I am nought but a Farmer. I know what I know, and that sorts me. I never thought, in all my days, that this duty would fall to me. But if that's how the Seven wills it, then it must be done."

He was half talking to himself, and Cam was finding it difficult to follow.

"What duty?" he asked.

Gismay closed his eyes and brought his hands to his face.

"May Etavïr give me wisdom enough for this moment," he said, a hushed tone now entering his voice, then looked at Cam earnestly.

"I have no doubt that you and friend Sonia have been through a terrible ordeal, and I wish that you had not. For your sake. But, well, what's done is done and all that, and here you are. Here. In my house."

He wiped his brow and started to pace about the small room.

"What is the last thing you remember?" he asked eventually, speaking carefully as if choosing each word one by one.

Cam fought against his confused mind to piece together what had happened to them. Flashes and snippets came back to him, but they were muddled and out of order; some were clear as day, others hazy half-memories.

"I... We were at work. I'd lost my phone. I went to find it. Sonia had come with me. The lights went out. There was... lightning? And a figure. They were trying to scare us, at least I thought they were. The floor gave way and we... ended up here."

He blinked and looked at Gismay, hoping beyond hope

that any of that made any sense. How could it?

To Cam's surprise, the Farmer nodded.

"Aye, then I saw aright. By my blood, I wish you could have a better welcome than I can give you. But if it is my place after all then I'd best to it. I will try and explain it as best I may. "

The Farmer came back to the fire pit and knelt in front of Cam, looking deep into his eyes.

"You and your friend have travelled. A very long way."

"How far?" Cam asked.

" You certainly ain't where you were last evening, let's put it like that for now," Gismay said, a little unease in his voice.

He stood and faced the fire pit, his hands resting on the edge.

"I don't rightly understand how, or why, but I've heard tell of it happening before. Not recently, mind. Not for a few thousand years, if truth be told, and even then it might be just stories. But, from what little knowledge I have, you come from... somewhere else."

Gismay turned and Cam could see the struggle on his face as the Farmer spoke.

What on earth was going on?

"At first I didn't think to believe it. I thought it was just a fierce bit of weather, what with the lightning. By the Seven, I thought it would tear the world asunder."

He paused and glanced meaningfully at Cam.

"Well, perhaps it did," he breathed, then shook his head, "point is that when I first found you I thought you and friend Sonia there had been caught out in the storm and come afoul of it. It was only when I noticed the strange cloth you both wore that it began to dawn on me what it was I'd witnessed. What you were."

"And what are we?"

Cam and Gismay turned their heads to where the voice had come from, and they saw Sonia had sat herself up amongst her furs and was staring intently at them both.

"Ah, friend Sonia," Gismay smiled, standing and

embracing the moment to break the tension, "it is good that you are awake. Don't be alarmed, friend Cam here told me your name. I am Gismay. Now, give me a moment."

He hustled away back over to the sacks of grain, no doubt preparing Sonia a bowl similar to Cam's.

Taking the opportunity Cam stood and, taking as many furs with him as he could, went and sat next to Sonia. She looked as tired as he felt, and he could see the nausea still swimming in her eyes, but she was seemingly unharmed by whatever they had endured.

"You alright?" he asked her softly.

She grimaced as she hauled herself over and allowed him room to share her bench.

"Well, I'm not dead," she said, a strained humour in her voice, "so I guess that's something. You?"

Cam smiled.

"Yeah, about the same."

Sonia flicked her eyes towards the Farmer.

"Who's that?"

Cam shrugged.

"I know about as much as you do. He's called Gismay and he lives here."

Sonia nodded.

"What happened to us?"

She had tried to sound calm and collected, but the slight quiver in her voice betrayed her. Cam did not blame her for whatever she was feeling in that moment, it was only the adrenaline coursing through his veins that had held him together up to this point.

"Not a clue," he sighed honestly, hearing the emotions in his own voice.

They shared a long glance and both saw tears forming in the other's eyes.

"Where are we?" Sonia asked, trying to hold her smile.

Cam shook his head.

"Not where we were last evening," he said, laughter and

sobs mixing in his words.

Sonia nodded again.

"OK."

They fell into each other and quietly let all of their emotions out. They were tired, confused, and all but broken. A faint hope burned in Cam that Gismay would be able to give them something, but for now that could wait. All that mattered to him was having his best friend next to him.

Gismay interrupted them by handing Sonia a bowl of food and the same leather flask he had given Cam. After waiting for Cam to confirm that the food was safe, Sonia cautiously tried what Gismay had given her.

She could not hide the immediate effect both had upon her; her eyes lost their glaze, and her breathing steadied itself. The emotions that raced within her were becalmed, giving her a much needed moment to compose herself and face whatever it was that lay ahead of them.

Cam took the flask from her and, with a gentle nod of approval from Gismay, he took another sip of the stuff himself.

"So," he said, steadied and grounded once more, "you were just about to tell us what we were."

Gismay smiled nervously.

"That I was. You are Travellers, though you almost certainly did not intend to become so."

"Travellers?" Sonia asked.

"Aye, though not in the traditional sense. Now, please forgive me, this is the bit that I don't rightly understand, but I will say as I may for you."

The Farmer took a moment to recompose himself. Sonia, almost without thinking, took the flask of Hocliquor from Cam and offered it to Gismay, who accepted it gladly. The effect upon him was less pronounced than it had been upon themselves, but it was still visible; his eyes now looked at them with a renewed focus.

"Where you come from and where I come from – that is to say, here – are two different places. Very different. They're not connected by roads, or oceans, or... well, anything like that. In fact they're not really connected at all, and nor should they be. But sometimes, according to them that knows more about this than I do, some folk can travel between them. And that's what's happened to you, if I understand aright."

He smiled at them weakly, hoping that his words had given them the answers that they wanted.

Cam stared back at him, blinking.

"I'm sorry, I don't..." he began, but Sonia cut across him.

"Are you saying that we're from different worlds?"

Cam looked at Sonia as if to say that she was talking absolute nonsense, but her face was deadly serious. He looked to Gismay hoping that he, too, would be incredulous, but his slow nod told Cam he was alone in his feelings.

"Come on," he said, scoffing, "you can't be serious. That's... impossible, for one thing!"

"Well, I thought so too," Gismay responded, "until I saw you both get dropped by lightning. There ain't no other explanation. And as I said, it has happened before. Not very often, and certainly not for a long while, but it's not unheard of."

"It is to us," Sonia said, a voice soft and vacant.

Cam went to speak but he had no words. He looked to Sonia, but she was deep in her own silent contemplation and did not meet his eye.

Different worlds? The words echoed as the tolling of a bell within his mind. That could not be it. There had to be something else going on.

A shared hallucination? Unlikely, they had not ingested or inhaled anything before they entered Fingall's Tower that might have caused something like that. Dreaming was also discounted very quickly as they had both definitely been awake when all of this started, and he had not felt tired or even closed his eyes from the moment they had met outside the Tower until after everything had transpired.

Maybe they had died? Had the lights suddenly going out in the control room been the place collapsing on their heads? He shook his head to dismiss the idea.

Ruling out all of those scenarios, Cam found has was left with only one highly implausible, but potentially possible solution. What if he and Sonia had indeed travelled somewhere? How had they done so, and why? And how did they get back to their own world? Could they get back? Did their world even exist any more? How long could they hope to survive in whatever world this was?

The touch of Gismay's hand upon his shoulder shattered his thoughts, the fragments cascading into the darkest recesses of his mind.

"Friend Cam?"

Cam shook himself. Whether he believed it or not, he was where he was. That would have to be enough for the time being.

"Right. A different world. OK."

His voice shook as he wrestled with the impossible truths staring him in the face.

He glanced over at Sonia and saw one single, silent tear rolling down her cheek. She brushed it away unconsciously, then looked back at him and gave a forced, watery smile.

"OK?" he asked her, uncertainly.

She nodded.

"We're here. Not much else to be said."

Her hand reached out to his, and they grasped each other once again. Gismay placed a hand on both of their shoulders and gave them a look of reassurance.

"But where is 'here'?" Cam heard himself ask.

"Ah, now I feel on firmer footing," Gismay replied in a deliberately upbeat voice. He stood and opened his arms wide.

"This is my farm," he announced proudly, "Lun Ridge, we call it. Been in my family for generations. I'll probably be the last one as, well, you can see I live alone. Even if I found a wife, I wouldn't bring her here in any case..."

Cam raised a hand.

"No, sorry, Gismay. That's great but... if we're not in our world, then where are we?"

The Farmer's face dropped.

"Ah, right, yes, of course. My apologies. This is Rhydariel," he said soberly, "specifically, the border between the Eislands and the Kingdom of Ebras."

Cam and Sonia glanced at each other. They were definitely answers, but they meant little to them.

"And what is... Rhydariel like?" Sonia asked.

Gismay thought for a second.

"Well, it's... Rhydariel, isn't it? It's hard to describe," he said, seeing their uncertain faces, "there's a lot in it."

"OK," Sonia soothed, "why don't we start with something smaller. Tell us about you."

Gismay sighed, and a look of relief crossed his face.

"That I can do, friend Sonia, and it won't take long either. I am but a farmer, and I live quietly out here on my farm away from the noise. When the spring's abounding I tend to my crops and take them to market, and when it's cold I look after myself here and try to keep the snow out."

He looked over at their disconsolate faces, and his heart sank.

"I'm sorry," he sighed, defeated, "I'm a farmer, not a scholar, and I don't rightly know why the Seven have chosen to land you on my doorstep. I'm not sure if it's a blessing or a punishment, nor who it would be for if it were either."

Cam shivered, and for the first time his body truly started to register the much colder temperature here than he had dressed for back in Welverleigh. Sonia was cold too, though her body and mind were so far removed from herself that it barely registered.

Gismay looked at them and stood.

"By Etavïr, you both must be frozen," he said as he did so, "and here I am being no use at all. Let me see if I've got some spare linens that you can change into."

A few moments later both Cam and Sonia were furnished with ill-fitting but warm woollen shirts and breeches. For Cam, Gismay had found a leather, front-buckled jacket that was about a size-and-a-half too big, whilst Sonia now donned a wool-lined, high-collared coat. They looked each other over and took in their new appearance; it suited both of them in their own way, but it also accentuated how different their lives had suddenly become.

"Well," Gismay said, adjusting Cam's jacket, "not perfect but a fair sight warmer than you would've been. Comfy?"

He looked to both of them for approval, and they nodded.

"Good," he continued, "and now that we've all had a fair moment to let our heads settle, I've been having a thought about our... predicament."

He motioned for them both to sit once more and then took a turn around the fire pit.

"Fact is, you're here. Like friend Sonia said, there's not much more to say about that. As for how or why, I am not the man to answer. Until last night I'd only heard of such things in stories and tales."

Cam shook his head and stared at the floor, while Sonia's eyes faced outwards past Gismay, as if trying to burn a hole through the log wall beyond.

"How do we get home?" she asked after a moment. "We can get home, can't we?"

Sonia and Cam glanced sidelong at each other whilst Gismay took another breath.

"Like I said, I'm not the man to answer."

The air in the room sank. Cam and Sonia's minds raced to keep their sanity from falling into the mire of emotions swelling within them.

How were they going to get home?

They had had no choice nor control over their arrival, so why would they have any agency in their return? Was this it then? Were they stuck here, in a world that was not their own, forever? What of their families and friends?

Cam's thoughts immediately went to his mother. She had asked him to be at home when she arrived. That was last night! She would be worried sick! He had no way of telling her what had happened to him. What would he have told her anyway?

How could he explain this to her, or to anyone? He could barely come to terms with it himself.

He reached his hand out to Sonia once more, who would be having all of the same thoughts about her life. She did not look at him but he felt her fingers tighten around his.

“But,” Gismay said quietly, his voice thick against the silence, “I will do everything in my power to help. And, while I may ultimately not be of much use in matters like this, there are people who can be. There are no promises, mind you, least none that I can offer. This sort of thing is beyond me, Etavïr knows.”

The two friends looked at him, no longer certain which of their emotions they should listen to.

“Thank you, Gismay,” Cam said, “I... that is, we, will take any help you can give us.”

Here, Gismay raised a stern hand and looked at them both seriously.

“Don't thank me yet,” he said simply, “Something like this is far beyond the normal troubles of the world. On top of that, it's the dead of winter outside and we could all be done in by frost in a week if we aren't careful, so travelling won't be easy. And that's even without the war.”

Cam and Sonia glanced at each other, a new fear bubbling up inside them.

“What war?” Cam asked, barely a whisper.

Gismay shifted and turned his eyes away from them.

“Between Ebras and Eismeer,” he said, “and a bitter and bloody one it is too. You were fortunate it was me that found you on the Farnhoc when you appeared and not soldiers. By my blood, I daren't think what would have happened if they had.”

He shook instinctively, as if he were truly unnerved by the notion.

“Who's winning?” Cam asked, but Sonia cut across him once more:

“Who's side are you on?”

Her eyes fixed upon the Farmer, who raised his head to meet her gaze before replying.

“To the second question; I pay my dues to Lord Fohenk of Eismeer. But being on the borders I have to tread carefully, if you take my meaning.

“To the first? Well, now, that is more difficult. The last big battle that happened was about half a year ago, away westward,” the Farmer motioned vaguely with his hand, “and there are some that tell of Eismeer getting the better of it, and others who say Ebras forced Eismeer from the field. Either way it was a nasty fight, so much so that neither army has had it in them to fight openly again since. There's been skirmishes, of course, but nothing big like that.”

He sighed as he finished this last sentence, and a heavy silence once again descended over them.

Gismay took himself over to the fire pit and began preparing some sort of midday meal; the sun outside the windows had risen high during their conversation and they would all soon be in need of nourishment. Cam and Sonia, meanwhile, sat and contemplated everything that had happened to them and all that Gismay had said.

A new world. A war. No-one certain how they could get home, if they could get home at all.

It was all impossible, and yet there it was.

Cam's thoughts turned once again to his mother. She would be beside herself. The Police would have been called, there would be an investigation, and they would find nothing. No clues whatsoever to tell them that he and Sonia had fallen through reality and landed somewhere that, to all intents and purposes, did not exist to their world.

What was it that Gismay had said? Not connected by roads or oceans, in fact they should not be connected at all.

By that measure, them even being there in the first place was too big a mystery to solve, let alone getting home.

Gismay now came over and handed each of them a clay bowl filled with a sweet and hearty smelling broth. It had in it somewhat recognisable ingredients – this world's equivalent of carrots, potatoes, and peas – yet it still felt otherworldly. With it,

Gismay gave them some torn bread, and the three of them sat and slowly ate this hearty fare with the crackling of the fire the only accompaniment to their meal. When they had finished, Gismay poured them each a small cup of what smelled like weak mead.

They were snapped from their thoughts by a knock at the door.

Gismay jumped to his feet as soon as he had heard it, a gesture that made Cam and Sonia nervous.

"What is it?"

Gismay gestured that they should remain silent. He stepped slowly towards the door and looked cautiously out of a crack in the wood. Whatever the Farmer saw was hidden from Cam and Sonia, but he pulled his face back suddenly and looked frantically around the room.

"Gismay?" came a voice from outside.

"One moment," Gismay called back over his shoulder, and quickly grabbed one of the larger furs. He then walked over to Cam and Sonia.

"You must hide," he whispered quickly.

"What? Why?" Sonia hissed.

"Because not everyone will be as welcoming to you as I have been," came the hushed and hurried response, "I will explain when we get a moment, but now you must hide!"

He ushered them into the corner with the barrels of grains and all but forced them down and threw some furs over them. He quickly assessed that they were sufficiently hidden from the rest of the room, then turned to face the door.

Doing so as quietly and quickly as possible, Cam and Sonia repositioned the barrels so that they could see. They watched as Gismay stepped slowly forward, carefully raised his hand, grasped the door-handle, and opened the door.

"Oh, it's you," he said, a tone of slight surprise in his voice.

Gismay was pushed back and three men, all with broad shoulders and muscular forms, entered the room. Two of the men had longer hair while one had a shorter style, and all wore chain armour. The man at the front, one of the longer-haired pair, had a stern face with piercing brown eyes that looked about the room. Upon each of the three backs hung a quiver filled with arrows, along with a bow, and at each waist hung a sword.

Soldiers.

The man with the deep brown eyes stepped into the centre of the small room and regarded the Farmer.

"We need to talk, friend Gismay."

Gismay betrayed no signs of emotion towards the man. Cam and Sonia watched them as they stared at each other, trying to gauge what the outcome might be.

Cam focussed on these two for a moment: the one with the longer hair had a thinner face than the man who had spoken, and his black, slick hair hung straight down from his scalp like a waterfall of oil. Grey-blue eyes peered out from the pale face, casting their disdain over the room before looking Gismay up and down with an expression that was close to disgust.

The third man had hair which was pulled back into a high pony tail and shaved close to his skin around his ears and the back of his head giving him a raw, almost savage look. His eyes were darker and had a wild edge. His armour, though otherwise identical to that of the other two, had no sleeves, leaving his huge and muscular arms bare for all to witness.

"What would you like to talk about, Captain Dunwald?" Gismay asked. "Long has it been since I was graced with such company."

"There is a matter of import we must attend to," replied the Captain, brusquely.

The Farmer gave Dunwald a quizzical look.

"I have paid my gold, Captain. A quick glance at the ledgers in your city would tell you such."

"This is not about gold, Gismay."

"Then, Captain, I am at a loss."

One of the other soldiers - the one with the slick, black hair - rolled his eyes.

"Captain, must we hear any more of this?"

"Hush, Aglorar," the Captain ordered, "If friend Gismay truly does not know of what I speak then we must make it clear for him."

"What's going on?" Cam hissed into Sonia's ear.

"No idea," she hissed back, and made a gesture that they should do as Gismay had asked and stay silent.

"How has the winter been treating you, friend Gismay?" the Captain was asking.

The Farmer once again shrugged.

"As the many which have gone before it have done," he said, "fortunately the crop this year was better than most so I have a fair amount of grain kept back."

Dunwald nodded, a friendly smile on his face.

"It is good to hear so," he said, walking up to Gismay and placing an arm around his shoulders, "Lord Fohenk will doubtless be pleased to hear of your good fortune, would you not say men?"

The two others made noises of vague agreement as the Captain laughed with Gismay.

"And it does me good to please my Lord," the Farmer said, an audible relief in his voice, "now, friends, what was it you wished to speak to me about?"

Captain Dunwald clapped Gismay on the back and stepped back toward the table. He smiled as he looked down once more then again back to Gismay.

"Who else is here?"

The smile had not moved, but there was a fire behind the eyes that flared as he spoke. Gismay looked confused for a moment and was doubtless about to ask what Dunwald meant, but Cam and Sonia saw that the Captain's hand was gesturing towards the three empty bowls on the table.

"I... uh..." Gismay stumbled, but he got no further.

"Find them," the Captain ordered, snapping into a standing position and drawing his sword.

This he pointed at Gismay as the two other men began to

ransack the house. Before Cam and Sonia could think, the fur had been flung off them and a pair of muscular arms hoisted them up with a frightening ease and threw them down unceremoniously onto the floor. The man who had picked them up held Sonia by the collar whilst the man known as Aglorar took a firm hold of Cam's shoulders.

"A bumper crop indeed," the Captain said as he eyed the two figures now before him, "friend Gismay, are you not going to introduce us to your guests?"

Gismay, his eyes focussed upon the very sharp point of the sword trained on his chest, swallowed hard.

"They are of no importance," he said quickly, "just an extra pair of farm hands that helped me through the end of the season."

Dunwald grinned.

"Is that so? You've kept them on many weeks after the harvest, and they are no doubt a drain on your supposed ample supply of grains? And," the Captain added, motioning to Cam's new jerkin, "to dress your farm hands in what looks like armour seems an unnecessary expense."

"They are of no importance," Gismay repeated, more forcefully, "and need not be dragged into any of our business."

"We shall see."

The Captain turned and faced Cam and Sonia at last. His eyes took in every inch of their appearance and considered them deeply. His gaze made them both feel very uncomfortable, and neither of them could endure it for long.

"Who are you? What is your business here?"

"Cam," came the automatic response.

Dunwald nodded, showing no reaction to the name.

"And you?"

"I'm Sonia."

"Your business?"

Cam and Sonia looked to each other, but neither had an answer for the other.

"They are foreigners in our lands, Captain," Gismay cut

in, “They came to me searching for work and lodging. I have offered them my protection. I would ask that you respect that, lest I be proved faithless.”

Dunwald turned to face the Farmer once more.

“I have already given you more courtesy in this matter than my Lord would normally allow, and that is only because of good faith between us. Do not presume to test that faith too far.”

The Captain now began circle them slowly. With each step he took they could hear the gentle clink of his armour and the rattle of the sword in at his waist.

“From whence do you come, friends?” he asked them.

Again, a frantic silence ran between them as they desperately tried to think of an answer that would make sense to the Captain. Sonia shot a quick glance at Gismay, but the Farmer was already ahead of her.

“The Crescent Isles,” he blurted out.

The Captain nodded.

“As you say. Friend... Cam, was it?”

“Yes.” Cam tried to sound as confident as he could.

“Thank you. Friend Cam, which sect of King Yolanda's House are you from?”

The silence as Dunwald waited for an answer throbbed in Cam's ears. How was he supposed to answer that? He looked to Gismay, but the Farmer was staring at the floor.

“Merchant,” Cam settled on, “I'm part of the Merchant sect.”

The Captain stepped through he and Sonia and sat himself on the bench where Cam had woken up a few hours earlier.

“Ah, of course. And, you?” He pointed to Sonia, and leaned back expectantly.

“I'm also a Merchant,” she said quickly.

“What do you sell?”

The question was aimed at both of them.

“Portraits.” Sonia's voice was strong and resolute.

Dunwald's expression changed from expectant to impressed.

"And very talented you must be to have the coin to afford the crossing, not to mention resourceful for finding work with such a reputable man." he cooed. There was a glint in his eyes that made them feel uncomfortable.

The Captain stood and smiled at them all.

"Well," he said, "it seems that my instincts have led me astray. Your answers are well given, and I applaud you for your bravery in making the dangerous voyage to our lands. May your stay here be a pleasant one."

He nodded curtly to them both, and strode past them towards the door. Cam and Sonia both gave inward sighs of relief. Gismay, though, still looked cautious.

"There is just one thing," the Captain said, turning back into the room and striding towards them once more, "something that you said, friend Cam, concerns me."

Cam closed his eyes and felt panic rising within him once more.

"Oh?" he asked, trying to sound calm. "What did I say?"

He felt Dunwald come close to his face and speak into his ear.

"Yolanda is a Queen, not a King."

A hand grabbed him roughly from behind and wrenched his arm behind his back.

"These are no more Crescent Islanders than you or I."

The Captain now turned back to Aglorar and spoke quickly.

"Bind them," he spat, thrusting Cam into Aglorar's hands.

"What?" Cam protested, but he was cut off by Aglorar roughly wrapping a coarse rope around his wrists. The third soldier had stepped forward and done the same to Sonia.

Dunwald stood before Gismay.

"Captain Dunwald," the Farmer began to plead, "I ask that you do not do this. They are of no consequence to you!"

"Silence!" the Captain snapped.

He once more began to circle the room; a predatory motion that sent shivers up Cam's spine.

"You must think me a fool, friend Gismay," he growled, "and your lies are more foul than I had dared believe."

"What lies?" Gismay spat back.

"Shall I go through all of them?" the Captain exclaimed. "There is not enough time in all of the Seven for me to do that."

"Captain Dunwald, I have never..."

Dunwald flashed the back of his glove across Gismay's face, sending the Farmer to the floor with the force of the blow.

"How long have you sent missives to Ebras? How many reports have you written? How many of your own kind have you sold out for coin? Did you even accept payment, or was the damage you could do to Eismeer enough for you?"

Dunwald grasped Cam by the scruff and, without warning, dragged him forcefully across the floor until he now stood in front of the Farmer's face.

"Tell me where they came from."

Gismay lifted his eyes to meet Cam's, an apologetic and painful expression. He opened his mouth, which Cam could now see was swollen following the blow from the Captain, but he said nothing.

"Tell me!"

"The Crescent Isles," the Farmer forced.

"Liar!" Dunwald threw Cam to the floor, then moved away.

Gismay looked at Cam once more, but Cam's attention was focussed entirely on Sonia. Dunwald had approached her and knelt in front of her, his eyes looking directly into hers.

"It is unfortunate that you chose to be under this man's care," he said, an almost earnest tone in his voice, "for you have not only lived beneath the roof of, but worked for, a traitor."

Sonia did all she could to keep her composure.

"A traitor?" she breathed.

Dunwald closed his eyes and nodded.

"I fear so, for he has been spying for King Hedradour. Our sworn enemy."

He stood once more and strode back to Gismay.

"I ask again: how much information have you given to King Hedradour, spy?"

For a moment, Cam did not believe that Gismay would answer. Even with the revelation about his actions, he wanted no more harm to befall the man. He had, after all, made them welcome, fed them, and clothed them, all without their asking for it.

After a moment, Gismay spoke..

"Enough. More than enough."

The Captain did not move his gaze from the Farmer.

"What information? For how long?" he demanded.

Gismay smiled up at him.

"You will never know. Not until the sword of Ebras is at your throat and your city is on its knees."

There was a hint of laughter in the Farmer's voice, as if he had scored some points in this game he and the Captain were playing. Dunwald smiled back at him, and looked around the room.

"Is that all you have to say?"

Gismay, still smiling, nodded and let his head fall forwards.

"Very well," the Captain sighed, "it is something that you admit to it. Though it still baffles me that you would hide these two from us. If they were indeed simply workers in your care then why would it matter?"

A beat of silence passed as Dunwald paced in the centre of the room.

"Unless," he said slowly, "they are indeed foreigners in our lands. But not from the Crescent Isles, that much is plain. Where do you think they could have come from Aglorar?"

The oily-haired man gave a look of mock confusion.

"Perhaps the Bowalt, Captain?"

Dunwald shook his head.

"No, for there is enough work in those lands for twice their population. They would not need to travel this far to find employment."

The Captain stood over Cam and looked down at him.

"No, I think I have the right of it. Why else would friend Gismay hide them, and defend them indeed, if they were not fellow spies from Ebras?"

Cam looked up at him, fear suddenly gripping his heart. Why did this man think they were spies? But then, why would he not think that? They were dressed in the clothes of the only world that Dunwald knew, and even if they told him the truth what would he say? Gismay himself had said that while travellers like them were not unheard of, it had not happened in many years and he would not have believed it if he had not seen it.

The feeling of cold dread that rose through Cam's body paralysed him.

"We're not spies!" Sonia cried, but anything else she wanted to say was smothered by a hand from the man holding her.

"My Lord Fohenk will be the judge of that," the Captain breathed, "for all of you."

Before Cam could do anything to stop it, the room exploded into chaos.

Dunwald spun Gismay's body and pinned him down upon the ground. The Farmer grunted in pain as his arms were twisted back and his wrists tied before being unceremoniously pulled to his feet.

"Gismay of Lun Ridge, I hereby charge you with High Treason against Lord Fohenk of Eismeer. Your two accomplices are charged with aiding and abetting you in that Treason. You will return with us to face the Lord's Justice for your crimes."

Dunwald looked to his fellow soldiers.

"Lekkon, get them on the wagon."

The man with the ponytail nodded at his Captains order, then grabbed Cam and Sonia, dragging them towards the doorway. Outside, the freezing temperature of the air cut deep into them. The vague shape of a wagon loomed into view. It had high sides and a gate that stood open at its back.

When they reached the spot, Lekkon dropped Cam to the ground and lifted Sonia heavily into the wagon. Seconds later Cam too was hoisted upwards and deposited, his head cracking down against the wood. Before he was fully aware of what had happened, Gismay's body landed heavily on top of him, forcing the air out of his lungs. The red explosion of pain was followed by a blue haze.

Lekkon laughed as he closed the metal door of the wagon, then his footsteps made their way toward the front of the wagon. It shook and pitched sickeningly for a moment as the three men clambered aboard.

Cam felt them lurch into motion. Gismay's body rolled off him, allowing him to suddenly inhale; the fierce rush of oxygen overwhelmed him, and black specks began to mix with the red and blue clouds that raged across his vision. Another wave of nausea passed over him, his body gave in, and he knew no more.

Chapter Four

Into Winter

When Cam next awoke, the dim gold of evening was in the air.

The cold stung him, his body shivering beneath his leather jacket, and his breath steamed as it met the air about him. He coughed involuntarily, the sound stinging his ears, and then lay there panting for many moments.

He became aware that the wagon was not moving.

Prising himself off the wooden boards beneath him, Cam gingerly raised his head to look about him. Over him was a simple metal cage, while to his left lay Gismay and to his right, Sonia. She stirred, obviously having heard him wake, and looked at him.

"Cam?"

He smiled at her. She smiled back for a moment, then shivered.

"I'm cold," she breathed.

"I know," Cam nodded.

"Where are we?" Sonia asked.

Cam hoisted himself up and looked about.

A few yards away, the three soldiers were sat laughing and eating around a fire. Cam paid them no heed and scanned the area around them.

The terrain was difficult to make out in the gathering gloom, but the ground seemed to be covered with thick gorse-like shrubs, and a smattering of snow lay about. To his left he thought he could make out the vague, distant outlines of mountains, but in the dim light he was not certain. The land stretched out for many miles in all directions, with no other discernable features or landmarks.

He settled himself back down next to Sonia and puffed out his cheeks.

“Not a clue,” he breathed, “miles from anywhere, by the looks of it.”

Sonia closed her eyes and let her head fall.

“This is getting ridiculous!”

“Yeah...” Cam sighed. He did not know what else to say.

“What do we do?”

Sonia's question hung in the air for many moments.

“I'm not sure there's much we can do,” he conceded, then raised his bound wrists, “our hands are quite literally tied.”

He had done his best to sound humorous, but even he was not convinced.

Sonia started either laughing or crying, Cam was not certain which.

“None of this makes any sense! You don't just jump from one world to another! Christ, I didn't even know it was an option until this morning!”

She shook her head and looked up once more. The gentle glistening on her cheeks revealed she had wept, yet she had an uncertain smile on her face.

“This is mental,” she said, half laughing at the absurdity of it all.

Cam coughed out a laugh as well, and the two friends leaned against each other and enjoyed the briefest of bright moments.

Despite everything, all the peril and the uncertainty, neither of them would have chosen to be marooned with anyone else. It was doubtful whether either of them would have been as stable as they were without the other for support.

As they sat there, leaning on each other, Gismay rolled over and began to stir.

“Gismay?” Cam breathed. “Are you alright?”

The Farmer groaned and struggled against his bonds for a moment before answering.

"I am whole," he said with difficulty, "how fare you both?"

"We're alright," Sonia sighed, "just battered, bruised, and cold."

Gismay looked at them both earnestly.

"It will only get colder from here. They are taking us to Eismeer, the city of Lord Fohenk."

"What's it like?" Cam asked with as much enthusiasm as his body allowed.

"The City by the Frozen Lake, Jewel of the east," Gismay said, mocking grandeur lacing his voice, "where sits the Tower of the Eis and the Throne of the Eismen. Its walls keep out everything but the cold, or so they say."

"Who are those men?" Sonia asked.

"They are soldiers of Eismeer," the Farmer spat, "the keepers of law in these parts."

"And what do they want with us?" Cam hissed

"We are to be taken before the Lord Fohenk, where he will pass his judgement upon us for the supposed crimes we have committed. The 'Lord's Justice', they call it, though what passes for justice in this part of the world is not wholesome."

"What is the 'Lord's Justice'?" Cam asked, suddenly aware his throat was dry.

"They will kill me. It will not be quick. I will be made to suffer before they let me perish."

The Farmer bowed his head.

"I fear that the Seven's choice to put you in my hands for safekeeping has proven to be a poor one. For that I apologise not only to you, but to the Seven themselves if they can hear me."

The darkening night now seemed to press upon them as they sat, bound and caged, on the edge of the circle of firelight with Gismay's terrible admission washing over them.

Next to him, Cam felt Sonia beginning to shake. Whether it was fear, rage, or despair, he could not tell. He did not even know which one of those he himself was feeling.

“And what about us?” Sonia breathed.

Gismay did not meet her gaze, simply staring at the wooden floor of the wagon beneath them.

“If they truly believe that you are working with me,” he said quietly, “then I suspect you will be given the same fate.”

Silence, total and deafening, engulfed them as Gismay's words thundered into their minds. All three of them were to be sentenced to death?

“Shouldn't we try to escape?” Cam blustered. “Or make a deal with them or... something?”

“We are three unarmed, against three not only armed but trained,” the Farmer said, almost laughing, “and even if we did overcome those odds we are in the middle of nowhere in the depths of winter. Believe it or not our best chance of survival, for now, is here in this wagon.”

“We can't just sit here and wait to die!” Cam hissed, leaning into Gismay's face, his emotions threatening to boil over.

“If you can open that gate,” Gismay responded calmly, motioning his eyes towards the end of the wagon, “then I will follow any plan you concoct, friend.”

Cam looked round at the gate, then at Sonia, then back to Gismay. Seeing no immediate support from either of them, he pulled himself across the wooden boards and took up a position in front of the lock. For a moment he simply stared at it, willing it to open, and realised how far out of his depth he was. He could not even tell what kind of lock it was; it looked simple enough but heavy, like one of those he had seen around Edgeborough Castle. Then he realised he had nothing to pick it with, and that he would have no idea how to do it even if he did.

Feeling utterly small and futile, he spun his legs out from behind him and aimed a weak kick at the gate. The shoes Gismay had given them were warm but not sturdy, and certainly not designed with such violent acts in mind. The force of his strike reverberated back through his feet and shins, making him feel even more wretched. His head fell forward on his chest, his breath rasping and misting in the half-light around him, and the cold sting of tears was on his cheeks. More kicks against the metal out of pure frustration, more pain in his legs, and then he was spent.

He heard Sonia behind him at the other end of the wagon. He could not make out if she was crying or not, but he knew that she would be feeling much the same as he was. He slid himself back to sit next to her and there they lay, their heads together and their minds blank. They did not notice as the soldiers got back up on to the wagon, the sudden jerk as they set off again, nor the fingers of sleep as it closed their eyes.

They felt nothing.

* * * * *

The dawn brought with it a flurry of snow and the land about them changed. The gorse had become sparse, giving way to short grasses and frost-covered tundra.

Cam blinked himself awake against the jarring motion of the wagon. The lock, taunting him, was the first thing he laid his eyes upon, but he paid it no heed. Looking beyond the wagon, he saw that the shapes of the mountains were considerably closer and clearer now.

Sonia was asleep upon his shoulder; her face was peaceful, but Cam doubted she had slept well. His shoulder ached from the unnatural position they had slept in, but he dared not move before she awoke. He gently pressed his lips against the top of her head, and silently thanked whatever powers that be that they were together.

Turning his face away from her, he saw Gismay for the first time. The Farmer had managed to crawl over to the left of the wagon, his forehead leaning against the metal bars. So still was he that only the wispy fog of his breath confirmed he was alive.

"Gismay?" Cam said, quietly.

When no response came he went to speak again. But, before he could, Gismay began to sing.

In times long lost in the mists of ages
When the world was bright,
Our Lord walked the Earth, and the lands were merry
In the fine sunlight.

The days were golden, the sky was clear
When Etavïr walked as men.
The world was calm, the world was good,
Before darkness crossed the fen.

From the flesh of the Earth came the foul creature
The hand of good upon its shoulder
Where once was light now darkness and flame
That never would grow colder.

Then the Godking fell, our world left broken,
All fire turned to frost.
Then the Godking fell, the world left broken,
The light of hope was lost.

The final notes of Gismay's song hung in the air about them for many moments. He had done his best to remain quiet so that Dunwald and their captors did not order him into silence, or worse, but the final verse had touched him so much that the farmer had not been able to contain himself.

"That was... beautiful..."

Cam looked and saw Sonia, wide eyed, staring at Gismay.

The Farmer did not look back, but he seemed to let out a quiet laugh.

"It'll serve, though I am no minstrel."

"You should be," Cam said earnestly, "what was it about?"

"It's part of a much longer tale that would take those far

more talented than I many days to tell properly. It's called the Lay of Naïyr."

"Could you tell us it?" Sonia asked, heaving herself off Cam's shoulder and into a more comfortable position.

After a short moment of silence, Gismay nodded.

"I'm as much of a tale weaver as I am a minstrel, but I will certainly tell you what I may.

"Many ages ago the Earthgod, Naïyr, Last of the Five, sought favour amongst the court of Etavïr, the Godking and First of the Five."

"'The Five'?" Cam asked.

"Ah, of course," Gismay said, raising an apologetic hand, "I forgot for a moment that you... well, you wouldn't know, would you? We had five Gods. Naiyr was the last of them to take form, and so we name him and all the other Gods in that fashion.

"Etavïr was the Godking, Lord of all Creation, and First of the Five. Then there was Bænïr, Second of the Five, Lord of Time, of Mortality, of Life and Death of all things; Gohmïr and Alberí, Third and Fourth, Lord and Lady of the Sky, the Sea, and the Seasons; and Naïyr, Last of the Five, Lord of Growth, and of Man, Mer and Beast.

"These Gods, though stalwart protectors of this world, did not allow their work to affect or touch them. They kept themselves distant and objective, as to do otherwise would be dangerous; the temptation to use their powers to change the natural order would be too great otherwise, and the world must be allowed to master itself.

"And for Naïyr it was more dangerous than most, for he created and cared for the mortal creatures of this world. He it was that gave the birds desire to soar and wings to achieve it; he gave horses hooves and the desire to run; he gave man the ability to create and the knowledge of how to master it.

"But when he saw how the seasons challenged and betrayed his creations, how the cruel and merciless seas devoured them without question, how mortality crippled and destroyed them, Naïyr was touched by the plight of his creations.

"He had come to know and understand the emotions he had given them, and had almost come to admire the inner workings of his human and animal creations, and these had begun to affect his own being. It was this empathy with his creations that set his path upon the destructive course it would wind through the ages.

"Driven by those same emotions that he had gifted us, Naïyr wanted to prove to Etavïr, the Godking, that he was as powerful as the other Gods. Being the last to form he was seen by the other Gods as but a child when compared to them, despite the complexity and beauty of his creations.

"This pained him greatly, so to prove his worth he created the Angekyn. These were a new, powerful race of beings that, though human in form, would serve as a personal guard to Etavïr. He created them from the rock of the mountains of Rhydariel, and of Mount Vorgaril in particular, and presented them to the Godking in a great show of pride and loyalty.

"Such was the surety of the Gods that they scorned and mocked Naïyr for his actions. While none doubted that he had indeed crafted a fine race, worthy of the task, they doubted the task would ever need to be fulfilled. Who would the Angekyn protect Etavïr from? The Gods had no enemies that were powerful enough to challenge them. Naïyr's actions were labelled a waste; the acts of a petulant, attention seeking child.

"This angered Naïyr beyond all his bounds, and he sought for a way to prove himself once again. He found himself cursing his fellow Gods, desperate to show them that his creations were not only worthy but necessary. He purposed that their pride would be their downfall.

"But then his own pride overtook him, and a terrible plan formed in his mind. He would build a creature that would be able to test the Angekyn – test, mind, not defeat – and then the others would see the wisdom of his creating a personal guard for the Godking.

"Once more he journeyed to Mount Vorgaril, but now he plunged deeper, driven half-mad in this moment by his own selfish desire. The emotions spreading into his soul were new and exciting, and he wished to know their full extent.

"As he hewed at the rock and shaped it into the creature he would send to test the Angekyn, he felt himself losing the emotions that had engulfed him. In his single-minded state, he believed this to be the simple release we humans feel after weeping or screaming or cheering. But it was not so. He could no longer feel his emotions because they were no longer within him. They were within his creature.

"When it was released upon the world, the creature made straight for Etavïr's Halls and began to destroy the Angekyn. Only now did Naïyr see his folly; the creature fought without forgiveness, without thought, and it did not relent. Within mere moments the Palace of Etavïr was in flames, dead figures of Angekyn strewn about the place.

"Fearing the power of his mistake, Naïyr fled back the Palace and sought to save any he found.

"Gohmïr and Alberí lay dead, their godly forms ripped asunder by the creature, and Naïyr searched the Palace for the Godking and what remained of his court. When he at last came upon them, Etavïr cursed him for his actions, and banished him to our world. He ripped his power from him, forcing him to live by the emotions he held so dear.

"Then, using the last of his strength, Etavïr delivered his house from their peril. They retreated from our world, vowing never to return. The barriers between mortals and immortals had been forever sundered by Naïyr's transformation, and they were no longer safe from the perils of this world. Naïyr they left to face his creation with what remained of the Angekyn, and to serve the land he had soured for the rest of time."

Gismay sighed, as though a great and terrible burden had just been laid upon his shoulders; his face was drawn and his eyes weary from the effort of his tale.

"That's one hell of a story," Cam croaked.

"It is the doom of our age," Gismay continued, almost as if Cam had not spoken, "and it was never said if Naïyr defeated his creation or not. We have thus named it 'Tûlfang' – the unending blight. Many believe that it is still out there, diminished but not destroyed. Whether Naïyr is there also, lost in the miasma of his own despair, I do not know. I believe that he still fights for us, and that, one day, he and the Angekyn will finally rid the world of the Tûlfang, and perhaps in that hour Rhydariel will know once more what it is to be graced.

"Until that moment, I caution that you have come to our lands in dangerous times. We are a Godless world, friends."

"You would do well not to add blasphemy to your crimes, Farmer!"

They all looked to where the voice had come from and saw Aglorar looking back at them over his shoulder, a wicked grin on his face. He eyed the three of them with utter contempt.

"You're all in enough trouble as it is," he spat.

"An Eisman, faithless and cursed, would know much of blasphemy, and would do well not to invoke it!"

Gismay's voice was harsh and venomous, but Aglorar laughed in response; a vicious cackle that echoed in the frigid air.

"Hear this? A spy for the Elderking calls our people cursed? That is fine indeed!"

"Enough," snapped Dunwald, "Lord Fohenk will determine what blasphemies have been committed. And, if we make good time, we should be within his walls by noon tomorrow."

Aglorar's gaze lingered for a moment, focussed upon Gismay, and them he faced forwards once more. A sudden jerk as the horses began to accelerate, and Cam, Sonia, and Gismay were sent sprawling back onto the floor of the wagon, and the journey eastward continued.

Cam must have dozed, off and on, for the day drew past and the sun arched across the sky, and yet no time seemed to pass at all. When he finally did bring himself fully back to the present, the last signs of the tundra had been left behind and they now cut through an unbroken expanse of pure, thick, white snow.

To the left and right of them the mountains rose up, sheer and foreboding, and the land began steadily to rise. Ahead of them the ranges drew together, closing about them to form a snow-filled bowl within the landscape.

Squinting forward to make out as much as he was able, Cam could see no possible way that they would be able to pass through the wall of rock that now rose before them.

Gismay and Sonia had joined him against the side of the cart, seemingly sharing his desire to find out where they were.

"We are passing the western-most reaches of the Glacier Mountains," Gismay said, pointing to their left, "and there stands Mount Vorgaril and its foothills."

The Farmer motioned with his head across the snow to the other mountains that enveloped them. Twisting their necks, Cam and Sonia saw that the central peak of these rose swiftly to meet the clouds. It was far taller than the other mountains around it, and it appeared to be formed of a darker rock that the rest. It loomed over them, proud, mighty, and untouchable. All three felt a shiver pass through them at the sight.

"Mount Vorgaril?" Cam breathed. "Isn't that..?"

"It is the very place I spoke of earlier, where Naïyr cut the rock to shape the Angekyn and the Tûlfang," Gismay said, "thought there is no such danger there now."

"I don't see any way through," Sonia said, her voice a whisper.

"We are making for the Glacier Gates, a narrow pass that cuts through the rock. Barely wide enough for a wagon such as this."

Cam and Sonia shared a glance.

"Is it safe?" Cam breathed.

"It is not a pleasant place; a sliver of a path with huge fissures on either side, so deep that you could fall forever and never reach the bottom, or so I've heard. If there was any place I could believe that true evil lurked upon this world, it would be within those fissures. I have passed this way many times and, though I have never come to harm, a strange feeling followed me whenever I rode there. Truth be told, I wasn't in any rush to come back this way."

"It's getting colder," Sonia shivered next to him.

"Aye, it will," Gismay said, "night is falling and the wind will be howling through the pass and up to meet us long before we get there. I doubt Dunwald will attempt the journey at night, no matter the haste."

As if in answer to Gismay's words, the horses slowed as they approached a small stone building standing alone in the ocean of white, seemingly a guard post for these Glacier Gates. Dunwald turned the wagon towards it and, as he did so, the setting sun appeared behind the mountains and revealed, for the first time, the pass that they were to take through these mountains.

A thin shaft of pure, shining gold cutting through the dull grey rock, inviting them to test their luck in the failing sun. The snow lay thick all about it yet there seemed to be troughs at either side of the central way where only an inky blackness loomed, untouched by the gold cutting through the peaks above. The wind rushed through to meet them, whipping up the powdery top snow and flinging it into their faces.

The wagon stopped, and the three Soldiers dropped to the ground.

"Aglorar, check inside. Lekkon, with me."

Dunwald strode purposefully to the back of the wagon and unlocked the gate. He then stepped up and, without any further warning, hoisted Sonia to Lekkon who dropped her onto the ground. This was then repeated for Cam and Gismay, by which time Aglorar had returned.

"It is empty, Captain, though there is store of firewood and food."

"Good. Get a fire going. Lekkon will cook us a fine meal. Now, let's get these inside and secure."

A strong shove in Cam's back directed him to walk towards the hut. But after near two days of being bound and lain in a wagon his body did not find it an easy direction to follow.

Nor, it seemed, did Sonia or Gismay have the strength to walk on command.

A laugh from the two Soldiers was followed by them all being dragged forward until their legs could obey their captors' orders long enough to make it to the door. Aglorar held this open and, as he did so, he lifted his foot and caught Cam's shin, sending him falling helplessly to the floor.

Before he could think, Aglorar had grabbed the back of his shirt and dragged his body across the floor. Cam felt himself thud heavily against the stone walls, the air being knocked out of him. He heard Sonia and Gismay being given similar treatment, and their bodies slumped next to him.

Taking a glance about him, Cam saw that they were in a sparsely furnished room, covered in a thick layer of dust. A fireplace, crudely cut into the wall on their left, was being filled with wood and tinder by Aglorar, while barrels filled with whatever passed for rations stood on the opposite wall. Here also was the only window into the room from outside, though in the dusky gloom it did little use.

In a short while, the Soldiers were sitting around the fire eating whatever it was that Lekkon had prepared for them. It did not smell especially wholesome, but it did make Cam and Sonia aware that they had not eaten since Gismay's farm nearly two days before. The small portions of stale bread and water that were afforded to them did little but exacerbate their hunger.

The embers burned low as Dunwald sent Aglorar to keep watch. Out of the window, Cam thought he caught a glimpse of the moon high in the night sky, but his tired and uncomprehending mind floated between dream and reality. Only when the sickly light of a wintry morning began to filter into the room did his mind cling to waking, and even then it was a tenuous grip.

The morning was much the same as the previous night; a good, hearty breakfast for the Soldiers and more bread and water for the Prisoners. Then, with the crumbs having barely hit the floor, Dunwald ordered everyone back onto the wagon, and the small company moved eastward. After a quarter of an hour or so, the Mountains loomed over them, all but blocking the sky above from view. The wind howled towards them, bringing not just snow but also fine stones from the path ahead into their eyes.

Like the maw of some great beast awoken from age-old slumber, the entrance to the narrow pass yawned itself open in front of them. Slowing to near a crawl the wagon rattled gently over the rocks and gravel beneath the snow, and they passed into the Glacier Gates.

The path was a little over six feet wide, with the sheer drops that Gismay had described delving away into complete blackness on either side. Looking ahead, Cam saw the sun's light blinking at them, with only its thin reflections off the sheer, grey-blue rock walls to illuminate the pass.

Yard by yard they trudged forward, the echoing sounds behind and about them growing steadily louder and more intrusive as they advanced through the roofless tunnel. The wind gave little respite, making their eyes water and casting clouds of snow into their faces. An oppressive silence embraced them, penetrated only by the echoes of the horse's hooves against the treacherous, icy ground beneath. More than once Cam feared that they would be pitched into the sickening black pits that lined their way, but each time Captain Dunwald, with simple, quiet commands, ensured that they kept a true course between the gaping chasms.

After perhaps an hour of this treacherous path, the walls of the mountains began to slowly recede and allow the sun's light to fall upon them. The echoing of the horse's hooves became less regular and oppressive as the rock fell back, and the air about them became less heavy. The pass dissipated and Cam saw they had emerged on a small plateau of unbroken snow that looked out over the lands beyond.

These seemed to sweep in perfect unison towards an indistinct blur against the horizon that Cam could not make out. Between the blur and them, barely a mile ahead, he saw the reddening sunlight glisten off a surface that was subtly different to the ice and snow ridden plains about it; it seemed to seep out of the very mountains themselves, like ink pooling on a page.

The wagon now lurched down a narrow path that cut its way through thick grass that somehow managed to maintain its life beneath the snowfall. This new way was rough, the wagon bouncing uncomfortably as the horses strove to control their speed down the incline. Now the lands changed from the tumbling rises of mountain foothills into flat plains which their path wound its way slowly through towards the new surface that he had seen earlier. From this proximity Cam could see the deep blue tint to it.

"The Eismeer," Gismay's voice cut through the clamour of the wagon, "the great frozen lake. We will follow its shores for the remainder of our journey."

The Farmer fell silent, receding into his own thoughts. Cam turned his face to watch their three captors once more, but could read nothing in their backs. They simply sat, unmoving, staring out across the whiteness.

The journey was slow and deliberate, Dunwald seemingly unwilling to increase their pace. Neither Lekkon or Aglorar challenged their Captain's decision to elongate their passage, nor did Dunwald appear to offer any explanation. As the sun reached its height at midday, however, the Captain motioned to his companions that they should indeed push the horses a little more. The wagon lurched forward and from that point on the frozen lake became a white-blue blur next to them. Cam stared ahead to see if there was any reason for this sudden change of plan.

The smudge on the horizon he had witnessed before began to grow. Within half an hour it was discernible as a walled city. A huge tower seemed to rise out of the walls, pointing its stony finger at the clear sky above. The entire structure was formed of polished rock, and the sun's light glinted off it in white and blue flashes. As they drew closer, the walls began to loom up to their full height and, when they were at last fully within their shadow, they stood forty foot high with towers double or triple that punctuating them at regular intervals. Two of the largest of these watchtowers stood either side of the great wooden gates that Dunwald was making for. The Captain did not call for the wagon to slow as, at a single order from the guard atop the walls, these split themselves perfectly down the middle and allowed them entry to the city itself.

The city of Eismeer, named for the frozen lake it overlooked, was prosperous. The streets about them were clean, and even the poorest-looking of its inhabitants were dressed in well made cloth. A myriad of sights, smells, and sounds threatened to overwhelm their senses as the wagon rattled along the cobbled streets that lay in the shadow of the Great Tower, looming over the city it served.

They followed a circular inner wall for a short time before delving through it and out onto the wide courtyard that lay beyond. This was filled with gardens, green and verdant despite the wintry world around them, and these were separated from each other by blue-grey paths of stonework, all leading to the Tower at the courtyard's centre.

Cam's eyes glared in wonder at the structure; it rose three hundred feet tall, glistening and beckoning the wagon towards it, and looked as though it had been hewn from the rock of the mountains themselves.

The wagon lurched away from the main path and plunged down into a tunnel that ran beneath the courtyard. The peak of the Tower loomed for one final moment, then became obscured as stone walls rose around the wagon. A shadow engulfed them and soon they were trotting slowly once more. When the tunnel did at last flatten itself out, the air became warm and close. The walls here were lit at regular intervals by torches, a sickly, red-orange glow dancing all about them.

Finally, the wagon stopped in a wide hall that was lit by what seemed like hundreds of these; it was circular and had a pair of simple, heavy doors that stood opposite them.

Dunwald and his companions clambered down. The Captain himself strode forward to speak to the pair of guards that stood either side of the door. These wore heavy, gold-tinted armour that bore a sigil of angel wings bisected by a thick icicle. This last was stained a pale blue, causing it to stand out from the rest of the armour. They had cloaks coloured with the same dye, and helms of gold that covered much of their faces. Swords hung at their waists, and their eyes were stern and cold.

The sound of the gate at the back of the wagon being opened drew Cam's attention. Aglorar's arms reached forward and grabbed him. He felt his body leave the safety of the wood, hang in the air for but a moment, then his knees and shins collided heavily with the rough stone beneath him. He let out a harsh cry of pain, which Aglorar answered only with a single laugh, and then wrenched Sonia from the cage, just as roughly. The sound of Gismay's form being hauled unceremoniously from the wagon by Lekkon followed soon after.

The Soldiers heaved their forms toward the door where Dunwald was speaking to the guards.

"Keep them under close watch," the Captain was saying, "make them as uncomfortable as you wish. Lord Fohenk will deal with them tomorrow."

One of the guards nodded, then thrust the doors open. Aglorar dragged Cam and Sonia into the dark, dank passage way beyond. The floor here was uneven and rough; pools of water splashed beneath the man's boots, while the squeaking and scurrying of rats and other vermin could be heard. Little light penetrated the darkness, save for the occasional torch.

A dungeon.

For many moments, past countless cages, Aglorar dragged the pair of them. Finally he reached a cage that was unoccupied and threw them both into it.

The sound of the lock clicking under the key's urging was the last thing that Cam remembered.

Chapter Five

Eismeer

The dripping of the water was merciless. Sonia's head was splitting. She could feel many new grazes and cuts that she had acquired, though they had at least untied her wrists which was some small comfort.

The cell they had been thrown into was probably not much more than six feet across. Two bunks hung off the back wall with simple, rough-looking cloth for bedding, and there was no light from any windows. The cells next to them on either side were empty, as was the cell opposite.

Cam was lying on one of the bunks; apparently he had had enough strength to drag himself up onto the thing before sleeping. Sonia smiled softly to herself, and gave him a quick look over to see if he was badly hurt. There was a cut on his right temple that looked a little nasty, but he would live. She placed a hand on him and took a moment to just feel the steady movements of his breathing.

The dripping shook her again. She turned her head to see where it was actually coming from, but she saw nothing save the darkness of their cell. A faint breeze managed to find its way through a hidden opening, stirring her hair. Running her fingers through it, Sonia suddenly realised just how much they both needed a shower! It had been three and a half days of freezing cold, being thrown around, and fear; their hygiene had begun to pay the price.

She knew it would not take much time before she and

Cam succumbed to some disease or other in this place; one rat bite or piece of mouldy bread could see to that. The water and reeds on the floor would have shared this space for months, years even, and all manner of creatures and bugs would inhabit them. It was surely only a matter of time. Maybe they would not even need the trial Dunwald had promised them.

A movement accompanied by a groan told her that Cam had begun to stir. He blinked his eyes open and, for a moment, she saw confusion within them. He looked at her in surprise, then around them, then he closed his eyes tightly in an expression of denial.

"Cam? Are you OK?" Sonia asked softly.

Cam managed a wry smile, which Sonia returned, and sighed.

"Sorry. Stupid question."

"How long was I asleep?" Cam croaked.

"Without a watch?" Sonia mused, "I don't know. But about an hour. Maybe two."

Cam nodded, barely hearing her answer. He slowly slid himself up, sitting back against the wall of the cell. It was cold and damp.

"Are we the only ones in here?" he asked, glancing about him.

"I think so, yeah," Sonia's voice echoed around the empty cells, adding to the eerie atmosphere.

"Any sign of Gismay?" Cam breathed.

Sonia shook her head.

"Not since we first got here. I think they took him somewhere else. Why bring him to prison if they're just going to..?"

The words stuck in her throat, the reality of where they found themselves taking over her thoughts.

"I want to go home, Cam..."

"Me too."

Sonia found herself grasping him, holding him close in desperation.

"My God, what's going to happen to us?" she breathed.

"Damned if I know."

Sonia felt him gently take her hand in his and it looked as though he was about to speak, but the door at the far end of the corridor was flung open and they watched as Aglorar swaggered up to their cell. His placed his hands upon the bars and stared at them with palpable arrogance.

"Comfy, are we?" he sneered.

Cam hauled himself weakly to his feet and placed himself between the man and Sonia.

"We'll keep."

The man's lips curled into a twisted smile.

"Pity." The smile held for a moment longer. "You, boy, must come with me."

Aglorar unlocked the cage, the door swinging back with a hideous screech.

Cam glanced sidelong at Sonia, then stepped out into the corridor to join Aglorar.

"I won't be long," he said.

Aglorar smiled, then locked the cell door on Sonia and dragged Cam away.

The hand that grasped around Cam's upper arm held tightly, leaving the blood flow to his hand non-existent. Though it was the least of the pains he felt in his body at that moment, he found that it was this one that hurt him most acutely as Aglorar dragged him through the maze of underground corridors. Eventually they came to whatever door it was that Aglorar was seeking, and Cam was thrust through it.

The room was dark and musty, dust hanging in the air in front of his eyes thick as morning mist. It caught in his throat whenever he breathed, making him cough and splutter, and the stuff clung to his eye lashes.

The Soldier dragged him through the noxious space to a chair in the centre of the circular room, where he promptly dropped his arm. Cam did not have the strength to hold himself up, so he allowed his body to fall backwards into the seat he had been tacitly offered, sending a thick plume of age-old dust into the air.

"Christ..." Cam coughed quietly.

Aglorar closed the door behind him, plunging the room into a new, thicker darkness that was broken only by the a single shaft of light from the centre of the ceiling. He then slowly dragged a second chair from the darkness and sat opposite Cam.

"This is the deepest room in our dungeon. While you are within these walls, no-one will hear any questions I ask, nor any sound you make. We are alone and will not be disturbed until Lord Fohenk himself sends for you."

The quietness of Aglorar's voice and the steady tone with which he spoke told Cam that this was not an empty threat.

"Alas for our Lord's impatience, for it leaves with me with very little time. Tell me of how you came to Gismay's farm."

Cam coughed as much dust out of his mouth as he could, and then simply stared at the man before him. He looked calm and assured, and he was certainly not threatened by Cam in any way – why would he be? And there was something else that Cam could not quite put his finger on; a flicker behind his eyes, or perhaps just an aura or a strength that he had not encountered before in his life. The hairs on his arms began to stand on end as he regarded him, and a strange feeling permeated the room.

"Speak, boy," the Soldier growled, "and be sure you do not lie to me."

What the hell was he supposed to tell him? The truth was too far-fetched and any lie would be exposed straight away. Even Gismay had said that while what had happened to them was not unheard of, it had not happened in a long time so why would this man even believe the truth?

"I don't remember..." Cam croaked through the dust.

Aglorar laughed and let his head fall forward for a moment.

"I am many things, boy," he said, "but a fool is not one of them. My Captain may have been blind to the events prior to our meeting, but I am not so blinkered."

Cam shook his head.

"I don't know what you're talking about," he said, as levelly as he could.

The Soldier's head snapped back up and his eyes had become harder and more piercing. They held Cam's gaze for but a moment, yet the feeling of fear that clutched his heart as they did was severe.

"I saw the storm, and the lightning, and I know what it signifies and what you are. You may not know why but you most certainly know how you got here!"

Aglorar leaned in so that they were almost nose-to-nose.

"Either I am right and the lightning brought you to Gismay, or I am wrong and you are Ebrahiim spies that are working with him against my Lord. The truth. Now."

Cam looked back at him in shock for a moment before the relief began to sweep over him.

Aglorar knew what had happened. He had seen the lightning and everything else and come to the same conclusion as Gismay. Perhaps he knew more than Gismay did, maybe even how to reverse it and get them home.

He stopped. Gismay had said that others would not be as kind to them as he had been, and Aglorar had certainly shown no signs of softening his demeanour towards them at any point in their short time together. Why should Cam believe that he was in any way interested in helping him?

Aglorar seemed to read his expression and rolled his eyes.

"Boy, if I wanted to hurt you or kill you I would have done so by now. Look at where you are, and consider what I said about this room when I first brought you here. I have not lied to you, nor have I wittingly caused you any harm."

Cam coughed out a laugh.

"You've thrown me around enough," he spat, "and dragged me, shoved me, pushed me... Is that how you treat your friends?"

Aglorar raised both his hands in a submissive gesture, and nodded slowly.

"You are right, I have indeed done so. And for that I must

apologise. Captain Dunwald is learned in many ways, but his wisdom in such matters as yours is lacking. He believes you to be spies of Ebras and I had to treat you as such to avoid suspicion."

Cam looked at the Soldier. His expression was earnest and his voice was apologetic, and he had in truth done no real harm to Cam. The other soldier, Lekkon, had manhandled them more roughly from what little details of the last few days he remembered.

"Still," he said cautiously, "why would you go to all this trouble? If I am just a spy then all your effort has gone to waste."

"True enough," Aglorar countered, "but if you are not then we can be of great use to each other. I am here not solely as a representative of Lord Fohenk, but also as a herald for others who know of such Travellers as you."

This was all sounding too good to be true, but Cam could not shake the feeling that Aglorar was telling him the truth. Every word he spoke simply sounded honest, there was no other way Cam could explain it.

"What others?" he asked, still trying to sound non-committal.

"Those who know about such matters," Aglorar responded, "and would do everything they can to help you leave our world. Travellers are not common, and knowledge of how, and why, it happens is the province of very few. It is passed down the ages to a select group, who guard it with their lives so that it cannot fall into the wrong hands and be used for unwholesome purposes."

He looked at Cam once more, then leaned in conspiratorially.

"Such power could lead to great and terrible evil for not just my world, but yours. The Balance is put into jeopardy when such events as your being ripped, unasked, from your world and into this one come to pass. We seek only to redress the Balance and to protect all of creation from being undone. The swiftest and surest way to do that is to send you, and your companion, home."

With these last words he smiled. It was a surprisingly pleasant expression and, to Cam's eyes, his face looked different now. It was as if his very appearance when they had first met at Gismay's farm was part of the front he put on when in the presence of his Captain.

"You are important to us," the Soldier continued, "as is your safe return to your own world. I cannot promise the process will be quick or easy – it has not even been attempted in many lifetimes – but it is in all of our interests to make it happen, and for the sake of my world I will do whatever it takes. You have my word."

Aglorar offered Cam his hand, and looked at him. A quiet pleading was in his eyes and the smile on his lips wavered a little. He truly did look like a man who wanted nothing more than to stop some terrible future coming to pass.

Cam breathed in heavily and nodded.

"Alright," he said, shaking Aglorar's hand and feeling a weight the like of which he had never known lift from his shoulders, "alright. Ever since we arrived we've wanted to go home. But everything's happened so quickly that... To be honest it's just nice to hear someone say they can help."

Aglorar nodded earnestly, a caring gleam in his eyes.

"I can believe it, friend," he sighed, "there are few who could possibly comprehend what you and you companion have been through. Let us help."

Cam felt a new, stronger wave of relief pass through him, and everything seemed to change in that moment. All the worry, the stress, and the fear evaporated from within him and it was replaced with the pure elation that, finally, he had found a way to get he and Sonia home.

"You have no idea how much this means, Aglorar. I... I don't know what to say. Thank you!"

"Think nothing of it," the Soldier said, "it is what we do. Now, to business. Our members know of Travellers from several different worlds. Before we can do anything, we will need to know which world you came from. The process to send you back is different depending on where you call home, or so the Masters say. And the more information I have to give to them, the more help they will be able to offer us."

Cam looked back at him, relief pulsing through his body and tears beginning to well in his eyes.

"This is... I mean... Well, I'm not sure what to tell you," he stumbled, a myriad of thoughts colliding within him.

Aglorar smiled warmly at him.

"Perhaps tell me a little about your world and your part in it?"

Cam took a moment before he spoke, not entirely sure how he should answer the request.

"Yes. Right," he began uncertainly, "well, I'm an actor. I work at a Castle, believe it or not. Edgeborough Castle. Sonia works there too, but she's a photographer. She takes pictures of people. It's basically what we told you at Gismay's farm."

Here he stopped and looked at Aglorar, the pit of his stomach falling away.

"Where is Gismay?" he asked.

Aglorar's warm smile stayed exactly where it was, and he reached a hand out to Cam's shoulder in a comforting way.

"He is being attended to," the Soldier said softly, the words immediately reassuring beyond measure, "you need not worry for him."

"Good," Cam said, breathing a sigh of relief, "I'm glad to hear it. Where was I?"

"You were telling me what you and your companion do in your world."

"Yes! Yes, of course! Sorry. So, like I said, we both work at a Castle, but we do different things. We were working together, actually, on the day we travelled here."

"Really?" asked Aglorar, leaning in.

Cam smiled. He always loved having a captive audience, and seeing how drawn in to his story Aglorar was only added to the euphoria he was feeling.

"Yes," he continued, starting to talk more animatedly, "but it all happened after work had finished. I'd left my mobile in Fingall's Tower, but when we both went back to look for it strange stuff started happening! There was someone in a cloak, speaking some weird language that I'd never heard but somehow understood. To be honest, I was terrified! All I wanted to do was go back home!"

"Ah, now," said Aglorar importantly, "home. That is a very powerful thing in these matters. You will need to focus on your home with all your thoughts if we are to be successful. Bring those thoughts to the front of your mind, so that they are fresh when the time comes."

Cam nodded excitedly.

"Of course! Well, I live with my Mum. She's called Charlotte, and we get on like a house on fire! She's always looked after me, on her own for most of the time. I was only three when Dad went so I barely knew him, and Mum doesn't really talk about him. When she does it's mostly just standard stuff, not positive or negative really. Just facts. She said once that the house feels empty without him, but that was a while ago and I don't think it does since I can't remember him being in it."

Aglorar moved his chair in closer, a fascinated expression and a glimmer behind his eyes.

"Good, Cam. This is very good. Tell me about this house. What is it like? Where is it?"

Cam could hardly have stopped himself talking even if Aglorar had not asked him the question. He did not know what had come over him, but the words were pouring out of him. Perhaps it was simply the knowledge that he would indeed see all of these things again that brought all of these thoughts cascading to the surface? Whatever the reason, it felt good for his mind to immerse itself in such mental delights.

"Our house is pretty big, for two people anyway. It's outside the town, in a little village in the countryside. There's loads of great walks and miles of fields around us, and I honestly don't think I could have wished for a better place to live! I miss it so much, and I can't wait to get back there!"

Aglorar now held him by the shoulders, his excitement beginning to match Cam's own.

"And where is this house? Where is it you wish to return to?"

The atmosphere in the room reached an absolute fever-pitch. Cam could not help himself. He raised his head upwards and shouted in an ecstatic voice:

"Welverleigh!"

The shout echoed about the room to infinity, and the release of energy that soared through Cam's body was more intense than anything he had ever felt in his life. Everything in his soul wanted to go back, every fibre of his being throbbed with the desire to see his home again. In that moment, he doubted there was anything anyone, even Sonia, could say to dissuade him from his course.

He was going home, whatever it took.

"Welverleigh," he repeated breathlessly, and let his head fall forwards to his chest.

He became suddenly aware that he was sweating. The euphoria still surged through his veins, but the thoughts of home began to fade from his now exhausted mind. He let them recede, for he now knew that he had a means to recapture them properly. They would not remain mere memories for very long, he would see to that.

He felt Aglorar clap him heartily on his back, and he then allowed the Soldier to lift him to his feet and lead him out of the room and back down the corridor they had come through before all of this started.

"You have done well," he heard him say in an earnest voice, "you have earned your rest."

When Cam looked up, he saw the figure of Sonia sat huddled in their cell. He smiled broadly at her, though with everything that had just happened to him he was not certain if it came across as he intended. He felt euphoric, almost drunk, but he revelled in it. He saw her look up at him, fear and concern in her eyes.

"Cam? Are you alright?"

She had stood quickly and come to the bars.

"I'm brilliant," he sighed with genuine pleasure, "we're going home, Son! Aglorar is going to help us!"

He lowered himself onto the spartan bunk that was within their cell and let himself be immersed in his emotions. He saw at the edge of his vision Aglorar place a hand upon Sonia's shoulder.

"Come," he was saying, soft and friendly, "it is time we spoke. Do not fear, it is as Cam says. I wish to help you."

Sonia looked at Cam uncertainly, but he did not hesitate in nodding his agreement with Aglorar.

"He's going to help us. We're going home."

The energy that had thrummed through his body began to dissipate and he felt his eyes closing.

He did not care.

"We're going home," he sighed as he drifted into a truly peaceful sleep.

* * * * *

The pressure on Gismay's arm had receded a little, though this did not relieve him. He had spent the night chained by his wrists and ankles to the wall of Lord Fohenk's most vile cell and been allowed only a brief respite before one of Eismeer's guards had taken to flogging him. For an hour Gismay knew only the stinging and lashing of leather against his flesh, and the warmth of his own blood running over his raw, contorted skin.

He had said nothing.

He was dragged along a stone corridor to a room where his freshly wounded back was then thrown onto a huge block of ice. The relief from pain had at first seemed like an uncommon mercy, but then he had been taken to another room where he was laid over a pit of molten-hot coals. His newly numbed back was barely a foot above the searing flames and he had begun to scream as the ice-water was boiled from his flesh.

He had let out his first cry of pain, but screams were the only sounds he made.

He had boiling pitch dripped slowly onto his chest. It was aimed at one spot – just above his heart – and the burning touch seared him, making him dizzy with agony and nausea.

Still no words passed his lips.

Before he could reach the blessed black of unconsciousness he was wrenched up a long flight of stairs, his knees and shins clattering into each stone step as he was dragged and his blood staining every one. From here he had been led across a mercifully smooth marble floor, through a huge pair of double doors and dumped where he found himself now. He was not yet being subjected to any form of torture, though he knew that would only be a temporary respite; he would either tell them all he knew or be kept alive until they decided he was no longer sport.

This room was different to all the others he had been in since his arrival. It was large and airy, not as warm or claustrophobic. Though he had never been here before, he knew exactly what room it was. There was only one room it could be.

This was the Throne Room of Eismeer, the seat of power in the Eislands and the domain of Lord Fohenk himself.

The light glinting off the marble below him, along with the near total silence that engulfed the chamber, told him that it was early morning. His head hung limply down against his chest, doing all it could to avoid the blackened skin from his final torture. His legs and back cried out in excruciation, blood slowly dripping from his wounds, the tatters of his shift matted together and sticking to his surviving flesh. His breathing was little more than a death rattle.

He was in no condition to face what he was about to be put through, exactly as intended no doubt.

The sound of a door opening and steady, purposeful

footsteps crossing the marble signalled the arrival of the Lord Fohenk. The guards either side of Gismay's fragile form snapped to attention, though the Lord himself would not have acknowledged it. The feet passed briefly through his field of vision before continuing toward the Throne itself.

A click of fingers.

"Bring him here," said a well-used voice.

The guards grasped Gismay's arms firmly and moved him forward perhaps six feet, no longer bothering to lift him from the floor.

"Leave him. He will not trouble me."

The guards snapped to attention once more before turning on their heels and striding from the room. The great doors through which Gismay had been dragged closed with a shuddering boom that hung in the air for many moments.

The Farmer took a long, deep breath.

"You have done well. Many better men than you would have broken by now. Do you not wish to end your suffering?"

Lord Fohenk's voice was even, though the slightest tremor at the ends of his words belied the age hidden behind it. He spoke softly, confidently, and Gismay nearly relented in that moment. He did not desire to die, nor endure further agony, but his desire to serve his true King overrode all other feeling in his body.

No, he would not give in.

"You are a good man, Gismay," the Lord continued, retaining his even tone, "your father served me graciously all his life. Would you throw that all away? All you need do is tell me what you know and you will be spared."

A single, harsh laugh passed the farmer's lips.

"No."

"Do not test my patience, Gismay. My leniency does indeed have limits, despite my grace. I do not suffer traitors gladly."

Another silence passed between the two men.

"How long have you worked for them?"

No, Gismay asserted silently to himself.

"How long?" Fohenk's voice showed his emotions for the first time.

Still nothing from the Farmer.

Sighing with frustration, Fohenk clicked his fingers. Gismay heard another door open, followed by footsteps and something wooden being dragged across the floor. The sound came closer and closer, stopping barely three feet away from his left shoulder, then arms sat him down upon whatever had been brought in.

For the first time since his arrival Gismay's eyes flashed their gaze across the interior of Eismeer's Throne Room.

The ceiling stood maybe thirty feet above his head, the grey-blue rock carved with ornate figures of winged warriors in all manner of heroic poses. The walls cascaded down from this height as dark waterfalls frozen long ago, and tapestries hung off their now stilled forms. These were faded with time and exposure to the light that flooded in from the great windows running the entire length of the wall to his left, next to the door that had just been opened. A single maroon and gold rug stretched from this door to the double doors Gismay had originally entered through.

Directly opposite him was the Throne of Eismeer. It was a finely crafted work of dark marble with maroon velvet coverings. It stood perfectly in the centre of the wall, commanding the entire room from its raised dais.

Here sat the Lord Fohenk himself with his long-fingered hands lying upon his lap, the powerful grey eyes staring at the farmer across the short distance between them. His long, greying-brown hair hung from underneath a simple circlet of gold, framing his healthy yet thin face, and reaching his blue and gold robes at his shoulders. His clean shaven mouth was set and his features betrayed no clues toward his feelings.

Gismay's attention was snatched back to his own battered body as the men who had hoisted him onto whatever contraption he was now sitting upon strapped his wrists and ankles to the thing. A sickening creaking filled the air as one of them turned a wheel behind his back, and Gismay felt his limbs being pulled back and apart from each other.

"If you will not tell me of your treachery, perhaps you might reveal who these two others my men have brought with you are? I am told you claimed that they are from the Crescent Isles, yet they did not even know who their Queen was?"

A dark amusement laced the words, and Gismay could just imagine the smile that would be curling across the lips as they spoke.

"Since that lie has already been punctured, what harm would it do to simply tell me who they are? Where did they come from? Are they allies of yours? Were they perhaps there to extract information from you by force? If you were to say so, I would undoubtedly believe you."

Gismay forced his head to look at the man before him, focussing his eyes as best he could through the pain.

"They're under my protection. You'll hear nothing of them from me."

Fohenk sighed.

"A regrettable choice, Gismay son of Hytol, but it is your stubborn will that drives you. You are indeed your father's son, though his loyalty to me was wholesome."

"If believing that makes you feel secure in that tainted seat you call a Throne," the Farmer forced, "then please continue to do so. Because you're right – I am very much my father's son."

Fohenk's eyes widened for a moment.

"Then this punishment is meant for two."

The wheel creaked and the Farmer's limbs were wrenched back once more. He snatched an inward breath at the motion, and at the sudden pain in his back as his muscles were forced to tighten. His raw flesh rubbed itself against the hard wood.

"This chair will rip your body in two if I so desire, Gismay, and do not presume that I would not order it. For your treachery, you would know the meaning of pain before the deed is complete. Will you not relent? Will you not tell me what you know?"

Gismay, summoning all his available strength, spat from his dry mouth onto the marble.

Another creak, and his arms were splayed out as if he were being crucified. His ankles had been pulled further apart, twisting his knees at a strange, excruciating angle.

Still Gismay made no sound.

"Ebras will not win this war, and all your bravery will have been for nought!" The Lord's tone was suddenly harsh and insistent.

The wheel creaked again and Gismay's face contorted into a silent scream as his arms were pulled back behind the line of his shoulders. He could feel his heart straining, the searing pain in the muscles of his chest and beneath his arm pits reaching heights he could not have guessed at in even his darkest nightmares.

A sickening snap and a flame of agony in Gismay's right leg told all present that one of his muscles had finally given way. The Farmer finally allowed himself the relief of a scream, hardly noticing his arms being forced back almost straight behind his head, his shoulder blades threatening to shatter against the pull of the bonds that held him.

One last creak and Gismay's left shoulder popped. His arm now was pulled away from his trunk, the skin around the joint already blackening. He no longer had the strength to cry out, but his eyes bulged with agony and his mouth howled a silent wail into the air.

"Take him."

Fohenk's final exclamation of disgusted frustration was the last thing that Gismay heard.

Whatever happened to him now was immaterial.

The guards released the bonds about his ankles and his wrists. His body crumpled. They dragged him across the floor, back down into the dungeons, and toward the torture chambers once more; their hands deliberately pressing on his dislocated shoulder.

He did not care.

As they led him through the great iron door behind which the deepest depravities of his tormentor's will could be realised, all he knew was that, no matter what lay ahead of him, he had not betrayed his people.

* * * * *

When Cam awoke to the sound of Sonia being led back to their cell, the feeling that Aglorar had awoken in him had all but spent itself. His mind and body were now mired in a post-euphoric daze that left him feeling heavy and cumbersome. His eyes were dry, his fingers numbed, and he had to concentrate deeply to pull himself up to a sitting position to welcome his friend back to their spartan accommodation.

He watched her as she stumbled slightly, a misty grin on her face. She caught herself on the bars, holding her body there for a moment before allowing it to slide slowly toward the relative safety of the bunk.

"Hey," Cam breathed.

Sonia waved a hand in response.

"You OK?"

She nodded in an exaggerated manner.

"Just like you said. He wants to help."

Cam nodded, then felt his own body sliding back down toward the bunk that he occupied.

"Yeah. Very nice of him."

He rolled himself onto his side so he could see Sonia.

"What did he ask you?" he forced from his dry mouth.

"Oh, lots of things," Sonia replied airily. "Where I was from, what our world was like. He really wanted to know about my house! Weird, but if it helps..."

She stopped as her head lolled forwards and for a moment Cam believed that she had fallen asleep. He closed his eyes and allowed himself to do the same.

“He said that we wouldn't have to wait long,” Sonia continued, her outburst shaking Cam rudely back into the room, “that it wold all be sorted soon.”

“Uh-huh?” Cam replied, quickly being retaken by the drowsiness within.

“Yeah... I can't wait. It feels like I haven't been home in... decades. Millennia! I wonder if they will have fixed those pillars when we get back.”

“What pillars?” Cam asked dreamily.

“I know, right? I didn't even remember we had them! But we do! The two broken pillars by the grey door. Overlooking the garden.”

Lazily Cam's mind tried to dredge images of Sonia's house from the recesses of his memory. He could not picture what she was describing, but then who was he to argue? She lived there after all. If she said there were pillars, then there were pillars.

“Oh?” he sighed. “Well, I hope they have fixed them. I'd like to see them.”

“They are gorgeous! Golden flowers grow around them in the summer.”

Cam did not have the energy to respond nor to hear anything else that Sonia said. He slipped back into a state of half-slumber, with visions of pillars and flowers and grey doors floating across his mind.

Then he saw his mother standing at their own front door, smiling and beckoning him home. The sight rejuvenated him beyond all measure. He ran to her, leaping up the steps from the road and along the garden path. She laughed joyfully to see him, tears of happiness upon her face. Cam felt he was crying as well, the sheer emotion of finally being back with her taking over every part of his body.

But as he reached her she faded, and was replaced by the bars of his cell once again as he floated back to the surface of his consciousness. The feeling of joy faded as quickly as the visions that had brought it, and the stark reality of their situation came back to him.

Even though Aglorar had offered them help, they were still stuck in this cell.

He groaned loudly at the thought, and hoisted himself up on his elbows. How long had he slumbered? It felt like mere moments, but the sleep in his eyes told a different story. He wiped it away with the back of his hand and clicked his tongue against the roof of his dry mouth.

"Sonia? Are you awake?"

His head swam at the sound of his own voice. His head was pounding. He massaged his eyes with the tips of his fingers then let his head fall back and stared at the ceiling.

After what he felt was far too long, he realised that Sonia had not responded.

"Sonia? Are you awake?" he repeated, slightly louder and more forcefully.

This time he made certain to focus and to listen. There was no response.

"Sonia?"

He turned and looked over at her bunk and nearly jumped out of his skin, for where Sonia was lying the last he looked now sat Aglorar.

"Bloody hell! How long have you been there?!" he panted, putting his hand to his chest to calm his thumping heart.

"Not long," the Soldier replied quietly.

Cam almost laughed with the adrenaline.

"Sorry," he said as calmly as he could, "I just wasn't expecting to see you. Where's Sonia?"

"Safe," Aglorar said simply, "you have my word."

He smiled at Cam, who instantly felt calmer.

"Ah, good," Cam sighed, then looked at the Soldier expectantly. "Did you need something?"

Aglorar nodded.

"As a matter of fact, I do. I have spoken to Lord Fohenk on your behalf."

Cam shifted himself round so that he was sat facing his

new-found friend.

"Oh? And what did he say?"

"He wishes to speak to you, as soon as may be. I believe he was receptive to my words."

Cam smiled broadly.

"You really think so?"

Aglorar returned the smile and nodded once more.

"I am certain of it."

With a sudden burst of energy, Cam pulled himself to his feet.

"Well, let's not keep him waiting."

Aglorar clapped a hand on his shoulder.

"Indeed not," he agreed, and led Cam out of his cell.

Chapter Six

The Lord's Justice

As dawn broke, Captain Dunwald of Eismeer looked out over the vista that lay before him. The entirety of the Eislands could be seen from his vantage point atop the walls that surrounded the city.

To the north were the eastern-most tips of the Glacier Mountains, the jagged natural barrier between them and the inhospitable wastes known as the Glacier Pass, and to the north-east stood the market and border town of Harling. There the Kingdom of Fohenk met the ancient lands of the Volarian Ward, ruled over by King Miravár ó Volarian. That was a proud land which had never much troubled with the Eislands, for their strength throughout the history of Rhydariel had always been superior than that of the Eismen, and both saw how prudent a treaty between such prosperous neighbours would be.

Behind Dunwald, away eastward, lay the great port at Daggerok. The seas and coasts around the Eislands were not kind to her people, and scant count of locations were suitable as a harbour, save for Daggerok. Yet even there the rocks and cliffs that jutted from the cold, deep water remained a constant threat to all maritime endeavours. Many men had lost their lives in its creation, and more had died in the years since, falling to the vengeful wrath of the sea that did not wish for their intrusions.

The people of the Eislands, though, were tough and hardy, resourceful and proud. They did not accept their land's refusal to grant them access to the sea, and so defied the very earth to create the master-work of stone, iron and wood.

Only once had Dunwald himself ever visited the place. He remembered gravely admiring the huge, fang-like pinnacles that perforated the water's surface at the entrance to the port. The waves had ripped between them as the wind howled through the maze of cliffs so fiercely that the spray was almost constant, creating a thick, grey-blue fog that obscured all but the largest ships from view.

Turning his thoughts away from the seas behind him, Dunwald cast a glance over his left shoulder to the south and west. There lay the old mining villages, untouched now for many years by ought but the sands of time. That had been the great wealth of the Eislands in their founding years, millennia ago, for they had discovered great natural caves running beneath the shore and sea that contained an abundance of the most sought after gem in all the lands.

Gildestone.

Its surface was as clear as the very air itself and its centre veined with the most perfect shades of violet and golden yellow. Such was the clarity of the stone that many believed it to be a gift sent directly from the Gods; a few such people also believed that, so strong was the stone's link to the Divine, it would enable any who bore even the smallest fragment to commune directly with them.

Such tales were too far fetched for most, Dunwald himself included, but it was on this legend that the value of Gildestone soared for many hundreds of years. The Eismen had constructed many great mines within the cave systems, plundering the hidden wealth as deeply as they dared, with villages and settlements springing up all along the southern coastline to take full advantage of this natural resource.

During the Civil War and Rebellion of Ebrahir, only a year before the War of the Whitesword had begun, these villages and their inhabitants had split their allegiance between Lord Galforth and Ebrahir the Blasphemer. The fighting that had taken place devastated whole families; sons fought with their fathers, sisters held to ransom so that their families would side with the brother.

After nearly three hundred years of prosperity, the entire region decimated itself within a a matter of weeks. Those who survived either joined the war or fled into the hills and mountains; many would fall prey to wolves, and those that managed to avoid that fate went on to live in secret fear or shame for their choices – or despair for the folly of their lost family members – until they passed, unremembered and unnoticed.

Dunwald knew all of this, and could have stared out at the beauty of the world and thought about what lay at all the points of the compass but, alas, he heard the approach of a Messenger.

The Messengers of Fohenk were the swiftest, fittest, and most agile young subjects that could be found. Often these were boys or young men who wished to serve their Lord or, more often than not, whose Fathers had wished them to gain apprenticeships at the Palace but who showed little aptitude for battle or crafting. If they could run fast and hard for long periods of time then Lord Fohenk put them to work as his Messengers, delivering news to all corners of Eismeer and passing urgent words and letters between the Lord and his forces, wherever they should be.

A young man of about eighteen years stood now before Dunwald. He saluted the Captain in the traditional Eismen manner of clasping the right fist in the left hand directly over the heart.

"Captain Dunwald, the Lord Fohenk demands your immediate presence on a matter of utmost importance."

Dunwald nodded his acceptance of the message immediately and, with only a short forlorn glance out over the western reaches of the Eislands, he made his way from the walls and down into the streets of Eismeer.

He strode through the market district and took in the scents and colours of all manner of items; fruits, seeds, grains, cloths, livestock, breads, jewels. Then came the Guild District where he was greeted by the sweltering steam and choking soot of the smithies, the clamour and thick odour of the stables, the quiet, meticulous workings of the fletcher.

After this he came to the gates of the citadel proper. They loomed up, two great teak structures defying any who dared breech the walls of Eismeer. Beyond these lay a large square that was often used as an additional market place during the high season, and as a gathering place for festivals and celebrations. It was also designed to be the location for any last stand before falling back inside the Palace Walls; two great towers of stone, manned by hundreds of archers, stood either side of the gates, overlooking the square.

Dunwald made his way to the base of the right hand gate tower and ducked inside the doorway. He passed through into the Citadel grounds and crossed them as directly as he could. Within moments, he was encased in the cool air of the Tower of the Eis.

The entrance to the Throne Room stood before him; another pair of teak doors, this time emblazoned with a huge, iron depiction of the Eiswings, with two of the Lordsguard – Fohenk's personal soldiers – stood upon either side.

At a nod from Dunwald they pushed the great doors open and moved aside to allow him entrance. Lord Fohenk was sat upon his Throne with a great tome open on his lap. He did not acknowledge the Captain's arrival, nor was he reading the book.

His eyes were focussed two figures stood before him.

"My Lord," the Captain tried softly at last, "you sent for me?"

Still Fohenk did not speak. He did not, in fact, do anything – he simply sat in his Throne and stared outward.

Only now did Dunwald take note who it was that stood in front of his Lord. His eyes landed on the figures of Aglorar and Cam. A moment passed as his mind processed what he was being confronted with.

"Lieutenant?" he began uncertainly.

"Lieutenant Aglorar has been having a very interesting conversation with our young friend here," Lord Fohenk cut in calmly.

Dunwald flicked his eyes between his Lord and the other two.

"What sort of conversation?"

Fohenk raised his hand and gestured that Aglorar should speak.

"Of course, my Lord," the Soldier said, bowing gracefully, then turned and faced Dunwald. "Do you remember the night before we reached Lun Ridge Farm, Captain?"

"Yes, I believe so," came the slow answer, "we camped perhaps ten miles east of the farm. The weather was particularly foul, even for this time of year."

Aglorar nodded.

"Quite so. And do you remember anything specific about the foulness you mentioned?"

Dunwald considered for a moment before answering.

"There was a fierce storm," he said, "thunder claps from the Seven themselves, and lightning the like of which I have never seen."

"The lightning," Aglorar cut in, clapping his hands, "well remembered, Captain. It was, my Lord, as Captain Dunwald has said, truly a storm for the ages. Lekkon had already raised the possibility of turning back in the face of such tumult, but the Captain and I agreed that we should press on. I volunteered to take the first watch, though I could see very little in such conditions. But what I could see, clear as the sun, was the lightning."

"Forgive me," Dunwald said, stepping towards the Throne, "but what does any of this have to do with the boy?"

"What indeed, Captain?" Fohenk responded. "It is precisely that question that caused me to summon you. I need your wisdom."

Dunwald snapped himself to attention.

"If it is within my power, my Lord, I will offer what wisdom I may. But I fear that I am still at a loss as to what we are discussing."

"It would appear that we have a Traveller in our midst."

Lord Fohenk's voice was soft, but the words hung heavy in the room. He looked to Dunwald with a neutral expression, passing no judgement on the validity of the statement, and spoke no further.

Dunwald blinked for a moment, considering what he had just heard.

"A Traveller?" he asked, trying not to sound too incredulous. "But such a thing has not happened in... thousands of years."

"And yet here he stands," Fohenk responded, nodding to Cam. "Tell the Captain what you have told Aglorar and myself."

Dunwald looked to the boy Cam as he turned his head and smiled.

"It's true," Cam said simply, "I'm not from here. I'm from another world. So's Sonia."

The tone of the boy's voice was odd, almost as if he had been drinking. It was all that Dunwald could do to keep himself from laughing. Surely Lord Fohenk was not going to be swayed by this?

"That is certainly a lofty claim, boy," he said as levelly as he could, "do you have any proof to back it up?"

"Nothing physical, no," Cam shook his head, but Aglorar laid a hand upon his shoulder.

"Tell the Captain where you come from, friend Cam."

Dunwald watched as Cam slowly turned his head to look at Aglorar. The motion was smooth, unnaturally so, as if his whole being was moving slower than the world around him. The Captain heard him take a breath as he nodded to Aglorar, then looked back to Dunwald once more.

"I live in a place called Welverleigh."

This Dunwald had not expected; indeed, it was his bearing as Captain that prevented him from showing any emotion in response to the words. He looked from the boy to Aglorar, and then to his Lord, trying to decipher where they stood on what was being said to them, but they simply stared back at him awaiting his response.

"Like I said, a lofty claim."

Cam shrugged.

"It's just where I live," he said.

Lord Fohenk nodded, then waved to two Guards that they should come forward.

"Return this boy to his cell, and give him his daily rations. Do not treat him roughly, but let him speak to no-one."

The Guards nodded and each placed a hand on one of Cam's arms, then led him away. Dunwald watched as the boy smiled gleefully, sharing a glance with Aglorar as he left the hall.

When the great doors to the Throne Room had closed, Lord Fohenk regarded his two men gravely.

"What think you both?" he asked urgently.

Dunwald did not quite contain the disdainful snort that came from within his chest.

"You surely cannot believe the boy, my Lord?" he asked, as forcefully as he dared. "The chances of such a thing happening are beyond the realms of common sense."

The room stood silent for what felt like an age.

"My Lord Fohenk?" Dunwald pushed, his incredulity beginning to take hold of him.

At long last Lord Fohenk's eyes raised themselves to meet those of his Captain.

"Tell me," he said steadily, "what do you know of the history of this city?"

The question had caught Dunwald off guard.

"As much as any man can, my Lord. I know all of your ancestors, as far back as the founding of the Tower of the Eis herself..."

The Lord waved a dismissive hand.

"I am well aware of your knowledge concerning those matters, Captain. I speak of the greater history – that of events, not names or titles. Lords come and go, Captain, but their people linger. What do you know of the history of the people of this city."

Dunwald took a moment to consider the Lord's request.

"I know that we have passed through a great many hardships," he settled on at last, "and that we have always fought bravely and truly. Of which events would you have me speak?"

"What do you know of the War of the Whitesword, Captain?"

This question was asked by Aglorar, who stepped forward and took his place next to Lord Fohenk.

Dunwald stared back at him.

"Is it now the practise in this hall that Lieutenant's can question their Captains, Aglorar?"

"Answer the question, Dunwald," Fohenk replied forcefully, "for on this matter, and no other, Aglorar has my authority to speak freely."

"May I ask why, my Lord?"

"All will become clear, Captain," Aglorar cooed, "I assure you."

For a moment Dunwald felt ready to chastise his Lieutenant for speaking out of turn, but he held himself.

"I know much about that conflict, Lieutenant," he answered stiffly. "What would you have me recount?"

Fohenk's eyes changed; where before they had been confused and, perhaps, a little fearful, they now became dark and forbidding.

"The conversation we are about to have must not leave this room. The knowledge we will speak of is not common and I would not have it become so."

Dunwald regarded his Lord carefully for a moment. So far as he knew there was little about the War of the Whitesword which was not known by many; the Civil War of the Eislands, the disappearance of the Nendolusians, the coming of the Great Evil and its eventual vanquishing by Whitesword himself. All of this was widely spoken of throughout all of Rhydariel, and many songs and tales were sung and told about it.

"What knowledge do you speak of, my Lord?" the Captain hazarded.

"You remember the lightning of which we spoke just now?" Aglorar mused.

"Of course, Lieutenant," Dunwald responded curtly. He

did not like answering to a subordinate in such a way.

"While to most it is simply part of the weather, to those such as I it carries a deeper significance."

"Those such as..? What in the Seven are you talking about, Aglorar?"

"I apologise, Captain," said Aglorar, "for I have not been entirely honest and open in my time serving you. I have kept certain things from your knowledge. All for the good of our people, you understand, and at the command of our Lord."

Dunwald could barely contain the anger building within him. A Lieutenant had been keeping secrets from him? And with the knowledge of Lord Fohenk? The very idea made his blood boil.

"If our Lord deemed it was best to lie hidden," he said aloud through somewhat gritted teeth, "then I am certain it was for good reason. Now, what did you keep from me, Lieutenant?"

He emphasised the final word so that Aglorar was under no illusions as to his place. The Lieutenant nodded, but did not look any more reproachful than he had before Dunwald spoke.

"I am part of a small group who hold some measure of knowledge of such Travellers to our world as this Cam claims to be. We work, in secret and oft unaided, to unravel the mysteries of how and why such events happen. And how they may be undone."

"Undone?" Dunwald asked.

"Such events are not part of the natural order of things. They can affect the Balance, and the very fabric of not just the Traveller's world but our own. The only way to protect us all is to return a Traveller to their own world."

Dunwald genuinely could not believe what he was hearing.

"My Lord, with all due respect," he began, but Lord Fohenk cut across him.

"I deem that Aglorar has authority on this particular matter," he said, "and there is also evidence to support the boy's claim."

"Evidence?" Dunwald cried.

For the first time Lord Fohenk now lifted the tome that had been resting upon his lap for all of this time. It was old, and the pages thick. It had been read many times judging by the condition of the spine and the many marks upon the leather binding.

"This is the journal of Wargrum, our chief scholar during the time of the Whitesword. He writes of how a great storm, resplendent with blue lightning the like of which not seen by our world before or since, ravaged the skies above Eismeer. The very next day the Whitesword appeared to Lord Galmorn. We know the Whitesword to have been a Traveller, and he appeared in an almost identical fashion to this boy."

Dunwald shook his head again.

"My Lord, I implore you. The lightning we saw, while certainly more violent than is usual for the season, was nothing more than that. And while I accept the similarities, I do not believe that they are enough to say that this boy is a Traveller!"

"There is more, Captain," Aglorar said softly, "and I believe it is something that we should take into account."

Dunwald was about to speak, but he stopped. Lord Fohenk turned the pages in the book upon his lap for a few moments then, when he had found whatever he was searching for, slowly and deliberately moved his hands underneath the book upon his lap and manoeuvred it so that it now faced Dunwald. He tapped his finger against the page, indicating a short paragraph.

"Read it," came the simple command.

The Captain accepted the tome and did as his Lord had bid him.

Amidst all the descriptions of battles, and the stains of time and dust, was a line of scripture. Though its context was long known and understood, it could well be the herald of a new era of war and woe for Rhydariel.

If the boy was telling the truth.

Dunwald read the words once more, even now hoping they had altered their message:

Whitesword, who hails from Welverleigh.

He read it again and again, half expecting and half wishing the words to change and make sense, but they did not. They remained resolutely as they had been scribed nearly forty centuries ago.

"This is why I have called you both here. I require wisdom. Both your councils have long been prized by me, especially yours Captain Dunwald. And this day it holds a value greater than ever before."

Now the Lord looked at both of them levelly, a simple and dignified plea in his eyes.

"What do I do with him?"

A long silence passed.

"If... if I had to judge, my Lord," Dunwald said carefully after many moments, "I would say that the boy is lying. He gave the answer under duress, and was probably fearing for his life. If he has seen many more than twenty winters then I will be deeply surprised. One so young might have simply said anything that he believed would save him from death."

Fohenk nodded slowly.

"And if he is telling the truth, Dunwald?"

"The chances of that are small, my Lord. You know this. When we found him he had no other possessions than the clothes on his back, clothes that are of Ebran design. That evidence which, if I may, I hold in higher esteem than the writings of a scholar long dead, points to he and his companion being Ebrahiim spies that were colluding with Gismay. He had certainly given them food and aid, and he asserted that they are under his protection. They are, to my mind, traitors. And we cannot allow any traitors, even ones so young as these, to live on the basis of whimsy and innuendo."

The Lord ran his long fingers across his chin, considering Dunwald's response.

"You may be right, Captain," he conceded, then turned to

the Lieutenant. "Aglorar? You questioned the boy, and you said that he was greatly receptive when you offered him your help?"

Dunwald looked at Aglorar with a mix of fury and disbelief.

"You offered him help?"

"I did," Aglorar replied, "because I wanted to see his reaction to being offered a way home."

"And what was his reaction?" Dunwald pressed.

Aglorar shrugged.

"That which you would expect from someone who had been through such an ordeal. He was happy to accept."

"So you believe him?"

Here the Lieutenant paused and looked to both his Captain and his Lord.

"Not in the least," he said. "I have dealt with many such as him who truly believe, or convince themselves, that they are such a Traveller. But he is clearly lying to save his skin. Why else would he and Gismay concoct that ridiculous story about them being part of Queen Yolanda's court? And let us not forget that Gismay hid them from us. No, I fear that, whatever lies the boy has convinced himself to be true, they are indeed simple spies."

The surprise that they were in agreement was plain on Dunwald's face, so much so that Aglorar smiled.

"Whatever you may now think of me, Captain," he said, a gentle laugh beneath his words, "I am still a man of reason."

Dunwald nodded, then turned to Lord Fohenk.

"I believe we have a commonality, my Lord," he said, "both Aglorar and I believe the boy and his companion to be traitors, along with Gismay."

Lord Fohenk smiled at him.

"Would that it were so easy for me," he said, "but the burden of decision lays not upon your shoulders. It is not that I doubt your advice, it is that something in my heart that troubles me. If you are wrong, and this boy is exactly as he says he is, then we cannot risk harm to him."

“Why not, my Lord?”

“The Planes, Captain. When the Whitesword first appeared to Lord Galmorn, the Planes were moving. If such a thing is happening now, and I do nothing to stop it, what kind of Eisman could I claim to be?”

“Allow me, my Lord,” said Aglorar, “to offer some small wisdom in this regard. The Planes are, indeed, bound up with the Travellers, and if this boy were such a one then I would indeed council you to consider this most catastrophic of possibilities. But I assure you he is not. Please, put all such thoughts from your mind. Eismeer is safe, and the sooner you rid her of these spies the better.”

“I agree with Lieutenant Aglorar,” Dunwald added, “and, if I may be so bold, if it is the burden of choice that weights heavy on you, I would offer you some advice in that regard.”

Lord Fohenk nodded.

“It would strengthen my heart to hear it.”

“I believe that you are given three choices,” the Captain said. “The first is that we leave the boy to rot in the dungeons and ignore him completely. This, in either case, I do not advise. The first obligation of a prisoner is to escape, with or without outside help. We do not know what information he and Gismay shared with each other before we arrived, and we cannot risk him taking any more with him should he be successful.

“The second choice is that we believe his word. You must then take him into your council, and trust that he is who he says. If your choice is ill then we could put him exactly where our enemies would wish him to be, and he could well prove our downfall.

“The third, and the road I believe shows the most diligence, is that we do not believe his word. It is the most likely of all the outcomes that he is lying or simply desperate to save his own life. Either way, it is my firm belief that he is a spy. The Lord's Justice cannot be ignored in these matters, as the laws laid down by your ancestors dictate.

“If you chose aright in this then you will rid the world of

yet another unfaithful soul. If, by some cruel twisting of designs, you are proven wrong then we will have to face the consequences, dire as they may be, as true Eismen – with bravery and steadfastness. That is my council, Lord, for good or ill."

Dunwald's words echoed about the Throne Room for many moments after he had spoken them. The very air about him grew heavy with their implications and Dunwald could not help wavering a little under the weight of the implied consequences.

If he was wrong then, by the Seventh, there would be a steep cost.

"Lieutenant?" The Lord's voice was a whisper.

"I agree with the Captain," Aglorar said, "and I believe the only true course is to put all three of them – the boy, his companion, and Gismay – to the Lord's Justice."

Fohenk ran his hand across his chin once more, then stared at the tome Dunwald held. His eyes told the Captain that a decision had been reached.

"You both speak well," he sighed, "and I believe that you are most probably right. He was aided by the traitor Gismay and has given us no true knowledge of himself.

"Though I agree the consequences will be dire should my choice be wrong, I cannot over look the sheer odds against that reality. Inform the Executioner that all three will face the Lord's Justice at noonsun today."

He stood and cast one last glance over both of the men stood before him. The expression was a difficult one to read, though the Captain discerned the same relief that he had felt once a decision had been reached and agreed upon. However, there were also traces of foreboding, uncertainty and defiance.

"Until then," Fohenk finished, and strode from the Throne Room.

They both saluted once more and watched their Lord go.

"Aglorar, you will go an inform the Executioner. I will return this," Dunwald said, gesturing Wargrum's tome, "to the Library, then I have another matter to attend to. Once you have spoken with the Executioner, make sure the Lordsguard are ready. Such a group of traitors will no doubt bring forth a crowd."

Aglorar saluted his Captain before spinning on his heels and striding from the room. Once he had gone, Dunwald tucked the book within his cloak and followed. However, when he passed out into the cool air of the courtyard he did not turn left toward the Library of Eismeer, but instead strode straight to the same gate he had entered when he had received his summons.

He pulled his hood over his head and wrapped his cloak about him, then he made his way back to the Market District. He used side roads and back alleys, keeping his head down and his grip upon the tome he had sequestered tight.

With every turn the air about him became thicker, the light dimmer, and the streets smaller. He was very quickly in an alley that ran around the base of the inner circular wall; very little light reached the stones here, and his boots struggled slightly for grip on the thin layer of permafrost beneath them. The noise and smells he had strode through earlier were nowhere to be found in this half-forgotten corner of Fohenk's City, but Dunwald knew it well. He had made it his mission as a Captain of the Lordsguard to know every street and alley under his watch, and because of that he knew this place was perfect for his needs.

He came to a low door that would not be noticed if you did not know it was there, and ducked through it into a barely lit tavern, though perhaps that was too grand a word. There was a bar that had certainly seen better days, and the Proprietor seemed be in a similar condition. What little light that came from the rather pitiful candelabras that stood in the centre of each table did not seem to penetrate the gloom that festered here, and it was only because Dunwald knew what he was looking for that he noticed the single patron sat in the darkest corner.

The Captain approached the bar and nodded to the Proprietor, who simply reached down and produced a bottle. From this he filled a glass, and slid it unceremoniously forward.

Dunwald nodded, then reached into the pouch tied to his belt and place two coins on the counter. This was far more than the drink was worth, but enough to make certain his presence here was kept a secret. He picked up the glass and stepped quietly over to the table to join the other patron. Dunwald settled himself, and regarded the figure with whom he now shared a table.

The man had about him a dark cloak that perhaps could have been green in hue, though it was difficult to tell in the quarter-light of the candles. The hood of the cloak was pulled up and over his face so that very little detail could be made out. Around the hem of the hood, and indeed the entire cloak, ran a design of golden flowers with dark, intertwined stems. This was the only colour that Dunwald could discern clearly against the flickering light.

He went to lift the glass to his lips.

"I wouldn't," came a voice from beneath the hood.

Dunwald stopped himself and looked uncertainly at the drink in his hand.

"Poison?" he asked.

The man shook his head.

"No, you are quite safe. But I saw which bottle that came out of. If you wish to be of any use to me later, I would ask you not to drink it."

The Captain took another quick glance at the liquid, then slowly replaced the glass on the table. A bestubbled smile came from beneath the hood, and a gentle laugh rose with it.

"Have you been successful?" the man asked.

"I have," Dunwald nodded, "to a point. The executions will take place at noonsun. That was the best I could do. Any other path presented too many obstacles."

The man nodded.

"It will suffice. What of the Lieutenant?"

"As you said it would be," Dunwald replied, "he had garnered information from the boy, and helped lead Fohenk to this."

Here the Captain revealed the tome hidden within his

cloak. The man took it and quickly wrapped his own cloak about it.

"You have done well. And is the boy what we believe him to be?"

Dunwald nodded silently.

"Then we must proceed," the man said gravely. "What state are they in?"

"I had to keep up some level of pretence," the Captain replied uncomfortably, "so whilst the younger two have been reasonably protected, Gismay will carry reminders of his time in Eismeer for the rest of his life."

"He knows the risks, as do you," the Figure said pointedly, "and you have both performed your duty. Let us hope that I can do the same."

"You have doubts?"

The Figure lifted his head and made eye contact with Dunwald at last; the deep green eyes that looked out from under the hood were aged, but not old. They glimmered against the faint, red-orange light that managed to penetrate the darkness about them.

"Do not be troubled. What we do, we do for Rhydariel. That is cause enough to ignore such doubts. Be ready at noonsun."

With that, the Figure stood and strode out into the cold of the morning. Dunwald watched, the cloak billowing out behind the man to reveal the sword that hung at his waist, and took a long inward breath.

It was going to be a difficult afternoon.

* * * * *

After Cam had been taken back to his cell by the Guards, he had fallen immediately into a heavy slumber. He was not revisited by visions of his home; indeed, he did not dream at all. When he first awoke from this blank sleep a feeling of relaxation and contentment had taken hold of him, and he moved to stretch his arms.

He found he could not.

Looking down, he saw that his wrists were bound by a thick cord, and also that the clothes Gismay had given him had been removed and replaced with a sackcloth shirt and breeches. These were secured to him tightly about his waist with a rope dipped in heavy tar. The stuff was thick and viscous, and Cam could feel its mass against him.

He shivered, and saw that he was no longer in his cell, but in a wooden room that was constructed against one of the stone walls of the city. It was outside, judging by the sudden drop in temperature his body was now adjusting to. The floor he was lying upon was mud covered with reeds and straw and no furniture or adornment was to be found; indeed the only break in the walls was the door that stood to his right. From beyond this came an icy breeze which chilled his body to the very core.

He breathed out hard, trying to control himself and keep from shivering. It was only then that he noticed another bundle of sackcloth in the corner opposite him. It was deep red in colour and, even from this distance, Cam knew why.

Blood.

Cam now saw a small, pitiful plume of steam rise from behind the red bundle, and he saw the sackcloth rise and fell of its own accord.

It was alive.

A sudden fear gripped Cam that he already knew what, or who, he was looking at. Crawling as quickly as his binds would permit him to, Cam pulled himself across the small space and turned the bundle.

The figure that stared back at him was the most horrific thing that Cam had ever seen.

Gismay's face was covered in blood. What little skin could be seen below was mottled with bruises erupting within the Farmer's flesh. His left arm hung unnaturally, while his right leg was bent at a peculiar angle.

Christ, Cam thought to himself, barely able to contain his nausea, *what have they done to you?*

A hacking, weak cough from Gismay's mouth answered him and Cam jerked up, staring at the man in astonishment.

"Gismay?" he gasped, gently shaking the man awake.

The Farmer's eyes managed, miraculously, to find some semblance of focus and he gingerly turned them toward Cam.

"My friend," he croaked, almost inaudibly.

Cam nodded, beside himself with relief that the Farmer had not yet succumbed to whatever terrible things he had been forced to endure.

"Yeah, it's me. What the hell did they do to you?"

Gismay grimaced, a strangely amused expression.

"Nothing that matters. My promise to King Hedradour remains unspoiled. How fare you, friend Cam?"

"I'll live," he answered, a half-hearted laugh lacing his words.

He looked at Gismay with what he had hoped was a genuine-looking smile, but saw that the Farmer did not share in his mirth. If anything, the expression that met Cam's gaze was one of resignation and apology. Cam raised his eyebrows.

"What?"

Gismay closed his eyes, and Cam could not be certain but he thought there were tears starting to form in his eyes.

"I am sorry," the Farmer said earnestly.

A sudden, horrible feeling exploded in the pit of Cam's stomach.

"What are you sorry for?" he croaked, but his brain was ahead of his question.

There was only one logical answer.

Before Gismay could speak, the door to the outside burst open and two guards strode in, followed by Lekkon. He motioned to the guards and they hoisted Cam and Gismay to their feet. Only now did Cam see the full extent of Gismay's injuries and dis-figuration. His right leg hung uselessly from his hip, and his left arm, clearly dislocated, swayed sickeningly from his shoulder.

"I am sorry," Gismay repeated, "I never meant for you to become involved in all of this!"

Cam barely heard him against the storm brewing within his mind.

"Shut your mouth, spy!" Lekkon spat. "Take them!"

The guards kicked the door open and dragged them both out into the full force of the cold beyond.

A mist hung about them, thick and grey, obscuring the way ahead of them. The path that Lekkon was leading them down seemed to be little more than an alleyway ducking between the Citadel and one of the inner walls of the city. From beyond the wall rearing up to Cam's left came the sounds of a great many people. Squinting ahead, Cam saw that the passage took a sharp downward turn to their left, presumably through the wall and into whatever lay beyond. Snow clung to the stone on either side of them and the path beneath his feet was frosted and slick.

He looked up at the guards and saw they were heavily armoured in plate and carried long swords. Even in a fully fit condition, Cam doubted that he would have stood even the slightest chance against either of them, let alone the pair plus Lekkon. All hope of a miraculous escape from whatever lay ahead of him dissolved from his mind.

The passageway narrowed so that the guards now had to walk in single file. Gismay was dragged ahead of Cam and roughly hurled around the corner. When Cam reached the spot he, too, was manhandled and thrown to his knees. Looming over them now was a wooden gate set imposingly within the stone wall. All that Cam could hear was the muffled crowd awaiting behind the gate, and the pounding of his heart.

He only now realised that he was crying. His breath was shaky and his body trembled with it. He knew why he was there with Gismay, but only now was the full reality showing itself. It was all he could do to keep himself from collapsing under the weight it.

It was clear now that Aglorar had failed to convince Lord

Fohenk that Cam was who he said he was. Well, why would he believe him? It made the most sense for the Lord to believe that he was a spy working with Gismay, after all.

So, that was that.

They were going to execute him.

He could feel Gismay next to him. The Farmer, too, was shaking. For a moment, Cam was angry at him. He was at least part of this world, and he was a spy! What did he expect would be the end for him? Cam had done nothing except get dumped on his doorstep at the wrong time! He did not deserve to die!

His snatched a breath of cold air and, to his own surprise, Cam found his anger dissipating slowly. Gismay had done everything in his power to protect both he and Sonia from the first moment when Dunwald had burst into his farm house and, in his heart, Cam was far more grateful for that than he was angry. And, he noted, Gismay had not given the order for his execution. That lay in the hands of Lord Fohenk.

In that moment Cam did something he had only ever heard of in tales and stories, and something he never thought he would do.

Silently he swore that, if he ever got the chance, he would get revenge on the person who was responsible for he and Gismay being executed, though the thought sounded hollow and childish in his head. What was he thinking? He could never get revenge on anyone, let alone the Lord of an entire Kingdom.

His thoughts were broken by Lekkon stepping past them and putting his hand on the gate.

Cam shot a quick look at Gismay. The Farmer simply stared at the floor.

"We're not done," Cam whispered, as forcefully as he could.

Gismay simply closed his eyes and nodded.

"May the Seven have mercy on you both," Lekkon growled, "because this lot won't!"

He pushed the gate open.

Noise exploded all about them. People were shouting with

words that Cam could not understand. He felt himself hoisted up by the guards and thrown forward. He collided heavily with the stony street, and he heard Gismay land heavily next to him.

After a moment, something hit him hard in the small of his back. He recoiled instinctively but soon something else hit him, this time on his shackled arms. Another object was hurled towards him but missed his head by mere inches. Raising his chin, Cam managed to cast his eyes over the thing. It was unfamiliar, but it appeared to be some form of fruit or vegetable. It had a deep purple pulp and a green skin, with its juice forming icy droplets on the ground.

Craning his neck forward, ignoring the continuous barrage of missiles and sound, he strained his eyes to focus through the mist and discover what was ahead of him.

On his left side stood the inner wall of the city, while on his right was a mass of people. Most wore the simple cloth of the working classes of Eismeer; some were old and grey, some barely even old enough to walk, but all were hurling what he imagined was abuse towards he and Gismay.

Without warning the guard pulled him to his feet, gave him but a moment to balance himself, then shoved him forward with a stern hand in the centre of his spine. Cam staggered for a few paces then slipped on the frosty ground and crumpled to his knees. Jeering rose from the crowd, electrifying the very air with their hate. Mist swirled around his eyes. More fruit hit him hard on his right hand side.

“Where's Aglorar?” he called out to Lekkon.

The man grinned evilly at him.

“You seek someone to speak on your behalf, boy?” he asked, grabbing him roughly by the scruff. “It's a little late for that, don't you think?”

Before Cam could reply he was thrust backwards, stumbled, and collapsed once more to the ground. The sound of Gismay's limp form crashing downward to join him upon the stones mingled with the taunting and the abuse from the crowd.

“Get up, traitors!” one voice taunted.

"Let us see what strength the Planks has given you!" called another.

The guards laughed along with those who heard the remark, while Lekkon simply watched in sick amusement. As the laughter reached a fever pitch, the guards stepped forward and hoisted Gismay as high in the air as his arms allowed, the Farmer's toes dangling six or seven inches above the stones.

"See here what comes of betraying our Lord," one of the guards called out. "Glory to Eismeer! Glory to Fohenk!"

"Glory to Eismeer! Glory to Fohenk!" the crowd cried in response.

The guards smiled, and dropped Gismay.

The Farmer's body clattered sickeningly into the ground. A cheer went up, a cacophony the like of which Cam had never experienced before; he could physically feel it in his ears.

"Should we drag these traitors to the Lord's Justice?" the guards beseeched the crowd, continuing the informal ritual.

"No!" the masses answered.

Lekkon now stepped forward, taking his first part in these grimly theatrical proceedings.

"Say you that only a coward would not face the Lord's Justice upon his own feet?"

"So we say!"

The answering shouts were laced with laughter. An air of celebration permeating the scene.

"What would you have us do?" Lekkon cried.

"Make them walk! Make them walk!"

The chant rang through the streets as hands dragged Cam to his feet once more, placing him in a standing position and holding him there. Lekkon removed a belt from about his armour, and Cam felt Gismay being placed behind him so that the two prisoners were now back to back. The weight of the Farmer pressed against Cam as his frame fought to keep itself upright.

"Make them walk! Make them walk!"

Lekkon wrapped his belt tightly across Cam's chest and

under Gismay's arms, buckling it roughly underneath the Farmer's ribs. He grinned evilly for a moment then motioned to one of the other guards to kick Gismay's legs from underneath him. The sudden extra weight brought Cam crashing to the stones, the air forced from his lungs.

"Up," Lekkon ordered.

"Cowards!"

"Make them walk!"

Cam tried to force his limbs to lift him upwards, but Gismay's weight was too much.

"Stand to face your death!"

"The Executioner is waiting!"

Once more Cam tried, but his body would not obey him.

"Shall we show them how merciful our Lord can be?"

"Yes! Make them walk!"

"Get them up," Lekkon ordered, and the guards promptly hoisted the two unstable forms to their feet. Cam felt for a moment that he would stumble once more, but to his surprise the guards held he and Gismay upright until they were as steady as they were going to be.

"Make them walk! Make them walk!"

Still the masses jeered and taunted.

Now Cam felt the guards position themselves next to him and lock their arms into his. They were taking his weight.

"See now the final mercy these traitors will be afforded by our just Lord! Let them see that Lord Fohenk and his people will not let even their enemies die without dignity!" Lekkon cried, his voice filling the scene. "Glory to Eismeer! Glory to Fohenk!"

"Glory to Eismeer! Glory to Fohenk!"

The crowd roared at what had transpired before them, and their cheering continued as Cam and Gismay were walked forwards once more through the ever-thickening mist. Lekkon had positioned himself at the head of their small procession, ceremoniously holding his sword in front of him. The feelings of celebration began to ebb away form the crowd and be replaced with a more sombre, circumspect air.

The street now turned through another door in the wall, beyond which was the courtyard in which the Tower of the Eis stood, the very centre of the city. What better place for the Lord to be seen disposing of traitors?

As they entered this place the noise of the crowd became hushed. Their footsteps echoed loudly through the ever thickening mist, and Cam thought he could hear a drum beat accompanying them. Lekkon had slowed their pace to a crawl, no doubt allowing as many citizens as possible to see the 'traitors' before their unceremonious end. Cam heard whispers all around him, and there was a strange tingling against his skin. The whispers sounded like prayer, and the tingling must have been the cold or adrenaline. Or maybe it was just his own mind beginning to shut out the world about him and prepare for what was inevitably coming next.

Ahead of them was a large opening in the sea of people, in the centre of which stood a gallows with three nooses already prepared.

Suddenly his human fear of his own mortality welled up within him and he forgot all thoughts of defiance or bravery.

He did not want to die!

Had he had more strength he might have gone manic, tried to twist and writhe his way out of the constraints that had been placed upon him, wept and begged for mercy. But he had nothing left within him for such things. All he had room for was a crippling terror which told him he was about to die.

Then his mind stopped.

Three nooses?

A terrible, cold, creeping dread took him as his mind now saw the final piece of the puzzle of their doom.

Arranged in front of the gallows were Lord Fohenk and a number of his personal guard, all of whom neglected to look at either Cam or Gismay as they walked across the square. Once they were at the bottom of the steps leading to the wooden platform, the guards swiftly removed Lekkon's belt and pulled them like sacks of grain up and onto the platform.

Lekkon himself took up his position next to Lord Fohenk.

Cam was vaguely aware that he and Gismay were pulled apart from each other and forced to stand with a guard holding each of them up to face both the crowd that had gathered, and Lord Fohenk.

A cheer rose somewhere in the crowd to their left, an an excited murmur spread out from it like a shock wave through the assembled masses. After a moment another figure appeared out of the fog and slowly walked through the crowd towards them. It was Aglorar. He was slowly followed by two more guards, each with a hand upon the shoulder of another figure.

Sonia.

Fear and rage exploded in Cam's body and he began to move towards her, crying out as he did so, but he was stopped dead in his tracks by the guard holding him with a grip that threatened to break his arm if he dared to defy it. For a second Cam thought he might as well carry on and let them break it – he was about to be hanged, what was one limb? But he stopped; if they would hurt him, then they would almost certainly hurt Sonia. He did not want her last moments to be spent in any more pain than necessary.

He looked at her, hoping that he could silently show how sorry he was, how much he wanted to save them, but he was met with eyes that were cold and unfocussed. Initially he thought that this was because of despair or fear, but he had seen Sonia scared before. This look was different; less emotional, more disassociation.

He watched as she stumbled on the icy stones beneath her feet, and she made no attempt to stop herself falling. Her arms stayed by her sides, her eyes did not so much as blink. She did not fall because the guards with her made certain of it, another example of Eismeer's 'mercy', and kept her on her feet.

She did not react to any of it.

Aglorar led her, as Lekkon had Cam and Gismay, to the steps before the gallows. She was not, however, dragged up them, rather Aglorar simply stood behind her and directed her forwards. Cam watched as she obligingly walked up the steps and across the platform.

"Sonia?" Cam whispered, desperate to share one last word with her.

She did not look at him. Cam could only watch, helpless, as she stepped past him and allowed herself to be led to the final noose by Aglorar.

Cam stared after her, then glared at the Soldier.

"You said you were helping us!" Cam called after him. "Aglorar?"

The Soldier simply strode away and put himself next to Lekkon. He did not look at Cam.

"Aglorar? Tell them!"

Cam's voice echoed around the now all but silent courtyard, before it dissipated into the fog that shrouded the scene.

Lord Fohenk motioned to Lekkon, who strode across the platform and roughly tied a length of dirty material around Cam's mouth as a gag.

"Fine last words," he hissed as he tightened the not, then strode back to Fohenk's side.

Cam fought to free his mouth so that he could scream their innocence at all of them, but he could barely breathe through the thing. All he could do was watch as Lord Fohenk looked about him to see that all was as he wished, then nodded curtly to a man stood at Sonia's right. The man was plainly the Executioner, for he wore a black hood and a leather jerkin and at his belt was a small but sharp axe. He stood next to a large wooden lever.

The temperature in the air about Cam seemed to plummet.

"People of Eismeer," the Executioner began loudly, "today it is my proud duty to serve you and our Lord Fohenk, may his spirit be praised, in the act of sentencing these three traitors to face the Lord's Justice!"

A great cheer went up from the crowd at his words. The fog seemed to thicken at the sound. Cam shivered in the freezing broil.

"On this day, Gismay son Hytol, is charged with, and found guilty of, the crimes of treason, spying, and allying himself with our enemies. He is declared a traitor. His name shall be struck from all city records and his possessions reclaimed by the people whom he abandoned!"

Another cheer. The guard holding Gismay walked him forward so that he stood directly beneath the noose appointed to him, and then slipped it casually around his neck.

Ice began to form seemingly from nothing on the platform, covering it in a thick sheet. Even Cam's noose, hanging forebodingly in front of him, had icicles dangling from it that were non-existent mere seconds ago.

"And these, simply named Cam and Sonia, are charged with, and found guilty of, treason, plotting against our lands, aiding and abetting our enemies, aiding the traitor Gismay, and the crime of blasphemy!"

The strange tingling sensation grew stronger and began to crawl over Cam's flesh.

The guard at his back pushed Cam underneath his noose. The rope, icy and frozen solid, was placed underneath his chin and around his neck.

The platform beneath him sounded hollow.

"With your blessing, my Lord Fohenk, I will perform your Justice in service of the defence and maintenance of your Kingdom. I perform this act for the glory of Eismeer, and in the defence of her people!"

"Glory to Eismeer! Glory to Fohenk!" the crowd cried.

Snow began to fall. The clumps were some of the largest Cam had ever seen.

He turned his head, noose and all, to stare one last time at Sonia. She was not looking at him.

"Do I have your blessing, Lord of the Eis?"

The ice had begun to freeze Cam's chin to the rope.

Out of the crowd stepped a man in a green cloak who reached for a sword at his waist.

"You have my blessing," Fohenk responded.

The man skirted round the front of the crowd towards the steps to the platform. As a guard moved towards him, the man drew his sword.

"Then, by your will, as Executioner of Eismeer..."

The man ran the guard through with a simple motion, then sped up the steps and onto the platform.

A gasp and angered cry went up from the crowd.

The snow was now almost forming snowballs in the air. They thudded heavily onto the wood and the stones beneath.

Sonia turned and met Cam's eyes.

"...I will hereby carry out the sentence of the Lord's Justice upon these criminals..."

The man turned and kicked the first of the pursuing guards heavily in the chest, sending him sprawling backwards on top of his comrades.

The snowfall had become clumps of ice, huge and heavy.

Cam's eyes strained to see Sonia through it all.

The man now advanced on the Executioner.

"... and they shall die!"

The Executioner pulled the lever.

The man thrust his sword deep into the Executioner's back.

Sonia screamed.

The world rushed upwards in front of Cam's vision, and then all hell broke loose.

Chapter Seven

Northward Flight

The rope holding Cam snapped taught, but his neck remained unbroken. For a few sickening moments he hung there, choking, with the ice that had formed about his chin pulling mercilessly at his skin. Then, without warning, the rope stopped holding him and he dropped through the mist and down onto the stones beneath him.

Dizzying seconds ticked by as he wrestled the noose from around his neck with his still bound hands. He finally ripped the thing off and felt the air surge through him, touching every nerve and sinew and bone. Everything that had failed him, everything that had given up mere moments before, suddenly began to waken. He felt his strength, such as it was, buoyed by his sheer desire to live.

Looking swiftly to his right he saw that Sonia had also fallen. Cam hurled himself forwards, almost swimming across the stones, and took his place at her side.

“Sonia? Sonia?”

She yanked her on noose from around her neck and threw the thing as far as her bound hands would allow.

“I'm alright, I'm alright,” she panted, “I just need a minute.”

“I don't think we have a minute,” Cam called back to her over the clamour.

The atmosphere around them had entirely changed. The freezing fog had now fully engulfed the courtyard and they could not see much more than a few feet in front of them. The excitement of the crowd which had surrounded them before had been replaced by screams.

The platform above them suddenly shattered in a shower of snow, ice, stone, and splinters. Cam threw himself over Sonia to protect her then, when the tumult had passed, he twisted his head around to discover what had happened.

Before him, covering the wreckage and remains of the platform, was a huge ball of ice. Its lower half had shattered upon impact with the stone, but the top was strong and untouched. The thing loomed over him, an opaque blue sheen glinting against the mist. It was larger than anything he had ever seen, and his eyes quickly saw that there were more of them crashing down all about him.

"What the..?"

A hand grabbed him fiercely and pulled him upwards. Half expecting to see another guard, or even Aglorar, stood behind him, Cam wheeled about as swiftly as his body could allow. Staring back at him was the man wearing the green cloak.

The man who had killed the Executioner.

Instinctively Cam tried to back away and put himself between the man and Sonia, but he was too slow. The man already had hold of her and was hauling her up from the ground. Before either of them could react they saw a small, sharp blade appear in his hands. He raised it.

"No! Wait!" Cam cried.

With two swift movements, a knife whirled through the air and cut the bonds about both their wrists.

"Come with me," the hood growled at him.

For a moment neither Cam or Sonia could not move, fear and shock rooting them to the ground. Then they noticed that the man was carrying something, slung unceremoniously across his back.

It was Gismay.

"Now!" the voice commanded.

The shattering of another ice block, closer this time,

brought them out of their thoughts.

"Alright," Cam said quickly.

The figure nodded, then silently turned away and carried Gismay's body. Glancing at each other, Cam and Sonia joined hands once again and followed him, ducking through the already half-destroyed square.

The storm had decimated the place already. Buildings that had taken the full force of an ice block were piles of rubble, while any people who were unfortunate enough to get in their way were beyond all hope. The city of Eismeer was being besieged by the weather, and its streets were littered with debris, ice, and the dead.

None of this perturbed the figure in the green cloak as he led them through the destruction. Cam marvelled at how sure footed his guide was – the man barely even lost his step despite all the carnage and devastation around him. What was even more astounding was that he carried Gismay easily through all of it.

Onward through the streets they went, ducking away from icy explosions and splintered stone. With every step they were surrounded by death and destruction as Eismeer was battered and torn apart from the heavens. Soon they reached the outer wall of the city, and they turned to their right and followed the wall for many moments. Cam assumed that the man was searching for a part of the structure that had been damaged sufficiently for them to slip through unnoticed, but he was wrong.

Soon a building loomed up out of the fog. It was wooden and attached to the stone around it by a slanted thatch roof. As soon as they came in sight of it the man began to move quickly and look about him, as if this was somewhere he expected to face trouble.

A splintering crash to their left as another block thundered down beside them.

The impact threw Cam and Sonia down, sending them skidding under a myriad shower of ice sparks and stone splinters. Amazed that they had escaped unscathed, they both pulled themselves up as quickly as they could and looked around frantically through the dust, desperate to find Gismay and their new guide.

The man, with the Farmer on his shoulder, found them first and strode purposefully towards. He barely seemed to have registered that any of the last few moments had taken place – his cloak was free of all but the smallest signs of ice.

“We must keep moving,” he said, simply.

He strode off through the mist towards the wooden structure they had been making for before the impact. Cam stared after the man in disbelief and mounting frustration. He allowed himself a moment to check both he and Sonia were still whole before hurling himself forward to follow the man.

Their guide had already ducked inside the relative shelter of the wooden building. Following through the door, Cam and Sonia found themselves inside a stable. There were few horses left – many would no doubt have simply bolted at the first sign of any danger – and those that were left were only there because they had been tied to posts that had not collapsed or splintered. Cam hastily managed to count seven of the creatures that still stood waiting for riders that might never arrive.

His guide had taken Gismay over to what was, presumably, his horse and already sat the Farmer's comatose body on the saddle. He then took out his small blade once again and cut the restraints on all of the other horses, freeing four of them to bolt to safety. The last two to be cut free he held, leading them over to stand beside his own. Only once this had been achieved did he turn to Cam and Sonia and motion them closer.

“We will await my companion here,” the man said, curtly, “but not for long. If you have questions I can answer in this short time I will do so, but of my full purpose I will not speak now.”

Cam and Sonia were both taken aback by he forthrightness of the man's words, and suddenly found that any questions had dried up.

“Companion?” Sonia stammered.

“An ally of mine in the city.”

He pushed past them both to fetch a large leather pouch

that he had hidden with a hay bail.

"Where are we going?" Cam asked.

"I cannot tell you until we have put many leagues between us and these walls."

"But..."

The sound of a door being thrown open stopped Cam's question dead. All of them looked over to the where the sound came from and saw Dunwald burst through, battered and bloodied.

"You arrive at last," the man was saying, "we must make all haste."

Dunwald scowled at him.

"Do you think I do not know that? Have you any concept of how difficult it is for the Captain of Eismeer to escape unseen ?"

"Do you have everything you will require?" the man asked, seemingly ignoring the Captain's words.

Dunwald nodded, then took one of the horses that the man had cut free. He led it over to Cam and Sonia.

"This horse is named Tibern," the Captain panted, "he shall bare you both."

Cam and Sonia glanced at each other, then stared blankly at the horse. It was huge.

"Do you ride?" Dunwald pressed.

Sonia shook her head.

"Not since I was thirteen."

Dunwald now looked to Cam, who immediately shook his head.

"Never so much as sat in a saddle."

"We cannot tarry," came an urgent voice from behind Dunwald.

Moving quickly and without warning, Dunwald gripped Cam firmly beneath the shoulders, lifted him roughly, and thrust him into the saddle. The position felt horribly unnatural and perilous to Cam, but he had little time to adjust before Sonia was similarly placed in front of him.

"You can't be serious..." she breathed, as she was handed the reigns.

"Wrap your arms around her waist tightly," Dunwald was telling Cam, who did so without thinking. The Captain now turned to Sonia.

"Sit up and grasp the reigns as tightly as you can. You will not need to direct him, for Tibern knows our course."

"We make for the mountains," the voice of their guide called back to them. "I will lead and Dunwald will hold the rear."

With that he reared his horse and sped out of the open door and into the wintry wastes beyond. Within moments he had disappeared into the fog.

Dunwald glanced sidelong at them.

"Hold on," the Captain ordered, and slapped Tibern's flank hard.

The world wheeled about them as the horse reared up and charged, headlong, out of the door and into the mist. The wind billowed past as Tibern galloped forward through the ever thickening broil. They were surrounded by swirling torrents of air and the sounds of a million explosions; all around they could feel the impacts of ice blocks, but somehow Tibern contrived to swerve between them.

All of Cam's energy was focussed on clasping tightly to Sonia. His knees dug deeply into the ribs and flanks of the animal, so much so that Cam felt certain he would be hurting the poor creature. But if Tibern felt any discomfort, or the nervousness of his riders, then he showed no sign.

He flew across the snow, unbelievably sure-footed and swift. Soon they could see the outline of Felgaron's shadow forming through the mist ahead of them. Tibern galloped hard and was quickly level with the man. Cam dared to turn his head and see how Gismay was faring, but the wind in his face had caused his eyes to water so violently that he could not hope to see anything.

However, a low rumbling to his left soon told Cam that

Dunwald had caught up with them, and for what felt like an age the three horses pounded their way across the frozen earth; never stumbling nor breaking stride. Tibern's motion became easy, recognisable to Sonia. She began to understand how the creature ran, began to remember the feeling of each leg as the muscles expanded and contracted within his frame.

Cam simply clung to her, hardly daring to open his eyes.

What little light the mist allowed through its clutches began to become steadily brighter as they rode. Still they pushed on, even though the worst of the storm was behind them. The air had begun to feel slightly warmer than it had during the height of the destruction, but the man still seemed desperate to outrun whatever remnants of the storm pursued them.

Through the afternoon they rode onward, pushing their horses to what were surely their limits, and by the time their guide finally allowed them to rest the air was all but clear, with only a light haze hanging over the small company as the horses slowed to a gentle canter.

They had come to a small hollow, a rocky dimple in the otherwise unbroken landscape, and stopped. Steam rose from the backs of the animals as their riders dismounted. Cam's legs threatened to collapse from underneath him as he lowered his battered, aching form to the ground. He steadied himself as best as he could, then helped Sonia down. They looked at each other and did not know whether to laugh, cry, or simply fall where they stood.

Dunwald had set about helping their guide tend to the horses. The beasts were fed and watered, then the two men began unpacking their burdens. In only a few moments there was a basic but well equipped camp standing before them. Only when all of this had been accomplished and Dunwald was beginning to start a fire and prepare a meal for the company did their guide turn to them.

“We will eat and rest here,” he declared, “we have come far enough, and should make the mountains by noontide tomorrow. We can afford respite.”

Cam and Sonia shared an uncertain glance.

"Come," he urged, "you will need strength for tomorrow's ride."

He now turned and went to the packs, then came back to them carrying two bundles of clothes. They looked thick and woollen. He carried also two pairs of furred boots, and two sleeping bags. These he handed to Cam and Sonia who, despite their misgivings, accepted them without question.

"These will protect you as well as any clothing in the landscape we find ourselves in."

Cam and Sonia took the bundles, then shared an uncertain glance.

"You need not fear me," the man said calmly.

"Who says we're afraid?"

Sonia's words brought another smile from the man.

"Put them on. You will feel better for it."

The two friends once again shared a glance, then did as they were bid.

Slipping the new clothes over his tattered sack-cloth, Cam immediately began to feel their warmth upon his skin. They were indeed similar to woollen clothes, but the material was less coarse. The breeches were of an earthen-brown colour, while the long-sleeved jerkin was a paler, tan-like hue. The boots were leather with fur lining, and they were laced with the leather thongs that criss-crossed over his shins.

Cam was now vaguely aware of Dunwald and the man laying Gismay's seemingly lifeless form next to the fire, wrapped in as many furs and blankets as could be spared. The man examined him for a moment as Dunwald watched on, an expression of nervous remorse upon his face.

"He will live," the man sighed, "for now, at any rate. I cannot treat him properly in such a frozen wasteland."

"But he can be treated?" Dunwald pressed.

The man nodded slowly.

"I believe he can. How full a recovery he will make I cannot judge," he added, a cautioning note to his voice, "for

Eismeer's techniques are efficient."

He shot a knowing sideways glance at the Captain, who could not bring himself to meet the man's eye. He simply stared down at Gismay's stricken form.

"Do whatever you can, and whatever you must, for him," Dunwald growled, then turned away from the Farmer and focussed upon finishing whatever meal he was preparing.

Cam and Sonia, not knowing what else to do, stepped forward into the firelight so that their new outfits could be seen, and feel the heat that managed to permeate the biting wind.

"Thanks for the clothes," Cam said quietly.

The man smiled and sat himself next to the fire, motioning that they should join him. Slowly they did so, then he passed to each of them a wooden bowl. These held a small amount of some form of soup or broth that Dunwald had prepared. A faintly sweet smell rose from the stuff, but they both regarded it cautiously.

"Eat," he said.

The tone was not angry or combative, but it did not invite further questions. Being too tired to press further in any case, Cam spooned a large mouthful of the stuff from his bowl. His tongue exploded with flavours, familiar and unrecognisable at the same time. Warmth seemed to spread outward from his mouth and into the rest of his body, erupting down his throat and touching every cell within him. Though it was fresh form the fire, the heat did not burn or discomfort him; his tongue was untouched except by the sensation of taste. Next to him he heard Sonia take a sip from the end of her spoon. Her reaction told him she, too, found the sensation rejuvenating.

Dunwald forced a smile onto his lips.

"It contains a small amount of Hocliquor. It will aid your rest and restore a measure of your hurts."

"Now," the man said, placing his bowl down by the fire, "our introduction in Eismeer was hardly appropriate for those who will be travelling together. I can only apologise for the necessity of our haste. But now we have a quiet moment, my name is Felgaron. I am a friend of Dunwald and of you, though we have never met."

"Why should we believe you?" Cam's question was pointed and harsh.

"I did just save your lives," Felgaron said, smirking.

They both stared at the man, not sure what to say.

"Look... we understand... Thanks," Cam said carefully, "I'm Cam, this is Sonia."

Felgaron smiled back at them, an earnest expression.

"I know," he said simply.

Another silence, broken only by the whistling of the wind.

"Where are you taking us?" Sonia ventured.

"Beregle," came the curt reply, "a town in the mountains west of here, and the seat of Marn, Lord of the Beregland. I judge we should reach his hall in no less than eight days, if the mountain passes are kind to us."

"And let us hope we do not find more trouble of the sort which plagues Eismeer," Dunwald mused.

Felgaron nodded at the Captain's words.

"That is sooth indeed. What has transpired in that city troubles me greatly."

The Captain looked up at him.

"Angestaf," Felgaron added, darkly.

Dunwald swallowed the last of his broth and seemed to shudder slightly.

"That would truly be an ill omen for Rhydariel if you correct."

A heavy silence passed between the two men which was broken only by the crackling of the flames and the sigh of the wind.

"What's Angestaf?" Cam ventured.

"A ruin," Dunwald answered immediately, "and an ancient one at that. It was a village of Eismeer. It was destroyed thousands of years ago by..."

"Not now," Felgaron cut in, "for before long the last shadows of the sun will be cast upon the land. Now is not the time for such talk. We must rest, for we have a long journey before us."

Dunwald slowly nodded his agreement, then he and Felgaron positioned themselves on the far edge of the firelight and stared back in the direction they had ridden from. The fire burned brightly against the gathering gloom, casting dancing orange flares against their backs. Between them was Gismay, as if they were two sentinels protecting him from all the troubles of the world.

Cam now looked at the Farmer, and saw that the only clue to life still being within him the faint wisps of steam that rose from his shallow breaths.

A movement next to him drew his attention, and he saw Sonia staring uncertainly at the sleeping bag Felgaron had handed to her.

"What's up?" Cam whispered to her.

She shook her head, trying to dismiss something in her own mind.

"We nearly died."

Cam looked at her, trying to order his own thoughts.

"But we didn't," was the only reply he could come up with.

"Gismay might."

"Felgaron says he won't."

She nodded blankly.

"Can we trust them, do you think?" she asked, motioning toward the two men.

"We don't really have a choice," Cam sighed, reluctantly.

They looked at each other, and embraced. The two friends stood, holding each other close, for many moments, and in that time it was as if everything else about them faded away and they were the only two left in all the world.

"Come on," Cam said, putting on the best smile he could muster, "let's get some sleep. It's been a long day."

They both settled themselves and lay next to each other on the ground. The wind howled over them, and the stars in the now cloudless sky blinked down from the heavens, yet they were both, for now at least, at peace.

*   *   *   *   *

They awoke the next morning to aching muscles and cold faces, but they had at the very least had a full night's rest. As they stood and stretched in the cool sun of the dawn, they saw that the fire had burnt itself out during the night, and the smell of the charred wood and the remains of Dunwald's broth hung about them.

As he went about his business, Felgaron managed to find a moment to hand them each a portion of something they presumed to be food.

“We call it Hocram,” he said, “it will sustain you for many hours on a march.”

It was a doughy mixture, like half-baked bread, flecked with purple spots. These looked like berries but Cam could not be certain. He slowly lifted into his mouth, and Sonia followed suit.

The stuff was was stodgy to start, but with each passing moment it became sweeter and softer. The berries burst as soon as their teeth touched them and the liquor they released was sweet and full; it cured their pains and reinvigorated their hearts. Despite this, the day ahead still seemed to stretch out before them in an unending vista of cold and barren wastes.

Before they finally prepared to leave, Felgaron announced that he had one more gift for them. From his pack he produced two cloaks, both of dark brown material. No adornment was upon the fabric save for a brooch of pewter, heavy despite its small size, shaped as a four-pointed star. Cam and Sonia gratefully accepted these and hung them over their shoulders swiftly. They were warm and thick, and kept out much of the wind.

The riding pace that Felgaron set for them was slower than that of the previous day, but no less urgent. The morning passed almost unheeded as the remains of the mist were burned off by the slowly climbing sun. The land was less snow covered here, with a few patches of bracken and gorse punctuating the white expanse, and ahead of them was a huge range of mountains. Digging deep into his memory, Cam seemed to recall the Gismay had named them the Glacier Mountains. They made their way up the gently rising ground towards the foothill of these peaks for much of the late morning, and it was well past noon before Felgaron called a reluctant halt to proceedings.

Though the mists had cleared, pregnant wintry clouds hung over them with the weight of promised rain, and a steady breeze began to blow. Cam unconsciously wrapped his new cloak tighter about him as he and Sonia manoeuvred themselves from Tibern's back and down to the ground.

"We have time for only a short respite," Felgaron was saying, "then we must continue. The passes will be hard, especially if the weather does not hold."

As if in answer to his words, a slow roll of thunder rumbled across the sky.

"Be ready in ten minutes," he ordered, then went about his business.

Dunwald glanced up at the sky before tending the horses.

Sonia looked at Cam.

"If we don't get killed by the cold or exhaustion it'll be a bloody miracle!"

Cam looked at her, a wry smile on his face.

"Come on," he said, and set about gathering what few possessions they could now claim in this world.

When Felgaron ordered them to saddle their mounts once again, Cam watched with a twisting pain in his heart as Gismay's helpless, lifeless body was hoisted once more atop Felgaron's mount. How could the man believe that Gismay would be alive when they reached the end of their journey? And, even if he was, what state would he be in?

Their pace was slower now, for the ground rose unceasingly towards the feet of the mountains. The threatening, black rain clouds they could see behind those peaks only served to exaggerate the sheer scale of their bulks.

After perhaps three hours, Cam felt a change in the air about him. Looking up, he saw that they had reached a small cleft at the foot of one of the mountains. A gravel path led away from the far side of this place, thrusting itself upwards between two almost sheer faces of rock. Its entry was marked only by a pair of scrawny looking firs, one either side of the cutting, and but for these it might have eluded Cam's sight altogether. Snow lay thick on the rocks above the path on either side, but the way itself seemed sheltered from any falls by the heights that flanked it.

This was clearly Felgaron's destination, for he slid himself gracefully off his horse and landed neatly on the scree-covered ground.

"Dismount, my friends," he ordered solemnly, "for here we say goodbye to our mounts."

Cam stared at him.

"We're not taking the horses?" he stammered.

"Alas, no. It is not a choice I have taken lightly, but these passes are narrow and the horses may actually hinder us rather than help. My horse, Kithran, will lead them west and northward, where they will find grass and safety. With luck their tracks will also lead any who try to follow us astray."

The Swordsman seemed genuinely saddened by the imminent departure of the beasts.

"What about Gismay?" Cam thought aloud.

Felgaron looked at Gismay's body, still sat precariously atop Kithran.

"We will all take turns at carrying him. With luck his body will have recovered sufficiently enough to endure stronger medicine in, perhaps, three more days."

Dunwald spoke next, his voice thick with emotion.

"I will bear him first. He has been a great servant to King

Hedradour for many years."

"What?" Cam cried without thinking. "The last time you had anything to do with him you threatened to kill him! You had him tortured!"

"Cam..." Felgaron began in a cautioning tone, but Dunwald raised a hand.

"Let him speak, friend Felgaron. We have not yet revealed to him my part in all of this. I fear he will not trust me unless we do."

After a moment's thought, Felgaron nodded.

"As you wish, friend Dunwald."

Dunwald inclined his head softly toward their companion, then slowly returned his gaze to Cam and Sonia.

"I understand you do not trust me," he began, "but not all things in this world are as they appear. I am one such thing. Gismay and I are one and the same. We have both served King Hedradour of the Boardwalks in secrecy."

Cam blinked.

"So you're a spy too?"

"Indeed. I have been for many years. The current war between Ebras and Eismeer began many centuries ago, but there have been many since Ebras came into being four thousand years ago.

"The Kingdoms of Ebras and the Eislands were once a united people. Then, one of Eismeer's Generals disobeyed a direct order from the Lord and was cast out. He was well loved and respected throughout the army and the populous, so the city was divided. Many stood firm to the banner of Eismeer, but many others decided to support the General. Those who did so were declared traitors and ordered to be killed.

"To save his people from the slaughter, the General led an exodus away from Eismeer and into the lands we now call Ebras, to the west. There they founded The Boardwalks, the City on the Water, and the Hall of Barrandel was built. And the two factions have been enemies ever since."

"That's all fascinating," Cam said impatiently, "but it

doesn't explain what the hell is going on!"

"You must understand the past before you can understand the present," Dunwald cut in, "for though the General took as many of his loyal followers as he could, some had no choice but to remain behind. Those that were discovered were hunted down and murdered in cold blood. But some managed to remain undetected.

"These few dedicated souls created a secret association, a pact that they would work in the shadows to help our true homeland of Ebras as best as they could. My ancestors were part of this pact."

"But you're a Captain in Fohenk's army!" Cam interrupted again.

"The General had supporters in all quarters of the city," Dunwald answered hotly, "and my ancestors were some of the most loyal he could have ever hoped for. My Grandfather was a Watch Captain of Eismeer, as was my Father, and they both aided Ebras all of their lives. I used my family's standing to get myself as close to Fohenk as I could. The closer I became, the more delicate and important the information I could pass on to King Hedradour to aid the war!

"Little did I dream that I might become First of the Royal Guard. I have been able to help Ebras in ways that I never thought possible, and had access to information that has saved the lives of thousands of us!"

"You were about to kill Gismay! And you had me and Sonia locked up for helping him!" Cam screamed.

"Lord Fohenk threw you into his dungeons! Lord Fohenk tortured Gismay! Lord Fohenk ordered your execution!"

Dunwald stepped forward and pressed his face against Cam's.

"The only active part I have played in all of this was to save your lives!"

"You took us to Eismeer in the first place!" Sonia cried, forcing herself between the Captain and Cam.

"The first moment we met I was surrounded by Aglorar

and Lekkon, my Seconds in Command! I could not reveal my allegiances and risk one of them revealing to Fohenk who I was. If that had come to pass then it would have jeopardised all of my comrades in arms. Their blood would have filled the drains of Eismeer for many weeks."

Cam glared at the man, livid.

"So all of this was to protect your own skin? How far would you have gone for that, eh? Would you have let Gismay die? Would you have let me and Sonia die?"

Dunwald looked at him, keen eyes burning with a fire Cam had not seen before.

"If the safety of our people could be preserved by doing so, I would have killed Gismay myself. It would have broken my heart to do it, but I would have had little choice in the matter. He would have done the same if our places had been reversed. Any of us would!

"As for you," he growled, "that is a more complicated question. Felgaron and I could not rescue you from the Dungeons. That would draw too much attention and we two, fine swordsmen that we are, cannot take on an entire garrison. We needed you out in public, somewhere with no walls or cages. A public execution was a slim hope, but a far better one than infiltrating the dungeons. At the very least we could cause enough chaos to slip away in the crowds or through the back streets."

Cam shook his head

"And who came up with that ridiculous plan?"

"I did."

Felgaron's voice cut across them all as he stepped forward.

"Why?" Cam asked, rounding on him without thinking.

"Because it was necessary. Now, come. The sun is beginning to sink and we must use what light remains to get as far into these passes as possible. The time for talk," he pressed, stifling Cam and Sonia's sounds of protest, "has passed. All you need know for now is that we have rescued you both and that you can trust us to keep you safe from all harm. If you do not believe me then you are both welcome to wander in any direction you see fit."

For a long and terrible moment Felgaron's eyes burned deep into Cam's, holding his gaze with an invisible and unbreakable grip. An involuntary shake of frustration ran along his shoulders which Cam did nothing to hide.

"Alright."

"Gather your possessions. The mountain passes await and the weather will not remain kind to us for much longer."

Felgaron turned on his heels and, muttering something to Kithran as he did so, ushered the horses on their way. The sound of their hooves galloping westward underpinned the glare that Cam threw at Dunwald. The Captain did not respond, he merely turned away and slung his own pack across his back before gathering Gismay's arms about his shoulders and lifting him as gently as he could off the ground. Cam watched him for a moment, adrenaline surging through him. Sonia placed a comforting hand on his arm.

"Come on," she said grimly.

As they both set about gathering their things, Cam's mind began racing.

After all that had happened to them – travelling between worlds, being imprisoned, questioned, and all but hanged – they found themselves somehow still alive and whole. And these two men were responsible for that, Cam did not deny it. But Dunwald had also played a large part in putting them in danger in the first place.

He was the kind of man who was willing to injure, even kill his friends to serve his cause. That was fanaticism, not bravery or loyalty, it seemed to Cam.

What would happen to them if they unwillingly found themselves standing in Dunwald's way?

And, perhaps more importantly, who the hell was Felgaron?

Chapter Eight

Shattered Ice

The gentle light that filtered through the slowly breaking blanket of clouds above the great Citadel in Eismeer belied the chaos and grief of the people below.

The events of the day before had left the city in a state of near total ruin; entire streets lay buried under rubble and huge blocks of ice, while the central market place was a gauntlet of barely stable debris that threatened to collapse and swallow all beneath it without a moment's warning. Against the dull, tuneless backing of the breeze that breathed through the streets was set the music of families crying out in loss, pain and confusion.

Mothers held children tightly in their arms, huddled in what remained of their homes, whispering half-believed words of comfort; husbands pulled the rubble apart with whatever strength they had left, ripping the rocks away until their fingertips bled, desperately searching for any who might yet have survived. The few members of the City Watch that had made it through that terrible day did what they could, but morale, strength, and will had been sapped almost utterly.

The city of Eismeer lay broken.

It was through this turmoil that Aglorar and Bryndain, the two highest ranking officers that remained in the Eismen Army, walked slowly, surveying the damage and distress in equal measure.

Bryndain's blue-grey eyes looked painfully over the scenes before him. With every passing moment his soul felt as if it was being ripped from his body; to see his people like this, reduced to scrabbling amongst the rubble and searching the gutters for food was more than he could bear.

He ran his hand through his thick, blonde hair and subtly wiped a tear away from his left cheek. Aglorar glanced at him sidelong, and twisted his lips into a casual grin.

"Your heart will prove your downfall, Captain Bryndain," he said gruffly, "even if it is from a wholesome place. A warrior cannot be sentimental."

Bryndain shook his head fervently.

"It is not sentiment," he spat, "it is pure grief and rage. Are we not a proud and strong people? Have we not followed the guidance of Lord Fohenk, and of Etavïr, even of Naïyr, to the letter? Are we not a good people?"

Aglorar considered the man's words for a moment, passing a casual eye over a woman kneeling in the snow. Her forehead was pressed against the ground, and she was mumbling some prayer or other.

"Eismeer has ever been a righteous place," he responded after a moment, "I see no way we could have angered the Gods."

"Then why?" Bryndain turned and placed a forceful hand on his comrade's shoulder. "Why have they let us fall in such a manner? Why have they forsaken us? By the Seven, Aglorar, our city lies in utter ruins! Our people are broken, unable to fend for themselves! What could we possibly have done to call for such a terrible fate to be visited upon our people?"

Aglorar shrugged non-committally.

"What the Gods wish can never be guessed at. We are but mortals, Bryndain; the creations of Naïyr, sanctified and damned by him in but a breath."

"No," Bryndain seethed, "this is deeper. If it were against all mortals then other cities would have fallen. This is something... different."

Aglorar laughed softly, barely audible.

"For mortals such as us to even begin to guess or interpret the actions of the Gods is foolish. They are utterly beyond our comprehension. They do what they do simply because they can.

We are nothing but playthings to be taken out and used when they see fit. If the Gods decided that Eismeer must be punished, for whatever reason, we are no more likely to discover their thoughts than we were to have stopped them attacking us in the first place. We are but men, Lieutenant Bryndain. We cannot fight such forces. We can only hope that we will survive them."

"The people of Eismeer have never just 'survived', Aglorar. You know that as well as I!" Bryndain retorted, forcefully. "If the Gods have been angered then we must atone for whatever offending actions we have taken. We will restore the Balance! Lord Fohenk will not allow our people to be downtrodden or abused, even by the Gods!"

"We must not forget our place, Captain," Aglorar hissed in a cautioning tone, "it would not do for either of us to pre-empt our Lord's actions. He will do what he believes to best for our people. Come, I received word that he wishes to speak to us – that is why I came to find you. He will be waiting."

Aglorar swiftly made his way along the ruined streets, not even waiting to see if Bryndain had followed. He knew that Fohenk would only summon them both in such a hurry if there was something of great need or worry upon his mind; Aglorar had known the Lord for nearly a decade, serving him first as a soldier, then a Lieutenant and, until recently, was second only in his councils to Captain Dunwald. Given the news of the Captain's disappearance, Aglorar had already begun to guess why he himself was being summoned.

As for Bryndain? Perhaps he was to be promoted also. He was a good and loyal soldier, young and fierce of temperament, and this afforded him much respect and love within Eismeer and it's people. His vision of the future for the Eismen, however, did not match Aglorar's own.

If Aglorar's fate was indeed to take Dunwald's place as Lord Fohenk's personal Advisor, then he would make certain that his Lord knew all about Bryndain's inadequacies. Too much work had been done to allow for one over zealous soldier to jeopardise it.

No, he chastised himself, *now is not the time*.

His plans had succeeded in the main and all of the work had not been for nothing. Eismeer was on the course he deemed right for her and her citizens. There had been mistakes, yes, but he would not allow such small blemishes to stain his record. The time would come when all such things were forgotten, when he would prove to his Lord that he was the right choice for such a task.

And that time was coming soon.

Bryndain quickly caught up with him and marched alongside as the two men made their way through the ruins of Eismeer toward the Citadel.

The tower itself had, mercifully, managed to avoid great damage; a part of the spire at the top had been broken off, littering the courtyard below with fragments of ancient stone, but that was the worst of it. Lord Fohenk himself had been hurried away as swiftly as was possible to his private sanctuary, the Underkeep.

As soon as the Storm had passed, however, the Lord had retaken his place upon his Throne as a gesture of strength and solidarity to his people. Though many of the Royal Court had argued against it, Fohenk had deemed it important for the people of Eismeer to know that their Lord was not afraid; that he would stand tall, as had his city, against any and all threats.

The greatest miracle of the storm was that the only damage caused to the interior of the Citadel was cosmetic; wall hangings displaced, oil lamps spilling their contents across the floor, ceremonial swords and shields being thrown from the wall. A sure sign, the people said, that the Gods still favoured Lord Fohenk even if his people had offended them.

The Lord Fohenk himself was sat in his Throne, his eyes glazed with the sorrow for his people that ran deep within him. He had always loved his subjects, those that followed him loyally and with honour, and Aglorar knew that to see them pushed to such extremes would have broken his heart.

He was a good man and a fine leader, and the only one

who could raise his people up from their icy ashes and back to the days that they longed for; the better days of his ancestors that had been lost in nearly forty centuries of war with the thrice-damned Ebrahiim.

"My Lord? You sent for us?"

Aglorar's voice was soft so as not to offend his Lord by breaking the silence which he had requested about him, an act of mourning for his people. It was only as his words echoed about the place that Aglorar became truly aware of the emptiness of the Throne Room. There were no other advisers or guards; no-one else there but himself, Bryndain and Lord Fohenk.

"My Lord?" Aglorar pressed gently.

Fohenk shook his head slightly out of whatever slumber or thought he had induced within himself and looked over to the two men as if they were not known to him. Then the moment passed and he saw them clearly once again.

"You have come. That is good. I would speak to you, Aglorar, in a moment, but first I must have words with Captain Bryndain here. Come forward, Captain."

Bowing before he did so, Bryndain stepped toward his Lord and stood to attention.

"What does my Lord command of me?" he asked levelly.

Fohenk smiled.

"You are a good man, Captain, and a fine soldier. And there is no more skilful archer in all of the Eislands. You have proven yourself worthy of honour and great recognition. The honour you have earned without my help, but the recognition is something I would give you personally. With the recent... departure of Captain Dunwald, there is great need for our armies to have a leader, a figure head on the battlefield. Someone to rally to."

Bryndain bowed his head.

"My Lord, they have but only to look to our gracious leader to find what they seek. Any and all who serve Eismeer do so because you are our soul and our heart."

Fohenk could not stop himself smiling at the words.

"As I said, a fine and good man. But I cannot be there at all times, and the armies need someone to turn to in these moments. I would have you become that man. You have earned much respect amongst our people. They look up to you. Your skill and your leadership in battle have been proven many times. I would name you General of the Eislands, and Captain of my Lordsguard."

"You are gracious to say so," Bryndain breathed, "and I thank you, my Lord. I gladly accept your offer and hope to serve you and our lands with honour and reverence."

"I have every faith that you will do just that, General Bryndain. Now, go. Leave us to talk privately. I will see to it that a more public ceremony is held when the time is right."

Bryndain bowed quickly and, with only a passing glance at Aglorar, strode proudly from the the Throne Room to begin his duties.

Aglorar watched him go, then turned to face his Lord.

"The public ceremony is a wise decision," he said slowly, "it will no doubt give your people something to cheer. That feeling is long overdue in these dark times."

Fohenk nodded, a movement that was almost imperceptible.

"I must agree with you, Aglorar. The tides of the world have ebbed and flowed much these last few days, and not all of their currents have been favourable to us. But I fear that this storm is but the first stone in an avalanche that approaches."

He sat silent for a moment, seemingly collecting whatever thoughts he had in his mind. Aglorar watched him, trying to discern what it was he was puzzling over.

"Dunwald has gone, Aglorar. He will not return."

Aglorar sighed.

"I fear you are right, Lord. And even if he did return, the only course of action would be to enact the Lord's Justice upon him. His actions are high treason, it is beyond any doubt. He will know this."

Fohenk nodded again, more openly this time. Raising his

hands to a point before his lips, he looked Aglorar squarely in the eyes.

"I need an advisor. One who knows my people and this city, but also one who knows Rhydariel for what she is. One who has seen far and experienced many things. One who can help me guide my people through the perilous times ahead. I want that person to be you, Aglorar."

Feigning surprise, Aglorar stared back at his Lord and allowed a small utterance of shock to pass his lips.

"It would be my honour, Lord Fohenk. I desire nothing more than to serve you honourably in whatever capacity you desire of me."

"You have served me well these last ten years. I would see that service and loyalty rewarded. You worked closely with Dunwald, saw many things that he has seen, shared his experiences, but you have never been disloyal to me. From one such as you it is greatly appreciated, even though I do not show the appreciation as often as perhaps I should."

Aglorar bowed low, a dismissive smile on his face.

"My Lord, you do not need to show appreciation. Your job is to command and mine is to obey. I will ever do so unquestioningly."

This time Fohenk's gaze was serious and dark, his voice strong and determined.

"A Lord cannot control his people with just power. He must know how to temper it with grace and honour. I have ever striven to be an honourable leader for my people as Galmorn was."

"And you have achieved such greatness, my Lord..." Aglorar began, but Fohenk's voice curtailed his words.

"I fear that in these last days I have made a most grievous error of judgement. I can only hope that the price I pay for my mistake is not yet more terrible than that we have already experienced."

The Lord stopped, lifting his hands to his face as if to hide away from whatever truth he felt he had revealed to himself. For many moments he sat there in silence, breathing into his palms, as Aglorar simply stood and watched, waiting for his Lord to finish addressing him.

The hands dropped slowly away and Fohenk's eyes met with his newest Advisor's gaze once more.

“The boy is what he claims to be.”

The sentence hung in the air of the silent Throne Room for a beat before Aglorar could form his reply.

“That cannot be, my Lord.”

Fohenk looked at him gravely, a fear beginning to form behind his eyes that Aglorar had not seen before.

“Alas, it is so. I made a mistake in sentencing him to hang, placing him out in the open where any and all could reach him, and as penance he has been taken from our grasp.”

“My Lord, if there is an error here then it is mine,” Aglorar said in a repentant tone, “for I advised you that the boy was nothing more than he appeared. And while I apologise if you feel my words have led you astray, I still believe that it be so. He is just a boy.”

“There is more, Aglorar. More that you did not know, that none of us knew at the time. I place no blame upon you, for you could not have seen without the knowledge that I now have.”

“What knowledge do you speak of, my Lord?” Aglorar breathed.

From within his robes Fohenk produced a scroll; it was sealed with the symbol of a single icicle that bore a crown. This was used for secret documents that were for the Lord's eyes only. Fohenk stood from his Throne and held it outward towards Aglorar, who accepted it cautiously.

The seal had not been broken.

“Do you trust me, Aglorar? Would you serve me through whatever may betide our people, fight for me to whatever end may await us against whatever enemy marches upon our borders?”

Aglorar stared back at him, dumbfounded.

“Certainly, my Lord.”

Fohenk nodded gravely.

"Then open that scroll."

"My Lord, I cannot open this. It is not meant for lesser eyes..."

The Lord of Eismeer waved a dismissive hand.

"I already know what it contains. Or, at the very least, I fear that I know. If I am right then I cannot bear the shame of it. You have my blessing. Open it and read it so that I might hear the doom of our time delivered by one I trust, one who will not judge me."

After a moment's hesitation, Aglorar slowly slid his fingers beneath the wax and broke the seal. The words upon the parchment had clearly been scrawled in great haste and the stains upon the edges suggested it had been dampened in its travels.

He read the words before him slowly and deliberately:

My Lord Fohenk, I write to you with strange tidings.

On our northern borders we spied a pack of what we believed were wolves. We followed the pack for many days, until eventually we came to the slopes beneath High Top Fort.

As we crept closer to the creatures, we saw that they were misshapen. Their front quarters were muscular, and we thought they were holding things in their paws. If I had not seen them with my own eyes I would not have thought it possible, but there they were. My Pa used to tell me of them when I was an Eisling, but I never imagined I would see his words walking in front of me.

Bereun.

The pack split before we could follow them further, some going eastwards and some heading into the mountains. We, too, have split our forces so that we may ensure that neither pack encroach further upon our lands, and I have sent this letter with my fastest rider that our city might know the danger.

Etavïr be with you, and with all of us.

Kelred.

Aglorar let his hands carry the note away from his eyes. His troubled thoughts must have been clear upon his face, for Fohenk spoke in answer to them.

"I see I was right?"

Aglorar nodded slowly, handing the scroll back to his Lord.

"Bereun in our lands? A boy who claims to be a Traveller from Welverleigh? This storm? All the signs point to one thing and one thing only. The Planes are moving."

Aglorar regarded the figure before him; proud and strong like his people, yet there was a new age and depth to his eyes beyond even his long years. His shoulders sagged beneath the burdens he now found hung upon them.

"If," Fohenk continued, "the boy has indeed come from Welverleigh – from Holmfast – then a great and terrible doom is upon us. It is written that such a time would come again to our world... I had hoped greatly that I would not be alive to see it."

Aglorar shook his head.

"My Lord, I understand the implications of what Kelred has reported but the Planes have not moved in many thousands of years. Why would the Gods choose this time to move them again?"

Fohenk stood and stepped forward, so that he was close enough to Aglorar to be heard even in a whisper.

"It is not up to us to understand why, Aglorar, you know that well. But there are some questions that must be answered, and that we can answer."

Aglorar met his gaze levelly and hardened his resolve.

"What would you ask of me?"

"Answer me this: why did Dunwald go with them? He has ever been loyal to me, served me with honour and diligence. He was my advisor, by the Seven!"

A silence filled with realisation passed between the two men.

"You already have an answer to that question in your mind, do you not my Lord?" Aglorar asked slowly.

Fohenk nodded.

"I do, and I fear that I am once again to blame. He told me that the boy could not be what I believed. You saw yourself how angered he was that he did not know of your knowledge in this area, and his relief that the two of you agreed? Then the boy, and that accursed Farmer, are rescued from the gallows and escape the city with his help? Damn him to the Seventh!"

The Lord's outraged cry reverberated around the great Throne Room into infinity.

"He knew! He knew what was happening, and he said nothing!"

Without warning, Fohenk spun and landed a blow with his fist into the seat of his throne. As he did so he let out a howl of rage, snarling through his teeth. Then his anger was spent, for the moment, and he collapsed forward onto his elbows and rested himself against the base of the throne, panting with fury.

"How did you know what was written on this scroll, my Lord?" Aglorar asked quietly.

Fohenk, without looking up, spoke gravely.

"I had heard disturbing reports from our spies along the borders with Strewel and Ebras. Wolves that were larger than any previously seen in our lands. I hoped against hope that they were nothing more than stories, but I sent Kelred and a small band northward to investigate. They were under strict instruction to only send word if they had found anything of note. As you can see, they have."

Aglorar nodded.

"If we assume that the Planes are moving..." he began slowly, but got no further.

"Oh they are, there is no longer any doubt of that," Fohenk hissed, "Bereun do not roam our passes freely! They have always been the first sign, for they are creatures of the Dark Power; they roam only where he holds dominion. His hand is stretching forward to claim what will soon be his, as has always happened in such times. We do not have long, but we have a moment. When Dunwald and the boy reach the Boardwalks the moment will be gone. We must not let that happen!"

Aglorar gave his Lord as questioning an expression as he dared.

"The Boardwalks, my Lord?"

Fohenk snorted.

"Where else would he go? We are cordial with Beregle and Strewel, and we have few dealings with the Bakslá. Why else would he take not only the boy but Gismay? No, I am certain that they will make for the Boardwalks, and that they are taking what they know to that Seventh-damned traitor!"

"Even if that is so, they will only get so far, my Lord," Aglorar said softly. "I have sent Lekkon to track them down. He is a good and loyal soldier, he went without urging."

"Good," Fohenk cooed, "if we can get him back, and kill that fetcher Dunwald and their companions, then no-one else will know. We shall be the only ones! We will have time to prepare against the darkness that gathers, time to ready our people for the struggle ahead! We can find a way to survive this, to stand against the Dark Power!

"Don't you see, Aglorar? Eismeer will lead the charge against the enemy! We will save the world, and then we will rule it! We can force all others to recognise our people for what they are – the born leaders and rulers of Rhydariel! And you will be my right hand, Aglorar. The Chancellor of Rhydariel, sitting beside the first High King! There will be a golden age, and we shall be at its head."

The smile, half mad and half righteous, that had spread across the Lord of Eismeer's face was intoxicating. Aglorar found himself drawn into the emotion of the moment, the visions of what was being described to him dancing wildly in front of his eyes.

The thoughts were truly enticing.

"If Dunwald knows," Fohenk continued, his voice becoming a snarl, "he will want to press the same advantage as I. They fled north, did they not?"

Aglorar nodded, a gesture which made the smile on Fohenk's face widen.

"Of course. Why did I not see it before?"

"See what, Lord?"

"They could not flee westward for, even though the city was in turmoil, there are too many of our forces protecting our borders with Ebras that way. To the east and south is the sea. Their only way was northward."

He paused and looked at his new Advisor with a significant expression.

"They are going to Beregle."

"Beregle?" Aglorar asked. "Why would they go there? As you have said, Lord Marn is not our enemy."

"He is not," Fohenk agreed, "but that is not why they have gone to him. The only way to Ebras they can take is across the Bowalt and through Lundang. After the mountain passes, which will be slow for them, it will take them a week at least to reach the Boardwalks... Yes, we have time..."

Aglorar raised an eyebrow to his Lord's words.

"Time for what, Lord Fohenk?"

A dangerous gleam began to shine in the depths of Fohenk's eyes; a fire had begun to burn and was spreading through his mind, fanned by his ambition and the chance to make his people the envy of the entire world now presented to him. If he succeeded he would not only equal his ancestors memory, but he would go beyond them and be greeted in the Halls of Etavïr with reverence and pride.

And all he had to do was say the word.

"Time to press our advantage," he said, barely containing his emotions, "how many ships do we have at Daggerok, and when could they sail?"

Aglorar paused, taken aback by the question.

"Perhaps ten, maybe twelve that are fit to sail. I deem they could be ready by tomorrow evening. Why?"

"Send out riders and tell the garrison there to assemble every man able to bear arms and load them onto the ships. They are to set sail the moment night falls tomorrow evening.

"You and Bryndain will march westward at first light tomorrow with the force of this city. Leave only my Lordsguard and enough of a garrison to help with the rebuilding. You are to meet with the ships south of Farn Bridge, destroy the fortifications there, then move on to the Boardwalks. You will sail up river and attack from the lake. Destroy as much of the city as you can. I want them unable to interfere with our preparations for the greater war that is to come. We must be allowed to continue with our plans unhindered.

"And, when the dust of battle settles, you will capture Dunwald and the boy. They are to be unharmed. I want them both for myself."

The fire behind Fohenk's eyes flared once more, brighter and more vicious than before.

"Go, Aglorar. May Etavïr go with you."

Bowing deeply, Aglorar turned on his heels and left the Throne Room. Lord Fohenk watched, letting his emotions bubble within him. Soon all of Rhydariel would know the true strength of the Eismen.

Chapter Nine

Paths Of Scree

The small company that had fled from Fohenk's city trudged into the mountains, with Dunwald carrying Gismay's body forward with as much ceremony as the task allowed. Within half an hour the lack of mounts had begun to tell; Cam's legs, already aching with the strain of riding for two days, now had to pull him across the loose and treacherous stones of the thin valley floor. He and Sonia walked together, keeping each other's spirits up and making sure the other did not fall prey to their fatigue. Even Felgaron seemed to find the going tough here; the path was littered with slick, smooth stones and pebbles that afforded the company little or no grip.

The clouds that had been merciful for so long finally betrayed them a little over an hour into their sojourn, and the rain now fell heavily and swiftly. Cam and Sonia were grateful for Felgaron's gift of their cloaks; without them they would have been soaked to the bone within moments. Felgaron pushed them as quickly along the pass as they could manage, but the air had already begun to grow darker about them with the downpour and the sun would not hold its small domain between the clouds and horizon for much longer. When the last light failed then their journey would cease to be troublesome and become perilous, if not impossible.

The ravine through which they stumbled had already gained a small torrent along it's floor. Cam's toes were quickly submerged and he and Sonia were finding it increasingly more difficult to steady themselves against the slickness of the wet, unordered stones they walked upon. The way was no more than four feet wide at most, but there were occasions where it narrowed to perhaps a little over two, forcing the company to turn their bodies sideways and step gingerly between the rock faces.

It was in these moments that Dunwald had the most trouble with Gismay, but Cam gave him what assistance he needed. The Captain called his thanks through the rain, but Cam could not bring himself to answer; what he did was for Gismay, not Dunwald.

Eventually, after what felt like an age of struggling and discomfort, Felgaron found a wider spot in the path hidden from as much of the rain as could be expected by a high shelf of overhanging rock. Despite offering them the best protection from the torrents they could hope for, the weather gave them no hope of starting a fire for warmth.

Felgaron announced that this would be where they would spend the night, and that he would take the first watch. Using spare blankets from Felgaron's supplies, Cam and Dunwald silently fashioned a bed for Gismay's body in the driest part of the camp, then they both turned their attentions to their own comforts.

Cam saw that Sonia had found a relatively dry section of the floor to array their sleeping bags, but even this was scant consolation against the continuous barrage of the rain all about them.

Sonia, exhausted and battered, fell asleep almost instantly despite the weather, but Cam could not find rest so easily. And when sleep finally did come, he wished that it had not.

He dreamt he was in Eismeer once more, standing at the gallows.

All about him were the people of the city, and Lord Fohenk stood once more in the centre of the courtyard. To his left was Gismay. The Farmer's flesh hung limply off his frame, tattered as if it was ripped sack-cloth, leaving his bones and organs open to the elements, and his face was black with dried blood. To his right was Sonia who looked peaceful, almost as if she had no cares in the world. In front of him, on the ground of the courtyard, was Dunwald. The Captain had his hands pressed together as if he was praying, and he knelt down and placed his forehead upon the frozen ground.

Fohenk raised his arm and the hooded figure of the Executioner yanked the lever once more, but this time Cam did not fall. He felt his entire body hang in the air, free of the rope but unable to move. Cam watched in horror as Gismay dropped to the ground and shattered against the stone. A flash of golden light went up from the spot where the Farmer fell.

The ice-blocks came again, shattering the gallows platform and splintering the stone where they landed. Felgaron ran suddenly across the scene, a trail of blood behind him yet he himself was bathed in brilliant light. Cam tried to move, to place his hand across his eyes and shield himself from the glare, but some invisible force held him still.

He looked outward, and saw Sonia now stood before him. No, she was not standing – she was floating. She was clad in a golden robe and her hair billowed behind her amidst the destruction. Her eyes were raw with crying, but she was smiling the broadest smile Cam had ever seen. She raised her left hand towards him slowly, palm forwards.

It was only now that Cam noticed Aglorar standing next to her, his entire form shrouded in a black cloud, ever shifting and distorting his outline. He had his arm about Sonia's shoulders and seemed to be comforting her, but where he rested his hand upon her right shoulder Cam saw darkness flowing steadily, like blood from a wound.

A huge ice block flew past Cam's right side, bound for Sonia. Before it struck her, she crumpled to the floor with her smile unmoved upon her face, and Aglorar's shadowy form slowly lifted his fingers to his temples. The ice block slowed to an almost immediate stop and then was sent hurtling directly towards Cam.

Without warning, a great gout of flame shot across his

eyes and evaporated the block. The now boiling water splashed itself all over Cam's skin, burning him instantly. He screamed but still could not move to wipe the stuff away.

A hand gently pressed itself against his shoulder.

Cam? Cam?

Still screaming, he suddenly felt himself free to move. He sat bolt upright, scrabbling at his face to get the boiling vapour off. Only when he had stopped screaming did he realise that he was not in pain.

Looking about him, he saw the concerned yet hard face of Felgaron staring down at him with a questioning expression. It was his hand resting gently upon Cam's shoulder while Dunwald and Sonia looked on.

It was the morning, but the rain had clearly continued to fall through the night.

Cam shook himself.

"I'm fine," he panted, "just a bad dream."

Felgaron nodded and stood. He offered Cam a hand to his feet, which was unsteadily accepted.

"It is an hour past dawn. We must move on quickly. There is a small scout's hut some distance from here. I wish to gain it by nightfall this evening. Come, help us make ready."

Cam nodded his agreement, then glanced at Dunwald. The Captain studied Cam for a moment, a genuine concern traced across his features. Cam felt himself scowling in response. Dunwald simply turned away and gathered his things as Sonia stepped forward and studied her friend.

"You alright?" Cam asked, speaking before she had a chance.

"Me?" she gasped. "What the hell happened to you?"

"A bad dream, like I said."

"Cam?"

"What?"

He rounded on her, his voice snarling the question out. Sonia flinched back and stared at him.

Cam raised his hands in a defensive gesture.

"Son, I'm sorry. I didn't mean to... I'm tired. I'm sorry..."

Uneasily, Sonia nodded her head in assent to his words, then stepped away from him and began to gather her few possessions. Cam closed his eyes and silently scalded himself for being so heartless.

They were both tired, both facing the same impossible situation, yet when he had woken there had been an unnatural rage inside his chest. He had not felt anything like it before. It had threatened to consume him in that moment, yet it had come on suddenly and vanished just as quickly.

What was happening to him?

His curses were his only companion as Felgaron announced that he would carry Gismay for the first portion of their journey himself; Dunwald knew the passes here as well as he did, apparently, so he would be able to lead them. Cam would carry the Farmer later in the day. With Dunwald leading, Felgaron with Gismay on his shoulders, Sonia close behind, and Cam bringing up the rear, the small company began their day's march.

The rain was as unrelenting as it had been on the previous day, and the path became even more treacherous. The mud that lay beneath the stones had been softened by the water, causing Cam's feet to slip and skid with what felt like every step.

Slowly the path began to curve to their left, and slope very gently upward toward the peaks of the mountains they were slowly cutting their way through. The further they walked, the faster the water flowed around their feet, but the rock they walked upon mercifully began to change from broken stones to smaller pieces of gravel that were embedded in the mud. These proved to have slightly more grip and allowed for a more comfortable journey.

Even so, by mid morning Cam was utterly exhausted. His eyes stung from squinting through the constant downpour, his face and hands ached from the impacts of rain and stones, his mouth was dry, and his stomach felt empty.

Their first respite eventually arrived after three hours of

walking, and it was far too short. Felgaron lowered Gismay steadily against the walls of the ravine as Dunwald handed out small portions of Hocram for each of them. The liquor of the berries within went some way to restoring them, but it was not the same as a full meal and an hour's rest. Felgaron afforded them at most fifteen minutes before ordering that they should continue on their way. The rain had begun to relent a little, which came as some small relief, and when they started off again the clouds above them had changed from charcoal to a lighter, less threatening grey.

Still, the air was cold and the path treacherous as Cam, with Gismay's arms now locked around his neck, trudged forward behind Felgaron. Sonia was behind him with Dunwald guarding them at the rear. Although he did not complain, the added weight of Gismay placed a great strain upon Cam.

After half an hour of walking he began to feel more tired than he had done at the end of their morning's march. He did all he could to move at Felgaron's speed and to not slow the company down, but he did not have the strength of the other two men.

Dunwald saw his discomfort and ordered that he allow Gismay to pass to him. Felgaron made no comment or gesture as Cam, grateful but reluctant, accepted the Captain's offer. As they moved once more onward the company managed to increase their pace somewhat, consolidating Cam's fear that it was indeed he who had been slowing them down.

At long last the rain broke and the last drops cleared themselves from the air. It meant at least that their vision ahead was cleared, but the cold wind that whistled down the ravine chilled their sodden bodies to the bone.

When their turmoil had begun to affect even Felgaron's resolve, he halted them for a moment and produced a flask from his belt. He handed it to each of them in turn, even pouring a small amount into Gismay's mouth.

When it reached Cam, who hesitated a moment before sipping, Felgaron spoke.

“It is mead,” he said, “it will bring warmth and refreshment. Only a sip is needed, I assure you. It is the finest brew from Lundang.”

Cam had never drunk mead before. He sniffed the neck of the flask and recoiled a little – it did not smell like the kind of alcohol he enjoyed. If he had been back in Welverleigh he would have needed lemonade, but there was no hope of such a thing here.

Steeling himself, he took a swig. The sensation was not an enjoyable one, for the taste was unpleasant to him, but he could not deny that Felgaron's promise of warmth was answered immediately. It spread through his veins to all the corners of his body.

He passed it to Sonia who, after her sip, managed a half hearted smile of gratitude before handing Felgaron back his flask. With a quick glance at Cam, she followed their two companions along the path once more.

That break was the last that Felgaron afforded them until the mid-afternoon when, mercifully, he ordered that they would halt for food in a small, circular hollow that crossed their path. Dunwald started a fire once more with what little tinder he and Felgaron had brought with them that had remained dry.

“We shall stop for an hour,” Felgaron said, a tone of voice that did not invite argument.

Sonia went and settled herself down against the wall of the hollow and wrapped her cloak about her, while Cam watched as Felgaron began to tend to Gismay.

“Is he going to be alright?” he asked quietly.

“He will live,” the Swordsman answered, “but we cannot hope to carry him much further.”

Cam felt a pang of guilt at the words.

“If you mean earlier when I..?”

“No,” the Swordsman cut in immediately, with a note of kindness in his otherwise gruff voice, “there is no blame on you. I fear only what would happen were he in this state should we encounter enemies of any kind.”

As he spoke, Felgaron seemed to be examining the heights of the mountains about them, scanning them for any signs of whatever enemies he was afraid of.

"You fear we may be followed?" Dunwald asked, stepping next to them and handing Felgaron a bowl of warm water.

"Possibly," Felgaron said evasively, accepting the bowl, "but by who I cannot be certain. And what of you, friend Cam?"

The question had caught Cam off guard.

"What of me?" he repeated uncertainly.

"Your sleep last night was troubled, was it not?" Felgaron's tone suggested sympathy but there was an underlying current that Cam could not quite catch.

"Yeah," Cam began uncertainly, "it was just a bad dream. I'm... I'll get over it. I've had a few recently."

In his mind flashed images of white walls, archers, and ungodly creatures as they had done on the day he found himself transported to Rhydariel.

"Honestly," he said, shaking himself from his own head and smiling weakly, "I'll be fine. I just have a vivid imagination, that's all."

Felgaron nodded.

"As you say. Now, get yourself some food."

Cam made to go, but the sight of Gismay in front of him compelled another question.

"What are we going to do about him?"

"I am loathed to do so," Felgaron began earnestly, "but I fear we cannot hope to travel as swiftly as we need to if he cannot walk. Rhydariel needs him to stand. I will heal his physical wounds as best I may then I will administer stronger medicine.

"Now, eat and rest," the Swordsman urged, turning to Cam "I will call for you when it is time."

Sensing once again that there was no discussion to be had, Cam reluctantly turned away from Gismay and stepped over to the fire that Dunwald had built.

Sonia had already shifted herself away from the wall and

sat, cross-legged, within the circle of warmth that it gave off. Dunwald hunched himself over the cooking pot once more, seeming to enjoy this role he had been given. The broth he made smelled to Cam the same as the one had had created on the previous night, but Cam's attention was drawn always to Felgaron's movements around Gismay.

Through the corners of his vision he witnessed the man first tend to the wounds on Gismay's face, cleansing them with a little of the warm water that Dunwald had heated for him before cooking. He then gently lifted the man's left shoulder into his arms and braced the Farmer's torso against his own. With one swift action he snapped the limb back into place.

The sickeningly staccato movement, followed by the dull thud of the bone relocating itself, made Cam choke for a moment on his broth. Sonia and Dunwald looked up briefly from their own meals, but the Captain needed only a swift glance behind him to understand.

Cam stared at him.

"Don't you even care enough to watch?" he seethed quietly.

"I am a soldier," Dunwald replied without looking up from his bowl, "death is as much a part of my life as air or water."

He now met Cam's gaze with an iron expression.

"My hope and desire for Gismay's health cannot aid him. We have done all we can."

Without another word, Dunwald returned his attention to his broth and ate in quiet contemplation.

Stifling all the fear for his friend, Cam finished the remainder of his broth and allowed himself at least a few moments of numbness in the face of everything. He consciously decided that he would focus on nothing except the inside of his own eye lids.

It worked too well, for he woke perhaps half an hour later. He discovered that somehow he had laid himself down upon the wet ground and settled himself as close to the fire as he could.

It was Felgaron who had once again shaken him gently out

of his dreamless slumber.

“Come,” he said, a strange smile across his lips, “Gismay is awake.”

Cam sat himself up and rubbed the sleep out of his eyes.

“What?”

Felgaron's smile broadened.

“I had thought the news would please you. Both of you.”

The Swordsman inclined his head to Cam's left where he saw Sonia lay sleeping.

“I also suspect this news would take precedence over any harsh words you have shared.”

Felgaron's voice was soft and kindly, and Cam took his meaning well. He nodded and, despite the feeling in the pit of his stomach, reached out and placed a hand on Sonia's shoulder.

She responded instantly, as if she had not been fully asleep or indeed had slept at all. She rolled over and with only a quick glance at both he and Felgaron for confirmation, stood and went over to Gismay. Cam closed his eyes and cursed himself, then pulled his aching frame up onto its feet and followed them.

Gismay was sat against the rock, looking as comfortable as one in his condition could be expected. As Cam and Sonia approached, he smiled broadly at them.

“Well don't you both look a sight for sore eyes. It's good to see you again.”

“And you,” Cam said, feeling himself getting emotional.

Sonia did not speak, but she placed a hand on Gismay's arm and smiled warmly.

Gismay pulled himself up onto his elbows and took in his surroundings.

“This is certainly not the dungeons of Eismeer,” he said, almost chuckling and looking at Felgaron, “I imagine there's a tale to our escape?”

Felgaron nodded.

“There is, though it will take some telling indeed,” Felgaron said earnestly, “but I am afraid I have more to ask of you. Rest yourself now, and take nourishment. Captain Dunwald will fill you in, no doubt."

Gismay's eyes widened into what Cam assumed would become a fearful expression, but it was a knowing smile that crossed the Farmer's lips.

"Will he, now?" he cooed.

Dunwald stepped over to them and handed Gismay a bowl of broth and a mug of mead, both of which were accepted gladly.

"I will certainly tell you what I can," the Captain sighed, settling himself next to Gismay, "though first I would speak of my sorrow for what has been done to you. Even though we both took our oaths and knew our duties..."

"We did, and we performed them to the letter," Gismay cut in, "and that's all we'll say on it."

A flash of dismay and guilt ran across Dunwald's features.

"That as it may be," he said thickly, "I want you to know that you served our people with honour, bravery, and selflessness. When next I speak with him, King Hedradour will be made fully aware of all you have done."

"As much as I agree with Captain Dunwald's words," Felgaron said, gently, "we have not all day. Eat and rest as much as you can, for we must make way soon."

"Where are we making for?" Gismay asked.

"Beregle," Felgaron answered, "though that is still some leagues away. We must continue the journey soon."

"How far do you need from me?"

"Today? Perhaps another three hours."

Gismay smiled determinedly.

"You'll have them."

Felgaron placed a hand on his shoulder.

"Do what you can. Nothing more. Now, eat and rest. We will not break camp for another half hour at least."

Gismay nodded, and returned his focus to his food and drink.

Cam, after a glance toward Felgaron, went and busied himself with finding some food. It warmed his heart to see Gismay awake and talking, but still there was a nagging vitriol clawing at the back of his mind. Even the news that the Farmer would live had not quashed it completely.

He picked up a bowl, but it slipped from his wet hands. A sudden red mist across his vision as he picked the thing back up, and the bowl was hurled against the rock in front of him. It clattered loudly, bouncing back past him and into the centre of the hollow.

Everyone was staring at him. He could feel it.

The gentle touch of Sonia's hand against his back roused him as the mist cleared. He half turned his head but did not face her.

“Cam?” she whispered.

“I'm fine.”

“Cam?” she pressed.

“You need to rest. We've got three hours of marching ahead of us.”

“Listen,” she continued, trying not to sound frustrated.

“I don't want to talk about it.”

Her hand on his shoulder again.

“If you do, I'm here for you. OK?”

“Yeah. Fine.”

Why did she keep touching his shoulder? Did she think that would help?

“I'm always here for you.”

Why was she still talking?

“I heard you. Thanks.”

He turned brusquely, passing close to her shoulder, and picked up the bowl. He then stomped back and carried on sorting himself some food.

Sonia had not moved. Why not? He was clearly busy. Why was she just watching him?

“Cam, I think we need to talk...”

He spun round to face her.

“What about?”

Instinctively Sonia had taken half a step back from him. Why? What the hell was she afraid of?

“W-well...” she stammered, uncertainly, “we've obviously both been through a lot lately...”

“Have we? I hadn't noticed!" Cam tried to stop every single word that came out of his mouth, but he could not. It was as if someone else was speaking for him.

Stop talking! his mind screamed. But who was it screaming at? Him or Sonia?

Sonia's worried expression changed to one that was harder and more defensive.

“Yeah, *we* have! I'm in this as well, just as scared and confused as you are!”

“You're right, you've had it really tough! I'm sorry for being so selfish!”

“Don't you dare!” Sonia seethed back at him, unable to control her temper. “Don't even think about it! That's not what I'm saying!”

Why was he still talking? Why would Sonia not leave him alone? Why was he angry?

“And what are you saying, exactly?” he heard himself fling at her.

Sonia blinked back at him, dumbfounded.

“You know what? I don't know. I don't know why I bothered to try and talk to you. From now on, I'll just leave you to it.”

Don't say anything. Just let her go. This can stop now.

“Good idea. I don't need your help anyway. I've made it this far!”

Sonia stared at him, disgust and rage mixing horribly on her face.

“Fuck you,” she spat quietly, then stalked off to the other side of the hollow.

For half a moment Cam wanted to scream at her again, to tell her that he had every right to feel aggrieved, but the thought died on his lips. His heart sank in his chest and the bottom of his stomach fell through the stones beneath him.

What was wrong with him?

He abandoned sorting any food out for himself and sat, numb and alone, away from everyone else and stared at the rock for what remained of their rest.

Gismay, as it transpired, was able to stand and hold much of his own weight, though he would certainly continue to need assistance on the journey ahead. Cam volunteered to help during the next march, if only so he had something to focus his mind on.

The final three hours of the day were a blur. Throughout, Cam's eyes strayed to Sonia's back; she walked perhaps five paces in front, but never once looked around to check on him. He could not blame her. He was livid at himself for being a bloody fool.

He made a conscious effort to shift his focus from the empty, lost feeling in the pit of his stomach to the figure of Gismay upon his left hand side.

"I never got the chance to properly thank you for your help back at your farm," he said as airily as he could.

The Farmer, puffing his cheeks out, looked at Cam with a perplexed expression.

"And why should you? I failed. We both ended up in the dungeons of Eismeer."

Cam smiled and rolled his eyes.

"Well, if you look at it like that. But, seriously, thank you. You've done a lot for us and I just wanted you to know we appreciate it."

Gismay nodded, shifting his weight against Cam as he did so.

"You're welcome. Thrice welcome, in fact, though all I did was what the Seven demanded of me."

They trudged on in silence for a few short paces, before Cam felt a question forming in his mind.

"Gismay, you remember what you told us when we first met? About Sonia and I being Travellers?"

"I do," the Farmer sighed, "and some help I've been so far in getting you home."

Cam shook his head.

"That's not what I'm worried about. Not right now, anyway."

"Oh? And what is it that worries you, friend Cam?"

Cam took a moment to consider his next words before speaking them. He had not really thought much about some of the things that transpired during his time in Eismeer, but now he had the chance thoughts had floated to the top of his mind that he could not shake.

"When I was in the Dungeons, that soldier, Aglorar, asked me some questions."

Gismay looked sidelong at him, an expression that could have been concern.

"What kind of questions?"

"About how me and Sonia got here. He said he represented a group of people that knew about Travellers, that would want to help us."

Gismay seemed to stiffen a little at Cam's words.

"There are some that have knowledge about these things, it's true," the Farmer responded carefully, "and Eismeer will no doubt have its fair share of them. But I'd be surprised if they counted Lieutenant Aglorar within their number."

"So there are groups that would want to help us?" Cam asked, trying not to sound too excited.

Gismay nodded cautiously.

"There are," he said.

"Is *he* part of one of them?" Cam asked, motioning towards Felgaron.

Gismay looked at the man's back and smiled.

"No, I don't believe so. Why do you ask?"

"I just can't figure out why he would do what he did – save us, I mean – if it wasn't because of that."

Cam's words seemed to perplex Gismay, and the Farmer took a moment before responding.

"Ain't it enough that a good man saved your life?"

"He killed two guards to get to us!" Cam cut in. "I mean,

fair enough, you're a spy. But me and Sonia aren't from this world. The only reason he would have to take us as well as you is if he knew we were Travellers. And the only two people that knew that were Aglorar and you."

The Farmer now regarded Cam seriously for a moment.

"You're observant, friend Cam, I'll give you that. All I can tell you is that what Felgaron chooses to do, he does for his own reasons. As for anything he knows about you, it ain't come from me."

Cam shot a meaningful look at the Farmer.

"So he does know something?"

Gismay smiled.

"I'd be surprised if he didn't. He's one of the few men I've met in Rhydariel who truly knows what goes on in our world."

Cam gazed at Gismay for a moment, then looked to Felgaron.

He strode ahead of them with his green cloak billowing behind him, beneath which was a simple leather hauberk and a sword he always gripped by the hilt. His boots and trousers were tattered and in need of repair, while his scruffy, stubbly beard framed his hard and muddied face. The only striking thing about the man was his greyish eyes; they seemed to physically hold you when they demanded your attention and their grip was unbreakable.

"Really? Him?"

"Aye. And, as you've already seen, he's a fine swordsman," Gismay said, matter-of-factly, "and has a friend in each court."

Cam raised his eyebrows.

"So he's a mercenary?" he tried after a moment's contemplation.

Gismay laughed in response.

"I doubt any could afford his skill. They say he's the best since the days of Whitesword."

"Whitesword?" Cam asked, his interest piquing, but he got no further.

Perhaps ten yards further along the path, Felgaron had stopped and raised a hand in caution. He looked about him as if he were sniffing the air.

Dunwald came up behind Cam and pushed his way past.

"What is it?" he called up to the Swordsman.

"I know not for certain," Felgaron replied quietly, striding backwards along the path towards them, "but I have been aware of someone – or something – following us ever since we last stopped."

Dunwald shrugged.

"There are few in these parts to follow us. Eismeer's scouts seldom patrol these passes."

Felgaron shook his head.

"I do not believe it is any Eismen that trails us."

The Swordsman looked up at the peaks arrayed about them.

Without warning, a single rock fell from some hidden precipice above and landed only a few feet away from Sonia. She leapt back to avoid being hit, then stared down it in shock.

For a moment no-one dared to move, then Felgaron slowly knelt down to inspect the thing. When he had looked it over, he handed it to Dunwald.

The Captain, perplexed, took it and, as he did so, he eyes widened in disbelief.

"As I said, it is no Eisman that hunts us."

Felgaron's words hung in the deathly quiet air about them.

"What is it?" Cam asked, an uneasy fear growing in his body.

Dunwald handed him the rock. Cam looked closely at it. He could feel Gismay reposition himself upon his shoulder so that he might see also. The gasp in his left ear told him that only he and Sonia would not understand whatever there was to be read in the rock.

It was almost spherical, and it had a number of small but clearly visible scratches. Upon closer scrutiny, Cam saw that they were in a most unusual formation: at the top of the rock were three evenly spaced marks, and there were two more that sat at roughly four and eight o'clock.

They were fresh and clean.

“What are those?” Sonia asked, taking the rock and indicating the marks.

“Claw marks,” came Gismay's quiet and instant reply, “Etavïr preserves us.”

“Claw marks?” Cam asked in confusion.

“Something threw this at us?” Sonia gasped.

“Aye,” Felgaron growled, “one of the most fearsome creatures this world has ever seen. A Bereun.”

“What's a 'Bereun'?” Cam tried nervously, the word sounding strange upon his lips.

“A wolf, for want of a better description,” Dunwald said.

Cam almost laughed once again.

“Wolves can't throw things,” he replied, doing all he could not to sound too unnerved.

“They are no wolves,” Felgaron spoke slowly, “they are abominations. Evil creatures twisted and corrupted to suit their dire purpose. Let us hope we can outrun them.”

Sonia stared at him.

“And if we can't?”

“Then let us hope there are not so many as to overpower Dunwald and I. Come, we must make all haste. The sun will set on us shortly and I do not wish to meet these creatures in the dark. The Guard House I seek is perhaps half an hour's march from here. At least there we can barricade ourselves in if we must.”

He turned on his heels and sped up the path.

Dunwald turned and took Gismay from Cam.

“I will bear him, for speed is of the essence,” the Captain urged.

Cam helped the Farmer settle himself upon the Captain's shoulders, then they and Sonia sped off after Felgaron.

The path here was flat for the most part, but all along its length it was followed by the shelf above them. Felgaron looked up and behind him at intervals, and every member of their small company could not help but follow his example. Alas, the shelf was too high and the rock face too steep for them to see if their enemy was close to them.

Onward they pressed, the darkening sky above them their only indication of how long it had been since that rock had been cast down amongst them. Occasionally Cam thought that he could hear more rocks falling behind them, but whenever he looked back he saw nothing.

His heart was racing.

Dunwald had said it was like a wolf, but Felgaron had said that they were abominations. The word conjured up terrible and nightmarish visions in Cam's mind, his imagination threatening to overwhelm him. Even if they did manage to outrun them, he doubted that he would find any sleep tonight with such thoughts running through his head.

Felgaron began to push them harder, breaking out into a half-jog when they rounded a sharp corner. The rock to the left of the path here began to fall, revealing a steep and rugged vale, at the bottom of which were a few hardy trees and plants standing beside a greenish-blue stream that reflected the last, waning light of the sun.

Suddenly, Sonia tripped on a jutting rock, and she stumbled dangerously close to the edge of the precipice. Cam caught her instinctively, then set her safely in the centre of the narrow path.

She stared at him, conflicting emotions of thanks, shock and anger on her face. She looked for a moment as if she would speak, but instead she simply nodded then turned and followed Dunwald onward.

Cam positioned himself beside her and on the outside of the path, but the way grew even narrower, forcing them to slow their pace lest they all tumbled to the earth below. The ledge above them had disappeared further back along the path, delving into the mountains above them, but still they felt the threat at their backs.

At long last, they rounded a curve in the path and reached the plateau upon which stood the Guard House. It was a simple affair, cut into the very rock of the mountainside, with what remained of a wooden door hanging awkwardly on rusting iron hinges.

The plateau itself was fairly wide, its edge perhaps ten or fifteen yards away from the Guard House. Felgaron forced the door open and ushered everyone inside.

Ducking through the opening, Cam saw a small central space with a fire pit in the middle of the floor. Upon further inspection, the place also contained a bunk room and some form of supply cupboard or pantry. The place was empty of furniture save for a metal spit that hung above the fire pit, and the furs that constituted beds in the bunk room.

Dunwald immediately set to work at the fire, once Gismay had assured him that he could hobble safely to the bunk room and rest his still healing limbs. Not wishing to watch the man struggle, Cam propped him up without invitation and led him through to the room. Gismay assured him that he would need no further assistance, and that Felgaron could almost certainly make better use of him. Cam nodded and went back into the central room.

"Need any help?" he panted into the air.

Felgaron looked up at him.

"There is little else to be done. Dunwald and I will share the watch this night. I fear the creatures will come on us in the dark. We must be ready if they do."

"Can they get in?" Cam found himself asking.

"I know not. The door is not strong, but if they are not numerous then Dunwald and I may be able to hold them off."

The fire in the centre of the room began to crackle behind him. Cam looked over his shoulder and saw that Dunwald was building a blaze far larger than any he had in the wild.

"Actually, friend Cam," Felgaron said, a thought seeming to strike him, "go into the other rooms and bring us any lengths of wood you find. The longer the better."

Cam nodded and quickly began to search. All in all he managed to collect perhaps fifteen pieces of wood that he thought might match Felgaron's description. Upon his return, the Swordsman ordered that he pile them as close to the fire as he could, making sure that they were within easy reach.

Whatever Felgaron was planning, Cam hoped that he would be successful. If he and Dunwald were overcome, the other three did not have much hope; he and Sonia were not fighters, and Gismay could barely walk much less take on a wolf.

Fear threatened to grip his heart. Had he and Sonia escaped the noose to get mauled on a mountain top?

He stopped and tried to control his thoughts. Panic would not serve him now. If he was to be of any use to anyone he had to keep himself calm, however impossible the situation was.

"Anything else I can do?" he asked out loud to the room.

Felgaron paused in his work for a moment and considered him, his eyes looking Cam up and down, then he reached to his belt and removed a small but sharp looking dagger.

This he pressed it into Cam's hands.

"You can't be serious?" Cam breathed. "I've never..."

"We may yet need every arm we can call upon if we are to escape this night alive."

"But..."

"You will find a way," the Swordsman said, a voice that was forceful but not unkind, "now make ready. The moment the sun leaves the sky tonight we are imperilled. Stay close to the fire. Dunwald and I will do the rest."

Once Dunwald was satisfied that the fire would burn as long as they needed it to, he and Felgaron took some of the shelves from the pantry and wedged them into the holes that served as windows on either side of the door.

Cam sat upon the cold stone floor with his back against the wall as he watched the last, blood-red rays of the sun slide under the door and mingle with the flickering firelight.

The dagger that Felgaron had given him was in his hands,

and he grimly admired the craftsmanship that had wrought it. He had held many of the castle replicas during his short time working there, and on a few precious occasions he had been allowed to handle one of the genuine articles.

This blade was of a far better quality than any of those had been, and it did not have the marks of time upon it either. It was perhaps eight inches in length, wide and thick at the centre, with no design of any kind upon it. The only extravagance was that the hilt was bound in leather so that it could be comfortably wielded.

Wielded? He had no idea what to do with it!

The natural light faded and an unspoken feeling of dread fell over the entire company. Sonia had gone to join Gismay in the bunk room where they both would remain hidden. Cam gave himself an excuse to poke his head around the door and check on her, and saw that she was sat huddled amongst the firs at the far side of the room.

"Son?" he said quietly, taking a few tentative steps towards her.

She nodded at him that she was alright, and went to settle herself once more. But then here eyes caught sight of something.

"What's that?"

She pointed at the dagger.

"A present from Felgaron," he said stiffly.

"Be careful."

Her voice was honest and clear, though the threat of tears clung to the edges of her words. Cam looked her dead in the eye, only just controlling his own steadily growing emotions.

"You too."

"Have no fear, friend Cam," Gismay said, his voice low and serious, "should the need arise I'll do all I can, you have my word. May the Seven protect you. May they protect us all."

Cam nodded then, with one final glance at Sonia, turned back into the central room.

Felgaron and Dunwald had taken their positions on either side of the fire, each of them holding one of the lengths of wood that Cam had brought for them, and their swords drawn. They stared silently at the door.

Before Cam could speak, Felgaron motioned that he should take up a position directly behind the fire. Cam nodded his understanding and crouched down.

A new resolve took him.

Whatever came through that door, he would meet it on his own terms.

The silence became total, only the crackling fire signalling the passing of each tense second.

Then there was a snuffling at the door.

The creak of leather as Felgaron and Dunwald tightened their grips on their weapons sounded inexplicably loud in his ears.

An impact that sounded like a stone thudding against the wood that Felgaron had forced into the windows rattled through the air, causing him to all but jump out of his skin.

A motion from Felgaron that he should stay still and quiet.

Cam was suddenly aware of how truly afraid he was, and whatever resolve he had managed to find began to dissipate.

Felgaron slowly moved his arm so that the length of wood he was holding began to catch the heat of the fire. Dunwald followed suit and soon both men held burning brands.

Another impact, this time on the door itself. More snuffling and snarling outside.

Felgaron raised his sword hand and lifted three fingers. Dunwald nodded his understanding.

More impacts against the doors and windows.

Finally, the fragile resistance of the wood in right-hand window broke, the flimsy barricade crashing down inside the Guard House.

Cam flinched once more, and his eyes widened in horror at what followed.

The shape of a muzzle appeared at the bottom of the window, sniffing desperately to discover what prey was huddled inside.

For a moment they all expected the rest of the creature to appear, but the window was mercifully too far off the ground to be climbed through.

Cam gripped his dagger tightly, his hand becoming wet with nervous sweat and the heat from his proximity to the fire.

More stones thudded into the door, and after a moment came the rasping of claws scrabbling at the wood.

Cam's heart beat hard and fast in his chest, his mind betraying him and conjuring all manner of nightmarish visions of what awaited him behind that thin, rapidly splintering barrier.

However, when the door finally gave way and the three creatures burst across the threshold, nothing could have prepared him for what he saw.

They were indeed shaped such as wolves, but their front quarters were far more developed; their front legs were muscular, with paws formed almost like human hands. The claws of these were long and sharp, but it was their faces that terrified Cam the most.

Their eyes were red, perhaps coloured so by the firelight, but their snouts were long with rows of razor sharp teeth. The muscles in their neck and jaw were so huge and defined that Cam doubted they would have any trouble with bone or even armour.

The dagger he held suddenly seemed totally insignificant.

Felgaron ripped his wooden spear out of the fire and thrust its flaming tip at the first animal's muzzle. The creature did not duck in time and yelped as the burning wood pierced the soft flesh of its nose.

Quick as a flash, Felgaron brought his sword crashing down, but the creature had enough of its wits to pull itself away so that the sword glanced across its flank rather than through its neck.

Dunwald joined the fray, charging at one of the other Bereun. The brand he wielded caught the thing's flank, and the smell of burning flesh and fur filled the room.

Howling, the thing used its overdeveloped jaws it

wrenched the stick from Dunwald's hand and send it flying across the room, out of the door and onto the plateau beyond.

Stunned by the ferocity of his opponent Dunwald paused only momentarily in raising his sword, but it was enough.

Seeing its opportunity, the second Bereun launched itself forward and crashed down upon the Captain, its front paws pinning him to the ground.

Crying out, Felgaron kicked his own assailant hard underneath the jaw and leapt across the room. In the same movement he plunged his sword deep into the thing attacking his companion. He missed the neck by mere inches, but the creature yelped horridly in agony. It slumped, incapable of holding itself upright, directly on top of Dunwald.

Cam suddenly felt himself spring forward, out from behind the protection of the fire, and force all his strength against the bulk upon Dunwald. Eventually, the broken body of the Bereun collapsed limply to the floor beside the Captain. He groaned in pain but managed to look at Cam and force a grimace of thanks in his direction.

A shout from Felgaron brought them both back to the present and Cam turned to see the Swordsman being almost overpowered.

Dunwald leapt to his feet and went to help him. Cam moved to follow, but something caught his vision.

At the door, having hardly moved, was the third Bereun. This was the largest of the three. It had been making for Felgaron, but it had stopped in its tracks when Cam had emerged from behind the fire. It had watched with growing curiosity as he had pushed the body of its fellow from Dunwald, and now it had chosen its new target.

Terrified, Cam slowly brought the dagger up in front of his face so that the blade was clearly visible.

The creature looked at it and seemed to smile. Slowly it stepped towards him, growling menacingly as it did so.

Cam felt himself trembling; if the creatures could smell fear then he would reek.

The thing's eyes burned into him, piercing his very soul with their menacing glare.

It threw itself upon him.

Instinct taking over, Cam dived away to his left but not soon enough to avoid the swipe of the creature's claws. He screamed as he went down and landed heavily upon the floor. He looked down, fear filling his body, and saw three deep claw marks raked through his clothes and upon his skin.

Once more the sight of his own blood was before him, and he felt sick.

Defying everything, he scrambled to his feet and faced the creature, holding the dagger out uncertainly in front of him.

The Bereun had skidded upon the floor, but regained its grip and rounded on him.

There was an air of arrogance about its stance.

Cam felt his feet moving him backwards away from the thing. He stopped as he hit the wall of the Guard House. He had nowhere left to run.

The creature seemed to read his thoughts and that horrible grin formed around its muzzle once more.

Cam could hear his heart pounding in his ears, the dagger now visibly shaking in his outstretched arm.

A brush of cold air touched his back.

The door!

Cam began gingerly making his way along the wall towards it. The Bereun stared at him for a moment, sizing up the situation.

Cam's fingers traced their way along the wall, stretched as far out as he dared so that he might find the frame.

The creature took two more slow, ponderous steps forward, waiting for its moment.

The tips of Cam's fingers finally reached the door, the chill of the night offering him some small measure of hope. With one more half step, he wrapped them around so that he had a grip on the shaped stone.

The creature leapt.

Using all his courage and strength, Cam pulled himself through the door and out into the cold night. Ducking as he did so, he felt the belly of the creature slide across his back and spine, the thing landing on the stone only feet away from him.

Looking up, Cam saw that the creature had landed heavily. It seemed to have injured one of its paws and was struggling to stand. It whimpered pitifully.

For half an instant Cam felt sorry for the creature, then he remembered what it was.

Mustering all his courage, he raised the dagger and strode over to it. The thing looked up at him with a pained and broken expression.

Ignoring his all too strong instincts to have mercy, Cam breathed out heavily, closed his eyes, and brought the dagger downwards hard.

The Bereun snarled triumphantly as it rolled out from under him, its paw perfectly in tact.

Cam fell forwards as his dagger cut through thin air. He collided face first with the rock, trapping his dagger underneath his torso as he did.

Scrabbling desperately to retrieve it, he twisted round so that he could see the thing once more. It eyed him almost pityingly.

Cam had used up the last of his luck. There was nothing else he could do.

The creature did not give him a moment to consider his fate.

Leaping forward with its front paws outstretched, it came at him, snarling and barking loudly. The cacophony would be the last thing Cam ever heard.

He felt his fingers close about the dagger's hilt and his arm lift itself helplessly forwards.

An ungodly howl pierced the air, almost deafening him.

His outstretched arm was wrenched backwards as the creature's momentum took it flying over the top of Cam towards the edge of the precipice. The dagger was snatched out of his grip by the force of the movement.

Opening his eyes against his fear, Cam saw that a viscous liquid was running down his arm, the light of the moon glinting off it in the cold night about him. He knew instinctively what it was.

Blood.

Looking over to the creature, Cam gasped, horrified.

It was stood on its hind legs, facing outward over the valley. Cam could see smoke puffing out into the cold air with every breath the thing took. It turned uneasily to face him and Cam saw that his dagger was sticking out of the Bereun's chest, embedded as far as the hilt. Blood oozed from the wound, dripping through the thing's fur and onto the grey rock below.

The creature stumbled for a moment, shocked, then it tried to grip the hilt of the dagger with its front paws but it was already too weak.

With one final look at Cam, surprise and anger beginning to mingle on the thing's face, the Bereun staggered backwards and toppled over the edge of the plateau.

There was one final howl, then silence.

Cam stared at the point where the creature had fallen, at the blood spots on the ground, and barely managed to breathe against his shock.

What had he done?

“Cam?!”

Felgaron ran out onto the plateau and grasped his shoulder.

Cam barely felt the man's touch.

“Cam? Are you alright?”

He turned to face the Swordsman, and instinctively held up his blood-stained arm.

“I lost your dagger...” he heard himself saying.

Then he was sick.

Felgaron, seemingly accepting of Cam's health, strode over to the edge of the rock and looked down.

“You did well,” he said as comfortingly as he could. “We

have survived this night."

A scream ripped through the night air. It came from within the Guard House.

Despite everything, Cam recognised it immediately.

"Sonia?" he said, his mind snapping back to reality. "Sonia?!"

Cam and Felgaron sprinted back into the Guard House and down the short corridor that led to the bunk room, Dunwald already ahead of them.

They burst into the room, and what they found almost finished Cam.

Sonia was huddled, shaking, amongst the fur covers of her bed. In front of her, at a most unnatural angle, was the body of the third Bereun. It lay like a grotesque rug, its eyes still holding the very last gleam of life.

For a moment Cam paused, relieved that she was seemingly unharmed, but then the true horror caught his eye.

Lying underneath the Bereun's front paws was Gismay. The furs from his bed were strewn across the room, and his clothes were ripped near the neck. Three huge claw marks scored his left cheek, and his right shoulder bled heavily from what was clearly a bite wound.

"He saved me," Sonia forced out between sobs and whimpers, "it ran in and came straight at me... I thought I was... Then he jumped down and... I think he killed it..."

She stopped, unable to control his emotions any longer. Dunwald and Felgaron moved as one to lift the creature from on top of him, revealing a mess of blood and furs.

"He did at that," Dunwald breathed, revealing that Gismay's knife still rested in the throat of the thing.

Felgaron nodded, then examined the Farmer.

"He is alive," he said, "but barely. The wound is deep, and creatures such as these will contaminate it still further by their very nature. By Etavïr that such an evil should take place while I defended him! We must offer what aid we can. Help me get him onto the bed."

Without thinking, Cam joined as Dunwald and Felgaron took Gismay's broken form and hoisted him from the floor. They laid him as gently as they could and, at Felgaron's urging, collected the furs and placed some of them beneath his head. The Swordsman then ripped a length of material from his cloak and pressed it hard onto the wound at Gismay's throat, and looked over every inch of the Farmer.

The others watched, helpless.

Gismay's body was barely recognisable from the one that Cam had first seen when he had woken in this world. How long ago had that been? A week, perhaps? Ten days? It felt like an eternity however long it was but, throughout everything, Gismay had been there. He had without doubt saved Cam and Sonia's lives by taking them in when he discovered them, and he had given them hope and reassurance when they had needed it most.

Now he lay before them, torn open and clinging to the merest thread of life, and there was nothing either of them could do.

Cam felt Sonia's arm wrap about his waist and he held her close. He could feel her sobbing into him, and he laid his head against hers and joined with her despair.

After everything – the farm, Eismeer, the storm – the thought that Gismay might die here in this cold, forgotten Guard House made Cam sick.

Felgaron stepped back, an unreadable expression on his face.

"Is there anything you can do?" Sonia breathed.

"This far from civilisation, without proper tools and skilled healers, there is very little," the Swordsman replied darkly, "but I will do what I can. Dunwald, bring me water and any clean cloth we have."

The Captain obliged swiftly, and soon returned with a filled bowl and a spare shift from their packs. Felgaron took them and ordered that Dunwald hold the material at Gismay's neck while he carefully set about cleaning the Farmer's wounds as best he could. But, by the time this had been done, even Cam and Sonia could tell that Gismay's breathing was more shallow than it had been.

The Farmer was running out of time.

Seeming to sense this, Felgaron shook his head.

"Conventional medicine will not work here," he breathed. "My pack."

Without thinking, Cam quickly went and found the thing and brought it to Felgaron. The Swordsman took it and pulled out a small, delicate-looking vial filled with the strangest liquid Cam had seen; it was purple-gold in hue, and seemed to shimmer even in the dim firelight.

"This is Deldylin," Felgaron said, not taking his eyes away from Gismay, "it is a specially distilled form of Hocliquor. It is more pure, and more potent."

Dunwald stared in awe at the vial.

"I have heard of the stuff, but never seen its application."

"It is seldom used save in the most desperate of moments," the Swordsman replied, "for the skill required both to mix it and to administer the correct dose is exceedingly delicate."

He paused and, unless Cam was mistaken, a nervous look passed over his face.

"By the First, I pray this is not folly," Felgaron whispered, barely audible to those around him.

With a gentle precision, he placed his right hand beneath Gismay's head and allowed a small trickle of the liquid to pass the Farmer's lips.

The effect was instantaneous.

He writhed in agony, his body desperately struggling to control the immense healing power that had exploded with its fragile shell.

His mouth warped itself into a scream as bright lines of gold and purple weaved their way across his broken skin. They flared as they reached the ends of each cut and laceration he had been forced to endure.

For a few terrible moments the Farmer contorted and

twisted, his hands reaching upward into the heavens.

Then the flames died.

Gismay's arms dropped, and the Farmer now lay still and silent.

None of the companions dared to move.

A sudden, deep intake of breath, and Gismay began to cough.

Felgaron rushed to his side, taking the Farmer's hand.

For a moment it was as if Gismay would expel all the air from within him, but the coughing relented and his breathing became steady.

He looked about the room for a moment, almost frantic, before his eyes settled on the Swordsman. He stared for the longest of moments, and then his face fell into a questioning expression.

"Felgaron?"

It was as if he was saying the word for the first time, but the Swordsman nodded reassuringly.

"Yes," he said softly, "I am here. As are we all."

Gismay stared at the Swordsman for a moment longer, then gingerly looked around the room. His eyes did their best to focus on the details about him. Cam marvelled that the man could take any of it in at all after his ordeal.

The Farmer's gaze now met his, and then that of Sonia and Dunwald. He nodded slowly, drinking in the scene.

"The Bereun?" he asked quickly, the memory suddenly coming back to him.

"You did well, Gismay," Dunwald replied calmly, motioning to the corpse at his feet, "for here it lies."

"You saved my life," Sonia breathed, then ran over and threw her arms about him.

For a moment Gismay was startled, but then he returned the embrace.

"My pleasure," came the earnest response.

Sonia released him, then gave him a thankful glance and sat herself on the bed next to him.

"Thank you," Cam whispered, "for everything. I'm... I'm glad Felgaron could help you."

Gismay smiled.

"So am I," he said, a gentle humour to his words, "and I've been very glad to help you and Sonia. Now, I'm whole, and I will continue to be so, if the Seven will it, and I should like to thank you all properly in the light of day. But I'm afraid I can't keep my eyes open much longer."

Felgaron put a hand upon the man's shoulder.

"Then sleep," he said kindly, "your body will need time to heal fully. Even Deldylin cannot complete its work in mere moments. You need, and deserve, a restful slumber."

He turned now to the rest of them.

"As do you all. Tonight has been hard, but you have survived. Sleep well this night, I will keep guard. Tomorrow we shall resume our journey to Beregle."

With that, the Swordsman strode out of the room. Sonia helped Gismay settle himself fully, then kissed him on the forehead before dragging herself back into her own bed and falling asleep almost immediately.

Dunwald hauled the body of the Bereun out of the room, no doubt so that he and Felgaron could dispose of it. Cam had offered to help, but the Captain had placed a hand on each of Cam's shoulders and gently urged him into one of the bunks.

Cam watched him complete the grisly task, then mechanically wrapped the furs about him, felt his head hit the simple pillow beneath it, and he knew no more.

Chapter Ten

Glacier Pass

The dreamless landscape that haunted Cam through the long struggle of his sleep did not allow him the rest that he needed. When the dawn came, far too quickly for his liking, he hauled himself to his feet and stretched.

He looked over at Gismay's bed against the wall opposite him, and he saw the Farmer lying still. For a moment Cam focussed his eyes on the furs that covered him, checking for the reassuring up and down movement of his breathing.

It was there, steady and deep.

On the floor before Gismay's bed lay Sonia, having moved herself closer to him during the night. She, too, was peaceful, and Cam smiled at the sight.

Dunwald stepped through the door into room. Cam motioned that he should be quiet, lest he wake their companions before it was necessary. Dunwald nodded his understanding, then beckoned Cam to follow him out into the main room.

Here, the Captain handed Cam a bowl of fresh broth and another portion of the doughy bread.

"How fare you?" Dunwald asked.

Cam nodded, taking a spoonful of the broth.

"I'll keep," he said simply.

The Captain placed a hand upon his shoulder.

"Of that I have no doubt," he replied, "for you have survived far more than would be expected of you. Especially given that our world is new to you."

They looked up to see Felgaron stepping in from the

plateau outside.

"The weather has changed," he said grimly, "it is colder."

He looked at the two of them.

"Are we rested?"

"Indeed we are," Dunwald replied, "and Sonia and Gismay sleep still. Even though haste is needed, I did not have the heart to wake them."

The Swordsman nodded, then busied himself with his pack.

"We can give them half an hour more," he said, "then we must make way. The path will tough, and if the weather is worsening I want as many miles under our belts as is possible."

The rest of the promised half hour was spent breaking their makeshift camp. When the time came, Cam gently woke both Sonia and Gismay then, after making sure the Farmer was indeed able to stand, Cam helped him through to the main room.

Once he and Sonia were breakfasted, the company stepped out onto the plateau outside the Guard House.

"We will make all haste that we can," Felgaron was saying, "for our goal is still many miles away and we are about to embark on the most perilous part of our journey."

"What peril do you speak of?" Dunwald asked, a concerned tone in his voice.

"Given the events of last night, we must move more quickly even than I had anticipated," the Swordsman said, "therefore we will go west, and approach Beregle from the south. Across the Glacier Pass."

These last words were said slowly and with such a weight that even Cam picked up on their significance, though he did not truly know what they meant.

"You would lead us to such a place?" Dunwald breathed. "Few men have ever dared cross that gorge in such a season as this one, and even fewer have lived to tell the tale! Wherefore is this madness called upon?"

"It is the most direct and secretive route to Beregle. There will be no patrols or guards to avoid, nor will there be any other travellers using that road. Such times call for such chances to be taken."

"But the very air will freeze us half to death," the Captain responded vehemently, "and that is without the snow and freezing winds!"

"If we can reach the edge of the pass before sunrise tomorrow then we have hope!" the Swordsman countered. "The seasons may move against us, but we can walk faster than they change. If the days were not so desperate I would not ask such a thing of any of you. But further argument will not help our cause.

"Friend Gismay," he continued, ignoring Dunwald's attempt to question him once more, "how fare you? Can you walk?"

The Farmer looked at him honestly.

"I'd probably need another day's rest to be of full use to you. That Deldylin stuff is good, but it's no substitute for a warm bed. But I can certainly keep up with you, provided I have help and we aren't doing too much mountaineering."

The Swordsman nodded.

"Good. I will do what I can to choose paths that are suitable, but this will be a hard march. Let us delay no longer. Come."

With that, he turned on his heels and stalked off. The companions looked at each other, then began to follow him. Cam gladly took Gismay upon his shoulder; after everything the Farmer had done for them, the least he could do was make sure he stood on his own two feet.

The path Felgaron now led them along wound steeply down, cutting across the mountainside back and forth. It had begun its descent by delving behind the rocks into which the Guard House had been built and scything into the mountain itself, then turning left and leading them out onto a narrow cleft below the level of the plateau.

From here it clung to the rock face and curled about itself on its way to the rocky floor some two hundred feet further down. Cam did not dare look in case he faltered and lost his grip on Gismay.

Their descent was hard; the rain from the previous day had loosened many of the stones and moisture still clung to the clay path, meaning that slipping, or worse, became a real danger to the company.

Still Felgaron pressed his pace as fast as he dared, and still they followed him without question or argument. They did not speak much, for all their energy was now concentrated on reaching Glacier Pass.

Finally, the path levelled out gracefully to meet the craggy, undulating surface of the valley floor that Cam had glimpsed from above the previous evening, and their treacherous descent came to an end.

Cam's eyes caught something to his left, hanging loosely over the top of a rock that jutted out from the ground.

The contorted corpse of the Bereun that he had killed greeted them as they left the scene, one final grim reminder of the terrible events of the night before.

The thing had been utterly destroyed by its fall, and the odour of flesh only hours dead wafted gently to them on the breeze.

Felgaron called a halt, then went over and examined the thing. When he returned, his jerkin and arms were covered in the thick maroon of blood. Not seeming to acknowledge what he had done, he came to Cam and pressed something into his hand.

The dagger he had lost.

"Thanks," Cam breathed, not knowing what else to say.

"Come," the Swordsman said in a low voice, "we must keep moving. We rest at noonsun, and that is many hours away yet."

Cam looked down at the dagger; it was stained with blood.

A little under a fortnight ago he had been an actor, just trying to make his way in the world. Now he was stuck at the bottom of a valley, holding a dagger, being led by a man he was not sure he trusted towards some place called Glacier Pass that another man he did not fully trust said might kill them.

His thoughts took him back to the time before all of this, back to Welverleigh and Edgeborough. What was going on there right now?

His mother would be utterly frantic. Nearly two weeks without sign or word from her son? The Police would be involved, and he might even be on the news, he mused darkly.

And what about Sonia? What would Mark and Ellen say if he did not get her back to them in one piece? What would they say even if he did? None of them would ever believe what had transpired! And what if she never got home?

What if neither of them ever got home?

These dark thoughts continued burning holes into his mind as Cam turned and followed Felgaron, Gismay doing all he could to maintain the pace that was being set.

Their trek across the valley floor was long and tough. Felgaron seemed to have ignored the main path, which had turned away northward soon after they had entered the valley, and followed smaller, less well trodden ways that cut through the rocks in the direction that they needed to go.

The land about them began to change, and the rocks gave way to more and more patches of grass and marshland. Eventually they came to a halt beside a stream, just long enough to eat some Hocram and refill their flasks with water.

Here Felgaron examined Gismay once more, ensuring that the Farmer had not undone any of the healing by exerting himself. Gismay professed that he was feeling as fine as could be expected, and that he would be no more of a burden to the party than he had been already. After the Farmer had reluctantly accepted a small dose of Hocliquor, Felgaron seemed satisfied and their break had run its course.

Their first task was to ford the stream.

The water was shallow but cold and swiftly flowing. It bit through Cam's thick fur boots, yet miraculously they managed to keep his feet dry.

Once they were all on the far shore they began another

march across the valley. After an hour or so, they finally found the path again. Felgaron explained that it would now head north and join the route of the stream they had crossed, and then eventually reach some place called High Top Fort before delving southward through a different range of mountains to come at Beregle from the north.

"If such haste were not needed," he had explained, "then this is the path I would have chosen to reach Beregle. But that circuitous route would slow us greatly, and take us within sight of Eismeer's northern patrols. We must cling to secrecy for as long as we may."

The rest of the day blurred into yet another long march for Cam, the company trudging relentlessly into the ever deepening gloom ahead of them.

Their path now turned upward into the mountains that reared ahead of them. All about them the mountain through which the path cut its way seemed to climb higher and higher, enclosing them within the stern, grey rock.

In truth, the path was no more narrow than any of the other mountain passes they had taken to reach this point of their journey, yet it felt as if the mountain was waiting for its moment to devour them.

For what felt like an age they forged onward, fatigue and aching muscles starting to claim each of them one by one. Yet somehow they managed to follow Felgaron's arduous pace.

The path at last began to level out as the sun made its final blaze across the eastward sky behind them, yet even when it had fallen beyond the horizon Felgaron did not allow them to stop. It was clear that while any light lingered he was going to forge ahead, and for a further hour he pressed the company on.

The sky was almost as black as the rock about them and the company mere passing shadows against the gloom when Felgaron finally allowed them to rest at a turn in the path.

The company gathered themselves along the outside wall of the curve and began to settle into camp. Cam found a dark, shallow sleep that passed blearily across his mind for what seemed little more than mere seconds until Felgaron woke he and the rest of the company to continue their sojourn.

The sun was not yet on the rise, and a thick, swirling mist had descended over the mountain path, accompanied by a bitter and harsh wind. The meagre fire that Dunwald had managed to light the previous night had been scattered, the greys and whites of the ashes twisting in the air, tainting everything in their path.

"If we reach the Glacier Pass before sunrise," Felgaron was saying, "we may yet have a chance to cross that terrible ravine by eventide. We cannot risk being caught in the freezing night that engulfs that place."

Half an hour later the small company was making its way into the fog.

Their going was slower than the previous day, hampered by tired and aching limbs and dimmed eyesight. Cam squinted hard to distinguish the outline of the rocks and mountains above them through the white broil, his eyes stinging with cold as he did so.

The weight of the Farmer upon his left shoulder seemed even heavier than before, and Gismay was not as mobile as he had been. Even Dunwald, who had been as strong as Felgaron up to this point, was showing worrying signs of fatigue; his steps were a little less certain and his head hung slightly lower, towards his chest.

Cam reflected that it was a miracle he and Sonia had made it this far at all, let alone kept the pace that was being set for them.

The dawn was approaching fast, the light struggling through the white wall of fog before them, yet the air was not warming. Indeed, Cam felt certain that it had actually become cooler since their march began. He was working hard just to stand up, using every ounce of strength and resolve to put one foot in front of the other; he should have been bathed in sweat with the effort, yet his skin was dry.

His lungs ached with the frozen air that was being dragged in and out of them, and the path beneath his feet had started to become slick; a treacherous film of ice forming over it.

He felt himself shiver against the air and shook his head.

"This is insanity!" he hissed.

"I don't disagree with you," Gismay sighed in response next to him, "and yet I have never seen Felgaron proven foolish in any endeavour."

"There's a first time for everything..."

Gismay was about to respond, but they were interrupted as Felgaron signalled for them to halt.

The Swordsman's gaze held itself into the fog beyond. Dunwald and Sonia gingerly took their places next to him and followed his gaze. Cam pulled himself and Gismay alongside them then felt the gentle pressure of Felgaron's arm across his chest, stopping him from going further forward.

Cam looked about him, trying to discover the reason for their pause.

Then he looked at the ground beneath his feet.

His toes hung over the edge of a tall cliff. If Felgaron had not stopped him, Cam might have wandered aimlessly forward and sent both himself and Gismay to their deaths.

Beneath the white of the fog lay the unmistakeable grey-blue tinge of ice. Cam's eyes followed it to the feet of another mountain range, rising in the distance through the slowly lifting broil. To his left and right the ice streaked out to the horizon. The wind that rushed up from the valley floor to meet them was colder than anything Cam had ever endured or experienced.

So this was Glacier Pass.

"I'd heard the stories," Gismay panted, "but never have I laid eyes upon it! How can we hope to breach such a barrier?"

"We will breach it," Felgaron answered resolutely, "and we must start without delay. The air now is as warm as it will ever get."

He delved into the packs and pulled out all of the spare blankets he had. Dunwald did the same.

"Wrap these about you," he ordered, thrusting the things at Cam.

“We'll freeze to death down there before we've gone a mile!” Cam cried.

“We will not,” the Swordsman pressed, “the journey will be difficult, and not without danger, but it will not prove fatal.”

He now knelt and retrieved his own blanket from his pack and wrapped the thing about his midriff and secured it with his belt. Gismay made to follow this example, but Cam stopped him and completed the task himself to save the Farmer any discomfort. He then secured his own blanket around him, as Sonia did the same.

Soon the small band were carefully negotiating the twisting path to the valley floor, every second filled with yet more numbing cold. The stones upon which they walked were slick with ice and cracks, and even Felgaron was not as sure upon his feet here.

Cam watched his steps as carefully as he could, the burden of Gismay upon his shoulders tuning his senses. Though the wind bit hard beneath his cloak and blanket, his hands held Gismay's arms as tightly as his fragile strength would allow him.

Felgaron pushed them on for what felt like days, and the only reward for their progress was the moment when they finally reached the bottom of the path and stood on the edge of the Glacier. The endless cold swirled about them, and the ever-present threat of a blizzard grew more foreboding as Cam looked out ahead of him. At this point the valley would be no more than a few miles wide, but the far side of it was obscured from their sight.

“We have done well,” Felgaron said, “to have come so far by noonsun is no small feat at all.”

“Noonsun?” Sonia exclaimed. “It's got to be later than that surely? It's dark!”

“It is dark,” Felgaron agreed, “for even the high sun will not penetrate the clouds here. But it is no later than noonsun. We shall rest here for a short while. Then we will begin to cross the valley. Stay as warm as you can, for I fear no fire will hold in this place.”

After helping Gismay to a comfortable spot, Cam sat himself against the rock they had just walked down and wrapped his cloak about him.

He could feel his eyelids becoming heavy and threatening to plunge him into darkness. He did not want to sleep, but he was so tired after the relentless march of the last few days that he could not hold himself up for long. He felt his head bob forward slowly, and his eyes blinked.

When they opened again he saw the face of Dunwald in front of him, a hand upon his shoulder.

“It is nearly time to continue,” the Captain said softly, “gather your things.”

Cam slowly hauled himself to his feet. The wind billowed into his face, freezing his bones with a chill they had never known before. Shielding his eyes against it, he looked about him and saw Felgaron stood a few yards away from the camp, staring out into the snowbound wilderness.

Cam doubted it would do him any good, for the weather had clamped in about them; the clouds above them had shifted from a white-grey shroud to a brooding charcoal that seemed somehow lower, almost dangerous.

Gismay's hand placed itself gently on Cam's shoulder.

“You are troubled, friend Cam?”

Cam made a non-committal noise.

“It's nothing,” he sighed dismissively, “just thinking. How are you holding up?”

“Don't worry about me, friend,” he said softly, “I'm alive and whole. Felgaron has seen to that, not to mention Deldylin's potency.”

Cam almost laughed at the man's humility.

“Gismay, it's a miracle you can stand! Why are you pushing yourself like this?”

Gismay looked at him with a stern yet friendly expression.

“There are some causes that are too important for anything to stop men pursuing them. What we're doing is one of them. Besides, I promised you back at my farm that I would do all I could to help get you and Sonia home, and I meant it."

"Thank you," Cam said quietly, "if there's ever a chance for me to repay you, though I'm not sure how, I will. I promise."

Gismay smiled once more.

"There's nothing to repay," he said simply.

The rest of the day passed without Cam even noticing. His body was numb to the cold and the wind and the gently falling snow, and his only thought was of the next step.

The company forced their way across the uneven surface of the glacier, ever watchful for crevasses that threatened to devour them after one false step. Every so often a great, deep cracking sound would rumble beneath them, causing them to pause and ensure that the ice upon which they stood was not about to collapse. The snow blinded their eyes and the cold numbed their limbs, with the wind threatening ever to knock them off their feet and send them skidding into the white oblivion that now surrounded them.

When Felgaron called them all in together to pass around the flask of mead, Cam could not guess how long they had been walking. As he cast his eyes around the small huddle, the faces that looked back at him were red-cheeked and drawn. All of them were panting against the freezing wind that had battered them, and their eyebrows and beards had snow and ice clinging to them.

Once this moment of warmth had been spent, they all turned their faces to the wind once more and pressed on.

Cam kept his head down for much of this second march, partly to shield his eyes from the snow but also to watch exactly where he and Gismay were stepping. Each of those steps was an act of defiance against the weather, a refusal to give in to the utterly inhospitable conditions that they found themselves having to endure.

Such was the concentration and resolve required to keep going, by the time Cam next looked up the mountains that had been lost in the mists were now looming down over them, perhaps another half a mile distant.

A feeling of unbridled joy swelled in Cam.

They had done it! Quite how they had managed it he could not guess, but they had crossed the Glacier Pass and had survived! Though, even now, Cam could feel the air about him gradually getting even colder than it had been throughout the rest of the day.

With one final push the group managed to make it into the shelter of the northern face of the valley and Felgaron allowed them to rest. He then went to scout ahead and ensure they were not in any immediate danger. The path he took was a steep climb that wound its way dangerously across the rock before them that was otherwise sheer.

While Dunwald attended to feeding them with what little survived of their supplies, Cam rested Gismay against the walls of a shallow hollow at the base of the rock wall, and then took a deep breath and stepped over to Sonia.

"You OK?" he asked, cautiously.

"Yeah," she sighed, "I'll keep. Bit tired, obviously. You?"

Cam nodded.

"Yeah, yeah. You know how it is."

A moment of silence passed between them, and neither quite knew what to do as it did so.

"Look," Cam began, "I'm sorry about the other day. When I shouted at you. I just... I don't have any excuses."

Sonia placed a hand on his shoulder.

"It's been a lot," she said, "I'm not going to pretend you didn't hurt me, but I get it. It's gone. Let's leave it there, shall we?"

The relief that washed over Cam was palpable. He embraced Sonia tightly.

"Thank you," he said into her shoulder, "for everything. I wouldn't have made it this far without you."

Sonia pulled back and smiled at him.

"I know."

Cam was about to laugh, but they were roused by the sound of a blade being drawn from a scabbard.

Looking up, Cam saw Dunwald, sword in hand, facing into the gathering gloom that was falling across the valley. Gismay was watching intently from his own vantage point also. There was no sign of Felgaron's return.

Cam instinctively drew his own dagger.

"Go to Gismay," he whispered to Sonia, who nodded, then he stepped next to Dunwald.

"Trouble?" he hissed.

The Captain did not look at him as he answered, keeping his vigil outward and facing the danger.

"I know not. I feel as though we have been followed for many miles now, though Felgaron did not react so I did not allow myself to believe it. He does not miss things such as this."

Cam glanced between the man and the snow-filled gloom ahead.

"But you think he's missed something this time?"

Dunwald nodded slowly.

"Stay back, for any who can track us through this are skilled. More so than most men. We will have a real fight if there is more than one of them."

Cam took two steps back from Dunwald, positioning himself between the danger and Sonia. Moments measured only by the heart beats in his ears passed.

Then, like a spectre, a figure appeared through the gloom. His sword was drawn and his cloak billowed about him as he trudged into view. As soon as he was close enough to make out any details, Cam recognised the man.

"Lekkon?" Dunwald called in shock. "I did not think to find you this far north."

"Nor I you, Captain Dunwald." Lekkon's voice carried easily through the night. The tone was uneasy, almost threatening.

"I would ask what you are doing here, Captain, but I fear that your answer would only be a falsehood."

Dunwald lowered his blade, though did not sheathe it.

"I do not understand your meaning, Lieutenant. I have

been tracking these traitors and have finally caught up with them. The boy here was about to resist me, but I feel he will think better of it now that you are here."

Dunwald turned and faced Cam, raising his sword.

The bastard! Cam saw it now! He was going to turn them all in to save his own skin! After all they had endured together, he would turn on them so quickly?

But then the Captain winked at him and smiled.

"As I said," Lekkon called back, "a falsehood. Captain Dunwald, I am here to place all of you under arrest. By order of the Lord Fohenk, Ruler of these lands, you will accompany me to Eismeer to face the Lord's Justice. If you will not follow willingly, then I have orders to cut you down where you stand."

Dunwald's smile lowered a little, a more dangerous expression upon his face now.

"You believe you can take all of us, Lekkon? You are well trained, but not that well."

Now a smile twisted across Lekkon's features as he surveyed the company before him.

"I see only one of you with a sword, and I doubt even you have the strength to fight after your journey."

Dunwald's eyes met Cam's once again.

"Let us see..."

Without warning, Dunwald swivelled on the spot and brought his blade crashing through the air. Lekkon, however, was wise to it and avoided the blow with ease.

While Dunwald reeled from his exertions, the soldier kicked him hard in the midriff, then once more in the head as he fell.

Dunwald was out cold.

Gismay cried out, but Lekkon's eyes were now already locked upon Cam, sword drawn and pointed squarely at his chest.

Cam backed away, raising his dagger in front of him instinctively. Lekkon laughed, a hollow sound that was easily lost in the night air.

"Do you know how to use that boy? Don't be a fool, drop it and come quietly. Lord Fohenk wishes to speak to you."

"I don't think so," Cam said uncertainly, playing for time and slowly stepping backwards, "we're not exactly friends."

Lekkon laughed again, more heartily this time.

"You have spirit, I will give you that. But that will not save you. If you resist I have orders to drag you back with me in chains. You will be left alive, but only as an example for those who defy Lord Fohenk. This is not my Lord's wish, but he sees no alternative if you do not come with me."

"And what about the others? If I go with you, what happens to them?"

Lekkon grinned evilly.

"My only orders are to bring you back alive, boy."

Cam's was desperately trying to think of something, anything to get out of this situation.

"Sorry," he heard himself say amidst the clamour of his thoughts, "no deal. Promise me their safety and I'll go, but not before."

He pointed the dagger more firmly in Lekkon's direction, but the Soldier did not pay it any heed.

"Ah, you fancy yourself the hero?" he sneered. "That is well. It would have been so dull if you had come without at least being of some sport..."

Cam saw the sword swing before he knew what was going on, and dived out of the way in plenty of time. Shocked at his own speed, he stared at the blade in terrified awe. Lekkon glared at him, dumbfounded that he had missed.

Roaring with anger, the Soldier launched himself at Cam once more. Again, Cam saw the blow coming almost before Lekkon had moved, and rolled smartly out of the way, unharmed and clear of danger.

Another strike, and once again Cam rolled to safety. Lekkon, now positively foaming at the mouth with rage, roared once more, but his stroke was truly wild and ill-aimed.

Cam avoided it with no difficulty but, in his haste, rolled

into the valley wall. His head clattered hard into the ancient, frozen stone, dazing him.

He felt Lekkon's form approaching him. The soldier was breathing heavily but Cam heard the remnants of a laugh forcing its way through the frustration of the man.

"It seems your luck has run out, boy," he snarled, and raised his sword aloft.

Cam held his dagger limply out in front of him, the last line of defence against the death blow that was coming.

He closed his eyes and waited.

From nowhere, a flash of white light illuminated the camp. Both recoiled from it, covering their eyes against the glare. It blazed for a moment, then receded.

Blinking, Cam opened his eyes and looked about him.

The world had changed, and what he now saw came straight from his nightmares.

The ground was ash and the mountains had crumbled to dust. Thick, broiling smoke billowed out of huge crevasses that had opened in the hellish landscape, and the sky was lost behind the impenetrable plume. All about him there was tremendous heat, it threatened to peel his very skin away and his vision shook in the radiance of it. After a moment, he realised this was the very pass he had been stood in mere moments ago.

However, between him and the hell-scape was a small yet piercingly bright ball of white light. It floated and danced before his eyes, following every move he made with his head.

"What the hell..?" he panted, disbelieving his own eyes.

A voice suddenly spoke in his head.

This is why you are here.

"What? What do you mean?"

This is why you cannot be allowed to die. Why you have been saved.

Cam blinked once more.

"Saved? By who?"

Movement in front of him raised Cam's vision. One of the fissures had opened wider and now he watched in horror as hundreds, no thousands, of 'things' clambered menacingly out of it and onto the ashen ground. They had black faces and hideous, deformed, evil-looking bodies.

He almost recognised them.

“What the hell is this?” he breathed.

This is what you must prevent.

Cam tried to take in the sheer scale of the devastation that was in front of him, but even with it so starkly presented his mind could not comprehend it.

“Me? How?”

Through whatever means possible.

Turning his eyes away from the horrific landscape, Cam looked about him and tried to find the source of the voice.

“Why me?” he pleaded to the Light as it began to dance in front of him.

It is your part to play.

“How can I be a part of any this?” Cam protested.

Your guide will tell you, when the time is right.

“My guide? You mean Felgaron?”

This time there was no answer; the Light simply floated before him, bobbing slightly.

Cam once more looked out over the destruction before him. His eyes locked on the fissure that had formed and the legions of foul creatures continuing to spew from it.

“I know those things,” he said, “they were in a dream I had.”

You are known to them as well.

One of them turned and saw him. Red eyes grasped his mind and would not let him look away. A wicked grin spread across the things face and it licked its lips, bearing its fangs at Cam as it did so.

Behold! War comes, terrible and bloody. You cannot escape it.

“But I'm not a soldier! I'm not even from here!” Cam retorted.

You must play your part. We all must.

"I don't even know what the hell is going on!"

Then learn!

A shadow fell across the thing as it snarled at him, and indeed across the entire scene. The air grew hotter and closer, and a terrific, intense feeling of menacing danger came over Cam. There was something else. Something greater. The cause of all this destruction.

Then he saw it.

Away on the horizon there now loomed a black mass, larger that anything Cam could ever have imagined. It was taller than the mountains it had felled, reaching the broiling mass that now covered the sky as it surveyed the total destruction that lay before it. The thing let out an ungodly noise. It might have been laughing, but the sound was harsh and evil.

Helrhûn, Lord of the Seventh. By some called The Dark Power, The Black King, The Great Evil.

"You want me to fight that?" he exclaimed.

No such victory can be won. This is not your true enemy.

Cam looked at the figure next to him, terrified.

"Then who is?"

Rhogân.

The ball of light blinked out of existence, engulfing him in darkness. He immediately felt that he was alone.

"Wait! Don't go!"

His voice echoed infinitely into the void.

We will meet again. I will be watching.

Once more there was silence, utter and total. Cam sighed and closed his eyes, at a loss.

When he opened his eyes again, he found himself transported once more.

Where he was he had no idea, but there was the sound of gentle waves lapping upon a shore. He looked to his feet and saw that there was indeed sand beneath them, but it was coloured with deep blue, purple, and black.

The atmosphere was odd; a green half-light, as if his eyes were viewing the world through the holes in cloth, hung over the scene, and a very strange tingling sensation was ever against his skin.

The beach rose swiftly from the dark ocean to meet rocky outcrops some fifty yards ahead of him, and beyond those Cam saw the outline of a huge, sheer-faced mountain rising into the thick, green-black broil of cloud that filled the sky, its peak hidden from view.

Cam was about to take a step forward when, out of the dark of the outcrops, there came a figure. For a moment he could not focus on it properly, but soon his eyes traced an outline they knew only too well.

It was the figure from the Tower.

Instinctively Cam stepped back, his right foot splashing into the seawater behind him. Before he could take a second step, however, a burning pain ran up his right leg. Looking down, he saw dark veins rising from the water. He was paralysed, unable to take his foot out of the stuff.

Frantic, he looked back at the figure and saw that it was almost on him.

Kyyyyynsssssaaaaaa...

The horrible voice that he had hoped never to hear again rang inside his mind, stopping all thought. He just managed to hold onto himself enough to keep trying to free himself from the dark waters, but it was never going to be enough.

KYNSA!

The voice exploded in his mind and Cam felt himself knocked backwards by an invisible force. He fell towards the dark water, but there was no splash.

He felt the shocking sensation of the cold beneath him again.

Looking up, he found himself back in Glacier Pass as he had known it. His head was swimming, and he barely held himself up out of the snow long enough to see anything about him.

Had he been able to focus, Cam would have seen that the small orb of Light was now floating in front of Lekkon's face.

"I did not think it was possible," the Soldier saying, his voice thick with emotion.

Cam felt sick. His head was swimming.

"I am yours to command!" Lekkon called out into the frozen air.

At the very uttering of his words the atmosphere changed. Cam could feel a strange vibration, a deep, low hum at the very edge of his perception. It only made his head feel even more strange.

He managed to collect himself enough to look at Lekkon. The man was staring at him, a look of fearful awe upon his face.

"I understand," he was saying, but to whom Cam could not tell.

The orb of Light flashed once more, then twinkled out of existence.

Lekkon closed his eyes and, as if compelled, drew his sword and threw it towards Cam. It was not an aggressive action, more one of surrender. The weapon landed harmlessly in the snow a few feet away from him.

"The Seven have indeed smiled upon you," Lekkon called, a strange note in his voice, "I will trouble you no longer. Take my sword. Play the part that I could not."

With that, the man closed his eyes and knelt, unmoving.

Cam hardly dared to move. What the hell was going on?

Take it. You will need it in the days to come.

"Why?" Cam breathed softly, his head becoming heavier.

He felt his body begin to fall to one side.

A figure stepped into his view and stood before Lekkon's form. The man did not notice it, and if he did he made no move or sign.

It held a curved sword in its hand, the crescent-shaped blade glinting in the darkness.

Cam could not fight his head any longer. He allowed himself to fall back into the snow, and closed his eyes.

The last thing he saw as the darkness came was the figure raise its sword, then bring it whistling down toward Lekkon.

Then there was darkness.

Chapter Eleven

The Western Lands

The Boardwalks, or the 'City on the Water' as some called it, had a long and chequered history. It was originally built as a safe haven for refugees fleeing from the terrible wars in the south of Rhydariel when the then Lord of Eismeer, Galmorn, ordered that his men would join with the men of Nendolus in their war against the Bakslá.

Nendolus was an island in the Finsae, the Greater Lake, in western Rhydariel. The people who lived there were an ancient, mystical race who cared little for the world around them, but Galmorn had persisted in aiding them in all their trials and tribulations to win their favour.

When word reached him of that the island was besieged by the Bakslá, he spared no time in pledging his men to their cause. How the war had started was never truly known; the men of Nendolus would not say what had angered the Bakslá, only that it had been the Bakslá who had started the war.

Galmorn's greatest General, one Ebrahir, said that his pursuit of the Nendolusian's favour was folly and refused to support the war. This decision caused two factions to appear; those that supported Lord Galmorn and those who supported General Ebrahir - The Ebrahiim.

Galmorn ordered that all who opposed him were thrown from the Kingdom and exiled. He ordered the death of Ebrahir, but Ebrahiim forces managed to rescue their General and escape westward.

Pursued by their own kin, the Ebrahiim had very little choice but to go into hiding in the mountains and wait for their moment to escape. Ebrahir was hailed as a hero for saving many sons of Eismeer, though their lives were hard for many years.

The war with the Bakslá ended in a bitter victory for Galmorn; his forces had defeated the enemy but very few of the people of Nendolus had survived the ordeal. The island now had less than one hundred inhabitants. Galmorn ordered his troops back to Eismeer, leaving a small garrison to defend the island in case of further attacks.

Meanwhile the Ebrahiim had taken their chance and crossed the River Lun in search of a new home. When they were confronted by Galmorn's returning troops many feared the worst, only to find that Galmorn did not order their immediate execution. He said simply that the Nendolusians had a power greater than any dared imagine and that this would serve his revenge far better than any torment he could inflict upon them.

The Nendolusians saw that he was right.

From the shores of the Lesser Lake, Ebrahir spied a small, rocky island, barely a quarter of a mile wide. In his hubris he ignored the proximity to the Nendolusians – a people he now believed to be of little concern to anyone – and declared that this island would be the new home of the Ebrahiim.

So began the construction of The Boardwalks.

Working as quickly as they could, the Ebrahiim built both on the lake shore and the rocks. From the shore they began to construct the great Walk that would eventually serve as the only entrance to their new city, and the rock became home to the Great Hall of Ebrahir - Barrandel. The word meant 'house of hope' in their language, and it stood proudly as the beacon to all those who believed Ebrahir to be righteous

All the while the remaining Nendolusians watched, waiting for their time to strike. They knew that using what little of their powers they could still command would consume them, but they were ready to sacrifice that much to bring justice to Ebrahir; the man who had abandoned his own people, leaving both the Eismen and the Nendolusians to face their fate alone.

In a little under a year the Walk was complete, with more people coming everyday to join this new city. Ebrahir pronounced that any who wished to live in freedom away from Galmorn the Warmonger, as he named him, could join his people in their new home.

This was a time of great celebration and hope, and the newly formed people of Barrandel revelled and drank in their merriment, heedless of the cares of the outside world. They finally had a King who would not simply lead them into war after war, searching for any political foothold he could find. King Ebrahir would usher in a time of peace.

It was on the evening of Ebrahir's coronation, when he was to officially be granted the title of King of the Boardwalks, that the Nendolusians chose to strike.

They stormed Barrandel. The revellers cowered as they spoke words of an ancient language, bringing forth the power of the earth itself to engulf Ebrahir in a cage of flames. They said that he must watch the world he had created, the world he had let take shape with his decision not to aid their people, for all eternity. Thus was Ebrahir cursed, doomed to live forever; to watch his kin and bloodline perish while he lived on to see the ends of time itself.

Then, their revenge complete, the Nendolusians used the final ounces of their power to engulf their island home in thick, dark mists, warning that any mortal who dared set foot on their land would be struck down in the same terrible manner. And they had stayed ever since, shrouded in legend and hushed whispers of fear.

Still, nearly six thousand years later, no-one had braved the mists of Nendolus lest the curse be placed upon them. And still, with his mind all but unravelled from the torture of seeing his entire bloodline pass before his eyes, Ebrahir lived on. His court had been granted to his nephew Aldamir, for the King had no heir, and it was his bloodline that now took the Royal Throne.

Barrandel had seen many battles since those fateful days,

yet no army had ever managed to breach the City on the Water. Its soldiers were renowned for their spirit and loyalty, and the banner of Ebrahir became well respected and even feared throughout Rhydariel. Yet the golden days of Aldamir's bloodline soon drew to a close; many lesser sons had been crowned King of the Boardwalks and for several generations they had posed no threat to Eismeer, their oldest foe.

Then had come King Lenandur, the Warrior King. Lenandur restored hope and vigour into his subjects, and for his thirty year reign there were many glorious battles with, and victories over, the Eismen, and for a time Eismeer was forced to retreat. These years of peace and prosperity were a true golden age for the Boardwalks.

Alas, Lenandur would meet his end fighting the greatest battle of their long war.

The two armies, after a long period of skirmishes and small, petty encounters, finally clashed in earnest upon the Felieren Plains, the great scrub-lands to the west of Eismeer. A pitched battle cost both sides many men, but it was in the final strokes of the battle that a chance arrow felled Lenandur. The Eismen had only just sounded their retreat and Prince Hedradour had grasped his father's arm to congratulate him on the victory.

In that moment, an arrow pierced Lenandur's heart and he fell into the Princes' arms, his last words being to confer the Throne immediately to his son and to swear that his bloodline would see the end of their war.

For the ten years since that fateful day, King Hedradour had led the Ebrahiim through some of their most turbulent times; Eismeer had once again begun pushing back towards the Boardwalks, whilst the Ebrahiim had simply maintained their borders, unable to take the initiative.

The people of Ebras had placed their hopes in this period of uneasy quiet so that they themselves might regroup and once more carry the fight to Eismeer.

Yet it was none of this that was occupying the mind of Chief Marshall Larin as he looked out of his window on the cold, misty morning that was dawning over the Farn Bridge, the eastern most outpost of Ebras.

It was a small outpost, set up on the only crossing of the River Lun, the great natural barrier that marked their eastern border. It flowed for many miles, running from the foot of the Spine Mountains southward to Archipelagos Sea.

The stone fort was manned by two-hundred and fifty of Ebras' finest warriors, hand picked for the duty by King Hedradour and Larin directly. They were the first line of defence and the last chance of warning should Eismeer decide to press the offensive. Each one of them would give their lives gladly for the defence of their homeland.

Larin knew this well, so much that even a true patriot such as himself felt an especially fierce pride in his heart as he watched them on their patrols. But even this sense of honour and pride could not sway the worry from his mind on that morning.

The period of quiet, calming peace had gone on for nearly three months now, far longer than anything he had ever known. The Eismen forces had not encroached on their territory, nor even been seen, for all that time. This showed great promise that this uneasy peace would last, but it still troubled him.

He had sent out a small scouting party to see if all was well three days ago, they were due to return that day. From the moment he had woken he had kept his eyes on the horizon, desperately searching for some indication of their impending arrival, but the dawn revealed only the silver-grey mist.

Shaking himself, Larin pulled his gaze away from the shrouded distance and took a long gulp of Wattemead – a warming mixture of alcohol and spices – and began to put on his armour.

His station afforded him the greatest work of the smiths of Ebras; his ceremonial armour was etched with golden designs and proudly bearing the great Black Bear of Ebrahir's line, while his battle armour was the finest, lightest and strongest steel, padded with thick leather, the Black Bear once again beaten into the chest. It was a great honour for him to have such gifts at his disposal, but he had none of these trappings with him at Farn Bridge.

Eight years previously, when he first been granted the rank of Captain, he had been assigned to that same outpost with nothing more than a leather hauberk, the only metal upon which was the chain beneath the arms. It was this same style of armour he wore now, feeling in his heart that it was only right he gave himself no more protection than the men under his command.

Finishing the buckles across his chest, he wrapped his sword belt around his waist and, stopping only to collect his brown woollen cloak to protect him against the early morning chill, he stepped out into the mist.

The morning was crisp, the air icy in his lungs as he inhaled, and the mist was beginning even now to lift against the slow encroach of the sun. It was going to be a cool but clear day, probably the last they would see for a while; even though Ebras was warmer than the bordering Eislands, their winters still brought with them a vicious, icy streak that lasted for nearly four months. These would not start in earnest for another two or three weeks yet, but the warning signs were there even now.

Larin was glad of his cloak as he strode out across the wooden structure, gazing eastwards over their enemy's lands. The stone towers that stood either side of the great span were joined at the higher levels by a single wooden bridge. Below this was a stone abutment above a pair of large oaken gates. These were strengthened with thick strands of steel running up and down their length, and the emblem of the Black Bear was once again prevalent in the centre of them.

Either side of this, the towers were octagonal and had many holes and slitted windows through which archers could pick off any enemies that dared to attack the gate.

If they managed somehow to break through this first line of defence, the space immediately behind the towers and the wooden walkway was rife with traps and murder holes, eager to loose their payloads of boiling sand and quick-lime down upon their opponents. The towers also had windows and small openings here for archers and, at the lowest levels, pikemen to impale the insurgents.

After that was the half-mile span across the River Lun itself. This was not a simple crossing, for the walls of the bridge had been fortified to such a degree that an army could only march six-abreast through the gauntlet; the fortifications being in essence stone passageways that were marked at every few yards with yet more gaps for arrows and pikes to be thrust through and, should any army manage to survive this onslaught, the western towers were identical in every way to the eastern entrance.

To top it all the span was built low to the river, barely twenty feet above the waterline, meaning that only ships with the smallest masts could pass beneath it. Most trade vessels from the rest of the Archipelago would drop their cargo at the nearby port of Talas Bay, from there being transported by road to either The Boardwalks herself or Lundang where it could once again be water-borne to the northern settlements.

This arrangement was inconvenient, but King Hedradour had deemed his people's safety and defence far more important than the complaints of merchants; Eismeer had its own port and a strong navy which could not be afforded entrance to the Lesser Lake.

It was across the wooden walkway between the two eastern towers that Larin strode purposefully, acknowledging each of the guards that he passed as they saluted him.

Once he reached the centre of the walkway he paused and looked out eastward, gazing through the silver-grey curtain that had covered the world. He could make out nothing save for the feint outline of trees and shrubs; even the outlines of the Glacier Mountains was hidden from his sight.

There was still no sign of he patrol he was expecting.

Ducking inside the south-eastern tower he began to descend the stairs towards the stone span proper. At the foot of the tower he entered the door into the small barracks that housed the soldiers who protected the eastern entrance.

These were those with the keenest eyesight, while the

fastest riders and runners were housed in the western towers so that they could reach the Boardwalks with news or warnings as swiftly as possible. Looking about the room, he found his second, Captain Maloran, readying himself for his duties.

Maloran was a fine soldier and a perfect candidate for Farn Bridge; he was ruthless and unerring in his devotion to both his King and his men, and he had served as a soldier there for much of his career. He knew the lands about better than anyone save perhaps Larin and Hedradour themselves and, most importantly, he understood the risks and dangers of the post.

With Farn Bridge being the only crossing of the Lun south of Lundang Port itself, it was imperative that it stood strong; if the enemy was so great that it could not be held, Maloran was to order three of his finest riders to make all haste to the Boardwalks using different routes, each taking roughly the same time to travel. This was so that should the enemy desire to stop the message reaching King Hedradour they would have to divide their forces.

But even this precaution did not diminish the need for the riders to gain as much of a head start as was possible. That came down to Maloran and his men. Whatever they faced, however outnumbered they were, they were under orders to fight as hard as they could for as long as they could.

Such was the burden that each of the two-hundred and fifty soldiers that now lined its walls had had to swear the Oath of Passing, granting their lives to the service of Hedradour and acknowledging his right to make their sacrifice for the good of the Boardwalks.

Larin held these thoughts in his head and allowed himself a smile as he sat opposite the Captain and helped himself to a slab of cheese and some bread and butter.

"Good morning, Marshall," Maloran said between mouthfuls of his own breakfast, "How fare you today?"

Larin laughed quietly to himself; Maloran had always been far too lofty in speech for his own good.

"As well as ever," he replied, pouring himself a fresh mug

of Wattemead.

Maloran eyed him over his food and cocked a single eyebrow.

“Oh? Well that is good news, Marshall. I had almost begun to worry about you.”

Larin busied himself with his meal, not looking at the Captain. After a moment or two of silence had passed, Maloran continued.

“There is, I take it, still no word or sign from your scouts?”

Larin shook his head.

“None. But the day is young yet.”

“Indeed it is,” Maloran agreed heartily, "though it is good to see the fact is not wasted on you, Marshall...”

“Captain...” Larin began, a note of caution in his voice, but Maloran continued unabated.

“...for I have heard from my men that you stood on the walkway last night until the moon had set, simply staring eastward. They say your eyes almost succeeded in pulling the horizon closer to us, such was the power of your gaze. And already this morning I have heard that you could hardly tear your eyes away from that direction...”

“Captain Maloran, I would remind you...”

“...if we had not known each other for nearly twenty years, Marshall, and if I did not count on you as a true and dear friend, I would almost be inclined to fear that you were hiding something from me.”

Larin sighed and threw his food down on to his plate, then aimed his gaze squarely at Maloran who returned it stoically.

“Are you finished, Captain?” the Marshall asked forcibly, emphasising Maloran's rank just in case it had been forgotten.

“No,” replied his friend almost cheerfully, “but I do not wish to be flogged more times than I have to be.”

Larin snorted.

“You have already overstepped your bounds. It is only because you are my friend I will overlook it. And... because you are right."

He rubbed his hands across his face and then looked at Maloran once again.

"My scouts are searching for signs of Gismay."

Maloran considered Larin's words for a moment, as if trying to remember something that he long pushed out of his mind.

"Gismay? The Lun Ridge farmer?"

Larin nodded.

"And this is what has been troubling you?" Maloran asked sincerely.

"It is," Larin answered, "for he has never missed a single report, yet now I have heard nothing from him for a fortnight."

Maloran sighed, thinking.

"It is strange," he admitted, "though I do not see why you have troubled yourself so greatly over it. The war is paused, neither us nor the traitorous Eismen are moving. Surely it is natural that he would have little or nothing to report?"

"Aye," sighed Larin, "that is true."

Maloran laughed and continued with his food.

"My dear Marshall, I fear you are worrying over nothing."

"Perhaps," Larin mused, then fell silent and stared into his drink.

Maloran laid a hand upon the Marshall's shoulder.

"Marshall Larin? Friend? There is more to this than you are telling me. What is it that is truly on your mind?"

Larin was about to respond but the sound of a horn, clear and crisp through the cool morning air stopped him. Both men raised their heads and listened. One long sounding, then two short notes, followed by another long drone.

"Your scouts have returned, it seems," Maloran breathed.

Larin nodded and both men rose swiftly from the table and strode out onto the span of the bridge.

There was a commotion from the guards as they busied themselves into defensive positions behind the slowly opening gate; this precaution was to protect the returning scouts should there be any enemies following or chasing them. Larin looked out through the gate and strained his eyes until the figures of three horsemen faded into view out of the haze.

Immediately questions arose in his mind.

As they rode in under the gate they called out to the guards above that no-one had followed them and that they had returned to their own lands unseen. Maloran then gave the order that the soldiers about him stand down and that the gates be closed once more. When this had been done, the riders dismounted and faced their Marshall, saluting him with grim faces.

"Marshall Larin," the Head Rider breathed heavily, "we have returned as you ordered us."

"You have not," Larin replied, "for I sent four riders and only three now stand before me. What of..?"

"Marshall," the Head Rider pressed, interrupting his words, "Gismay is gone. His house has been ransacked. We fear he is either dead or taken prisoner."

Larin stared at the Rider, disbelieving.

"Eismeer?" he heard his voice saying.

"Almost certainly. But there is more. We found evidence of a cart or wagon outside his house. We followed the tracks as best as we could, but they were leading toward the Glacier Gates. We dared not go further, lest Eismeer learn of our presence. We attempted to return immediately, but..."

The Rider fell silent, as if he had lost all courage or will to finish his sentence. He looked back to the other two men he had travelled with, though they simply regarded the stones beneath their feet. Larin and Maloran watched them, waiting for the last of the report.

"Well?" Maloran pressed after a moment had passed.

"It is... strange, Captain," the Rider continued disjointedly. "We did not believe it ourselves at first. Even after Halseth was killed, we could not comprehend..."

"Halseth..." Larin breathed. "Who did this?"

Without a further word, the Rider beckoned to one of his

companions who unhooked a bag from his horse's saddle and came forward. With very little ceremony, he tipped the bag up and dropped a wolf's head onto the stone.

It was only after a chance to stare at it properly that both Maloran and Larin truly realised what they were being shown.

"A Bereun?" Maloran gasped.

The Rider nodded.

"We were ambushed by a pack of them. This one killed Halseth. We avenged him but the rest of the pack was on us swiftly. We fled so that we might deliver our message as you had commanded us. The pack numbered nearly fifty. Perhaps sixty. I have never seen such a gathering of wolves of any kind, let alone these creatures..."

Larin stared at the head for a moment longer then turned from the sight, as if denouncing it. He shook his head then looked in turn at all the faces gathered about him. They would look to him for answers, but he had nothing to offer them.

"I had heard odd reports, some mentioning that one or two of these creatures may have been spotted amongst the foothills of the Glaciers and the Spines," Maloran breathed through his shock, "but I did not believe them. A pack of sixty, you say?"

He looked now at the Rider.

"Did they follow you?"

The Rider shook his head.

"I do not believe so."

Larin closed his eyes and sighed. There was only one thing to be done.

"You and your companions shall rest," he said, addressing the Rider. "You have done more than was asked of you, for that you and your men will be rewarded. Halseth's name shall be written amongst the Tomes of the Lost. He was a good man, and will be fiercely missed. The rest of you return to your duties. Captain Maloran, if I may?"

Larin gestured for the Captain to follow him towards the western towers as the men did as he had bid them. They walked silently for many moments as Larin led him across the half-mile span. After perhaps twenty steps the Marshall stopped and brought Maloran close to him and spoke conspiratorially.

"Prepare the fastest horse you have here, Captain. I need it saddled and ready to leave as soon as can be arranged. Then I want you to double your patrols and run extra drills. I want your men ready."

Maloran looked at him, and earnest and sincere worry crossing his face.

"Ready? For what?"

Larin looked at the Captain, a thousand dark and terrible thoughts filling his head.

"Anything. I must speak with Araht, then return to our King. If you see or hear anything unusual, send word to the Boardwalks immediately, even if it seems unimportant. Stay vigilant, Captain."

Maloran saluted him.

"Of course Marshall. I shall send for you when your horse is ready."

Larin watched as the Captain went off to the western towers to make the preparations he had asked for, but his mind was filled with the image of the Bereun's head that was even now being removed from the stones and taken into the cool darkness of the eastern barracks.

Why would such creatures appear now? Larin did not know, but he believed King Hedradour might. Whatever it was that was happening, the Marshall knew he had to move quickly.

Chapter Twelve

The Planes Of Reality

"Cam? Cam?"

Sonia's voice sounded concerned, though what about Cam could not guess.

He did not know how long it had been since his ordeal, but his head was still swimming and his limbs felt heavy. There was a strange feeling in the pit of his stomach, as if he was constantly on the very edge of nausea.

What had happened to him?

A hand brushed against his cheek.

"Cam? Can you hear me?"

The hand was warm, at least compared to the snow he had fallen into.

It moved back suddenly.

"Allow me," said another voice.

The next moment he felt a vial being pressed against his lips, and the familiar taste of Hocliquor flowed through his body. The nausea instantly dissipated, and his head cleared. He took a deeper breath in than he felt he had in an age.

"Thank God for that," he heard Sonia sigh as he blinked his eyes open.

The sky above him was brighter than it had been, and the air was much colder than he remembered it. Cam took a moment to allow his eyes to focus properly on where he was, then let them settle on the relieved face of Sonia as she leaned over him.

"Hi," Cam said, weakly.

Sonia grasped his hand.

"Don't you ever scare me like that again, you hear?"

There was just enough humour in her voice to belie the harshness of her tone. Cam simply nodded in response. Sonia leaned in and hugged him, then stood and went out of his sight.

Felgaron took her place.

"Are you hurt?"

"No, I don't think so," Cam said, trying to listen to his body for a more detailed answer, "I hit my head I think but I'm alright otherwise."

Immediately the Swordsman positioned himself so he could gently lift Cam into a sitting position and examine him.

"The wound is not deep," Felgaron said, "though it has bled. I think you should heal well, given time."

Cam was not truly listening, for over the Swordsman's shoulder he saw the lifeless body of Lekkon. He was laid on his side in the snow, a peaceful expression on his face.

He felt himself being lifted and hauled to his feet. After steadying himself for a moment, he saw that Gismay and Dunwald were near him also.

"Are you well, friend Cam?" Gismay was asking him.

"Yeah," he replied distantly, " how long was I out?"

"The whole night, from what we can tell," the Captain answered, "we had feared the worst."

Snippets of the night before started to come back to Cam; Lekkon attacking them, ash covered ground, that terrifying figure.

Felgaron stared at him, seemingly comforted.

"Take your time," he said comfortingly, "but we must away from here as soon as you are able. We still have a long march ahead of us."

Cam nodded.

"Yeah, I won't need long."

The Swordsman glanced at him briefly once more, then went and busied himself about the camp.

"I'll get you something to eat," Dunwald.

Cam simply stared ahead of him. His eyes had caught

something in the snow. Ignoring the gentle hand that Gismay had placed upon his arm, he walked slowly over to the spot and looked down.

"Friend Cam?" the Farmer called after him.

It was Lekkon's sword.

You will need it.

The voice came back to him now; echoing within his mind.

Gismay had come next to him.

"Are you alright?" the Farmer asked.

As if compelled, Cam leant forward and picked the thing up. It was light and well made, and had a hilt of teak with red leather wrapped about it. The pommel was a simple affair, formed of polished steel; so smooth was the thing that the snow it had landed in slid from it and left no mark. He pulled gently on the hilt and revealed the first few inches of the blade proper. It, too, had no design or motif upon it, but was crafted with the same care and skill.

Play the part that I cannot.

Remembering one of the weapon talks he delivered at Edgeborough Castle, he placed his index finger against the flat side of the blade, next to the hilt, and allowed the sword to sit upon it. It balanced perfectly.

It was a good sword, from what he could tell.

Seeing nothing else to do, he pushed the blade back into its sheath and stuck the thing into his belt. He then turned Gismay.

"Spoils of war?" the Farmer asked, raising an eyebrow.

Cam shook his head.

"No. He gave it to me. Something about playing the part he couldn't? I don't know. It's all a bit of a blur, to be honest. What was the light?"

The Farmer stared at him, confused.

"Light? What light, friend Cam?"

The confusion seemed genuine, which concerned Cam greatly.

“There was a flash,” he said, trying to piece it all together in his mind, “and a ball of light. I don't know where it came from, but Lekkon saw it too.”

Gismay shook his head.

“I saw no such thing,” he mused, perplexed, “and nor, I think, did friend Sonia. All we saw was that fetcher knock you down. We were afraid that would be the end, as neither of us could get to you quick enough. Thank the Seven for Felgaron. He came back in the nick of time, as you might say, and finished Lekkon off.”

In his head, Cam saw once again the ghostly figure standing over Lekkon's body. In that moment, as in this one, he did not believe he recognised the figure as Felgaron. Admittedly, he had only seen them from the back, and as he was collapsing, but he felt certain that it had not been the Swordsman.

“Are you certain you are alright, friend?” Gismay pushed.

Cam nodded, then rubbed his hand over the back of his head and felt the scab that had formed where he had hit it during the fight.

“I must've hit my head harder than I thought,” he laughed, “ignore me, I probably just dreamt it all.”

The Farmer gave him a concerned look for a moment, then nodded.

“Aye, as you say. Come on, you're food'll be ready by now I'd wager.”

They both went over to what remained of their camp and Dunwald handed Cam a small bowl of cheese and seeds, along with a piece Hocram. Cam ate it gratefully, and washed it down with a sip or two of the mead.

Sonia, clearly concerned for him, did not speak but seemed to forever be looking him up and down, as if expecting him to convulse or collapse at any moment. He did his best to show her that he was, physically at the very least, fine.

Was he fine?

He was certainly whole and uninjured, if very tired and with an ache in the back of his head. But after all they had been through, he was probably in as good a shape as could be expected.

Outwardly, he smiled at her, then made a point of very actively assisting with the breaking of the camp. She made no attempt to question him, but he could feel her eyes on his back as he worked. He put it from his mind and within half an hour the small company was on the move again, climbing into the mountains on the far side of Glacier Pass.

At his right shoulder walked Sonia, forever watchful of him, while Gismay rested himself upon Cam's right shoulder. Felgaron once again set as swift a pace as the landscape allowed and, though the first climb was ultimately short, it was nonetheless brutal. When they reached the more level path that scythed its way westward through the rock, they were already exhausted, yet still their guide did not relent.

For much of the day they flogged their bodies along yet more rocky paths, squeezing through clefts and cuttings. What respites they did have were quick and only when Felgaron deemed them necessary, and when he finally proclaimed they would stop for the evening the sun had long set behind the rocks ahead of them; such was his pace that he had lit them torches so that they might continue walking far longer into the night than would otherwise have been safe.

This last phase of the day's travel was more stressful than the others, as visions of snarling Bereun filled all their minds. Even Felgaron seemed to be on edge and looking over his shoulder every other moment.

The sleep they managed to achieve was short and uncomfortable, and when they were roused before dawn by Felgaron wielding fresh torches, a sullen mood had fallen over the company. A quiet, rushed breakfast was followed by another day of following small, barely remembered paths through otherwise solid, grey rock.

However, as the sun began to set and Cam and Sonia began to fear the appearance of more torches for the nighttime march, the landscape changed. They emerged from the mountain passes onto a small, narrow plateau that overlooked a larger outcrop perhaps forty feet below. Upon this outcrop was a dreary collection of stone and wooden structures surrounded by a high wooden palisade, punctuated at intervals by modest wooden towers. In the centre of all the buildings stood a large stone hall with a great thatched roof.

"Beregle, the City of the Bowalt," Felgaron said, barely a trace of fatigue in his voice, and turned to his gathered companions, "you have done well, friends. Now our ordeal is, for the moment, over. We shall rest here before meeting with Lord Marn in tomorrow."

Dunwald leaned over the edge of the precipice on which they stood and stared at the settlement beneath them.

"It has been a long time since last I looked out over the Bowalt, or the hall of Lord Marn. That time has not been generous to his people..."

"They're farmers," Gismay said non-committally, "and gold is hard to farm."

"Whatever the state of the city," Felgaron cut in, "know that we are amongst friends."

The Swordsman then turned from the parapet of stone and signalled to his companions that they should follow him. He led them to a narrow, sloping path and once more Cam found himself plunged into darkness, hidden from the view of the setting sun. Despite the cold, unforgiving climate about them, the closed in walls of the path somehow contrived to make the air within them stifling.

The ordeal, however, was mercifully short, and soon they had reached the bottom of the path. Here, Felgaron led them around a corner and along a level, steep sided cleft in the rock which eventually opened out into a wider, flatter area of grey-blue stone.

A large palisade wall stood twenty feet high and stretched across the entire width of the rock before them. Two wooden towers stood either side of a simple, single gate. Beyond these came the sounds and smells of Beregle; shouting from the market, the thick aroma of soot-ridden smoke, and the lone ringing of a blacksmith working at his anvil.

It seemed to Cam that Beregle carried an air of solemnity and a dark, bitter resilience emanated towards them. This place had stood for a long time on this barren, rocky outcrop, with lush grasslands far below and cruel mountains behind, as a meeting point of fertility and rugged harshness; the boundary between want and plenty. That is where Beregle lay, and its people, its buildings, even its walls hummed with the low vibrations of unease; a slow rumble of something long repressed but never forgotten.

The company paused for only a moment when they reached the gate so that the guards might open it silently and allow them entry. As he passed, Cam saw that they had deep blue hauberks, stained and frayed, emblazoned with a white dove set against the mountain, worn over rusty, ill-kept chain.

The streets about them were all but deserted, betraying the sounds Cam had heard before they entered. He doubted now that he had really picked out more than a couple of voices, and all the doors and windows about him were locked and dark. You could be forgiven for imagining the simple wooden dwellings were abandoned, though the smoke of fire pits and cooking ovens escaping from them gave away their inhabitants presence.

Felgaron led them into the quiet, brooding village, through the seemingly deserted streets, and eventually came to the central square. Here, at last, was some semblance of a settlement.

The square was lined by a motley selection of buildings; blacksmiths, tanners, various market stalls, all with their share of the few customers milling around. In the centre stood a small point of untouched mountain rock, out of which flowed a trickle of spring water.

Directly behind this was the Great Hall of Beregle; a huge, stone building that dwarfed the rest of the village. Two large oak doors barred immediate entry, whilst there were crude slits in the stone for archers. A pair of stoic guards stood either side, watching silently over the square. They cast their gaze briefly over the company before returning to a stony watchfulness.

For a moment Cam though that Felgaron would lead them up the small stone steps and approach the Hall, but instead he went around the square and brought them to the door of a tavern. It seemed simple and homely enough to Cam, though he felt a pang of nerves as the Swordsman opened the door to reveal the dark, smoky common room beyond.

The place had few patrons, and the scattered souls that did drink here were hidden within the shadows cast by the large open fire in the centre of the long room. The tables that were visible were all empty, and those in the cloak of darkness around the walls were seemingly taken by no more than three or four at a time. All eyes glanced warily upon the group of intruders as they crossed the threshold before returning their focus to their own conspiratorial conversations.

Felgaron led his companions to a table in the far corner of the room, out of the fire's light and directly across from the bar. He then quickly went over to the Innkeeper and, with a few quick words, man passed something into Felgaron's waiting grasp. The Swordsman nonchalantly placed a large bag of coins into the Innkeeper's hand and strode back over to the table where the company waited for him.

In his hands he carried what the Innkeeper had given to him; the cloth that had been wrapped around it, dirty and mouldy, obscuring its true shape. The Swordsman sat down and eyed his companions carefully, as though weighing up in his mind exactly what his next words were going to be.

"The Innkeeper bids you enjoy the finest he has to offer," he said softly, "I have seen that he has been paid for all the service he will give us, and for all those he has already rendered. You may relax here. It may not look it, but this is one of the true safe havens left to us."

His words were clearly intended to calm his companions, though his goal was not that easily achieved. Still Cam eyed the object in his hands, desperate to see what it was, and still

Gismay and Dunwald did not remove their eyes from Felgaron's.

“What's our next move?” Gismay breathed so as to break the silence.

“Tomorrow we shall meet with Lord Marn and his daughters. There are words that need to be spoken with them and I fear they must be spoken with greater haste than is preferable. But, for tonight,” the Swordsman sighed, “we are tired and shall rest here.”

The Company all silently agreed with him; they were at the end of their reserves and a night in a warm bed would go some way to replenishing them before the next stage of their journey began.

A few moments later the Innkeeper and one of his boys brought each of them a plate of food and a cup of weak mead. They eat heartily and spoke very little, heeding Felgaron's advice and enjoying the moments of respite that were being afforded to them.

Both Cam and Sonia had seemingly forgotten how hungry they actually were, for once the first bite of food has passed their lips their bodies cried out for more, and they gleefully obliged. The fare was rustic – bread, cheese, root vegetables – but afterward they felt filled and satisfied as they had never been before. This, mixed with the mead, weak as it was, had made them feel quite drowsy, so much so that when the Innkeeper told them that their room was ready the thought of sleep filled their heads.

The man led them to the corner of the tavern and down the dark flight of stairs to the guest rooms. A dank smell hung in the air here, and the few candles that lit the walls cast only a small, yellowish hue. Three doors along either side led to the chambers, and it was the nearest on the left hand side that Innkeeper opened.

This was, presumably, the largest room he had to offer; though dark and dismal, Cam could see that it was of a fair size and would have been some comfort to many a weary traveller.

A small dresser stood against the far wall, and a fireplace

was on their right as they entered. This held a small yet resolute fire, the smoke of which drifted towards them as the Innkeeper pushed the door inwards to allow them to enter. The thin wisps then drifted lazily towards them bed and hung in the air before the company as if contemplating their arrival.

There were five beds arranged around the walls, all made up with simple sheets and thin, uninviting pillows. Felgaron thanked the Innkeeper on the party's behalf and pressed another coin into his hand. The man nodded and closed the door behind him, leaving the company stood in tired but satisfied silence.

"Come," said the Swordsman after a moment, "make yourselves comfortable. You have earned it after many days in the wilds."

He then strode over to the far wall and laid the thing he had been holding since they first entered the tavern onto the bed, doing so with the utmost care and delicacy.

Sonia tapped Cam on the shoulder and motioned him towards the two beds on the right-hand wall. They silently picked which bed would be which, sat themselves down upon the surprisingly comfortable mattress, and sighed deeply. Neither of them had ever felt as exhausted as they did in that moment; everything that had happened to them since the evening in the Tower came flowing back into them and fed into their tiredness.

"Now that we have a moment," Felgaron spoke, breaking their slumberous thoughts, "I believe it is time we properly discussed some of the events that have come to pass, and those that will come to pass in the days to come."

He looked up at Cam and Sonia as he spoke and smiled warmly at them.

"I have not had the proper opportunity to welcome you both to Rhydariel, Travellers," he said, a grace to his words that neither of them had heard before, "so I do so now. Would that your coming to us was under better circumstances, but that is not the way of such things. I trust Gismay gave you a more fitting welcome when he originally found you?"

"He was very kind," Sonia said earnestly.

Gismay smiled and shook his head.

"I did no more than I would've done for any guest," he said.

"Come now, friend Gismay," Dunwald cut in, grinning, "do you mean to tell us that you hide all of your guests behind your wheat barrels?"

The Farmer glanced sidelong at the Captain.

"Ones that Eismeer wants to capture I do."

Dunwald clapped him on the back, then looked to Cam and Sonia.

"I feel I also owe you some words of welcome, for how we met was not how I would have chosen such a moment to pass."

"Don't mention it," Cam said, shrugging and trying to look and sound upbeat.

"Very good," Felgaron began, his voice low and foreboding, "yet despite my words when we first arrived here, I regret that we cannot yet rest fully. There are conversations that must be had, and I fear they cannot be held off any longer."

With this, he pulled the material that passed as curtains across the window and plunged the room into a dim twilight.

"Things have happened that we can no longer ignore. You two," he said, pointing to Cam and Sonia, "are part of it, as are the Bereun."

"The Bereun?" Cam asked, shaking the sleep from his mind.

"A terrible omen," Gismay breathed.

Dunwald nodded in agreement.

"They have not been seen in nearly six thousand years. If I had not seen them with my own eyes I would say that we were mistaken. I wish we were."

Felgaron had not taken his focus away from Cam and Sonia.

"Have you seen their like before, either of you?"

"No," Cam answered, "the wolves I know can't throw rocks."

“Quite so,” Felgaron agreed, “And that is because these are not mere wolves. Bereun are, much like yourselves, not native to our world.”

Sonia looked back at him.

“But they aren't from ours either,” she said.

Felgaron shook his head.

“They are not.”

He slowly paced the length of the room, positioning himself in front of the fire and turning to face his companions.

“It is a deeply held belief across Rhydariel that the universe is constructed from Seven Planes, each separated only by their pureness of heart and soul. These Planes are ruled by a force known only as the Balance; it controls all seven of the Plains and sees that the Universe remains in harmony within itself.

“Three of these Planes are immobile. They are Absolute; their Balance can never be altered without the direct intervention of the Gods themselves. The remaining four Planes can move and shift amongst themselves so that the Order of the Universe is maintained. Order and Balance are two terrible and decisive powers, and one contributes to the other.

“The two plains between the Fourth and First must make a perfect bridge from a balance of good and evil to perfect good, so their Balance is one of increasing purity. The two between the Fourth and Seventh must, therefore, create the bridge between harmony and complete evil. This Balance is one of decreasing purity.”

He paused for a moment, looking at both of them to ensure that they were following his words.

“So,” said Sonia slowly after a moment, “if we were to mark these ‘Planes’ out of ten, the First would be a ten, the fourth would be five, and the Seventh would be naught, with the others being somewhere in between, right?”

Felgaron smiled at her, impressed.

“A very succinct description, yes.”

Cam looked at Sonia, in awe of not only how well she was

taking all of this in but also how calm she was. He could feel his heart beating hard in his chest and he was barely holding himself together as the Swordsman explained, yet she was as cool and collected as if she was dealing with one of the customers back at Edgeborough Castle.

"The highest plane," Felgaron continued, "the First, is the blessed Neluiná. This is the plane of the Gods, a realm of purest good. No evil walks there, and nothing taints the land or its people.

"The Fourth Plain is a perfect balance between the two; a land which maintains a delicate yet vital harmony between the forces of good and evil. We call this plain Holmfast. I believe this is where you hail come from.

"The Seventh Plane, Hrúhnash, is the lowest and basest of all the realms of this universe. It is a haven of all things evil, where terrible and tortured forms of life are bred and cultivated. It is from here that the Bereun hail."

The silence that filled the small room was palpable. Dunwald and Gismay had both simply stared at the floor from the moment that Felgaron had begun speaking, and they had not yet raised their heads. Cam looked at all of them in turn, hoping someone there would help it all make sense to him. But none of it did. Even Sonia, who seemed to have some sort of grip on things, did not return his gaze. Whatever everyone else was thinking, he had no way of knowing.

"So," Sonia said, "Bereun are... Hell Hounds?"

"That's as good a description for them as I've ever heard," Felgaron replied grimly.

Sonia looked at Gismay and blinked.

"You saved me from a Hell Hound."

Not knowing what else to do, she reached out for the Farmer's hand. Gismay took it, but made no other move or sound.

"Hold on," Cam said, something finally clicking in his mind, "if they are Hell Hounds or whatever, why are they here? Shouldn't they be, you know, in Hell?"

Felgaron began to pace again.

"Now we come to the heart of the matter, the reason behind everything that has happened up to now and everything that will happen in the days ahead.

"Rhydariel – our world – was once, long ago, the Second Plane," he continued, a voice soft and thick with emotion, "these were the golden days of our world, a time of peace and tranquillity. The world was an altogether more wholesome place. However, such times cannot last, for we are not one of the Absolutes. Our world diminished, and our connection to the Gods was lost."

"How far did you fall?"

Sonia's mouth was dry and she barely managed to force the question past her lips.

"As far as a Plane can." Felgaron answered, darkly. "Our world became the Sixth, and was laid bare to the evil of the Helrhûn, the Dark Power, Master of the Seventh Plane."

Cam's vision flashed back into his mind, the dark shape filling his thoughts.

"What happened?"

"Rhydariel fought. You see, when a Plane falls it is because something upon that Plane is affecting its own Balance. To rise again, you must first discover what it is that is causing you to fall and defeat it. Only then can you hope for redemption."

Another, longer silence passed as the meaning of his words began to settle itself into their minds.

"Did you win?" Cam asked. "The last time it happened?"

"In a manner of speaking. The people of Rhydariel defeated a great part of the forces that were infesting our world, rotting its core, but they did not finish the task. A part of the evil plaguing Rhydariel survived. It had hidden itself from them, in a manner that none had ever considered. One that has, I believe, allowed that evil to survive until this very day."

"This still doesn't explain why me and Sonia are here though," Cam said.

Felgaron now sat back on the bed he had claimed and puffed out his cheeks.

"When a Plain moves, either in ascent or descent, the borders between it and the other Plains are weakened. If a border is sufficiently weak, the Order of the Universe can become distorted, causing curious and unearthly events to occur. One such event is to have people swap Planes, falling through as easily as rocks through water. That is how Travellers, such as yourselves, find yourselves in our world."

Cam felt the words and their implications wash over him, though he did not comprehend them. He had accepted that Sonia and he had somehow travelled to another world, but to hear the process laid out before him was unfathomable. Planes? Seven different worlds? Were they just worlds? Were they seven different galaxies? Seven universes? Seven entire existences separate from each other?

Everything he knew or believed evaporated in that moment.

"How do we get back?"

Sonia's question thudded into the empty, still air.

"Without the help of the Gods themselves, the only moment when travel between Planes is possible is that when two Planes pass."

Cam felt a small spark of hope within him.

"So when does that happen next?"

Felgaron smiled weakly, and met his gaze.

"I have been watching my world for what feels like an age," the Swordsman breathed, "observing, investigating. For a long while I believed I was seeing things that simply were not there; imagining portents in place of coincidence, significance instead of simplicity. And I nearly convinced myself that I was wrong. Then two things happened to prove that which I hoped was false.

"First, and most obvious, was your arrival here. When Dunwald sent me a missive to inform me that two unknown people had been apprehended by Fohenk, and that one of them claimed they were from Welverleigh, I knew. That should have been enough. But there was also something intangible, an instinct that I could not shake nor ignore. I was seeing that which I was convinced I could not.

"To put it as simply as I may, the world felt wrong. People were not themselves, the air felt less wholesome, forests became more foreboding. Even the sun seemed a little less bright, day by day. It started slowly, barely perceptible, but as time wore on the signs became more visible, more ominous. Streets became more dangerous at night, people were skittish and nervous, Lord and Kings looked more to their own borders and ignored the troubles of the outside world. I heard whispers of malcontent in dark corners, rumours and deceits in hushed voices echoing into the void. All about me there was a feeling of unease and uncertainty.

"I can still feel it now. It permeates the air we breathe, and I fear that whatever is causing this sickness is beginning to take hold of our people. The arrival of the Bereun was the final, utter proof. We have become the Sixth Plain, and our world is open to the Seventh once more.

"Know this: we are on the brink. A terrible evil is coming and we must hold fast if we are to survive. The powers at play are far beyond the simple forces of life and death."

At this moment, Felgaron looked hard at Cam and Sonia. They hardly dared to believe it, but both felt certain they could see tears silently rolling down the Swordsman's cheeks.

"There is a long and bloody road ahead, my friends," Felgaron forced through his own emotions, "for both you and my world. But it is my vow that if I can do anything to protect either cause then I will. Only by holding off the Seventh, and by defeating the evil that is taking hold within our Plane, can we hope to get you and Sonia home, and truly restore the Balance."

Another heavy and oppressive silence came over the company as they let themselves come to terms the Swordsman's words. Even Dunwald and Gismay, whom Cam assumed would know much of what Felgaron had told them, seemed to be stunned into submission at hearing it laid bare before them.

"What evil do you speak of?" Sonia asked, in a tone Cam had not heard her use before.

"The Wizards of the North."

If these words were meant to mean something to them, their effect was lost on Cam and Sonia. But the expressions that now appeared on the faces of Dunwald and Gismay told them both all they needed to know.

"Such an enemy is surely beyond the strength of men," Dunwald breathed, "for the power that they wield is enough to shatter the world, if the legends are true."

"Some of them are," Felgaron mused darkly.

"Who are these Wizards?" Cam asked, visions of robes, long beards, and pointy hats filling his mind.

"Evil creatures," Gismay growled, a ferocity in his voice Cam had not heard since that day at his farm, "honourless cowards who seek nothing more nor less than dominion."

"They have been the scourge of our world for time immemorial," Dunwald added, "though I believed they had been all but defeated in the War of the Whitesword?"

"All but," Felgaron said pointedly, "and that is why we find ourselves at the door of the Seventh once again. A more terrible foe we could not hope to find in our path. I would that it were not so. Though I say to you now that this fight is not beyond us. The Balance permeates all things, and where there are those who seek to wreak evil upon the world there are also those who seek to defend against it. And, there are powers that will aid them, if only they look for them."

Now Felgaron reached behind his back and produced the thing wrapped in the stained cloth. He held it upon his lap so that they could all see it in such a manner as to give the thing a significance that, at first glance, it truly did not deserve.

"What's that?" Cam asked.

"This," the Swordsman said grandly, "is the first weapon we have in our fight against the bitter odds that stand against us."

Sitting the thing more sturdily upon his lap, Felgaron slowly began to untie the leather strips that held the cloth in place. He then pulled back the cloth and revealed a small, battered chest. It looked old; the wood was rotten in some places and there were traces of rusted iron that were clearly once decorative.

At the front there was a makeshift lock using the remains of the old clasp and a comparatively modern looking nail. Felgaron removed the nail and slowly opened the lid.

Inside, covered in dust and clinging stubbornly to the musky odour about it, was an otherwise remarkably well preserved horn. It was of white metal and had golden bands around it, between which were etched several intricately carved scenes, though what they depicted Cam could not tell.

Dunwald and Gismay stirred next to him.

"By the Seven..." the Farmer breathed. "Is that..?"

"For six thousand years we thought it lost," Felgaron answered before the question could be completed, "but it was not so. I myself have searched for it for what feels like a lifetime, and at last I have been successful."

"Where?" said Dunwald, his mouth sounding dry. "When?"

"I went back to where no-one else thought to look. Sepelchor."

The Captain turned his head to face the Swordsman.

"Sepelchor? That accursed ruin?"

"It is not cursed," Felgaron cautioned, "though a ruin it most certainly is. Destroyed by the Dark Power when last his forces walked upon Rhydariel. Few dare to tread there now."

"I do not blame them," Dunwald answered, "for the ground is still scorched from that battle. The air about the place reeks of death and evil. It was the greatest massacre of men this world has ever known."

"It was," Felgaron agreed, "and that is why this has lain there untouched for all these long years. I knew the tales of Sepelchor, and still I went there."

"When?" Dunwald repeated.

"Perhaps a year ago now. I had travelled to Lundang after

I had heard whispers in dark places that Sepelchor held something of great value and power. I knew that if I heard these whispers then others would soon hear them also, so I paid one of the merchants to ferry me northward on the river.

"After a day and a night of sailing against the current, we reached the shore near Erkenweit Hill. When I reached the ancient walls that fortified the place, I saw the terrible remains of that battle. The ground was black, and still no grass grows there.

"I rested in the ruins of the outer gatehouse that night, climbing the ancient path to the keep the next day. The closer I got to the ruins, the more insistent the shadows of the past became. More than once I felt I saw the figures of men lost millennia ago, the wind becoming their screams in my ears.

"I forged on, reaching the keep just past noon. The crumbling, blackened stones that greeted me were also heavy with the effigies of their past, so I did not linger. I searched every ruined hall, every destroyed passage way and found nothing. With the sun setting behind me I all but abandoned my search.

"It was then that I discovered the door. It was unremarkable in almost every way, save for its very presence in that place. It was blackened and burned, but it still clung desperately to one of its hinges as if fulfilling a great task. It did not yield easily, despite its decrepit state, yet I eventually forced my way beyond it.

"The passage it protected was long and dark, and my torch did not illuminate far into the blackness, but I persevered and eventually reached a cave beneath the keep. Still it plunged down and still I forged on, feeling that I was being led toward my goal.

"For nearly an hour I stumbled forward along the slippery and treacherous path. Then, my feet kicked against something hidden in the blackness. Looking down, I saw the corner of that chest. It had been all but claimed by the rock, but it was there. I did not hesitate to look inside as I knew that my guess would be right. There it had lain, for six thousand long and dark years.

"The Horn of Etavïr."

Neither Dunwald or Gismay had removed there eyes from the Horn during Felgaron's story, and still they did not in the silence that followed his tale.

"Where did you take the horn after you discovered it?" the Captain asked.

"I first considered taking it back to North Bridge," the Swordsman answered in a lighter voice, "but I realised that if I had considered it that easily and quickly then others would also fall upon this conclusion. I knew that I needed to keep the Horn safe, so that it might not fall into the hands of those who seek to either destroy it or use its true power for their own ends.

"Many other hiding places crossed my mind, but most I dismissed immediately. None of the Lords could be trusted with it, as they would seek to use it to further their own ambitions. No, I had to find somewhere that no-none, not even I, would have considered looking.

"Then the perfect place occurred to me. Somewhere that no-one would ever conceive of."

"Where?" pressed Dunwald. "What place is strong enough or secret enough to warrant the honour of hiding such a precious relic?"

Felgaron did not speak, he merely glanced about the room meaningfully. For a moment no-one understood what he meant, but then it dawned upon them.

"You aren't serious?" Gismay breathed, half laughing and half horrified.

Felgaron nodded.

"I assumed you had merely left it while you journeyed south to Eismeer," the Farmer continued.

"You mean to tell me that you left the Horn of Etavïr, our Godking, the one single most powerful and precious artefact in the whole of Rhydariel, in a backwater tavern in Beregle under the watch of a simple Innkeeper?"

Dunwald's words were harsh and unforgiving, yet Felgaron did not let them phase him. He turned his head slowly to meet Dunwald's gaze.

"Would you have looked?" he asked, simply.

For a moment Dunwald stared back at Felgaron in such a manner that Cam wondered if he was going to punch him in the face; the tense silence hung in the room like a storm cloud threatening to burst. And, when it did, it was with the sound of the Captain's laughter.

"You play a dangerous game, Felgaron," he chuckled, "but you seem to play it well."

The Swordsman smiled slightly.

"Let us hope so."

"Sorry," Sonia cut in, her eyes marvelling at the artefact before them, "but why is this horn so special?"

"This Horn," Felgaron responded, "once belonged to Etavïr, the Godking, and he brought it to our world back in the golden days when Rhydariel was the Second Plane. He would use it to signal his arrival into our realm, so that our people might know that they were blessed with his presence. It is said that any who heard the call of the Horn knew no fear nor strife, only peace and happiness."

"But you just told us that the Gods went away thousands of years ago," Cam said, "this horn looks brand new."

"It was forged by the Gods," the Swordsman proclaimed, "and as such is not hampered by something as trivial as time. It will look as it does now in a thousand years, and for aeons after; until the world is at last unmade, its beauty shall never diminish."

"But how will it help us?" Cam pressed.

"It is a symbol, for one thing," Felgaron said, "a rallying call for all the peoples of Rhydariel to answer. And it does have some power in its own right, though for now it must remain hidden. The day will come soon when it must be brought forth more openly, but for now I ask each of you here to keep it, and its power, secretly in your hearts and minds in the days ahead. We are not without hope, however dark our time has become. We can survive the trials that await us. We will survive them."

With that, the Swordsman closed the lid of the box and

once again wrapped it in the discoloured cloth, tying the leather strips as tightly as he could. He then carefully placed it into his pack, and looked at them all once more.

"Now, friends," he sighed, drawing the curtains back from the window and looking out, "the sun is all but gone. Let us, for the moment, put such thoughts of darkness out of our minds as best we can. We have spoken much, and travelled long. I will now give you the rest that I promised. Tomorrow we will meet with Lord Marn. Until then, what remains of the evening is yours. I, myself, will go for a walk and take in the mountain air."

"I will join you," said Dunwald, standing, "for it is too long since I have been in friendly lands, and longer still since I walked the streets of Beregle."

The two men made for the door, opened it, then looked back into the room.

"What of you three?" Felgaron asked.

"I am in need of rest," Gismay said, his voice suddenly sounding exhausted, "and I fear my body will never forgive me if I do not take it while I can."

Felgaron smiled, then looked to Cam and Sonia.

For a moment Cam did not know what to say, but the tiredness in his limbs and the weight in his eyelids returned quickly to answer for him.

"Sleep," he said simply, "I don't think I can do anything else."

"Me too," yawned Sonia, already settling herself under her covers.

"Then rest, all of you," Felgaron said earnestly, "for the road ahead of us is still long and we may not get another moment such as this. I shall rouse you all after dawn, and when we have breakfasted we shall speak with Lord Marn. Until the morning."

With that he and Dunwald left the room, and before the door had fully closed all three of the remaining members of the company had their heads down and their eyes closed.

Chapter Thirteen

The Men Of Ebras

A chill wind blew through the fortifications of Farn Bridge. The Guards watched the horizon as the fires of their torches flickered about them, casting a dancing, golden glow into the air. The black of night was all about them, with the sky above covered by clouds and the encroaching river mist. The dawn was four hours away and the darkest part of the night was coming to them.

Another night was slowly drifting past, and Maloran could not wish it gone soon enough. The wind howling north from the Pelagos Sea, up the River Lun, brought with it what he could only describe as a wholly uneasy feeling. He had stood upon these parapets every day for eighteen years, and never had he felt anything like it at all. Something was very much in the air, but what it was he dared not imagine.

Maloran shook himself. He was a Captain in King Hedradour's army and he was letting a stiff breeze get inside his mind? Larin, were he here, would no doubt tell him the comfort and stability of his posting had made him soft. He laughed quietly to himself at the thought; he debated asking the Marshall for a change of posting, if only to see the reaction it elicited.

He turned and once more look outward into the gloomy night.

Something whistled through the air, high over his head. He looked, straining his eyes, but saw nothing.

A beat of silence passed.

A shape slowly appeared in the darkness above him. For a

moment Maloran believed it to be a falling star, and then the sickening truth revealed itself.

The body of one of his Guards, his armour caught by the torchlight as it fell, landed heavily on the stone next to him. An arrow had embedded itself in the man's throat. With little more than a gasp of shock, the Guard breathed his last.

A cry went up from the men above.

Maloran looked out into the darkness and scanned the horizon, his eyes squinting tightly to discern anything that would help him.

Fading slowly out of the fog like a spectre came the outline of a ship. No, two ships. Five. Eight. Twelve. Maloran stared out in horror as the silhouettes crawled towards the bridge, encroaching like the fog out of which they sailed.

"Ships!" came the cry from the garrison above. "Archers! Ready!"

Acting as swiftly as his terror allowed, Maloran examined the tip of the arrow.

It was glass and shaped as an icicle.

"Eismen!" Maloran cursed.

Another glass-tipped arrow appeared from the darkness, killing the man next to him.

"Hold your courage, men! These Eismeer dogs will not force us from this bridge! We will never yield! For King Hedradour!"

His war cry was picked up by the men who remained, and it echoed through the black night around them.

"Archers! Loose at will!"

The scream of two hundred arrows being sent toward their enemy filled the air.

For a moment there was silence in reply.

Then came the terrible whine of a catapult shot, alive with fire as it flew towards them.

It collided with the corner of the northern tower of the fort; the wooden structure crashing into the river below.

"To the bridge!" the Captain bellowed, but even as he did

so another shot thundered down from above and into the central span, shattering the stone beneath their feet.

"HALT!"

Maloran's command came just in time to stop he and several of his guards tumbling into the newly formed abyss before them. He had to repeat the command to the Guards who came running from the western watchtowers.

"What devilry is this?" called Maloran's Lieutenant across the chasm.

"Eismeer. Ships." Maloran responded. "They will be on us in moments. How many have you there?"

"Six of us were tending to the horses," the Lieutenant answered, "but that is all of us."

Maloran closed his eyes and nodded slowly. Only six? At least the casualties would not be total.

"So be it," he said, resolve in his voice, "You must take word to the King. The Boardwalks must be warned! Do not fail! Once Eismeer has finished here they will surely come to the Barrandel."

The Lieutenant stood his ground.

"Do not tarry!" Maloran cried.

"What of you?" the Lieutenant asked, a voice thick with emotion.

From the darkness now came the battle cries of Eismen bearing down upon them.

"We all took our oaths," Maloran said, looking at the guards stood beside him, "and we will fulfil them. Go, and may the First go with you."

The Lieutenant made as if to speak once more, but the screech of more arrows filling the air convinced him finally that his Captain was right. With a swift salute, he and his contingent left the bridge, not daring to look back.

Maloran turned now to face his own men. He took what little time he had to look them each in the eye, however briefly. He knew in that moment that they would perform their final duties valiantly.

“My life for the Elderking!” said, defiance in his voice.

The guards all drew their swords and stood with him.

“MY LIFE FOR THE ELDER KING!”

The cry went up, echoing into the air about them, and the small, doomed band turned to face the approaching Eismen.

“FOR EBRAS!” Maloran cried, the last words he would ever speak.

He and his guards charged headlong at the attackers.

The skirmish lasted barely five minutes.

Maloran was the last to fall, his sword claiming ten of his opponents before an arrow found its mark and embedded itself into his sword arm. He fell, dropping his weapon, and stared up at the Eismen Commander as he strode forward, raised his sword, and brought it crashing down.

The sound of the blow echoed into the dark world around them, and then there was silence.

Farn Bridge was lost.

* * * * *

The rain had begun to fall through the night, and it had only grown heavier as the light of dawn had crept over the world. The clouds were thick and the air humid over the Farnhoc, a region of low, rolling hills south-east of the Boardwalks. There was little in the way of trees or vegetation save for the most hardy of grasses, and even less influence from civilisation; few homesteads dotted the landscape, and none of the major roads or trails passed through, instead hugging the banks of the Finlos River to the north.

In weather such as this the few muddy paths that did pick their way through the fells became brown torrents, ultimately impassible in many places, forcing travellers to haul themselves up and down the contours of the undulating landscape about them.

A low, ominous rumble of thunder thrummed through the air as Larin, cloaked and hooded as best as he could manage against the inclement conditions, directed his horse to the top of one of the rises. He had ridden hard for two days, stopping only when necessity required, but now the first destination on his journey to Barrandel was in sight.

He crested the hill and saw the ramshackle structure he was making for. Its roof had many holes in, and the smoke from the fire within spilled out of the cracked chimney that rose at an unnatural angle.

Larin directed his horse to the crooked fence, dismounted, and tied the reigns as securely as the rickety structure allowed. Another horse, belonging to the occupant, was already tied there, enjoying a drink from a large bucket. The only cover afforded to both animals as protection from the rain was a hastily erected awning of leather that even now bowed under the weight of the swiftly collecting water.

Larin now stepped through the remains of a garden that surrounded the house, welcoming him to the dilapidated charm of the place. This was one of many such safehouses dotted throughout the lands of Ebras, all of which were in secluded, out of the way places such as this, though this had always been one that Larin held close to his heart for both its location and its occupant.

When the Marshall at last reached the door, he took a deep breath. He then knocked three times, then two, then four – the signal he had devised to let all his informants know it was he asking for entry.

A moment of silence, followed by slow, purposeful footsteps coming closer.

The door was opened a crack from within and, barely lit by the gathering gloom, half a face appeared, the single eye looking him up and down.

"Greetings my old friend," sad Larin, as airily as he could.

"It's about time," the thick, deep voice responded from within.

A chain was loosened from within, and the door opened to allow Larin into the relative comfort of the small house.

The occupant did not stand on ceremony, instead simply turning and walking back into the dimly lit room within. Larin sighed, unsurprised by his welcome, and stepped slowly over the threshold and examined the safehouse.

The water from the rain was getting in more easily than the last time he had visited, and the single rug that covered the boards of the floor was more muddied and threadbare, but things had not changed overmuch.

On the far wall were several perches, each with a raven stood upon it waiting to take to the skies with important messages or news for the King. For each of these, Larin's host now prepared bowls of seeds and water, carrying them over and placing them on the small shelf that accompanied each perch. He then busied himself with preparing a plate of food and mug of mead for himself; this was done slowly, no doubt to prolong Larin's wait.

The Marshall smiled wanly to himself. He had expected such a reception, but even for his host this was some of the finest lily-gilding he had ever seen. It was only their long and deep friendship that allowed him to get away with such behaviour.

This was Araht, one of Larin's oldest and most trusted informants. He hailed from the Bakslá, the sun-baked mudflats in the far north-west, a heritage shown by the darker tone to his skin, though he had long since broken his emotional ties to the place and its people.

He had defected to Ebras some twelve years ago, swearing fealty to King Hedradour and the Elderking and had provided sterling service ever since. Larin had long come to depend upon him for not only his scouting prowess, but his forthrightness and direct speech; he had kept Larin honest, both as a Captain and as Marshall, which was something Larin held in high esteem.

Finally, Araht settled himself into one of the two chairs around the small table in the centre of the room. He unceremoniously kicked the other chair out and invited Larin to sit.

The Marshall bowed graciously before stepping forward and accepting the invitation.

"You look well," he said as he sat.

"You look tired and worn. Why did you ignore my last report?"

Araht's eyes held an unflinching, piercing stare as the words settled into the room. Larin closed his eyes and nodded.

"Straight to it, then," he said, massaging his forehead with his fingertips.

Araht simply smiled, enjoying his moment.

"That is why you are here, is it not?"

"It is," Larin sighed, "amongst other things. I did not 'ignore' it, as you say."

Araht laughed.

"No response, no word, no acknowledgement of my sending it at all. What about this does not present as being ignored?"

"I simply had another, more pressing report to look into."

Araht held his gaze again, even more sternly.

"Indeed?"

Larin did his best to return the gaze.

"I am the Marshall of Ebras," he said strongly, "I have a myriad of matters to attend to."

"I don't doubt it," Araht cut in, ironic sympathy lacing his words.

"Sometimes my attention must be focussed elsewhere."

"This matter that demanded your attention," Araht mused, finally releasing Larin from his stare, "it must have been terrible news indeed for it to be more pressing than a Bereun pack roaming across the Farnhoc."

"It may have been," Larin forced, trying not to maintain his composure.

"I barely escaped without being spotted," Araht continued, unabated, "and I had to wander the wilderness for three days to ensure that they did not follow me back to this safehouse."

“I have not come here to debate with you. I have come here to tell you that you were right.”

Araht snapped his head back around to fix his eyes once more upon his Marshall.

“I know I was. It is not me that needed convincing.”

“Yes, and your point has been made! Halseth is dead!”

Larin threw himself forward out of his chair and strode over to the window, unable to look at his friend. As he stared out through the shimmering curtain of rain, it was all he could do to contain his rage at his mistake.

Halseth was a good man, and loyal to Hedradour to a fault. He had a young family of his own, a wife and child back at the Boardwalks, and a brother and sister that both lived in the villages along the banks of the Finlos. He had barely seen his twenty-first winter and now, because of Larin's mistake, he would never walk this or any other land again.

“Halseth? Dead?”

Larin nodded, barely able to speak.

“Aye. A Bereun pack on the Felieren attacked his scouting party.”

Araht walked slowly over to him and joined his vigil.

“Surely not the same pack I witnessed? They could not have crossed the Lun unseen.”

Larin shook his head.

“I do not believe they did.”

Araht looked sidelong at his Marshall.

“Another pack?”

Larin nodded slowly, not taking his eyes away from the window. The implications of the statement sank into both of them as their eyes scanned the veiled horizon. No signs of life were forthcoming.

“Nothing good can come of any of this,” Araht breathed.

“I should have listened to you, old friend,” Larin said, lowering his head, “perhaps then one less soul would be in Kamaht now. And my heart would not be so heavy with grief.”

Araht placed a hand on the Marshall's shoulder.

“Despite my words earlier,” he began.

“Do not,” Larin cut in, “I wish not to hear it. I know my part and I know I have not played it well in this matter. Nothing I can do will change what has gone before, and no words will comfort me. Only time and redemption can help me. And it is the second one I seek in this moment.”

He turned to face Araht, holding himself as proudly as he felt able.

“I fear what these packs mean for our people. To have two so close to our lands would be concern enough, but that Bereun roam our lands so freely and so openly... I am worried, Araht.”

His friend nodded, stoic and thoughtful.

“As am I. But, I am dismayed to say that these hell-wolves may only be part of what we should fear.”

Larin looked at him, questioningly.

“How so?”

Araht motioned that they should return to the table and, seeing that Larin agreed, fetched them both a fresh mug of mead. He placed one carefully in front of the Marshall, then settled himself back into his own chair and looked over his mug at Larin.

“As you know I still have contacts within North Sel, and one of them bade me travel north with as much speed as I could. They did not say why, only that it was a matter of urgency that could not be risked in writing. They asked that I meet them at North Bridge, save us being seen by unwanted eyes. I sent a raven on to Barrandel that I would be unreachable for the coming days and made my way north.

“Upon my arrival in North Bridge, my contact met me in the tavern there and handed me a piece of parchment. He explained that he could neither say more nor stay longer, for he was afraid that the Serpent's Guard was aware of his journey. This would be his last communication before he defected to King Miravar. He left eastward before I could ask any questions.

“I opened the parchment that he had given me, and realised in that moment that he had been rightly cautious to send its contents in a missive to myself or any other, which is why I also have not sent it on until now."

Araht now reached into a pouch that hung upon his belt and pulled out what Larin assumed to be the very parchment that Araht's contact had handed over. He slid it slowly across the table to the Marshall, who took it up and unrolled it.

Upon the now ragged page was a drawing, as detailed as Larin could have asked for, and four words.

The drawing was of a ship, large with many sails, at port. It was being loaded for what looked to be a long voyage, with many figures rendered going up and down several gangplanks that ran between the vessel and the quay. Emblazoned upon the main sail was a Serpent curled about a double-headed axe; the sigil of North Sel and of Chief Bharangâd.

Larin now turned his attention to the words at the bottom of the sketch, and only now did he truly realise the significance of everything else.

The first were 'Ja'Grahb Docks', which Larin knew to be a port located a few miles outside the main city of North Sel. He himself had never been, but his scouts – and Araht – had told him that it was the chief trading port in Bharangâd's lands, and a main staging area for their naval and military manoeuvrers.

Next was the word 'Northward', clearly indicating the direction in which the ship would be sailing. Larin did not pay much heed to it, as it was the fourth word that drew his attention and sent chills through his heart.

'Mythravia'.

Larin stared hard at the word. It had been many years since he had heard any man mention it, and even then it was done in hushed tones, or as a warning to children who were misbehaving.

He placed it slowly back on to the table and looked up at Araht, trying to hide his growing nerves.

"This contact is reliable, yes?"

"He was my best," Araht nodded, "and I would trust him and his judgement with my life."

Larin nodded absently and looked back at the parchment.

"Mythravia?" he breathed. "Has our world come to such a time? First Bereun roaming the wilds and now an alliance between the Bakslá and the Wizards! The days ahead are dark indeed."

"I had heard rumours," Araht said quietly, "though I doubted that any such thing could be possible. Even for Bharangâd, this is an evil choice. It appears that his desire for power is no longer satisfied by enslaving his own people."

The man spoke with a seething, building rage that threatened to overwhelm him, memories of his former life fanning the flames.

"We must away to the Boardwalks," Larin said, finding his resolve and grasping his friend by the arm, "I would have you deliver your reports directly to King Hedradour, and you are capable with a sword. I suspect we will need every strong arm we can muster in the days to come."

"I will gladly join you, friend," Araht responded immediately, standing out of his chair, "though if what we suspect is true, I doubt that any number of arms, strong or not, can be of much help us now."

"Let us hope that we are wrong, then. But if we are not, I swear to you that I will do all I can to make certain that your people are not enslaved by the two evils of Bharangâd and Mythravia."

Araht looked back at his Marshall, emotion burning in his eyes.

"I would gladly see it done," he said through gritted teeth, "but we have other matters to attend to. King Hedradour must know of this."

Araht stood resolutely and began busying himself around the room, gathering what he would need for the road ahead. His armour, a sleeveless hauberk of scaled metal, and his sabre were the first he took, then his padded shirt which he immediately dressed into. Over this went his armour, and he then wrapped a thick leather belt around his waist and hung his sabre from it, before unfurling a deep red cloak from the bottom of a chest and hanging it about him.

Only then did he pick up a battered, weather-beaten pack already stocked with provisions for a march. With a flourish he hoisted this up onto his shoulder and faced the Marshall, who had simply stared at him throughout.

"Shall we?"

Larin laughed, marvelling at the man.

"It seems we shall. Come, we must reach our King by nightfall in two days, and it will be a hard ride."

Araht marched past him and out into the rain. Larin followed, a vigour in his bones that he had not felt in far too long. They mounted their horses and, with only a short glance at each other, immediately spurred them westward into the drizzling gloom.

Chapter Fourteen

Beregle

Cam, Sonia, and Gismay were roused by Felgaron at dawn.

Despite their much more comfortable and restful sleep, their bodies still ached from their ordeal thus far. They pulled themselves slowly and painfully to their feet, got dressed, then almost as one staggered out into the all but empty common room.

"Good morning friends," Felgaron greeted them, "and a fine morning it is. Are we all rested?"

The three of them all nodded in groggy agreement.

"A little stiff," Gismay said, giving his best smile, "but nothing more than to be expected."

"This is good," Felgaron responded, "are you ready to meet with Lord Marn?"

Gismay nodded once more, whilst Cam and Sonia shrugged; it was an ultimately pointless question for them since they did not even know who Lord Marn was.

"Then let us to it," the Swordsman continued, "I would like to be away from here no later than noonsun."

"Where would we be going?" Gismay asked.

"The Boardwalks, and the Hall of Barrandel. King Hedradour must be made aware of what is transpiring in our lands, if he is not already."

"Are we telling Marn as well?" Cam asked, trying to sound knowledgeable.

"No," Felgaron said quickly, "not yet. He will not agree to my plan if Ebras has not already."

"What is your plan?" put in Sonia.

"Not here," he replied in a low voice, "while the Innkeeper and Lord Marn's house can be trusted, not all in Beregle can be. Come."

The Swordsman turned and led the party out onto the Square across which they had walked the previous evening. To Cam it seemed to have been cut directly into the mountain; on his right the palisades rose to meet sheer rock, while in front and behind him the village sprawled across the plateau. To his left was another large palisade and the western entrance to Beregle, and the shop-lined main street that led from the gate. Beyond that could be glimpsed a cloudless sky, but so high up were they that the horizon was hidden.

The Square itself had market stalls all about, and many shop fronts that opened on to it, though this morning all of these seemed to be closed. It was a little early, but Cam thought this was more to do with the prosperity of the place rather than the time of day.

Glancing at the rock upon which he stood, there seemed to have been some attempt made at carving a design into it, but what it was Cam could no longer make out. He doubted it would mean much to him anyway, even if he could.

Taking his eyes away from the ground, he now focussed on the building which they were making for.

The Hall of Marn.

It was the largest and grandest that could be seen, though Cam reflected that the bar for both of those was particularly low. It had a huge thatched roof, and was made of a thicker, darker wood than the rest of the town's structures. It stood, tall and proud, overlooking the realm of its Lord, unmoved by weather or time.

The Swordsman led his companions up the steps to the large double doors that stood at the entrance to Marn's Hall. With a nod to one of the Guards, the doors slowly swung open and revealed a large, dimly lit room, filled with tapestries and paintings. This was what Cam first noticed, as these were the only source of colour in the otherwise brown and grey room. Fires which crackled in two heaths on either side sent heat and red-gold light into the space, illuminating a huge banner with the white dove set against the mountain emblazoned upon it – the emblem of Lord Marn.

This hung from the roof behind the enormous Throne which stood at the far end of the room. From what Cam could see it was wooden and shaped as a mountain with a chair simply cut into of it. He marvelled at the intricacy and detail of the design.

Upon the Throne sat an equally impressive looking man. He wore a great, grey fur coat, maroon breeches and jet black boots. On his head was a circlet of gold, with small and surprisingly detailed mountains climbing about its circumference, and his long, brown hair seemed to flow downward from it before merging with the fur of his coat.

"Lord Marn," Felgaron called, stopping halfway down the hall and bowing at the figure sat before them, "it is good to be within your hall once more."

"Long has it been since you were here to see me," Marn replied in a deep, gruff voice, stroking his beard as he spoke, "though you are as welcome as ever. My land needs to see warriors such as you that fight for our cause. It gives them hope. And who is it you bring with you? Captain Dunwald of Eismeer?"

Marn's tone was one of playful banter. Dunwald responded with a smile.

"It is, though I am now throwing off the disguise. I stand as Dunwald of the Boardwalks once more. I hear that Larin has taken on the roll of Marshall with success?"

"Indeed he has," Marn agreed, "and he has been a good friend to Beregle in that short time as well. We shall not forget it when the time comes."

The Lord's eyes now rested upon Cam, Sonia, and Gismay properly for the first time.

"And who are these, pray?" Marn said, an air of

inquisitive cautiousness in his voice. "I do not recognise them."

The Lord's eyes pierced Cam, staring deep into his very soul. He did not look it, but Marn was a strong willed and strong minded man, and Cam was becoming more aware of it with every passing second.

"This is Gismay," Felgaron responded, gesturing to the Farmer.

"Gismay?" Marn asked, an air of recognition in his voice. "The Lun Ridge informant, yes? You and your Father have done fine work for King Hedradour. You are to be commended for your service, and you are welcomed here."

The Farmer smiled and bowed, but said nothing.

"And what of you two?" the Lord asked.

"Friends Cam and Sonia," the Swordsman answered, "they are allies from a distant land. They have travelled very far to aid us in our endeavours."

"Our endeavours, or yours?"

This new voice came from behind Cam.

He turned to see a woman dressed in full armour, a deep blue cape draped across her shoulders proudly bearing the Dove of Beregle. She carried herself proudly, her light brown hair cut short and a fine looking scabbard at her waist. From this protruded an intricate golden sword hilt, bearing a deep blue gem at the centre of the pommel.

She walked past Cam and gave him barely a glance. Her steps took her straight to Felgaron, her hand never leaving her sword hilt.

"Lady Ianor," Felgaron said, bowing deeply, "it is a pleasure to see you again."

Ianor did not return the bow, nor did she take her eyes off the Swordsman.

"A long and joyful time has passed since you last paraded around our hall," she continued, "wherefore come you to us now?"

Marn laughed heartily.

"My dear Ianor," he said, genuine affection in his voice,

"forever the Guardian of the realm. Felgaron is a friend of Beregle, and he and all who travel with him are welcome in our hall whenever they will. Friends, forgive my daughter. She is over protective of her father."

"Make no apologies for me, Lord Father," Ianor said, as curtly as she dared, "it is well known that Felgaron swears no fealty to any man save for himself. I merely seek to make certain that he is not using us for his own purposes."

She continued to run her eyes up and down Felgaron, but after a moment she stepped away and joined her father by his throne.

"I seek for no aid," Felgaron said defensively, "your Lord Father and I have been friends for many long years. I will admit, I have questions which the House of Beregle may be able to answer, so my coming here is not without pretence. If that makes me unwelcome in your eyes, my Lady, then unwelcome I must be."

Ianor turned and studied the Swordsman, as if searching for a reason to have him thrown from the hall.

"Send for my sister," she spat at a nearby Guard, then returned her gaze to Felgaron once again, "and if we suspect that my Lord Father is being misled..."

"I will make no apologies for you, daughter, if you will make no apologies for me."

Marn's voice was stern but not unkind.

"I am not yet a infirm old man, Ianor," he continued, gently chastising her, "I am more than capable of detecting counterfeits, be they from Felgaron or anyone else."

Ianor's response was cut off by the return of the Guard and, Cam assumed, Ianor's sister. She was not dressed in armour, but instead wore a heavy fur coat similar to her Father's. Her auburn hair was longer than her Ianor's, and her face was softer but still with those piercing eyes. At her waist was an axe of what looked like iron, but that was all she bore.

She also took up position next to Marn, and smiled at them.

“Welcome, honoured guests,” she said, “I trust that my Lord Father's Hall is to your liking?”

Felgaron bowed once more.

“As ever, Lady Carial. And what more could be expected from the finest House Maiden in all the lands?”

Carial's smile broadened at his words.

“Your words do me great honour, Sir Felgaron.”

“Indeed they do,” Marn chimed, a proud grin adorning his features, “such is the boon of having fine and worthy children. They bring honour unto you that you do not look for, nor deserve.”

He took a moment to regard both of his daughters, a genuine love and affection between all three of them.

“Now,” he continued, a more serious tone to his voice, “what words would you have with me?”

“I am here simply for news, Lord Marn,” the Swordsman said, “I need tidings of anyone or anything moving unexpected or unexplained thought your lands. I would know if there have been any unusual happenings within your borders.”

“Unusual?” Ianor scoffed. “That is a broad question. What is abnormal for one might be perfectly plain for another.”

“Indeed,” Marn agreed, gruffly, “I would ask that you give me more to go on, Felgaron.”

“I am afraid that I cannot, for these are delicate days and we must all tread carefully.”

These words were met with a sigh of frustration from Marn and a disdainful roll of the eyes from Ianor.

“You come to us for information,” she spat, “but you don't tell us what kind of information you seek?”

“Perhaps,” cut in the Lady Carial softly, “even delicate times, as you call them, can be afforded a small measure of candid speech? We all wish to help you, Felgaron, but we cannot if we do not know what help it is you need.”

Her tone was cautious but deliberately so, trying to act as some sort of mediator between Felgaron's enigmatic words and Ianor's hot temperament.

"My daughters speak true," Marn added, "though even if we knew what you were asking for I fear that we would have nothing for you. I have heard of nothing that might be considered out of the ordinary."

"Nor I," said Ianor stepping down from the Throne and looking Felgaron dead in the eye. "Not a sheath of wheat so much as out of place for many months. Now, if that is all you would ask of us in these 'delicate times', then I would take my leave. I have work of genuine import that requires my attention."

Felgaron did not avoid her gaze, he simply stared back at her for many moments. It was as if they were both waiting for the other to blink. Cam was not certain, but he thought he saw a faint grin form on Felgaron's lips as they tested each other's resolve.

"I have no more questions," the Swordsman eventually responded, a deliberate level tone to his voice, "and ask only that if you do hear anything unusual, however small, that you send word to me in Barrandel as soon as you are able."

Ianor nodded imperceptibly, then turned to face her Father.

"With your grace, my Lord?"

Marn was about to grant her leave when the sound of the doors to his hall being thrown open caused them all to turn. A soldier came running in, grasping a parchment tightly in his right hand.

"My Lord Marn," he called as he quickly crossed the floor.

"What news?" Marn demanded.

"I bring word from Farn Bridge, my Lord!"

"Let me see!" Ianor ordered, stepping toward him and taking the parchment.

She read it, though her face showed no clue as to what was upon it, then offered the parchment to her Father.

"My Lord," she said, her voice barely above a whisper.

Marn, concern upon his face, took it and looked it over. As he did so, Cam saw his body stiffen and his eyes widen.

"Delicate times, Felgaron?" he said aloud.

The Swordsman looked up at him.

"What has happened?"

Marn flung the parchment down to him, landing it at Felgaron's feet.

"Eismeer has taken Farn Bridge. They attacked during the night. They have ships making their way north along the Lun."

The silence that followed the Lord's words was heavy and deafening. Felgaron reached down and picked up the parchment.

The words written there were undeniable and unchanging.

Dunwald snatched the thing out of Felgaron's hand, shocked and seething. He turned to the Soldier that had brought the news.

"Survivors?"

The Soldier looked to Ianor, who nodded.

"Six men were seen fleeing westward. No-one else."

"Six?" Dunwald cried. "There was a garrison of one-hundred and fifty!"

"It would seem the Old War is opened again in earnest," Marn sighed, leaning back on his throne.

Ianor placed her hand on the Soldiers shoulder.

"You have done well. Go and rest."

The Soldier, breathless, saluted her.

"For the Mountain."

Ianor returned his salute.

"For the Mountain."

Everyone watched as the Solider turned on his heels and strode from the room.

"Time is short," Felgaron said, "and I regret that we cannot tarry here any longer. I thank you, Lord Marn, for your time and for your hospitality."

Felgaron bowed low to the Lord, but Marn waved a hand.

"You need not stand on ceremony, friends," Marn was saying, "go, and take the grace of Beregle with you."

The Swordsman nodded gratefully.

"Thank you, Lord," he said, then turned to his companions, "we make for Barrandel immediately."

Dunwald, with barely a glance at the Lord, turned and

stalked out of the room, barging through the doors onto the square. Felgaron followed him, and urged the others to do the same. Cam and Sonia were swept up by Gismay and felt themselves being propelled out and onto the square, and then back into the darkness of the Inn.

Before they knew what was happening, they were both sat back on their beds in their rented room watching as Dunwald paced up and down while Felgaron and Gismay busied themselves packing up the party's gear.

"That fetcher!" the Captain cried. "An Eisman he may be, but I always believed Fohenk was a man of honour! To attack in the dead of night?"

"There's nothing Eismeer does that surprises me," Gismay agreed, stuffing a sleeping bag in Dunwald's pack.

"I spent all those years at his side. I could have killed him! I *should* have killed him!"

"And what would that have gained you, except for a swift visit to the hangman's noose?"

Felgaron's voice stopped the Captain in his tracks. He wheeled around and faced the Swordsman, and for a moment looked as though he would strike the man in his rage.

"It would have saved one-hundred and fifty men!" Dunwald hissed.

"And reopened a war that has already killed thousands and will kill thousands more."

"I could have saved my people!" Dunwald forced, trying to make Felgaron understand.

"If the Seventh takes them, and the Wizards overrun Rhydariel, what comfort will it be for them to know that one Lord of men lay dead by your hand?"

The Swordsman's voice was sombre yet forceful.

"Without your help," he continued, grasping the Captain's shoulder, "I would not have been able to rescue any of our companions here from Eismeer. We would not be able to tell King Hedradour of the Planes, or of the threat of the Wizards. Cam and Sonia, the Travellers who are proof of what is happening and what our world must prepare for, would be dead. And my cause would be all but lost.

"Yes, Lord Fohenk would be dead, and one-hundred and fifty men might have been saved, but the entire world would fall, and you would be dead. Whatever you are feeling, trust me – the act would have achieved nothing."

Dunwald stared at the Swordsman for many moments, his heart and mind scattered and torn amongst all of the possibilities, the intangible moments that might have been.

"Damn you, and damn all the rest of them," he hissed, "I need to pack."

With that, Dunwald turned and positioned himself and his pack so that they were both facing away from the group, and he fell silent.

Felgaron now turned to Gismay.

"I will speak to the Innkeeper," he said, "and ensure that you are given room and board for as long as you need."

Cam stopped and looked at both men.

"Is he not coming with us?" he asked, disappointment in his voice.

Gismay shook his head.

"I cannot," the Farmer replied levelly, "my injuries have not healed sufficiently either for the swift travelling that will be needed to reach the Boardwalks in time, nor to be anything other than a burden during the battle."

"Which brings us to another point," Felgaron said matter-of-factly, turning to Cam and Sonia, "do either of you have any combat experience?"

The two friends looked at each other, a sudden fear coming into their hearts.

"I mean," Cam began cautiously, "we aren't soldiers. We never needed to... I'm an actor. I've done some stage combat. A bit of sword stuff, and some archery at work. But that doesn't really count."

Felgaron now looked to Sonia.

"And you?"

Sonia stared back at him, her eyes wide.

"No. Nothing."

The Swordsman nodded, a gesture of finality.

"Then you shall stay here with Gismay. Cam will come with us."

"What?" Cam breathed.

"No!" cried Sonia.

"This is not a discussion." the Swordsman pushed. "You are Travellers and, while it is true that I need you to help convince others that the Planes are moving, the prospect of battle means it is now too dangerous to take both of you. Make ready, Cam, we leave as soon as we are able."

Cam stepped forward, putting himself between the Swordsman and Sonia.

"I'm not going. Not without Sonia."

"Yes, you are."

Felgaron rounded upon him and drew himself up to his full height.

He was only an inch or two taller than Cam in truth, but in that moment he towered over him; his muscular arms and shoulders framing his barrel chest, all supported by his strong, powerful legs. This man had lived a hard, physical life, and had certainly seen battle – the scars on his arms, neck, and face indicated as much – and Cam doubted he would have any difficulty in simply ripping him in two if he desired it.

The fire behind his eyes once again burned, adding to his suddenly oppressive aura.

"I..." Cam stammered. "We came here together, and we're going home together."

"Commendable," the Swordsman said, "but the second can only be achieved if we save Rhydariel from the enemies that are plaguing her. To do that, there are many dark and bloody days ahead. Even if battle does not come to us at Barrandel, one way or another battle will find us. Neither the forces of the Seventh, nor the Wizards themselves, will be stopped without bloodshed.

"I need you both to help me save my world, and to help prove our cause not only to King Hedradour but the other rulers of the Five Kingdoms. You at least have some training with weaponry, however basic, much the same as any other when they first face the fires of war. Sonia is not so trained, and I do not have time to train her. Until such time as war marches upon Beregle itself, she is safer here."

Cam felt tears beginning to well in his eyes.

"Friend Cam," Gismay said, placing a hand upon his shoulder, "Felgaron speaks the truth. It'd be nothing short of folly to send both of you into danger, yet into danger one of you must go. I swore back at my farm that I'd do anything in my power to keep you both safe. I can't look after both of you, but I can and will protect Sonia. With my life, if needed."

Cam looked at the Farmer, pleading silently that he should convince Felgaron that his was not a good idea, that Cam and Sonia should stay together.

Gismay simply smiled and gripped his shoulder tighter.

For the first time since Felgaron had spoken, Cam and Sonia made eye contact.

Dunwald, his own pack hoisted onto his shoulder, went to the door. He then turned and looked back at them all.

"Well?" he said, barely containing the rage within him.

Sonia stared back at Cam, tears upon her cheeks. She reached out her hand, and he took it without hesitation.

Felgaron picked up his own pack, then motioned something to Gismay.

Cam closed his eyes, letting his tears fall.

In his heart of hearts, he knew Felgaron was probably right. If everything that he had heard was true, if these Planes really did exist, then to get home he and Sonia needed Rhydariel's Plane to pass their own again.

The only way to do that was to deal with whatever was going on here.

Gismay he trusted implicitly; he had done nothing to suggest that Cam should not. Indeed, he had already saved

Sonia's life once.

But Felgaron?

There was something, intangible but unmistakeable, that felt unnatural about the man. Something not quite right. Cam did not doubt that he was hiding something, but what it was and how important he did not dare to guess. Even if it was important, would it mean anything to he and Sonia if they found out?

More importantly, could he risk not doing what Felgaron and Gismay were asking of him?

He opened his eyes once more and looked into Sonia's, his heart breaking at the sight of her tearful face.

"I have to go, don't I?" he croaked.

Sonia simply stared back at him for a moment, then nodded. Her hand gripped his tighter, pulling him slowly toward her.

Cam stepped into the embrace and they stood, two friends in an unknown world, and allowed their sorrows to encircle them. Gismay's hand touched Cam's shoulder.

Sonia sniffed, then pulled herself away from him. She blinked tears from her eyes, then drew the best smile she could across her lips.

Cam, wiping his own eyes, returned the smile as best he could.

He looked down and saw that Gismay had handed him his pack.

Cam stared at the thing for a moment, then nodded and resigned himself that the moment truly had come at last.

He took the pack and slung it on his shoulders. It was heavy, pulling at his already aching muscles, but he paid it no heed.

To get he and Sonia back home, away from all of this, he would endure far worse.

As if in answer to this last thought, Gismay now handed him Lekkon's sword. This, too, felt heavy in his hands as he took it and attached it to his belt, and the knowledge he would have to use it – properly use it – made it all the more burdensome.

"Your cloak is in your pack," the Farmer said quietly, then stepped back.

"Thanks," Cam breathed, then looked once more to Sonia.

She smiled at him, doing her best to hold her emotions back.

"Look after yourself," she said simply.

"You too," Cam said, "I'll see you soon."

"Yeah," Sonia breathed.

"Come," Felgaron said, his commanding voice once again filling the small room, "I want to reach Barrandel in four days, before if we can. Gismay, friend Sonia, stay safe. We will send any word we can to you here. Etavïr be with you."

"And with you. All of you." the Farmer replied.

Dunwald, positively shaking with his eagerness to depart, could finally take no more and, throwing the door open, strode down out into the corridor. Felgaron looked at the rest of them with a knowing smile, then turned and followed the Captain.

Cam lingered for a moment longer, then walked out of the room and let the door close slowly behind him.

Sonia watched as her friend disappeared, then turned to face Gismay. She smiled as broadly as she could.

"Well," she sighed.

Then, without warning, she collapsed into Gismay's chest and wept.

Chapter Fifteen

The River Lun

For Cam, the rest of the day was a compete blur.

He vaguely remembered catching up with Felgaron and Dunwald outside the Inn in Beregle, then being led out of the main gate and along a steep switchback path that lead them down the mountain to the grassy plains below.

The march westward across these was relentless; the three companions stopping only for short respites when absolutely necessary. With every single step, Dunwald stared at the horizon before them and seethed, striding onward like a man possessed.

By the time the sun was beginning to fall from the sky they had covered perhaps thirty miles, such was the pace that the Swordsman set. The mountain still rose high behind them, but the details of the town upon it were no longer visible. By the time they stopped to make camp, near a small patch of thick bushes set a few yards back from the road itself, it had become shrouded by a thin mist.

They ate in silence, each of their minds brooding at the times they found themselves in. Cam's mind ever wandered back to Sonia, wishing that he would close his eyes and somehow suddenly find himself back with her, all talk of battles a distant, fading memory.

All too soon, and after a thoroughly ineffective sleep, Felgaron roused them as the sun was pulling itself above the horizon and another march began.

As they walked and the light about them grew, Cam saw that the land was beginning to change; rolling fields and hills gradually giving way to bracken and marshlands.

After perhaps two hours of walking they paused for a moment by a small stream to fill their flasks. Felgaron also handed them a slice of bread each with two Hochberries, and then they set out once more across the plains with renewed vigour.

Soon, with the sun climbing to its height, Cam spotted a tiny shadow on the horizon.

"What's that?" he called to Felgaron.

"Lundang," came the reply, "It still lies many miles from us. I judge we shall be there as the sun falls this evening, but not before."

The shadow on the horizon grew steadily larger until they could make out distinct shapes of roofs and outlines of buildings. The land about them, too, began to change once more; marshlands giving way to fertile floodplains, with small farms and fields beginning to border the road on both sides. The land became boggy in places, making the road they were travelling on sometimes little more than a causeway.

"When was the last flood?" Dunwald asked, gruffly.

"It receded just past a fortnight ago," Felgaron replied, "but Lundang was unharmed by it. The waters are not as ferocious as they once were."

"It is a wonder that it has survived so long without being washed away," Dunwald growled.

"It is," agreed Felgaron, "but the people of Lundang are strong and proud. If it were not for their loyalty, they would have long gained independence from Beregle."

"Be careful you do not let Lord Marn hear such a thing."

From the rest of their talk as they travelled, Cam gathered that Lundang was an old port, having stood on the same spot for millennia. It had begun as little more than a fishing village, surviving on its own until some war long ago when its importance as a strategic port came to the fore.

However, with this responsibility came a new danger: Lundang suddenly became a target.

The people petitioned to the then Lord of Beregle to give them protection, and he accepted. With this new backing the village quickly began to grow, with people from all across the lands flocking from smaller, unprotected settlements to take advantage of the might of Beregle to keep them safe; it was a time of prosperity and peace.

Then, the Lord of Beregle suddenly vanished.

No-one had any idea where he had gone. Search parties were sent all about his domain and further afield; to the Boardwalks, Eismeer, and one even to Strewel asking for news, but no-one had seen or heard anything of him.

It was said amongst his people that he had gone in search of a legendary treasure in order to gain his lands yet more renown and that, being the truly great warrior he was, he would return in glory and begin a new golden age.

So the people of the Beregland waited, but their Lord never returned. Lundang was all but forgotten, leaving the her people feeling unwanted and lost.

It was this feeling that hung heavily in the air as Cam followed Felgaron and Dunwald beneath the wooden archway that served as the entrance to this once bustling town.

The wooden buildings were damp, as if there had been a light fall of rain, and a thin layer of mud covered them. People walked to and fro, sullen and careworn expressions upon their faces. The streets wound and curved much through the buildings on either side, as if these had been simply thrown together.

Cam guessed that this was the area where the new settlers had come to reap the rewards of Lundang. If they could see their descendants now, he doubted that they would have come to the town with such enthusiasm.

The street opened out and the three companions came at last into the oldest quarter of Lundang. Organised streets stood about them which gave the feeling of a once proud place. The architecture here was far grander, with houses and shops built two and three stories high, and Cam could hear the sounds of the port beyond the skyline. Above the roofs he saw the tips of masts, and watched as gulls floated on the gentle breeze that danced through the streets.

Felgaron continued on through this square and out onto the docks themselves. Here they were met by a market, and a plethora of smells, sounds and sights that Cam had never seen.

All the stalls about him positively glowed with the variety of colours sat upon them; fruits, vegetables, grains, cloths, tools, everything that you could imagine was being sold. The vendors were calling out the deals of the day, bartering with sailors and Captains over the price of goods, trading what they had for precious items from far off lands.

The Swordsman led them through the market and out onto the jetties. The river ran past swiftly, with the sound of the water lapping against the wooden supports adding a different aura to the scene. There was also a different complexion to the men that worked these boats, for they all had olive skin. Cam had seen no-one with such features since he had arrived in Rhydariel, and he wondered where they called home.

As if reading his thoughts, Felgaron spoke above the clamour of sailors and boats.

"These ships are from the Crescent Isles."

"Where's that?" Cam asked, as if the answer would make a difference to him.

"A small archipelago to the south west," Felgaron answered, then his eyes were drawn somewhere to their left. "Ah, here we are."

He strode over to the smallest craft that Cam had seen at the dock and beckoned that he and Dunwald should follow.

It was a simple rowing boat, or at least it looked like one from a distance. As Cam got closer, however, he saw that it had what looked like a miniature thatched roof over one end, and a canopy stretched out over most of its remaining length.

Upon the deck sat a man, busily polishing some artefact or another. He had bright blonde hair that hung untidily from his head in a way that, even at first glance, seemed to suit the man perfectly.

The sound of Felgaron's boots on the walk caused him to look up from his work.

"I wondered when you'd get here," the blonde man said, "I've got me own schedule to keep, y'know! I can't be sat waiting all day, not even for you, Felgaron!"

"Agazi," Felgaron replied, "as well as ever I see."

Agazi climbed from his boat onto the walk and grasped the Swordsman's arm in a greeting.

"You should know better'n most, Felgaron, you can't keep me down! Especially not when there's trading to be done. Talking of which."

Agazi's voice tailed off and he simply smiled knowingly at the Swordsman. Felgaron smiled in return and produced a small leather pouch from his belt and emptied the contents into Agazi's hand.

"Ten coins, as we agreed."

Agazi's face lit up with a greedy smile.

"You are a man of y'word, I'll say that for you!"

Felgaron laughed and turned to Dunwald and Cam.

"Come," he invited, "meet my friend Agazi. No shrewder merchant has ever sailed the River Lun. Agazi, this is Captain Dunwald of the Boardwalks, and Cam."

The Merchant looked at the two men and smiled.

"Well, if you're friends of Felgaron, you're friends of mine. Besides, Dunwald's name is famous in these parts! Bravely going off to spy on Fohenk an' all!"

Dunwald stared at the Merchant.

"I suppose you know that my mission was supposed to be secret?"

Agazi looked affronted.

"O' course I knew, we all did! But don't worry, none of us would ever dare breath a word to anyone."

Dunwald gave the man a forlorn glance.

"How reassuring."

Agazi laughed heartily and invited them down to his vessel. The three men followed him and soon all were sat under the cover on the front section of the craft.

Cam felt it rock in the water as they all settled and grasped the side for comfort. Agazi ducked inside the thatched part of his boat and returned with a small flask for each of them. Passing them out, he took and quick swig from his own.

"I've just brought a haul of this from some of them Crescent Islanders. They call it 'Swamdra'. Say it comes from a rare plant they have over there. Whatever it is, it tastes like nothing you'll have tried here. Go on, give it a go."

The three men shared a quick nervous glance, not wanting to offend their host. Felgaron nodded at them and slowly took a draught from his flask. Cam and Dunwald cautiously joined him as Agazi waited expectantly for their reaction.

The taste in Cam's mouth was difficult to describe. It had hints of earth and herbs, giving it a very full flavour, but there was something else; an after taste that clung to the inside of his mouth. His lips suddenly felt as though they were very thin, almost like the fluid had burned away a layer from the inside of them. It reminded him vaguely of whiskey, which he had never liked, but it was far more harsh and sour.

Doing his best not to appear ungrateful for the sample, Cam simply swallowed and puffed his cheeks out as he blew a slow, steady breath to try and expel the taste. Dunwald and Felgaron, it seemed, had a similar idea.

"'S good stuff, isn't it? I reckon I could make a mountain on that. Maybe even enough to afford me own ship to go there meself!"

Felgaron nodded graciously.

"I daresay you will," he said with a strain, "and we thank you for the taste."

He handed his flask back to Agazi, trying not to look to eager. Dunwald and Cam decided they would follow his example, but Agazi waved a hand and took another swig of his own.

"No, I wouldn't dream of it. You keep that for y'selves. Can't have it all to myself, can I?"

All three silently wished he could.

Agazi wiped his lips on the tattered sleeve of his shirt and addressed them all.

“So, Felgaron tells me you're all off to the Boardwalks? Bad business with Farn Bridge and all that. You really think ol' Fohenk will attack King Hedradour? I thought that war had gone quiet?”

“We are indeed making for the Boardwalks” Felgaron said, cutting across the Merchant's words as politely as he could “and we need to them as soon as maybe. The river is well known for being the fastest route.”

Agazi smiled at him proudly.

“It is indeed. Well, since I'm going that way, I'm willing to take you, even if it is a bit dangerous all things considered. Especially since you've paid so handsomely. Now, are you ready to make way or do you need some more time on land?”

“No,” said Felgaron, “we are ready my friend. We can leave at your earliest convenience.”

Agazi leapt up from his seat and grasped the poles holding up the cover beneath which Cam had sat.

“Right then,” he puffed, “let's get to it. It’s a day’s sailing if the wind is kind, and twice that if it's not, especially with the current against you. And I want to be back before the fighting starts, if its all the same to you. Watch yourselves!”

He hoisted the two poles out of their supports and, with far less difficulty than Cam imagined, Agazi slotted them neatly into two cradles on either side of the thatch roof. Once secure, Cam saw that they were angled in such a way that the cover became an instant sail. It was small, but more than adequate for a boat of this size.

Agazi, not seeming to find any marvel in his achievement, leant past Dunwald and untied the mooring line then kicked them away from the docks and out into the current.

“Amazing…” Cam breathed aloud.

“I built her meself,” Agazi said proudly as he sat next to him, his arm taking the rudder, “got the idea off an Islander. Said this was how they build their fishing boats."

Cam quickly decided that these 'Islanders' were far more skilled at sailing than they were at brewery.

"She's served me well," the Merchant continued, an air of paternity in his voice, "the best friend I ever had. Come storms or maelstroms, this craft will see me right. Now, get some rest. You've done a good few steps today if I know Felgaron, so don't worry about giving me company. I've got the water, and it'll sing to me as we go. That's all the company I need."

The three companions gladly accepted Agazi's advice and, as sleep slowly encroached upon his mind, Cam curled himself up against the sides of the boat and thought once more of Sonia.

Her face filled his mind, and he held it there for as long as he could before the song of the water, and the exertion of the last two days, finally took him and sent him into the deep black of sleep.

* * * * *

The pale gold of dawn gently brushed against Cam's face as he opened his eyes, the flapping of the sail in the wind having stirred him from slumber. He looked up to see Agazi sat at the rudder. Felgaron sat next to him, his eyes closed and his head bowed upon his chest, while Dunwald lay opposite Cam fast asleep.

Deciding that he would not gain anything from trying to hold off waking any longer, Cam wrapped his cloak about him, clambered gingerly to his feet, and looked out over the water. It was gentle and easily allowed the boat to cut through against it with the wind in their favour.

Cam grimaced and rubbed his eyes.

"Ah," said Agazi, "I know that look. You've not slept on the water before, have you?"

Cam shook his head.

"No. Where are we?"

"About halfway to the Boardwalks. We've made good time. The wind has been kind to us. It'll get trickier as we enter the Lake - the water is treacherous there - but this little lady will get us through."

Agazi tapped the hull in a loving manner.

"Get Dunwald up," he added, airily, "we'll be docking in no time at all."

The morning carried on at a steady pace with Agazi skilfully guiding the boat upstream. By the time the morning mist had burnt itself away, they were at the mouth of the lesser lake. Here there were shallows and rocks waiting to catch the unsuspecting navigator, but Agazi's craft glided between all these obstacles and soon they were upon the glass-like water of the Lesser Lake with the outline of the Boardwalks barely a mile distant.

Cam's first sight of the city was with the sun casting its glory upon it, the tall roofs of Barrandel ablaze under the bright blue of the sky. He thought it one of the most beautiful sights he had ever seen. The sounds of a vibrant community drifted down to them, and there was even some small bustle at the docks which Agazi steered them toward.

Once they had reached these, it was the late afternoon; the sun's light had already become tinged with red and pink as Agazi secured his craft. Felgaron leapt up onto the Walk and took in a deep breath of air.

"There is nothing finer than the Lake in the sunshine," he sighed, "I have seen many sights in my time and this is one I would truly lament if it were to fall."

Dunwald joined him on the jetty and looked about them.

"On that we can agree," he said.

"If it's all the same to you gentlemen," Agazi said, gathering up a number of sacks and boxes from within his vessel, then clambering up onto the Walk himself, "I've got trading to do, and I want it done before Eismeer get here. May the Seven watch over you, and after all this has blown over come and find me in Lundang."

With that he bustled away, leaving the three companions to take in the scene in front of them. The threat of war was on their doorstep and yet still the day to day routines of the city did not stop. Cam marvelled that any of these people could even think of anything other than the imminent arrival of the Eismen army; he certainly could not.

"Come, my friends," Felgaron said, "We must speak to King Hedradour. However, I would caution that we leave all talk of our true mission until the threat of Eismeer has been dealt with."

Dunwald stared at him, wide eyed.

"You cannot be serious? The King must be told!"

"He will be," Felgaron replied sternly, "but Eismeer is the more immediate concern. What good would knowledge of Travellers in our world do if Barrandel falls? Let us survive this day before we face tomorrow."

The Captain glared at him for a moment longer, then gave a curt nod.

"As you say. Lead on."

Cam followed the two men and the city about him grew quickly. He was soon surrounded by tall roofs and wooden walkways, and everywhere they went they were accompanied by the sounds of the waters below them; lapping and dancing against the large struts that held the city above the waves.

After perhaps half an hour they reached the courtyard in front of the House of Barrandel and Cam saw it at last in its full glory.

It towered above them, gazing out over the city it protected with a watchful eye. The wintry sun glinted off the thick wooden beams, casting a golden-pink hue upon the scene. These beams reached upward to meet at the great, carved likeness of a roaring bear: the sigil of the Boardwalks.

Felgaron did not allow them to tarry at the sight, and soon the three men had entered the hall and found themselves in the darkness of the stairwell. Even here the sound of the lake water below could be heard, gentle yet insistent.

They climbed the stairs and came to a small but open landing, at one end of which were a pair of large, dark wood doors, guarded by a pair of stern looking men in leather armour, wielding spears.

Each of them gave a quick glance at Felgaron, who bowed with his arm across his chest. One of the guards then tapped on the base of the doors, which swung open to reveal a large hall with a high vaulted ceiling. There was also a large fire in the centre, behind which stood a stone throne carved from a rock that jutted through the floor.

In this last sat the figure of King Hedradour, a man in his late-middle years with long, auburn hair, and a clean shaven chin that sat below a pair of deep green eyes which flicked towards them as they entered.

Stood beside him were two other men, one in armour and a cloak similar to that of the guards throughout the city, and the other with darker skin and sleeveless armour.

Upon sight of Dunwald, the King stood and held his arms wide in a welcoming gesture.

"Captain Dunwald!" he said gleefully in a rich, clear voice. "It is a most gracious day to see you returned to us. Long has your mission been and much good has come of it, but overlong have you been away."

Dunwald bowed with his arm across his chest.

"My King, it is an honour to be upon the water once more, and to be in the presence of my Lord at last. The word is that Marshall Larin has stepped into his role with great success."

The King stepped down from his Throne and placed a hand upon the shoulder of the lighter skinned man, a warm expression on his face.

"He has indeed. I believe he is eager to hear any news you bring."

"I indeed look forward to it," Marshall Larin said, "and to welcoming you back, Captain Dunwald. Our city has been lessened by your departure, however necessary it was."

The King now turned his attention to Felgaron, and Cam noticed a subtle cooling of the King's mood.

"Long has it been since you have stood within my hall, Felgaron," he said, "and, while I cannot say I have had sleepless nights because of your absence, I bid you welcome also."

Felgaron bowed deeply and reverently.

"It is an honour to stand within your hall once more, King Hedradour, and I sincerely hope that I will spend many days here enjoying the hospitality of your people. It is good to see you, Marshall, and you, Araht."

Araht did not speak, choosing simply to bow. Larin, however, was not so circumspect.

"It is of no surprise to any that you return to Barrandel on such a day as this. I might even have placed gold upon the chance."

The King gave a cautioning look to his Marshall.

"You are welcome as long as you wish, as Larin well knows, but I too have known you for far too long to hope that your arrival here is merely by coincidence."

He returned to his throne and now sat, regarding the two men in front of him.

"I would have you tell me whatever it is you have brought to my door, and then allow us to prepare our defences for the coming of those accursed Eismen!"

Felgaron bowed deeply.

"Lord King, I do indeed have words that I would share with you," the Swordsman said tactfully, "but I fear they must wait until after the current crisis is over. Until then, we are at your service and the service of your City."

"That is well," cut in the Marshall, glaring at Felgaron, "for we have brought dire tidings to our King of great import."

"What tidings?" Felgaron asked, ignoring the man's tone.

The Marshall looked to his King, who nodded, then stepped forward and stared into the Swordsman's eyes.

"Ships from North Sel have been seen making the treacherous crossing to Mythravia," he said, tersely, "Araht brought me this information, and thus its integrity cannot be questioned."

Felgaron, with only a slight glance at Araht, nodded in acknowledgement.

"Long have we suspected the Bakslá have had dealings with that Isle. To discover we were correct is deeply troubling."

"It is more than troubling, Felgaron," the King cut in, his voice filled with barely controlled rage, "it is blasphemous and an act of outright war! No civilised people would have any dealings with that accursed rock, nor its inhabitants!"

"It is as my King says," Larin agreed, "and we must now consider what we are to do with this new revelation. Especially given the sightings of Bereun within our lands."

"What's Mythravia?"

Cam's simple question floated across the conversation and caused Larin and Araht to notice him for the first time.

"And who is this?"

King Hedradour's words were directed squarely at Cam, upon whom his eyes now rested for the first time since they had arrived.

Felgaron went to speak, but Hedradour raised a hand to silence him.

"No, I would hear it from his own mouth. Speak, man, and let me know you."

Cam looked once more to Felgaron, who half smiled and raised an eyebrow to him.

Seeing no other choice, Cam breathed in deeply, and did his best to bow as his companions had done before him.

"My name is Cam, King Hedradour."

"And where do you hail from, Cam," Hedradour asked, the name sounding unnatural in his throat.

"Lord King, if I may..." Felgaron began, but Hedradour cut him off immediately.

"You may not! I asked him to speak, and I would have him speak. I trust he will answer me honestly."

The King's eyes pierced Cam, leaving him naked and

exposed in the centre of the hall, which seemed to have grown. The distance between himself and the relative safety of the outside world now was insurmountable.

Felgaron turned to Cam, a knowing and thoughtful look in his eyes.

"Very well, Friend Cam. Answer the King honestly."

For a moment a vision of Edgeborough Castle and the life he had left behind floated across Cam's thoughts. It felt safe and welcoming, calling to him across the universe that now lay between him and his home.

Then he saw Sonia smiling at him as he approached Fingall's Tower, standing with Nikki, Jason, and Laura. And then he saw his house, and his mother, and he longed to back there and just disappear from the world. From all of the worlds.

The vision faded and he was left with King Hedradour's eyes staring deeply into him, a growing frustration and annoyance on his face. Cam suddenly became aware that he had been silent for many moments.

He took a deep breath, then began to speak.

"I'm a Traveller. I come from a village called Welverleigh. Me and my friend, Sonia, found ourselves here. We don't know how or why we got here, and we have no idea of how we're going to get home. Felgaron and Dunwald have been kind and helpful to us both, and that's why I'm here now – I have literally nowhere else to go. Except maybe back to Beregle, where Sonia is.

"All I want is to get us both home, and if there's anything you can do, King Hedradour, to help me achieve that I would be eternally grateful. Until then, like Felgaron said, I'll do whatever I can to help, though I don't expect that will be much if I'm honest."

Cam had not meant for so much to come out at once, but once he started the words flowed freely from him, all his thoughts and fears fighting to get themselves out into the open.

In a very strange way, Cam was relieved. The catharsis he felt hummed through his body; his shoulders relaxed, his head felt clearer, his limbs ached less, even his sight seemed sharpened.

It was only now that he realised that, quite literally, all eyes within the Throne Room of Barrandel were on him. Hedradour stared at him, disbelieving; Dunwald's face somewhere between impressed and unnerved; the various guards and advisors all stood, mouths agape, as if Cam had suddenly sprouted two heads.

And the silence! The deafening, total silence! As if the entire world both within and without Barrandel had stopped at his words. Even the sound of the lake lapping beneath them seemed quietened.

"Welverleigh..." Hedradour whispered.

"Indeed," Felgaron nodded, "Cam hails from Welverleigh. I am glad to see that his words are not lost upon you or your house, King."

Hedradour sat, lost in whatever thoughts were now swirling through his head.

"Whitesword who hails from Welverleigh..." the King breathed. "Have our days come to that?"

"It is so," Felgaron said, then he turned to Cam, "to answer your question, my friend, Mythravia is an island to the north. It is home to the Wizards we spoke of in Beregle."

The Swordsman now turned to face the King and his hall.

"Bereun are roaming your lands. North Sel is aligning itself with Mythravia. And now a Traveller steps forth from Holmfast. From Welverleigh, no less. I say to you all that the Planes of Reality are moving, and Rhydariel is in the gravest of peril. But, I have council for those that would hear it."

Here he looked pointedly at King Hedradour, who was still staring dumbfounded at Cam. After a moment, he roused himself from his stupor and looked to the Swordsman, his eyes filled with desperation.

"What council would you give? What possible council could you have against such an event?"

Felgaron ignored the King's tone and kept his voice level.

“Council against fear and despair. I know what time lies before us, and I say to you we will outlast. But all of Rhydariel must stand together. That is why I have come as Eismeer marches upon you. Not one hall nor village, no King nor serf, can be allowed to fall undefended! To survive the greater darkness that threatens all the world, we must first survive the twilight of Eismeer's hubris.”

The Swordsman stepped forward and placed a hand upon the King's shoulder.

“For the moment, and only for the moment, you must forget about the wider world and ensure the survival of your own people. Only when that has been achieved should we speak of the war that is to come.”

The King did not take his eyes off Felgaron.

“What do you say, Marshall Larin? “

Larin took a moment to compose himself before answering, his eyes darting between Cam, Felgaron, and his King.

“I would say,” he began carefully, “that Felgaron speaks aright. We cannot focus on tomorrow if it blinds us to today.”

The King nodded, still taking in all he had heard.

“And what of you, Captain Dunwald? Do you stand with Felgaron?”

Dunwald saluted.

“I stand with my King,” he said resolutely. “If we are to face the Seventh, it will darken our doors, Eismen or no. Let us look to our own people first, control what we can control. The forces of Eismeer are well within our capabilities.”

Hedradour, for a moment, looked to the floor, and it seemed to Cam that he bore all the troubles of the world upon him. Silence once more filled the Hall of Barrandel, none present even daring to breathe.

The King looked up.

“You speak aright indeed, Felgaron,” the King said at last, a new and dangerous tone to his voice, “and I will heed your words as if they were those of the Elderking himself.”

He turned now to all gathered before him, his eyes aflame.

"Marshall, you and Captain Dunwald are to prepare the city. All able to wield a weapon must be ready. Including you, Felgaron."

The King looked pointedly at the Swordsman, who simply stared back.

"I am going nowhere, King," he said levelly.

The King nodded, then turned his attention to Cam.

"You as well, boy," he hissed.

Cam gulped, barely containing his own fear.

"Yes. Of course."

His response was completely autonomic.

"Sound the horns," the King was continuing, "and send riders to all the nearest settlements. All swords are to come to Barrandel at the swiftest haste. Those from our city that cannot fight will be taken to the outlying villages south of the river and be sheltered there. Let us hope that Fohenk has eyes only for Barrandel. See it is done."

"My King!"

The two words rang out in chorus around the Throne Room.

The Boardwalks was going to war.

Chapter Sixteen

Before Swords Are Drawn

Cam felt the touch of a hand upon his shoulder, and a face close to his cheek.

"Come with me," Felgaron whispered.

He felt himself being led out of the Hall. They did not go back through the doors through which they entered, but instead went out of a side door onto a path that hugged the edges of the hall perilously above the lake below. The evening sun shone down on them both as they walked, Felgaron ahead and Cam following numbly.

Eventually, they reached a courtyard where the air was crisp and clear. The lapping of the water beneath blended perfectly with the birds that fluttered in and out of the trees that stood at the each of the four corners.

Felgaron strode over to one of the benches that sat beneath these trees and placed his pack upon it. He began to rummage around in it while Cam watched on confused.

"I apologise that your training will be brief," the Swordsman said over his shoulder, "but, alas, time is not on our side. I would prefer that you did not fight at all, but there will be more days than this when your sword arm is called for."

He stood and faced Cam.

"Take out your sword."

Cam fumbled at his belt to draw the sword that Lekkon had thrown at his feet in Glacier Pass.

It was lighter than he had remembered.

Felgaron regarded him for a moment.

"Have you ever used one of those?" he asked.

"Like I said, a bit of stage combat," Cam said.

He looked up at Felgaron, who stared back at him with an expression that looked dangerously close to being impressed.

"In battle?" the Swordsman asked, pointedly.

Cam looked at the blade once more. He suddenly felt as though he was holding something completely and utterly alien to him.

He swallowed involuntarily.

"No. Never in battle."

"Then listen and learn. I cannot teach you to become a master in the time we have, but I aim to teach you enough to keep you alive. Now, what about this?"

Felgaron held aloft a metallic bundle that he had pulled from his pack. Cam recognised it immediately as a shirt of chain.

"Yeah, I've worn that. Heavy stuff. Never liked it."

Felgaron unrolled the bundle to reveal the shirt fully. It was about Cam's size, though it had clearly been used before – there was evidence of repair work on some of the rings.

"It may well be the difference between life and death. It is yours now, as is this."

The swordsman now gave to him a simple, brown, padded jacket. This also had signs of repair, with some stitching holding in whatever Rhydariel used as padding. It had a leather lace to tie it up at the front, just like the ones Cam had used back in Edgeborough.

"Looks good."

"Put it on," Felgaron said gravely, "and do not tarry."

Cam did as he was bid, and found himself reliving an experience he had not even thought about since the day he and Sonia had arrived in this world.

Every day at Edgeborough Castle he had dressed himself in costumes just like the stuff he was now putting on; hose, jackets, cloaks, armour. And while his mind knew that this was a much more dangerous and deadly moment in his life, the fact that there was even the smallest level of familiarity about it calmed him.

In all of the chaos and things he had never seen, or heard, or even conceived of before, here at least was something he had a modicum of experience with.

The chain was heavy, and pulled on his shoulders, but it fit, and the jacket protected him against any further discomfort. Felgaron had also acquired for him a belt with a simple sword frog to hang his blade in. This he tightened around his waist securely and stood for a moment, enjoying the fact that his body felt at least slightly at home in his new garb.

Felgaron nodded.

"We shall start with some basics. Always deal with the man you can see ahead of you, do not get distracted. Every swing will be aimed to kill you. Do not turn your back on your enemy. If you do, you die. Do not hesitate if you see your chance to finish your opponent. If you do, you die. And, do not enjoy any strike or kill. If you do, you die."

Cam looked back at the Swordsman. He told the schools tours a similar thing, although in very different language.

In the movies, he used to say, *people stand over their enemies and deliver beautiful, Shakespearian speeches before they kill them. It never happened! You stab them, pull your sword out, and move on.*

The children and teachers always laughed. If only they could see him now.

"Understood."

"Good. To start with, I just want to see what you can do. I will swing, you block. Let us begin."

Felgaron stepped back and allowed Cam a moment to ready himself, then swung his sword hard at him.

It came from above, and Cam barely had enough time to register what was happening before feebly lifting his blade above his head.

It deflected the blow, but only just.

Suddenly Cam regretted not truly listening in the training

sessions with Jason.

"Too slow," Felgaron said simply.

"Yeah," said Cam, "I'm a little rusty."

He had meant it as a joke, trying to calm his own nerves, but Felgaron did not smile.

"Again."

Another swipe, this time from the left. Another poor parry.

"Again!"

And again. And again.

Cam was already beyond tired, sweat beginning to cling to his brow and his body straining against the weight of his armour. His breath began to rattle in and out of his lungs, his sight became blurry, and his reactions became slower.

Then, Felgaron aimed yet another swipe at him Cam's left.

Cam once again did not have time to parry it, but some long forgotten bit of training stored away at the back of his mind kicked in.

He stepped back, out of the reach of Felgaron's blade, then moved past him and aimed his own strike at the Swordsman's side. It was weak and poorly directed, but it brought a slight smile from Felgaron.

"Better."

Cam stood frozen in shock. To Felgaron this was a tiny, imperceptible improvement, but to Cam it was a stratospheric revelation.

"Do not rest on it," Felgaron continued, preparing for another strike, "your swing would not have hurt, let alone killed me. You cannot afford to be afraid to use your weapon properly. Either you kill them, or they kill you. It is as simple as that."

The reality of his situation once again loomed large in Cam's mind, evaporating the joy he had felt mere moments ago.

"Yeah. Sorry." Cam breathed.

Felgaron put a hand on his shoulder.

"I do not mean to chastise you. I simply do not want to see you die. Your world is not our world, and you have never seen battle. It is... well, there is nothing quite like it."

A vision formed in Cam's mind.

Men with fear in their eyes, blood on their hands and faces, doing all they could to survive. Blocking blows with their shields, swords, axe hafts. Arms and legs flailing outward in fits of instinct, using every part of their body to protect their lives. There was no form, no beauty, no grace in the way they wielded their weapons, just pure and simple necessity.

All about them were the screams of those who had failed. Half-conscious, dying bodies, confused in their agony; not knowing what had happened or how to stop it. Uncomprehending eyes looking up at the carnage about them, pleading for someone to end their suffering.

The vision faded and Cam sunk to his knees, his mind broken and his heart heavy.

He had arrogantly believed that he could possibly imagine what battle would be like – after all, he had seen documentaries and read books with contemporary historical accounts. He had even seen and held some of the more gruesome weaponry that mankind had developed to perfect the art of killing on another.

He could not have been farther from the truth.

"Felgaron," he breathed, sobbing, "I'm not ready for this. I can't... I... I can't."

The Swordsman knelt before him, a comforting hand on his shoulder once more.

"No-one ever is ready. And you never will be, no matter how much death you face. It will never be easy, and nor should it be."

Cam's body shook with fear.

He did not want to die! He did not want to fight! He just wanted to go home!

More than anything he wanted to be with Sonia, back at Edgeborough Castle, showing hordes of hot, grumpy, ungrateful, demanding customers into Fingall's Tower, where they were both safe from the constant spectre of death that seemed to have followed them from the moment that Dunwald had found them at Gismay's farm.

"Is there definitely going to be a battle?" he asked, attempting to pull himself into some semblance of equilibrium. "And if there is, can we win it?"

Felgaron looked up at him and answered earnestly.

"Eismeer would not have attacked Farn Bridge if they did not intend to attack Barrandel. It is too far away for a simple skirmish. As for the result of the battle? I know not. It shall be a tough fight. You can never predict how these things will go, nor should you try."

Cam looked at him, confused.

"Surely a battle is a battle?"

"Not so, though all battles begin in one of three ways. You either feel you will win, you know not how the battle will go, or you know you will lose.

"If you feel certain you shall win then prepare for your downfall. Such conceit can only lead to one result. If you are uncertain about the result then you fight if only because there is a chance you will prevail, a chance that you shall live to fight another day."

The Swordsman's voice tailed away, as if his own thoughts had dried up.

Cam looked at him and waited, but the Swordsman did not continue.

"And the ones you know you'll lose?"

Felgaron took a breath, casting his eyes to the sky.

"Who wants to live forever?"

Cam had not noticed until now worn Felgaron's face looked; the Swordsman's eyes had a grey tint to them and his skin was wrinkled far beyond what Cam would expect to see for one of his age. It was as though many years caught up with him at once.

"How many battles have you fought in?"

The question would ultimately solve nothing, but it at least moved the conversation, and his thoughts, away from the despair he found himself in.

Felgaron shrugged.

"I've lost count."

"How many men have you... you know?" Cam's voice was shaking. Did he really want to know the answer?

"I've lost count."

Felgaron's voice was flat, non-committal, as if Cam had asked him how many hot meals he had eaten.

This man had killed, many times over. That was a part of the new reality he found himself in; killing was a way of life, a necessity to survival. Cam did not know if he could ever bring himself to do it.

Sooner or later he was going to find out, and he was not sure he liked either outcome.

If he was unable to do bring himself to do it, then he was not willing to do whatever it took to get he and Sonia home, as he had promised her he would. But if he was able to kill? The deeply sickening and uncomfortable feeling in Cam's stomach told him all he needed to know.

"I don't think I could ever..."

"When your very existence hangs by a thread, when all you are and all you ever will be rests on one instantaneous decision, you will find out. Until that moment, you will never truly know who you are or what you are capable of."

Felgaron's eyes were serious, but they had a softer look to them now than they had before.

"There is no crime in simply staying alive."

Cam allowed the words to wash over him, and he saw the wisdom in them. He knew that he had the right to defend himself, but there was still the hideous feeling deep down inside him that said he could not do it.

If he did not, he would die. He would never get home, and Sonia would be left alone in this world.

But if he had killed, would she ever want to know him again?

Every answer posed new questions, and every question scared him to his very core. He wished nothing more than for the whole situation to just disappear and leave him be.

"Come," Felgaron urged gently, "we have little more time. I would offer you what training I am able. If only so that you can avoid being killed, even if you cannot bring yourself to do the deed."

Cam looked up once more at the Swordsman.

"Does not doing it, not even wanting to do it, make me weak?"

Felgaron shook his head, and there was a genuine look of comfort and reassurance on his face.

"Quite the opposite," he said, earnestly, "and the fact you would even ask that question says far more about you than you might guess. And it is why I will do everything I can to make sure you, and others like you, stay alive. Now, up. We have more training to get through."

Cam nodded, and the pair began their macabre dance once more.

With each swing, Cam felt himself getting steadily more used to at least having the weapon in his hand and using if defensively. But the reality of what he was soon going to have to do to simply stay alive was beginning to claw at his mind.

After another hour, Felgaron called a halt to their training. He offered Cam a flask of Hocliquor, which was gratefully, if breathlessly, accepted, and a small bite of Hocram.

The sun was beginning to lower toward the horizon as the last of the afternoon passed, and the breeze now had a chilling edge as they sat.

"You have done well," the Swordsman said, "I only wish there was more I could do."

Cam nodded.

"I've come this far," he heard himself say.

Felgaron looked at him with an impressed eye once more.

"You have indeed," he agreed, "and if I can have any say in the matter, you will go much further."

They both took another swig from the flask, and more vitality returned to Cam's body and mind. His thoughts began to reorder themselves from the jumble of emotions he had collapsed into earlier, and things he had not thought about in days surfaced within his mind.

"Who are the Wizards?" he asked aloud.

"Powerful beings," Felgaron answered, "whom I hope you avoid having to encounter for as long as possible."

He fell silent and stared at the floor for many moments, and a heavy atmosphere fell over the courtyard. The wind in the branches and the lapping of the water beneath their feet was loud in Cam's ears as he waited for the Swordsman to continue.

"To give you their full history would take time that we do not have. Suffice it to say that they have forever been a plague upon Rhydariel. Wherever there has been trouble, they are never been more than a step away."

Cam now looked at the Swordsman, searching his worn face for any secrets it might give away.

"What kind of 'wizards' are they?" he asked.

"How mean you?"

Cam shrugged.

"Where I come from, wizards are usually depicted as old men. Long beards, pointy hats, staffs, that sort of thing. And the only magic that we ever see is either trickery or technology."

Felgaron laughed softly.

"They are certainly not that," he said, his dark humour infecting his words, "and would that they were. It would certainly make the task that lies before us far easier.

"These are not 'wizards' as you describe them, and they are most certainly not magical. Their power is much more manifest, and when it is brought to bear it is enough to wipe all life from the face of our world. You have already seen a small portion of it in Eismeer."

The Swordsman turned his face to him with a meaningful expression.

"The storm?" Cam gasped. "They did that?"

"I am almost certain," Felgaron nodded, "for that was no weather of the natural world, and there are very few beings or powers that could create something as terrible."

Cam looked at his feet, gobsmacked.

"But if they can do that, how the hell are we supposed to beat them?"

He looked to Felgaron for an answer, but the Swordsman was deep in thought and did not appear to have heard his words.

A longer, deeper silence passed between them than any that had come before. If what Felgaron was saying was true – and Cam had no reason to doubt that it was not – then he and Sonia were in a far more devastating plight than he could possibly have imagined.

Once more his mind was filled with the notion that ever since that day in Fingall's Tower, every single step they had taken had led them both further and further from their life, their home, and their own world. And with each day that passed he became more and more disillusioned to the idea that they would ever find a way home.

As all of these thoughts flashed across his mind, an image of that day in the Tower rose to the surface:

The Cloaked figure.

Cam had now seen him twice; once in the Tower and then again in Glacier Pass. Whether it was dream or reality, Cam was still not certain, and he nearly dismissed the thought until a single word echoed about his mind.

"What does Rhogân mean?"

The Swordsman, seemingly awoken from his own thoughts, looked up with a curious expression that Cam could not read.

"Why do you ask?"

"It's just something I've heard," Cam said, trying to sound calm.

Felgaron leaned in and began to loom over him.

"Where? When?"

"After Lekkon attacked me in Glacier Pass," Cam replied, "I heard this voice in my head and I had some sort of... vision? Maybe? I don't really know. It could've been a dream. But I definitely heard the word Rhogân."

Even as he said the words Cam knew how they would sound, and he hoped beyond hope that Felgaron believed him.

"What did you see?"

"I don't really know," Cam said, trying once more to control himself, "it's hard to explain. There was this light, and a voice in my head. It showed me the Seventh, I think, and Helrhûn. Or maybe it was just what he would do to Rhydariel? Then the light disappeared, and I was on a beach. The sand was black and the water hurt when I stood in it. There was a figure. I'd seen it before, on the day we came here. It was a man, I'd guess, but I don't know for certain. He wore a black cloak, and there was no face under the hood. He kept shouting at me. Then I fell back and woke up in the snow."

He had not noticed it until he finished speaking, but Cam was panting and sweat clung to his brow once more. His heart raced as his mind was forced to relive things that had pushed it to the very brink of madness, and he felt the pit of his stomach fall away as the Swordsman looked at him.

He had hoped that his outburst would be met with an expression of derision, or reassurance; something that would prove he had only dreamt those terrible things, that they were nothing more than the creations of his addled imagination.

Yet Felgaron's face was one of resigned sadness.

"That figure you saw was Rhogân," the Swordsman breathed, "and he is the First of the Wizards of the North; their 'king'. That you have been shown him, or shown to him, as you travelled to our realm is... But then, you seeing him at all is deeply troubling."

Cam stared blankly at him.

"Why?" he croaked.

"Because Rhogân was killed six thousand years ago, and has never walked this Plane or any other since. Or, at least, that is what I believed. If his soul has endured then we are in more immediate danger than even I had guessed."

The Swordsman once again fell silent, a dark look upon his face.

“Felgaron?” Cam began, but got no further.

A cacophony of sound erupted about them, shaking them from their conversation.

First, Cam distinguished the sound of trumpets calling urgently across the city, and then the swiftly approaching sound of feet running along the Walk. Cam looked to where the sound was coming from and recognised the figure of Agazi.

“Felgaron!” the Merchant cried, his voice strained by exertion and what sounded like panic.

“What news?” the Swordsman called back, pulling his glance away from Cam.

Agazi rushed up to them and stopped, leaning forward to put his hands on his knees and catch his breath.

“Fohenk's ships,” the Merchant panted.

“How many?”

Agazi pulled himself up to his full height and face them both, sweat dripping from his brow.

“At least ten by my count,” he rasped.

Felgaron did not even blink.

“Has the King been informed?”

“Aye,” Agazi nodded, “when I saw them I sailed back as fast as the wind would take me and told every guard I could. Then I came to find you.”

“How quickly will they be upon us?” Felgaron pressed.

“The middle-night, perhaps before.” Agazi breathed, then looked about himself for the first time. “Where's Dunwald?”

“With the King,” Felgaron answered, “and that is where we must be. Come, both of you, to Barrandel!”

Chapter Seventeen

Dinner In Beregle

Lord Marn sat in his hall, staring into the flickering flames of the candles that lined the centre of the dining table that had been set for he and his daughters. He followed their dance avidly, letting his thoughts on the day organise themselves and slide across his mind.

Very little of any interest had happened in the days since Felgaron's visit, and life had trundled on without so much as a thought for the outside world. The news of Eismeer's attack on Farn Bridge had, of course, swiftly become public knowledge, and Marn doubted there would be a patron in the tavern that evening whose lips were not touched by the talk of war.

It had been a long time coming, he mused morbidly.

Whatever peace that had existed between the two nations, if one could ever have truly called it that, had always been fragile. It had held for roughly six months since the last skirmish, and even then there were constant scouting parties staring at each other across the River Lun in what was agreed upon by both sides as being 'secrecy'. Though an assault on the only fortified crossing of that river was certainly a more bold move than any Fohenk had attempted in recent memory.

War, all out and bloody, was most definitely on the horizon.

And then, of course, there was Felgaron himself.

Why had he spoken so guardedly? Marn had never known the Swordsman as one to mince his words or hide his thoughts, even from Lords. What could possibly be happening that would warrant such secrecy? He had not known about the attack on Farn Bridge before Marn's scout had arrived, or if he had he play-acted extremely convincingly, so whatever answers he was seeking surely were not linked to that.

Though, Marn mused, it was surely no coincidence that no sooner had Captain Dunwald, King Hedradour's spy, left Eismeer there was a reopening of hostilities. Had Lord Fohenk uncovered his true identity, perhaps? And why was he travelling with Felgaron at all? The Swordsman was never known to hold particular allegiance with either side.

A mercenary through and through, Marn reflected.

He focussed his mind once more on the candles as his household began to bring in the necessities of the meal, and he gladly accepted the goblet of wine that was placed before him.

A few moments later, both Ianor and Carial walked in from the family chambers and took their places at the table, bowing to their Lord Father as they did so.

"Welcome, my daughters," Marn said, a broad smile upon his face, "it does my heart good to see you again."

"And ours you, father," Carial cooed.

Ianor quickly flashed a smile at him, though behind it was a tired and worn expression.

"How has the day fared for you?" Marn asked her.

Ianor sighed.

"The news from Farn Bridge has put my soldiers on edge," she said tersely, "and I have put on extra drills and stationed more guards on the walls as a precaution."

"You believe we are in danger?" Carial asked loftily.

"It is my job to believe we are in danger," Ianor retorted.

Carial raised her eyebrows toward her sister.

"I thank you for your diligence, though I am not certain how Eismeer would feel to know that you don't trust them."

Ianor snapped her head up to respond, but Marn cut across her softly.

"It is not about mistrust, Carial, as you know well. Ianor is doing what she believes is best for our people, and she has my blessing to do what she deems necessary."

Carial nodded slowly and met Ianor's bullish gaze across the table.

The tension of the moment was broken by the serving of food, which had been expertly prepared by the household. The sight and smell of the meal took over the hall and eased their minds for a moment, and they ate heartily.

"What make you both of Felgaron?" Marn asked, seeking to break the silence.

"I make of him what I said at the time," Ianor said sternly, "I do not trust his motives."

"Wherefor?"

"Any man who refuses to pledge allegiance to any other than himself either has something to hide, no honour, or both."

"He has gone now," said Carial, a soothing note to her voice, "let him to his own business and focus upon your own."

"Would that I could," Ianor snapped back at her sister, "but there is something that unsettled me about his manner. What was his business, and what has it to do with father? And why would he not tell us more?"

Carial shrugged.

"I saw no harm in it. He asked a question we could not answer, so we did not. Now he has gone and will soon be King Hedradour's problem, if he is not already."

Ianor regarded her sister. Carial had always been the more thoughtful of the two of them and, while Ianor did not see this as a weakness, she did note that it gave her a tendency to overthink and ignore obvious, simple signs.

"But why should a mere swordsman need to know what transpires in our lands?"

"The lone agent can get where others cannot," Marn countered, as diplomatically as he could "as well you know."

Carial nodded once more.

"When you send out scouts do they not work alone, or only in small groups? Mayhap his business is personal and he simply did not want to burden our Father with the details?"

Ianor shook her head, then looked back out of the window once more.

“Then why come to us at all?” she mused. “No, there is something else going on.”

Carial laughed, a sound like delicate glass.

“You fantasise intrigue where there plainly is none,” she said, “such is the life of peace for a soul of war.”

Ianor once more opened her mouth to retort, a rage flashing behind her eyes, but Marn raised a hand.

“All good soldiers seek peace and know its true value,” he said calmly, “and your sister has no fear of living under its embrace.”

“Quite so, Father,” Carial agreed, smiling sweetly.

Marn returned her smile, and looked to Ianor.

“Have you any more concerns, daughter mine?”

“About Felgaron?” she asked, as gently as her emotions allowed. “No, not specifically. But...”

She looked both of them in the eyes for a moment, then shook her head.

“Pay no mind to it,” she said, busying herself once more with her meal.

Marn and Carial glanced at each other uncertainly.

“Pay no mind to what?”

Her father's question seemed to fill the room and drown out the sounds of their meal. Ianor did all she could to focus on her plate and not look up.

“Ianor?”

She felt Marn's eyes burning into the top of her head, which she kept down for as long as she dared.

“Everyone that is not my father, my sister, or myself, leave. Guards and household alike. We will call you when you are required.”

Ianor now looked up at met her father's eyes. He studied her for a moment, then nodded.

“Do as Lady Ianor says,” he proclaimed.

The sound of feet shuffling out of the room, accompanied

by the clink of mail, signalled that the request had been heeded, and after a few moments there was silence.

“You may now speak freely, daughter,” Marn said softly.

Ianor took a moment to collect her thoughts, then looked at both of them earnestly once more.

“I know how these words will sound to you, but I swear to you I speak the truth. I fear that there are forces at work, within and without our walls, that would seek to undermine not only your authority, Lord Father, but the world at large. I cannot explain it fully, but there is a feeling in the air that unsettles me.”

Ianor looked, pleading at both of them to listen to her and take her words as she said them.

Carial's expression changed from one of amusement, to one of confusion.

“What mean you?” she asked.

Ianor paused for a moment, uncertain how to continue.

“Speak, daughter,” Marn urged.

“I have heard... rumours. Nothing more,” Ianor began cautiously, raising her hand before the inevitable rebuttal, “but rumours that come from sources that are not fanciful or prone to whims. There have been shadows in Beregle.”

Carial blinked at her sister, uncomprehending.

“Shadows?”

“Half seen shapes in dark corners, figures at the edges of sight.”

Ianor's voice was dark and quiet, as if she feared she would be overheard.

“Some have told me that they have felt as if there were eyes behind their walls, or of hearing footsteps in empty corridors. There is something at work in Beregle and I fear that Felgaron and his companions might be a part of it.”

Now Carial laughed openly.

“My dear sister, you and those who council you are becoming paranoid of your own senses. 'Shadows' in Beregle? I've never heard such fanciful notions. Perhaps you should no longer seek your informants out whilst they are at the inn.”

For half a moment Ianor looked as if she would launch herself at her sister in unbridled anger, but the steely glint within her father's eyes told her this was not a wise course.

“Perhaps,” she conceded through gritted teeth, “and perhaps there is nothing sinister to all of this. But Felgaron's visit has put me on edge and it brought back a number of conversations I have had these past weeks.”

“And why did you not tell Felgaron of these conversations?” asked Marn, a tinge of annoyance to his voice. “This seems exactly the sort of thing he was describing.”

“I did not tell him because there's nothing to tell! They are only rumours!”

She caught herself, seeing the smile now spread across her father's face.

His plan had worked.

“Only rumours,” Ianor repeated.

Marn's smile was warm, and his eyes soft.

“Indeed they are,” he said, “and I do not blame you for holding them to yourself. If there were more to Felgaron's questions then perhaps your apprehension would prove to be founded. But, as things are, there is little to tell me that anything untoward is at play.”

“I believe our father speaks wisely,” Carial chimed, “and, though I trust your judgement in these matters more than any other in these walls, I fear that this time your instincts have led you astray.”

Ianor nodded slowly.

“You are both almost certainly right,” she sighed, “ but there is a nagging doubt at the back of my mind. I feel as though I am missing something, but what it is I cannot even begin to guess.”

“Then stop guessing,” her father said, with an air of finality, “if there is truly an answer out there then let it find you, rather than chase it into hiding. The watched pot never boils, as you mother used to say.”

Ianor sighed, resigning herself to the wisdom of her

family.

"I have perhaps created a mystery where there was none. I shall put it from my mind unless I hear something more certain."

"I think that is all for the good," Carial said, "and, as your loving sister, I will do all I can to keep you from any further flights of fancy."

Ianor looked at her, a genuine smile across her face.

"It would be appreciated," she said.

"Ah," Marn cried, a humorous lilt to his voice, "an accord between my daughters! Let us praise the Seven for the day they have sent!"

The three laughed and finished their meal, and talked of many other happier things as they did so. And when, at last, the final morsel of food and drop of wine had been dealt with, the three parted company for the evening; Marn to his personal chamber, Ianor to the barracks, and Carial for a turn around the village.

The air that greeted her outside was cool and crisp, the first snap of a long winter reaching out its fingers to the top of the mountains at last.

Carial revelled in it.

She wandered through the square and to a small door in the mountain wall, half hidden from view by barrels and sacks of grain.

Taking a key from her pocket, she carefully unlocked it and, making sure she was not followed, ducked into the passageway beyond.

This was cut straight into the rock and had, once upon a time, served as the entrance to a number of guard posts built within the side of the mountain, overlooking the switchback road that climbed from the fertile plains of the Bowalt below. They had been supplanted by two new stone towers that stood on either side of the road, leaving the old guard posts as storage that was seldom used.

As she strode down the gently sloping corridor, Carial ran through her sister's words at dinner once more, and smiled to herself.

She had managed to quiet Ianor's inquisitive mind with barely any effort whatsoever. So much for her much vaulted vigilance!

And, even better, she had done it in such a way that had kept her father closed to the idea that there was anything to her words. This would, no doubt, become more difficult over time, but by then all of her plans would be in motion and her sister would have no choice but to follow her.

She smiled broadly to herself as she entered the cool of one of the empty guardrooms. Detritus littered the place, untouched from the moment it was left here, but it would serve her purposes well.

Carial contemplated what she was about to accomplish.

For too long had Beregle sat at the fringes of Rhydariel's thoughts, forgotten by the rest of the Five Kingdoms, maligned and ignored. Not since the time of the Whitesword had Beregle commanded any respect from the other Lords and Kings, and that was all about to change.

She looked about her, making absolutely certain that she was alone. Once this was established, she once more checked the corridor behind her before closing and locking the door.

A banner fluttered in the breeze outside.

"You know that is unnecessary," said a deep voice.

Carial rolled her eyes.

"So you say, yet people are starting to notice you," she responded, "and one of us has to take precautions."

She turned to face the figure that had joined her.

Hooded, black robes with elegant gold trim hung above polished black boots. The hood covered the top of the face beneath it, and a golden half-mask covered the lower portion, leaving only the eyes visible. These were piercing, almost glowing in the dim light; two red-brown circles gazing back at her.

Though she could see no facial features, Carial knew that an expression of disdain was being aimed at her.

"You disapprove of caution?" she asked.

The Figure did not move.

"We disapprove of lack of faith," it replied simply.

Carial laughed.

"This from the people who demand I prove myself worthy of their trust? Now who is lacking in faith?"

The Figure's eyes flashed for a moment.

"We do not give our assistance to those who are beneath us. You will do well to remember that."

"But you are beginning to attract attention!"

"Attention is irrelevant. So are your concerns."

Carial scoffed.

"You are the one who told me your presence must be hidden until the appropriate time! And what do you do to hide yourself? Nothing! People are becoming suspicious!"

"Then control your people."

The response was calm, unmoved by her words. Its simplicity infuriated Carial.

"The people of Beregle are loyal to my father, and to his house. But I am not a Lord, merely the daughter of one."

The eyes brightened once more.

"And you wish to be more than that."

Carial wheeled round and stared at the Figure.

"I deserve to be more than that!" she spat. "And speaking of such matters, have you given thought to my offer?"

The eyes dimmed again, content that she was now back in line.

"We have."

Carial did all she could to hold her scorn.

"And?"

A cold, unblinking stare.

"No."

Carial glared back at the creature before her.

"But why not? Beregle would be a perfect stronghold for you! We are in the centre of Rhydariel, we have access to Eismeer and Ebras, we are well defended! What more could you need?"

"You and your people are weak. You have nothing to offer us."

Carial stepped forward, mastering her fear and facing the creature head on.

"The people may be weak. Indeed, my family may be weak. But I am not. I know what power I have within me, and I know what I want. Nothing, not even you, could stop me from achieving it."

The Figure regarded her with what she felt might be an amused expression.

"If that is so, why do you need us?"

"Because I would see Beregle retake its rightful place within Rhydariel! With you at my back I could achieve that and more! The people would rally behind me and flock to our banner! Not just those of the Beregland, but of Ebras, Eismeer, and the rest! The world would be at our feet!"

"But what have you to offer us?"

Carial stared at the Figure, her gaze unblinking.

"Myself. My father may be ignorant to our history, but not I! I know what claim we could have upon Rhydariel. I intend to stake that claim."

"Does your father know of us?"

"Of course not. I gave you my word. My father is not suspicious, yet, but my sister is of quicker wit than him. She has begun to listen to the murmurs and whispers of people."

"We know. We saw."

The voice was always so assured. Carial doubted the thing had emotions, or even a concept of what they were.

"So," she pressed as pointedly as she dared, "what of my offer? I will give myself, and Beregle, unto you if you will give me the nation of the Beregland as it once was. As it should be."

The Figure seemed to grin back at her.

"We will inform you of our decision."

The Figure turned once more toward the window.

"No!" Carial demanded. "I will not wait any longer! I will not allow you to..."

"Allow us?"

An invisible force suddenly filled the room, throwing Carial back against the wall.

The Figure span on its heels and grew to nearly twice its height, the eyes now exploding with colour and burning deep into her.

Carial choked for breath, her body flattened against the stone, all the while a deep throbbing within her ears.

"Do not forget your place, mortal. You are naught but the dirt beneath our boots, filth that is only allowed to exist by our whims alone. You answer to us. We do as we please. Understood?"

Carial tried with all her rapidly disappearing strength to croak out an answer.

"Understood?"

Summoning all the might she had left, Carial finally forced a single syllable out of her airless lungs.

"Yes."

The force dissipated immediately, sending her winded form crashing to the floor.

The Figure returned to its normal size, though the eyes did not lose any of their intensity. They looked down upon her, as a hunter on their prey.

"We will inform you of our decision."

Carial nodded her understanding.

The Figure looked away from her at last and stepped out of her sight.

A banner fluttered once more, and Carial was left alone.

Chapter Eighteen

The Battle Of The Boardwalks

After Agazi had found them both, Felgaron and Cam had moved quickly.

First, there was a brief and frantic council that King Hedradour had held where the plans for the defence of his city had been finalised:

A small group would row halfway down the walk pull the supports from beneath. This would mean that the city was safe from any of Fohenk's forces that wished to attack from the shores of the lake. However, the news of ships had meant that the city was not safe from the water. The Marshall had, as such, made defending the docks a priority.

After this, Cam remembered being led by Agazi, now donning his own, worn, leather armour, to the armoury of Barrandel. Here he had been handed a hauberk with plates of studded leather to wear over his mail shirt, a collar of mail to protect his neck, and then he had been handed a bow and belt quiver. The arrows he had seen before, but the bow was far larger than anything he had handled. He silently doubted he could even draw it back, let alone cause any damage with it.

That thought was not allowed to linger too long in his head as he and Agazi had been whisked away by Felgaron toward the docks.

A great column of soldiers of all types were marching

through the city to various defensive positions at the orders of their Marshall and their King. It was this host that they had followed until they came to the large and open quayside that ran the entire length of the eastern edge of the city, and acted as a buffer against any invaders in times such as this. They were lined with huge crossbows and towers for archers, and had three powerful catapults designed specifically to attack oncoming ships.

Felgaron ordered Cam and Agazi to join a company of soldiers that would remain hidden in the houses that stood behind the docks, awaiting a signal from the Marshall to charge out and ambush their attackers. He then bade them both farewell, and went away to help with the rest of the preparations.

What remained of the evening passed slowly for the men now gathered here, waiting as they were for the Eismen advance. Their scouts had confirmed that the enemy would be upon them by midnight, and that was but two hours away.

Many people, soldiers and others, were busy helping to get the final preparations in place. Arrows were being brought to the archers, rocks and stones to the catapults; all manner of essential materials for the fight about to engulf them.

The torches, both within the towers and upon the docks themselves, would soon be extinguished, making it less easy for the approaching enemy to make out their defences. All the fires and lights in the city itself, save for those essential for food and warmth for casualties, would also be extinguished.

It was in darkness that the men of Ebras would await their ancient enemy.

Cam found himself being utterly useless. He was not strong enough to lift much of what needed to be lifted, he did not know enough of war or tactics to be of any assistance, and he was still struggling to fully comprehend what was going on about him.

A movement next to him told him that Agazi had returned from finding them some food to fortify them before the battle.

The Merchant handed Cam a pouch of dried berries and

seeds, and a small flask of what smelt like mead, then smiled pleasantly as he sat next to him.

"Master Cam, what brings you here?"

Despite everything, Cam heard himself laugh.

"Oh," he said, trying to sound jovial, "the view mostly."

"Indeed, houses by the water are often sought after for just such a reason. Never thought I'd live to see the day where I could afford a property like this!"

Cam marvelled at the Merchant. To be on the verge of so much death and fear, and to still be making merry? He was either the bravest man in the history of war, or completely bereft of his senses.

"I've heard the prices are to die for," he said, without thinking.

Agazi clapped him on the shoulder, laughing heartily.

"The kind of man I want by my side in battle," the Merchant said brightly, "if you can't escape danger, you might as well laugh at it, eh?"

"Yeah, I suppose so," Cam sighed, and looked back out at the hive of activity that was the docks.

Agazi watched him, and the two sat in silence for a while, both contemplating that which lay ahead.

"Your first one?" Agazi asked, nonchalantly.

Cam nodded without looking at him.

"Aye, I know that look," the Merchant continued, "like a rabbit in a trap. If it helps, you're doing better than me my first time."

Cam looked sidelong at him.

"Yeah?"

"Oh, much better," Agazi mused, "by this time I was already sitting in a puddle of my own fear. And you can never properly get that out of your breeches."

He smiled at Cam once more, and the two shared another gentle laugh.

The entire situation still threatened to overwhelm him, and how Agazi could find it within himself to be amusing in such a moment was a complete mystery, but Cam was glad that he was there even if he barely knew the man.

“I don't mean to be rude but why are you here, Agazi?” Cam asked, a thought striking him. “You're a merchant. You've got your own boat. Even after you'd seen them and told someone, you could still have avoided the ships and been back home. Safe and away from all of this.”

Agazi nodded, a more serious expression on his face now.

“I could, but I'd only be delaying my battle rather than avoiding it. Lundang occupies a strategic point on the river. And though we are loosely ruled by Lord Marn, neither Ebras or Beregle truly wish to lay a claim upon us. We are alone.

“But,” he continued, a brighter note to his voice, “that also means that we are not counted among the Five Kingdoms. So, for a long time, everyone else has ignored us as well. Including Eismeer. But if that's about to change, if Fohenk has decided that he wants to claim the Western Lands for himself, Lundang will need to be defended. I don't see any advantage in waiting to face them. What about you?”

Cam took a moment to himself before answering; partly because he wanted to give the Merchant's answer time to settle in his own mind, but mostly because he felt that his gut response of 'I have no choice' did not seem adequate after Agazi's words.

“I... um... I have a friend. A very good friend. I'm worried about her. She's in Beregle at the moment. She's tough and can look after herself, but if Fohenk decided to attack Beregle then she would be in danger. We spent some time in Eismeer. It... We weren't very welcome there. Fohenk tried to hang us, actually. So I suppose I'm fighting for revenge, and to protect my friend.”

Agazi nodded at him, an genuine understanding in his expression.

“Worthy causes,” he said, “but I do wonder what you did to upset Lord Fohenk so much. He doesn't just mete out the Lord's Justice to your average criminal.”

“He believed we were spies,” Cam breathed, “along with another. A farmer, called Gismay. Who actually was a spy. And a good man. What they did to him... It wasn't right."

"Eismen have always had a cruel streak to them," Agazi said darkly, "so it doesn't surprise me to hear you speak of such things. Well, tonight you'll get to pay them back for what they did to you."

Cam sat, expressionless, staring out into the thick darkness beyond the torches of the docks.

He had never been the pay back type, and even after all he had endured could he really bring himself to kill? Was he going to have much of a choice when all was said and done?

The time dragged on slowly, minutes feeling like days as Cam sat in silent contemplation of the horrific task that lay before him. Agazi did all he could to keep the spirits of the men around him high, but very little could penetrate the malaise that lay upon the company.

Preparations on the docks themselves seemed to be going well, and whatever plans the Marshall was putting into action were being implemented without hesitation. Cam wished he could be involved, if only to give him something to do to take his mind off what lay before him.

The sky was the deep blue of night when Agazi tapped him on the shoulder, rousing him from his thoughts.

Cam stirred quickly, half expecting to see an army outside the windows. Agazi made a calming gesture to him, then gestured his head to the quayside.

Cam followed Agazi's gaze and saw the figure of King Hedradour, now resplendent in a blue, velvet hauberk bearing the emblem of the Black Bear of Ebrahir, walked into the courtyard.

The hauberk covered what looked to be a fine suit of silver-steel armour which gleamed red in the light of the torches. His helm was grasped under his left arm as he strode into the centre of the docks.

An expectant hush filled the air, the silence practically crackling with anticipation.

The King turned and eyed his army, a look of defiance

upon his face.

Slowly, with a deliberate motion, he drew his sword and held it aloft for a moment. The blade sparked in the firelight, leaving multicoloured trails in its wake as it cut through the air.

Bringing it down once more, he carved a line in the wood squarely in the centre of the docks. The ringing of his sword filled the deathly silence.

When he was satisfied he raised his sword once more before finally sheathing it. He stared out over his army for another moment before speaking in a clear, commanding voice.

"No further than this."

The air was now positively humming with the eager energy of one thousand men. Even Cam could feel the emotions rising in him; the desire to stop any and all who would bring harm to Sonia.

"The enemy comes," spoke Marshall Larin, "and we will meet them. Hold fast! For the King!"

Hedradour looked once more upon his army.

"Douse the torches!"

One by one, the light from each of the torches and braziers that lined the docks blinked out. Through all of this the silence was not broken; even the slightest sound might give the Eismen an indication of where their arrows should fly, and none wanted to give them even that chance.

For a few, sickening moments all was still.

Then Cam saw it.

Out of the darkness there formed the shape of a ship, it's prow cutting effortlessly through the waters of the lake. Its sails were full.

All eyes watched as it approached, only the fluttering of the sails and the gentle wash of the water breaking the perfect blanket of silence that hung over the city.

A whistle.

The sound of ropes being loosened.

A creak of wood and the woosh of something heavy being hurled through the air.

Cam watched as one of the catapults swung forward and sent a stone flying out across the water.

The loud splash that followed moments later told that the stone had missed its mark.

Another whistle.

Another splash.

This time two whistles.

A loud snap, and a hiss.

The bolt from one of the large crossbows thundered through the air and embedded itself into the side of the vessel.

Agazi looked uncertainly at Cam.

“Something's not right,” the Merchant breathed. “They haven't taken a single shot back at us.”

They both stared back out at the ship as it continued sliding silently towards them.

“I'm no expert,” Cam whispered, “but is that not going a bit fast?”

Agazi nodded at him, hurriedly gathering his weapons and pulling himself and Cam back from the windows.

“Aye, it is. Get down! Everyone!”

Everything happened at once.

Out on the docks, King Hedradour, Marshall Larin, Felgaron, Dunwald, and the rest had all come to the same conclusion Cam and Agazi had.

Men began to fall back from the quayside, scattering as the prow of the ship drew closer.

Those huddled in the houses awaiting their part in the battle watched in horror as the thing slammed hard into the wooden structure, cracking and splintering the wood.

One of the Watch Towers had its foundations destroyed by the impact, collapsing down into the maelstrom of chaos and taking the soldiers garrisoned inside with it. One of the catapults was destroyed also, much of it falling into the waters of the lake.

The sounds of screams began to fill the air as those who had been trapped in the rubble began to awaken to what had happened to them.

Then came the calls of those who were outside of the carnage; those who could give aid and assistance to the injured.

And then came the sound Cam had feared the most.

From the waters arose the battle cry of the Eismen.

As he looked out, Cam saw a number of other ships glide out of the gloom. Upon their decks Cam saw the glint of swords, spears, and all manner of other weaponry.

The Eismen wore armour that he recognised only too well – gold tinted, with the angel wings and the pale blue icicle resplendent upon their cloaks and banners. All the ships bore down upon them, cutting through the blue-green surface of the lake.

The first volley of arrows whistled down upon the defenders, and they were answered by the thrum of the bowstrings of Barrandel. For many moments the fight was fought from quiver and bow, hundreds upon thousands of arrows ripping through the air above the quay.

Agazi drew his bow, skilfully notched an arrow to the string, and let fly. Cam, feeling the desperation of one whose life now hung in the balance, took up his own bow and set himself to join the fray.

Against the clamour of all around him, he tried desperately to remember the very brief training Jason had given him back at Edgeborough Castle:

Hold the string not the arrow, pull it back to your cheek, and let go.

Cam did all he could to follow that distant instruction, but the bow he had now was far heavier than the ones he had been trained with; he could barely draw the string back halfway to his nose, let alone to his cheek.

His arm shaking, causing the arrow to bounce against the bow haft, he gave up and threw the thing to the floor.

He was not made for war.

As those all around him strung and loosed their bows with unwavering speed and agility, Cam watched on powerless.

From behind him another group of archers bustled through

to the windows, knocking him out of their way, and began to loose their own fury into the thickening sky.

A number of their arrows found their marks; the bodies of Eismen could be seen falling from the decks of the ships and into the dark water below. But soon the Eismen pinpointed the location of their attackers and targeted those hiding in the buildings.

The sounds of arrows thundering into the wood of the structures around them filled Cam's ears, but that was not the sound that unnerved him.

All too often the arrows flying towards them did not hit the buildings, but the archers and soldiers around him. The screams and gasps of those whose flesh was pierced by the glass-tipped arrows of their enemies rang throw the air; every one threatening to break his resolve.

An arrow scorched past him, so close that he felt the breeze as the thing narrowly missed his left ear, and embedded itself into the chest of a man stood but a few paces behind him.

He fell instantly, his heart pierced. He made no sound, but just dropped with a look of profound shock upon his face.

He could not have been more than two or three years older than Cam.

Cam's first and loudest thought was to run, escape the death and destruction that was heading squarely in his direction, and get back to Beregle and Sonia. From there they could find their own way, in secret, and discover those who had the knowledge and power to send them home.

Yet his feet did not move. And his heart did not waver.

His hands reached down, and grasped the hilt of the sword that hung at his waist.

Eismeer had caused him nothing but trouble from the moment he had arrived in this forsaken world, and he was not about to stand idly by while they attacked and killed innocent people.

His friends were before him, and beside him, and he would not let them down. When this was all over, they would all work together to find a way to get he and Sonia home.

Until then, any who got in his way – including Eismeer – would have to face the consequences.

Revelling in his new found fortitude, Cam watched as the rest of the Eismen ships reached the landings.

More cries went up, and soldiers poured forth onto the docks and the battle began in earnest.

Arrows continued to rain down onto the docks from within the demolition ship, now transformed into a makeshift citadel, many finding their marks.

Already the forces of Ebras were thrust onto the back foot, Eismeer having seemingly emptied upon them. The fighting was pitched and vicious, and Cam feared for his friends in that dreadful melee. He had already lost sight of Felgaron and Dunwald, though he could still make out the King and Marshall in amongst the chaos.

"We can't just sit here and do nothing!" he said, his new vigour cutting through his fear. "They need our help!"

Agazi nodded and looked about him.

"Aye," the Merchant responded, then turned to the assembled soldiers. "What say you? Shall we defend this city?"

A great shout went up, and Agazi held his axe aloft. The soldiers about him followed his lead and drew their own weapons – axes, spears, hammers, daggers, a few swords even.

Cam found himself caught in the wave of emotion and held his own sword high, letting out a guttural cry.

Their cries were taken up by the soldiers in the neighbouring buildings, and the sound echoed around the docks and into the night. Doors and windows were being thrown open to allow the newly invigorated forces of Ebras out onto the docks.

Agazi led their group, perhaps fifty soldiers, and Cam followed behind the Merchant, his fear temporarily evaporated by the wave of emotions.

The sudden eruption of noise and movement gave the Eismen pause for perhaps only two or three second seconds, but it was enough for the defenders who had nearly been overrun to regain their composure and face their foes on an equal footing.

Hedradour himself led a new charge with his Royal Guard, and they killed many with flashing blades, his Marshall Larin at his side always.

Dunwald and Felgaron were amongst the fiercest fighting by the landings, holding back the encroaching Eismen that sought to clamber up from the quayside into the fray.

Cam and Agazi found themselves on the fringes of the battle, with Cam doing all he could to not get hit by the flying blades that now surrounded him. The scene threatened to overwhelm him, and if it had not been for an Eismen Soldier beading down upon him then it probably would have done.

The man had marked Cam as his target and ran headlong at him.

Instinct took over as Cam watched his sword block the man's attack.

He staggered back under the strength of the blow, but managed to find his footing once more.

The man came at him again, and this time Cam was ready.

A swing at his head was easily dodged and Cam felt his arms thrust outward. His sword caught itself on something, then slid forward once more.

The attacker fell forward onto the blade.

Cam looked up in horror at what had happened; the trail of blood running down the blade to meet his hands. He pulled his sword back quickly and watched the man drop to floor.

Dead.

The shock, and the dizzying sickness it brought, consumed Cam for a moment.

Then he was aware of another man charging at him. He was forced to block another strong blow and thrust his sword once more into his opponent.

This second kill threatened to break him, but the vision of Sonia, and of their world, suddenly filled his mind and he shook himself.

Another soldier was upon him, and this time Cam was not prepared.

A swing came in at him from his right and, while he managed to just get his blade between him and certain death, the force thrust him to the floor. Cam closed his eyes, fearing for his life, but the end did not come.

He opened his eyes to find himself surrounded by a forest of boots, all desperately searching for grip on the now blood-covered Walk. Cam looked down at where he lay and saw that his head was in the sanguine river, the stuff already clinging to his skin and hair. He was unharmed, but he suddenly felt sick and weak. He tried to lift himself, but no-one around him knew he was there. He was kicked back down by unwitting assailants time and again.

A momentary panic struck him. He would surely be trampled to death.

A hand plunged through the seething mass of bodies and hauled him back to his feet.

Cam shook himself and looked at the face of his rescuer, half expecting to find an Eismen axe or hammer awaiting him.

It was Dunwald.

Cam barely had time to offer him a glance of thanks before two more soldiers were upon them.

He ducked and weaved past the wild swings of his assailant, and found himself thrusting his sword, unthinking, into the man's midriff.

He looked about him to see if Dunwald was as fortunate.

He had not been.

His attacker had more skill than Cam's, and was bearing down on the Captain with a large war-hammer poised to strike.

"DUNWALD!" Cam cried out and charged at the man.

He managed to knock him down, giving Dunwald a moment to gather himself.

Cam now aimed a kick at the Eisman, his boot colliding with the side of his head.

Dunwald send his blade thrusting down to end the man's

torment.

"Thanks," said Cam, "I owed you that!"

"Where is Agazi?" Dunwald called back, as he dispatched another Eisman.

"I don't know" Cam cried, but before any more could be said the battle swept them apart and Cam found himself on the edge of the landings.

Here the fighting was more fierce and desperate, the Ebrahiim being faced with fresh Eismen joining the battle from the boats.

With disturbing ease, Cam killed two more as they hurled themselves at him.

By now, he was finding it hard to keep going; his arms and legs ached from the strain of battle. He had been fighting for barely fifteen minutes and already he was reaching the limits of his fatigue.

Suddenly an assailant leapt at him and managed to force him to the floor, a particularly fierce swipe at his head had unbalancing him.

Cam found himself inches away from tumbling into the inky darkness of the water below him. With mail on he knew he had no chance of surviving such an ordeal.

He overcame his terror just long enough to see his attacker readying for the killing blow.

Somehow, Cam blocked the next swing, then managed to roll out of the way and use his sword to send the man plunging into the lake.

He watched as the stricken figure disappeared from view, already gasping for breath. Cam staggered back, panting against the adrenaline surging through his body.

What the hell was he doing here?

Another attacker launched at him, and Cam's instinct thrust his sword out to block the swipe that came his way, and his left hand swung a tired fist at their head.

It was weak, but it was enough.

The blow unbalanced his assailant, causing him to slip on

the Walk and tumble into the murky waters.

It's either me or the man who swings his sword at me, he told himself, desperate to keep hold of whatever humanity he was allowed under the circumstances.

He took this chance to run back up onto the docks proper.

What he saw was a sea of carnage, blood, and chaos.

King Hedradour and Marshall Larin were leading the defence. Both had killed many, aided resolutely by the Royal Guard.

They were setting about dismantling the leading Eismen battalions when a chance arrow cut deeply into Hedradour's shoulder. His armour managed to deflect the greater part of the arrow's force, but Larin quickly ordered that he be escorted back to the Palace.

The Marshall covered the King's retreat, but this break in the Ebrahiim line gave the Eismen the chance they needed.

A call went up from on board the demolition ship and several wooden barrels were hurled down from on high. Wherever they landed, they exploded in a shower of white powder.

Quicklime.

Any and all who were touched by the powder immediately cried out in agony as it burned their skin.

Men fell, clawing at their armour and helms, helpless against the hideous substance.

Barrel after barrel was thrown into the melee, indiscriminately.

Cam avoided any direct contact, but the stuff filled the air and he could feel his lungs beginning to get heavy as he breathed it in.

"Fall back!" Dunwald cried over the screaming tumult. "Archers!"

From the top storeys of the houses in which Cam and the other men had hidden themselves came volley after volley of arrows to cover the Ebrahiim retreat.

The Eismen, however, were beginning to make their

numbers tell.

Felgaron, Larin and the Royal Guard held the line as best they could in the centre of the dock, doing everything to give the rest of the defenders extra time to retreat and regroup.

Cam froze, caught in two minds; should he retreat to safety or help the man who had saved his life hold them off? He surely owed Felgaron that much? But had he the skill or nerve to be anything but a hindrance?

His body dragged him backwards, but his mind and willpower urged him forward towards the Swordsman.

Somehow his arms found the strength to lift his sword once more and kill another Eisman who threw himself towards him, but he doubted he could do it much longer.

The smells of blood and smoke, the visions of men lying dead, or close to, upon the Walk before him; all began to conspire against him.

Yet still he did not fall, ducking and weaving once again purely on instinct, fighting his way onward until he was, without truly knowing it, stood shoulder to shoulder with the Marshall and Felgaron.

The Swordsman glanced down at him.

"Get back, Cam!" he cried, his sword flashing through his foes. "I need you safe behind the line!"

"No!" Cam forced through gritted teeth as he just held off another Eisman.

"Go!" Felgaron ordered, pushing him back and out of danger. "This is no place for you!"

Defeated and too tired to continue the argument, Cam all but turned and ran from the battle to the relative safety of the city, when his eyes caught sight of a figure climbing down from one of the ships.

Aglorar.

"You!" he spat, levelling his sword at the man. His arm quivered with the weight of the blade and his own fatigue.

Aglorar saw him and laughed.

"Cam, go!" Felgaron ordered once more.

Cam stood his ground, a new strength seeping through him.

Where it came from he dared not guess, but it was abetted by the visions of Gismay's tortured and broken body, and of Cam's own ordeal back in Eismeer.

And it felt good.

He strode back to the front line, his sword raised and his eyes fixed on the man who had done him more injury than anyone else in his entire life.

"Come on, boy," Aglorar sneered.

Felgaron stepped between them and pushed Cam back.

"Retreat! That is an order!"

Cam threw his body forward against the Swordsman.

"He sent me and Sonia to the gallows!" he cried.

"Retreat!" Felgaron repeated. "Larin! Fall back!"

The Marshall, himself embroiled in a bitter one-on-one struggle, sent his assailant to the floor and lifted a war horn to his lips and sounded the retreat.

The Royal Guard raised their shields and positioned themselves as a screen against the onrushing Eismen so that those last few remaining on the docks could flee. They then stepped back and thrust their spears outward, keeping a distance between them and their enemies.

Felgaron lifted Cam off his feet and out of the heat of the moment, with Cam all the while hurling abuse at Fohenk's Advisor.

Larin and his men fell back into the shadows of the streets, and the battle transitioned into its next phase.

Finding a relatively quiet spot amongst the clamour and chaos, Felgaron dropped Cam back onto his feet and glared at him.

"Stay back!" the Swordsman ordered.

"He nearly killed Gismay and had me and Sonia hanged!" Cam spat. "You have no idea what I want to do to that piece of..."

"Enough!" Felgaron shouted, bringing Cam out of his

rage. “Getting yourself killed will not help you, Sonia, or my world. Leave the fighting to those who must, so that you can do what you must.”

Cam glared back at him, feeling his rage bubbling up once again.

“And what must I do, eh?”

“Stay alive.”

The Swordsman's answer was simple, but his tone was fierce.

Whatever bloodlust had threatened to take Cam in the moments before dissipated utterly and he felt spent. Tears that had welled when he saw Aglorar now flowed freely down his cheeks; a perfect mix of emotions, fatigue, and utter hatred at what he had allowed himself to feel.

“What happens now?” he asked in a low voice.

“The fighting will spread into the streets. I beg you do all you can to avoid it, for it will only get more desperate as the night draws on.” Felgaron pointed to a small alleyway some fifty feet behind Cam. “Down there, to the right, then up the stairs. There is one of our healing houses. Assist them.”

“But I want to fight! I want to do my part!”

“You will,” the Swordsman pressed, “but you are only of use to anyone if you remain alive. Not all glory is won with a blade. Now go!”

For a moment, the temptation to defy the Swordsman once again filled Cam's being, but it ebbed away as quickly as it had come.

Felgaron was right.

He was tired, beaten, and in no fit state to continue. His sword arm was leaden, and Cam doubted he could kill anyone else even if his life depended on it.

“Alright,” he said, “alright. Good luck. See you when it's over.”

Felgaron allowed himself half a smile before turning back and running through the streets to rejoin the fighting. Cam watched him go, the urge to follow him despite everything bubbling underneath his better judgement.

When he was out of sight, Cam sighed and turned to go where Felgaron had directed him.

"Not so fast, boy!"

A hand grabbed Cam's neck and thrust him into the wall of the building next to him.

Cam did not need to see his assailant to know who held him; he would have known that voice anywhere.

Aglorar grinned up at him, evilly, his teeth bared and his sword drawn.

"You did not think you could challenge me on the field of battle and escape judgement, surely?" His voice was thick with hatred. "Come, let us go somewhere we shall not be disturbed so I can show you the error of your ways."

A blow to his stomach took all the air out of him, and Cam felt his body being dragged along the backstreets of Hedradour's city, Aglorar's hand gripping the back of his neck.

All around them were the sounds of the battle, but Aglorar paid no heed to them.

Cam did not know for how long they walked, nor could he guess which way they had taken; all he could be certain of was that with each step the sounds of battle became quieter and more muffled.

A swift move to their left, followed by the sound of a door being kicked in, told Cam that they had reached whatever destination Aglorar had chosen.

A musty smell rushed out to greet them as Cam was hurled forward. He landed heavily on the wooden floor, the wind gone from his lungs and the will gone from his heart.

He had felt the sensation once before, when the noose had been placed around his neck.

Aglorar's footsteps slowly paced around the room. What was he waiting for?

"You have no idea who you are, do you?" the Lieutenant said, a rasp in his voice.

Cam did not even understand the question.

Before he could contemplate it, however, there was a heavy boot in his back holding him down flat into the floor.

"I've half a mind to tell you everything," Aglorar growled, "if only so that you might truly comprehend the joy I will get from ending your miserable existence."

Cam was no longer listening; he was too tired to hear. He longed for sleep, for all the noises to stop, for everyone and everything to simply go away and leave he and Sonia alone. He wanted nothing more that to open his eyes and discover it had all been one long, terrible nightmare.

He felt his body being rolled over on his back.

He opened his eyes and, to his eternal dismay, saw nothing more than Aglorar's face glaring down at him with a wicked grin and fearful glint in his eyes.

"But then I think I would enjoy you dying without ever knowing what was happening," he was saying.

Cam pulled the most determined expression he could muster.

"Whatever you're going to do," he forced, "just hurry it up."

Aglorar widened his grin.

"Oh, no," he breathed, "I am going to enjoy myself."

He pulled Cam up to a kneeling position, and kicked his sword away. He allowed him a moment or two to hang there, his knees barely able to support his own weight, and then punched him hard.

Cam's head thudded down into the timbers once more, and the warm feeling of blood beginning to run from his nose was upon his skin.

Aglorar now aimed a kick into his ribs, and another into his back. Cam opened his mouth to cry with pain, but there was no air left in his lungs.

"I will break you," Aglorar spat, another kick connecting with Cam's midriff, "and then I will kill you."

He grasped Cam by the hair and once more pulled his face up to meet his own. The look in Aglorar's eyes was one of a man possessed.

Another kick, this time to Cam's groin, followed by a fierce blow to the side of his head. It was so hard that a sickening dizziness erupted from his temple.

His body gave in and collapsed once more, panting and defeated.

"To think that the fate of our world," Aglorar continued, lifting him by his hair again, "rested at your feet. Pathetic little worm!"

Another punch, this time an uppercut to Cam's jaw. He was sent sprawling, his back bending awkwardly over his bent knees.

Every part of him screamed out in agony; he barely knew where he was any more, let alone being able to comprehend whatever Aglorar was talking about.

His body now folded sideways and allowed him the relative release of slumping down upon the wooden floor beneath. From this new vantage point his eyes finally saw some details of the room he was in.

It seemed to him to be some kind of store room, though it did not appear to have been used in a long time. Cobwebs hung above him, and empty, broken chests were stacked behind his head.

A sickening glimpse of his own blood splattered across the front of these made his head swim once more.

This was where he was going to die.

Aglorar loomed over him once more, his slick black hair blocking the room as it dangled into Cam's face.

The last face he would ever see.

"And now," Aglorar breathed, an unbearable stench, "the real game begins."

A golden gleam passed across Cam's vision, and a cruel looking dagger appeared between their faces. Its blade had the outline of a flame, the curved edges glinting in the candle light as it danced above him.

Aglorar toyed with it, teasing the instrument of Cam's

death with its prey.

He was going to die.

The point of the blade cut into Cam's cheek with startling ease, the warmth of yet more of his blood draining from his body at least giving him proof that he was alive for the moment.

He was alive.

"After all this time we will finally have our revenge..."

He was *alive*!

A sudden burst of energy exploded into Cam's veins.

He cried out, using all his force to push Aglorar away from him, and somehow found the strength within him to stand.

Looking at his foe, the hatred he had felt upon the dock came flooding back, adrenaline surging through his veins once more.

Aglorar staggered, winded, and fell to his knees. Cam's kick had landed more forcefully than even he had guessed.

Using the moment he had been afforded, Cam moved quickly and retrieved his sword. He pointed it towards Aglorar.

"Told you you should've hurried up," Cam panted.

Aglorar looked up, the wild eyes of a caged animal appearing between the strands of slick, oily hair.

"You think you can use that, boy?" he sneered. "You think you stand a chance against me?"

Cam heard himself laughing, a harsh and bitter sound in his ears.

"The way I see it, I don't have anything to lose. What about you?"

The wicked grin retuned to Aglorar's face.

"So be it," he hissed, and launched himself at Cam.

Thinking as quickly as he was able, Cam sidestepped the attack, causing Aglorar to miss him and thunder into the wall.

Pressing his advantage, Cam aimed a kick into the small of Aglorar's back, forcing the last air out of his lungs.

Cam swung his sword down towards his opponent, but Aglorar hauled himself out of the way, clambered to his feet, and aimed his own swing towards Cam's ankles.

Cam jumped the blade, but landed awkwardly and stumbled.

Aglorar was lunging toward him once more.

He ducked to his left, only just avoiding the point of Aglorar's sword, then kicked upwards once more.

His foot barely made contact, but in raising it he brought his knee hard into Aglorar's face. It was enough to knock him back and give Cam the chance to stand once more.

Wildly, he thrust his blade forwards.

This time his aim was true, and he landed a blow to Aglorar's right shoulder.

The Lieutenant screamed, though the point of Cam's sword had barely pierced through his armour.

When Cam pulled his sword back, the tip was stained with blood.

He readied the blade for another swing, and then stopped.

Something was not right.

Cam looked at the sword again.

It was not stained with blood, for what dripped from its point was golden in colour. Even in this world, Cam knew that men bled sanguine just as he did.

"What?" he breathed.

Aglorar rounded on Cam and a fire was in his eyes.

Cam took an instinctive step back and raised his sword up to block the coming blow.

It never came.

The Lieutenant held his left hand open, fingers outstretched and palm towards Cam.

The fire in his eyes burned bright, and Cam felt himself being lifted off the floor and held by some invisible force. No air found his lungs, no move he made broke whatever spell was being held over him. He simply hung, five feet in the air, helpless and gasping for breath.

Aglorar closed his fingers slightly and the pressure upon Cam's body increased.

"Not in six thousand years has the flesh of my kin been

pierced by mortal scum," he hissed, "you should consider yourself blessed, boy."

The words were spat, as if simply forming them left an unpalatable taste in his mouth.

"You can at least die knowing that."

His fingers tightened once more, and Cam felt as if he would be crushed. The very life was being squeezed out of him.

Who was this man?

What was he?

Cam watched on, helpless and terrified, as the fire within Aglorar began to spread out from his eyes and into his skin, his veins, his hair; the Lieutenant's whole being began to glow with the power within him. His eyes became pure white; two perfect, colourless orbs piercing his very soul with their gaze.

"Die now."

Aglorar's voice was distorted, inhuman.

His grip tightened one last time, and Cam felt his life begin to ebb away. His body was breaking, his lungs were empty, and his hope was spent. He had nothing left, no will even to try and fight against the tide that fate had set against him.

His left hand let his sword drop to the floor, and he waited for the moment of death to come.

Cam's last thoughts would be of Sonia, and of their home, their friends, their times together, and of his mother. He let the images of all fill his mind and soul, savouring each memory that came to bid him farewell. He felt no pain nor fear in that moment, but simply felt the peace of one who knew he would soon be home.

The world about him seemed to slow, as if time itself was halting to witness his passing.

His visions changed and his memories faded from before his eyes.

A new image filled his mind, an image he did not recognise nor conjure of his own will.

A face now stared back at him.

It had pale skin of a perfect complexion; no blemish or

mark was upon it, yet it was not a young face. The eyes, round and open, belied a vast wealth of experience and a deep well of age behind their piercing, silver irises. Short, white hair clung to the sides of the face, while the perfectly smooth scalp was encircled by a lapis corolla beset with many multicoloured and multifaceted jewels. No beard was there, nor indeed and other adornment upon the visage.

The scene about him had all but slowed to a stop.

Do not fear. I have you.

The mouth did not move, nor was there any sound, but the voice echoed within Cam's mind and he felt immediately comforted by it.

He had heard this voice before. Where?

The eyes now took on an expression of caring, and Cam felt safe within their gaze.

Your time is not come.

A silver-white light began to emanate from the eyes, filling the room. Air began to flow back into Cam's lungs, and his strength was returning to him. He felt his sword come back into his hand.

Go now. I await you in the Undrŷk.

Cam felt the soles of his feet gently touch the wooden floor beneath him. The face smiled at him, and faded away into the light which grew now to its blinding pinnacle. It flashed and then was gone, leaving the room in a moment of silent stillness.

Aglorar was looking about him.

"Bænír?" he breathed.

Now! Fight! Live!

The voice thundered into Cam's mind through the silence. He knew not what had transpired, but he heeded the call.

He raised his sword and charged at Aglorar, a vicious and sustained attack on the stunned Lieutenant.

He pushed Aglorar back, forcing him to the wall. Their swords clashed and for a moment Cam stared deep into his opponent's eyes and saw fear; a raw, primal fear that brought his heart joy to witness.

The visions of what this man had done to Gismay, and the emotionless face he had held as Sonia and he stood at the gallows, once more surfaced in his mind and, with all his might, he swung his blade above his head and down.

Aglorar lifted his own sword in desperate defence.

The half stop of a blade passing through something substantial.

A cry of anguish.

The clatter of a sword falling to the floor.

Cam finished his attack with a flourish and levelled the point of his sword at Aglorar's face.

Yet when he looked, Aglorar was no longer there before him.

The Soldier had crumpled to his knees, screaming in pain.

Cam looked down and saw that Aglorar's hand lay, still gripping tightly to his sword, several feet away from the arm it should have been attached to.

A pool of golden liquid had begun to form beneath it.

Aglorar wailed in agony, a sound that cut through to the very heart of Cam's soul.

What had he done?

He stepped back, utterly appalled by what had transpired.

A horn sounded outside. And another. And another.

Cam, hardly daring to take his eyes of his stricken foe, stepped gingerly over to the window and looked out.

To his surprise, he saw the growing light of dawn outside; the golden rays of the sun were creeping through the city streets, and he had to shield his eyes against it.

Yet when he and Aglorar had begun their fight it was perhaps an hour after midnight.

He saw the figures of soldiers running past, and heard their cloaks billowing in the wind as they did so.

“Back to the docks,” one cried.

“Retreat!” another called.

The figures shouting were those in the cloaks of Eismeer.

They were fleeing!

Cam had not only survived the night, but he was on the winning side!

The forces of Eismeer ran through the streets, hounded every step by the resurgent Ebrahiim, purging their ancient foe from their city.

“Ha!” Cam laughed aloud, “we won! Your lot are running, Aglorar!”

He turned back and stopped, bewildered.

No door had been opened, nor had he heard any movement from behind him, but Aglorar, leaving only a severed hand, had gone.

Chapter Nineteen

Dawn

Cam stepped over to where Aglorar's body had been, and examined the spot.

The severed hand had already begun to wither, the skin now grey and pallid, and the golden 'blood' that had pooled beneath it had congealed quickly upon the floor. There was no other sign of the hand's owner having ever been there.

A morbid curiosity came over Cam and, despite all his better judgement, he slowly reached out to touch the thing.

The moment his fingertips reached Aglorar's hand it crumbled into dust.

Cam pulled himself back, a cold sickness coming over him. The grim reality of all that had just happened came flooding back to him.

But what had just happened?

His thoughts were broken by the sound of the door bursting open.

Cam instinctively raised his sword and rounded on the figure who stepped into the room.

He immediately sighed with relief.

"Dunwald," he breathed, lowering his blade.

The Captain, bloodied and with rents in his armour, stood before him and smiled.

"Friend Cam," he said loftily, "it is a joy undimmed that I have found you alive. After you could not be found at the healing house we feared the worst."

Cam did his best to not look too shaken as he spoke.

"Yeah. Well, I'm tougher than I look. What happened out there?"

"The Eismen have been broken," the Captain declared proudly, "we have won, but it has been a hard fought battle. Many from both sides have been lost. They had pushed us back as far as the main square, before the very gates of Barrandel. But King Hedradour, even with an arrow embedded in his shoulder, led his men in a valiant charge. We broke their ranks and forced them into the lake! We are just rounding up the last stragglers now. And how goes it with you? Why did you not go to the healing house?"

Cam debated for a moment what his answer would be.

Did he tell Dunwald everything? Would he believe him if he did? And what reaction would the revelation that Aglorar had golden blood draw from him, or from anyone for that matter?

He decided quickly that the best course would be to wait until he had made some sort of sense of it all before telling any other what had happened.

"Oh, I, uh, got lost in the battle. Don't worry, I'm fine," he added, seeing Dunwald's immediate look of concern, "well, physically I am. I don't think I'll ever be quite the same again."

Dunwald stepped forward and clasped his shoulder.

"Battle and war will change any man. But take heart in the fact that you have survived long enough to be changed. That is no mean feat."

Cam looked up at his friend and gave what he could only hope was a smile. Whatever else had happened – the hurt, the blood – Dunwald was right.

He had survived.

"Come," the Captain continued, "let us find Felgaron. He will no doubt wish to see you are safe."

Dunwald led him out onto the Walk and Cam's senses were once more assaulted by the stench of war; the odours of blood and flesh hung in the air, mixing with the salted aroma of the lake. Gulls circled above, their calls echoing into the golden dawn.

All about him were bodies. Young, old, men, women, Eismen, Ebrahiim; all lay there, still and silent.

Cam dared not look at them overlong, lest the despair of what had transpired claim him utterly, but he knew that their number would be beyond count. Some lay with eyes closed, the longest peace upon their face; others looked out with unseeing, lifeless stares, frozen in the moments of their passing.

Keeping his own eyes firmly fixed in front of him, he followed Dunwald through the City.

The buildings themselves seemed to have escaped the battle largely unscathed; those nearer the centre of the city had endured the least damage, but as they walked closer to the docks the destruction became greater. The quayside itself was a tangled mess of wreckage, with the Eisman demolition ship still embedded in the outer planks.

Dunwald strode across the scene to the shattered remains of the guard tower that had been brought down by that same ship. Here stood Felgaron, Marshall Larin, and Agazi.

The Swordsman looked up as they approached and, for the second time since they had met, Cam saw a look of genuine joy upon his face.

"Friend Cam! You have survived!"

The Swordsman stepped forward and, much to Cam's surprise, embraced him.

He was not certain how to react, for he had never seen Felgaron show such open emotion. He slowly placed his arms around Felgaron and returned the gesture.

"I guess I did."

Felgaron released him and looked him over. A curious expression came over him as he regarded Cam.

"You have endured much," he said, as if he was stitching his thoughts together as he spoke them, "you are changed."

"I would say so."

The Swordsman looked as though he had more to say, but Dunwald cut across him.

“I do not know any who have not been changed by the fires of such a battle. This victory, and the sacrifices it required, will live in the memories of Ebras for many ages.”

Felgaron looked into Cam's eyes and, though he did not know how, Cam felt sure that the Swordsman saw some small amount of what was within his mind.

The Swordsman's eyes widened for a moment, but he said nothing else; he simply continued to stare. Cam, hoping beyond hope that Felgaron truly could see into his thoughts, did all he could to open his mind to the Swordsman.

“Aye,” Agazi said, placing a friendly arm around Cam, “it is good news that you are still with us, friend Cam. He fought well on the docks, I have to say.”

Neither Cam nor Felgaron took their eyes off each other; Cam silently wishing to tell the Swordsman everything, and Felgaron taking in every single detail about the man that now stood before him.

“All have fought bravely,” the Marshall declared, “though even in victory this is still a dark day for Ebras.”

“What news of the King?” Dunwald enquired.

All was so much background noise to Cam and Felgaron. Still they were locked in their gaze, and still neither spoke yet both understood.

“He is bruised but strong,” Larin was responding, “it will take more than a chance Eisman arrow to halt our King!”

Laughter. Why were they laughing?

Cam did not care. He screamed within his mind, laying bare to any who could hear his thoughts all that had passed between he and Aglorar.

“Your sword.”

Felgaron's voice was low, but it cut through the din surrounding them.

Cam nodded, and slowly raised the blade in his hands. He held it flat, and the dawn sun flared across the polished metal.

“What are you..?” Dunwald began, but got no further.

All now stared at the weapon being presented to them.

The rising sun caught the stain of gold upon its edge and tip.

Everything seemed to stop, as if all the world were focussing upon this single moment.

Cam held the sword before him so that all could see the glittering mark. The eyes about him looked hard and disbelieving, but they could not deny what they saw.

“What is that,” Agazi breathed.

“That,” Felgaron replied, a dark edge to his voice, “is the blood of a Wizard of the North.”

The words were leaden and thudded into the air.

“That is impossible,” Dunwald whispered, his eyes locked onto the blade.

“It seems not,” Larin cut in, “and it would seem that North Sel are not the only land to have dealings with Mythravia”

Dunwald shook his head.

“In all my time in Fohenk's halls, there have never been dealings with the Wizards. Fohenk himself has utter distaste for them. Whatever you may believe about the man, not for any price would he allow one of their number within his armies.”

Agazi looked at him, uncertain.

“You sure? This war with Ebras has been going on for six thousand years! Maybe he really wants to finish it once and for all?”

Larin shook his head.

“No, for no other has come across such a foul creature during this fight. There can only have been one.”

“But why? Why would one Wizard fight within the armies of Eismeer?” Agazi's question was loud, ringing through the air.

“Why indeed,” Felgaron mused.

“Enough!” Larin's outburst came with a voice hot with rage. “Who amongst them was one of those accursed creatures?”

“Aglorar.”

Cam had answered without hearing his own voice, and he still did not take his eyes off Felgaron.

He was suddenly very tired.

"Aglorar?" Dunwald gasped. "The Seventh, how did I not see?"

"Who is this man?" Larin demanded.

"He is one of Fohenk's advisors," Dunwald answered, "second only to me. It would not be unthinkable that he is now chief amongst his council."

"They may not be working with them," Agazi said, "but it looks like they might be working for them. Deliberately or not."

"Where is this thing now?" Larin spat, turning once more to Cam.

Cam shrugged, his heavy shoulders barely moving.

"He vanished. One minute he was there, the next... He nearly killed me. I cut his hand off."

Cam had no control over the words coming out of his mouth, and still he could not take his eyes off Felgaron.

The Swordsman returned his gaze, his expression growing more and more unnerved with every moment.

"The King must hear of this," Larin declared, and turned on his heels and marched towards the Hall of Hedradour. "Dunwald, bring the boy."

Cam felt Dunwald's hand grasp his arm and begin to lead him back through the city towards Barrandel.

The world around him blurred, Cam could not hold his focus on any one thing or person.

He just closed his eyes and mind to the destruction and the horror that surrounded him, and allowed himself to be led to the King.

* * * * *

The embers of the previous evening's fire burned their last in the hearth as Gismay dozed in his bed.

The room was still warm from the heat that the logs had produced though the small hours, though now the chill coming from the world outside threatened to undo their work.

The village of Beregle was quiet; even those that roused themselves early waited for the sun to crest the wall before beginning their day. The mountain birds could be heard with their dawn chorus, and for the moment their quiet intrusions were the only sounds to be heard.

Sonia lay upon her bed, restful and untroubled. Gismay smiled to see it. She had done all she could over the past day to make certain that he was as comfortable and happy as he could have been.

Over the days since their company had been parted, both Gismay and Sonia had waited for news to come of events at the Boardwalks, but none had arrived. Gismay had taken to sitting in the inn of an evening, listening to what the local gossip was.

In truth however, there was very little of such talk; the inhabitants of the Mountain had grown steadily more quiet and watchful since the news of Eismeer's attack on Ebras, with most conversations now being had in small groups, quiet and shrouded in shadows.

Whenever he returned to their room, the Farmer would always find Sonia simply stood at the west-facing window, staring outward in silent contemplation.

During the days, she would wander aimlessly through the town, sometimes with him and sometimes alone. She spoke little, and sometimes did not seem to hear everything he said to her. And while she did eat the food that Gismay brought for them, she seemed to be doing so out of habit rather than out of hunger.

Gismay felt a great deal of sympathy for her, and he wished with all his heart that he could offer her more solace than simply food and companionship. Though, he had thought to himself as he had settled into his bed the previous evening, it was some comfort that she was at least afforded a roof, relative safety, and a comfortable bed in which to sleep.

The only trouble was that she was not asleep.

She could not sleep, however hard she tried. Her soul was

filled with too many thoughts, too much anxiety. However much Gismay had tried to fill her days with distractions, her only thoughts were of Cam and of how alone she was without him with her.

They had been the closest of friends for many years, and she knew that neither of them would have survived their ordeal this far and this well without the other. The sight of him walking out of the door and off to battle had been almost too much for her to bear. Her grief at their parting had been torn in two; half was because she could no longer help and support her best friend, and half was because she was alone.

Gismay stirred in his slumber, breaking her train of thought.

Sonia smiled to herself. He deserved his comfort.

She greatly appreciated everything that he had done for both she and Cam since the day that they had arrived in this strange world, and she hoped that he did not think her ungrateful. She knew she had not been much company since Cam had gone, and she had not shown Gismay that she truly did appreciate all his efforts even if she was not showing it.

A gentle breeze fluttered in through the open window, catching the single piece of material that acted as a curtain and sending it fluttering into the room. Sonia's eyes followed it idly, and then came to rest upon the embers in the fireplace.

Thin wisps of smoke curled into the cool air of the room, catching the soft, golden light that glanced in through the window, as if the wood was breathing its last into the world before finally being spent. Parts of it yet glowed red, defying the chill breeze and threatening to burst into flame once more; these outlines were as of stained glass and made the embers look to her like rock.

As Sonia watched, the first true light of day crept in above the window ledge. Her eyes followed it as it crossed the floor, touching each board one by one, the fingers of the dawn inching themselves forward to banish the darkness from her temporary abode. It drew itself closer to the fireplace, emblazoning every slender thread of vapour that rose from the ashes.

Gismay stirred once more, snoring loudly.

It occurred to Sonia that this moment was the stillest and most peaceful one she had been afforded since the events that had brought she and Cam to this world. She breathed in deeply, savouring the calm and immersing herself in this precious moment.

For the first time in what felt like forever, she felt her eyelids grow heavy. Despite her worry she knew that sleep was necessary, and she knew that if it came to her she would not be able to fight it.

Another, stronger gust caught the curtains, making the smoke swirl and spin about itself in an intricate, indecipherable dance that snatched Sonia's attention from the jaws of sleep. She watched, enthralled, as the wisps gambolled amongst each other, cavorting upon the winds as leaves in the autumn. It thrilled her tired heart to see such simple beauty; it reminded her of a time before she knew of Rhydariel, or of different worlds and the roads between them.

How she longed to return to the days of the quiet, comfortable life she had lived before.

The dawn's light crept onto the grate before the hearth.

The last of the smoke was extinguished, and for a moment the room seemed to freeze.

Sonia took one last glance at the encroaching dawn through the window, and closed her eyes.

Her last thought before slumber took a full hold upon her was of Cam. More than anything she wished that she would see him again, safe and whole, back at Edgeborough Castle entertaining customers.

She sighed deeply, and allowed herself to fall to sleep and, for one moment more, everything was still.

Without warning ash exploded from the base of the fire, billowing out into the room.

The logs shattered, sending splinters and sparking shards into the air.

Gismay leapt from his bed as the newly ignited embers landed upon him, crying out in shock.

The window slammed shut, pulled by some invisible force, closing off the one way of escape for the smoke and soot that now rose from the cold hearth.

A grey-black broil began to fill the room as Gismay, doing all he could to keep the stuff out of his eyes, frantically looked about him.

He could make out very little in the chaos before him; the growing light outside was not yet strong enough to cut through the thick vapour, and his own sight was hindered by stinging tears. He stood, one arm across his face and the other reaching forwards trying to find his bearings.

He slid his feet slowly and cautiously toward what he thought was Sonia's bed.

Before he could get even half the distance, another explosion from the fireplace and something collided hard with his right hand side.

The impact sent his sprawling to the floor, his head thumping into the wall.

When he groggily regained his feet, still barely able to see in the swirling mess of ash and splinters, he nearly believed he had lost all of his senses.

Standing before him was a tall figure, clad in black robes with golden trim. A golden half-mask covered the lower half portion of their face, while all else but the eyes was covered by the dark hood itself.

Without touching him, it lifted Gismay from the floor and held him against the wall.

"You... cannot... have her..." he forced, the words taking all his strength to speak.

The figure regarded him for a moment.

"This is not your affair," it hissed.

"She... is under... my... protection..." Gismay forced.

The Figure gently cocked its head to one side, and Gismay could feel he was being looked over.

"You are, as you have always been, unworthy," it answered, the hint of a laugh within its words.

Gismay struggled hard against the force that was holding him.

"May the... Seventh... take you... Betrayer!"

The Figure stared at him.

"We are the Seventh!"

The force holding the Farmer was released suddenly, sending him crashing to the floor.

The Figure stared down at him, then slowly raised its hand.

Gismay felt his arm being lifted against his own will. He screamed as the skin above his wrist began to burn, though no flame was upon him.

When he looked down at the spot he saw a throbbing, black mark upon his skin.

The Farmer looked up as more Figures appeared from the broil. His pain-addled mind believed he counted eight in total, all clad in the same gold-trimmed black cloaks and half-masks. They had surrounded one of the beds above which, Gismay now saw to his horror, floated Sonia.

Her eyes were closed, and a look of true peace was upon her face, as if she was immune to all that was transpiring around her. Her arms were fully extended at her sides, hands outstretched with palms facing outward. Her hair and her clothes hung as if she was floating underwater, but no other sign of movement or affect was upon her.

The Figures began chanting:

Huch mil Dar
Huch mil Ros
Huch mil Fír
Ro mah nu Los!

The words at first were slow, rhythmic, but they grew in pace as Sonia's stricken form was lifted higher and higher above the bed.

As the pace increased, so did the pitch and within a few moments it had grown to such a level that Gismay had to cover his ears; the voices of the eight figures seemed to fill the room, reverberating through the air, their very sound increasing the pressure about him.

A white orb began to appear around Sonia. It glowed brightly for a moment, quietening their chanting, but soon from each Figure there came a spark of darker-hued power that licked and flashed at the surface of the orb.

Slowly the dark began to overcome the light, the surface of the thing fading and cracking, allowing the dark tongues to touch Sonia's flesh.

Now the chanting returned tenfold, pushing Gismay down into the floor once more and thrumming incessantly through the air.

He cried out as Sonia was engulfed entirely in this swirling devilry, smoke and soot filling his lungs.

The dark tongues now began to reach out and surround the entire gathering, Sonia and Figures alike.

The chanting stopped, replaced now by a crackling which filled the air as black lightning snapped and fizzed about the room, leaving ashen burns wherever it struck.

Gismay lifted his head to look once more to Sonia, but she and the Figures were now all but obscured by the power that had been unleashed.

There was a high pitched whine ripping through above all the other noise. It grew in pitch until Gismay could barely hear it and then, when it could go no higher, the black power spun impossibly quickly about itself and Gismay was thrown back once more to the floor.

There was a final, deafening cacophony of noise and then, as abruptly as it had started, the whine and the crackling fell silent, and the soot and smoke fell back into the hearth.

For many moments Gismay lay where he was, his body bruised and his mind overwhelmed. His wrist throbbed and burned, and his ears were ringing, but otherwise he was mercifully unharmed.

He took several deep breaths against his discomfort, then slowly pulled his shattered form up onto his feet and looked at the scene before him.

The beds lay as if untouched, the window was open, and the golden light of dawn now fully illuminated the room. Yet Gismay found no comfort within that truth, for his eyes told him all he needed to know.

"My Lady?" he breathed, knowing he would get no response.

Sonia was gone.

End of Book One

The story continues in Book Two, “The Five Kingdoms”

Glossary

Bakslá, The – A country in the north west of Rhydariel, encompassing the Selman Flats and the Bakslán Peninsula. Its capitol is North Sel, and it is ruled by Chief Baranghâd.
Barrandel – Hall of The Boardwalks.
Beregland – Common name for the Bowalt. It is ruled by Lord Marn in the capitol, Beregle.
Bereglan – Collective name for people of Beregle.
Beregle – Mountain village that is the capitol of the Bowalt.
Bereun – Wolf-like creatures that have over-developed front limbs, shoulders and jaws, and have developed the use of simple weapons such as rocks.
Blasphemers, The – Derogatory Eismen name for the Ebrahiim.
Boardwalks, The – Capitol of Ebras, also called City On The Water and The Planks. It is ruled by King Hedradour in the hall of Barrandel, and located in the west of Rhydariel upon the Finsae.
Bowalt, The – The lands ruled by Beregle.
Bovinian Mountains – Range of mountains that run through central Rhydariel. Beregle sits on a plateau on their western slopes.

City On The Water, The – Alternative name for The Boardwalks, often used by allies and vassals of the Kingdom of Ebras.

Daggerok Port – The port of Eismeer.

Ebrahiim – Collective name for the people of Ebras.
Ebras – Land ruled by The Boardwalks and King Hedradour.
Edgeborough – A small town in Central England.
Edgeborough Castle – A tourist attraction. Once played a small part in the English Civil War. Cam and Sonia work here.
Eislands – Country ruled by Lord Fohenk. Its capitol is Eismeer.

Eismeer – Capitol of the Eislands, located in the frozen south-east of Rhydariel.
Eismeer Lake – Frozen lake that fills much of the land between Eismeer and Mount Vorgaril.
Eismen – Collective noun for the people of Eismeer.
Erkenweit Hill – Ancient landmark in the centre of Rhydariel. Upon its top sits the ancient, ruined fort of Sepelchor.

Farn Bridge – Fortified crossing of the River Lun. It marks the border between Ebras and Eislands.
Farnhoc, The – Plateau of scrubland within Ebras.
Felieren Plains – Frozen scrubland proliferated by Hocwede and bracken. A region in the west of the Eislands.
Finsae, The – The great lake of western Rhydariel. Also called the Murky Water.

Gildestone – A rare and precious mineral, prized for its clarity.
Glacier Gates, The – Very narrow and treacherous pass between the Glacier Mountains and Mount Vorgaril.
Glacier Mountains – Range of mountains that stand to the north of Eismeer.
Glacier Pass – A valley between the Glacier Mountains and the Bovinian Mountains. The temperature here is rarely above freezing even in high summer.
Glewash – River in the northern Eislands.
Godswurd – Common language of Rhydariel.

Hocberries – The fruit that grows on the stalks of Hocwede.
Hocliquor – The healing draught made from distilling Hocberries.
Hocram – A bread-like food that contains Hocberries. It is designed to sustain travellers on a march.
Hocwede – A heather-like shrub. Its berries have potent healing powers.

Lordsguard – Lord Fohenk's personal guard.

Lord's Justice, The – Punishment by torture and slow death, sometime drawn out for weeks or even months, employed against traitors in the Eislands.
Lun Ridge Farm – Farm located north-east of Farn Bridge inside the borders of the Eislands. Home of Gismay.
Lundang – Port town on the River Lun.

Mortalis – Godswurd name for mortal men.
Mount Vorgaril – Highest peak in Rhydariel, located west of Eismeer.
Murky Water, The – Common name for the Finsae.

North Sel – Capitol of The Bakslá.

Pelagos Sea, The – The ocean surrounding Rhydariel.
Planks, The – Derogatory Eismen name for The Boardwalks.

Rhydariel – The land shown within the map.
River Lun – River that forms the border between the Bowalt and Ebras.
Selman Flats, The – The sun-baked mud flats in north west Rhydariel. It is part of the Bakslá.
Sepelchor – Ancient, ruined fort situated upon Erkenweit Hill.
Spine Mountains – Mountain range in central-eastern Rhydariel.

Tower Of The Eis, The – The central citadel of Eismeer.

Welverleigh – A small village in Worcestershire, England, where Cam lives.

ABOUT THE AUTHOR

Christopher Goldthorn is an actor, writer, presenter, and composer from Kidderminster, England. He first had the idea for the Heirson Chronicles in 2003, when he was 14 years old.

Since then he has worked on the story, gone to University, looked over the story, started a YouTube gaming channel, rehashed the story, got married to the love of his life, taken another crack at the story, helped run a theatre company, and finally sat down and finished his book.

He currently works at a Castle, and lives in Coventry with his wife and daughter.

Printed in Great Britain
by Amazon

f831cb85-3160-472d-872a-07cc8b4b4c8fR01